Convenient
Disposal

Books by Steven F. Havill

The Posadas County Mysteries
Heartshot
Bitter Recoil
Twice Buried
Before She Dies
Privileged to Kill
Prolonged Exposure
Out of Season
Dead Weight
Bag Limit
Red, Green, or Murder
Scavengers
A Discount for Death
Convenient Disposal
Statute of Limitations
Final Payment
The Fourth Time is Murder
Double Prey

The Dr. Thomas Parks Novels
Race for the Dying
Comes a Time for Burning

Other Novels
The Killer
The Worst Enemy
LeadFire
TimberBlood

Convenient Disposal

A Posadas County Mystery

Steven F. Havill

Poisoned Pen Press

Library of Congress Catalog Card Number: 2010923862

ISBN: 9781590586648   Trade Paperback

Poisoned Pen Press
6962 E. First Ave., Ste. 103
Scottsdale, AZ 85251
www.poisonedpenpress.com
info@poisonedpenpress.com

Printed in the United States of America

For Kathleen

Acknowledgments

The author would like to extend special thanks to Vincent Mares, Jeff Encinias, Leslie Fernandez, and Kathy Trujillo.

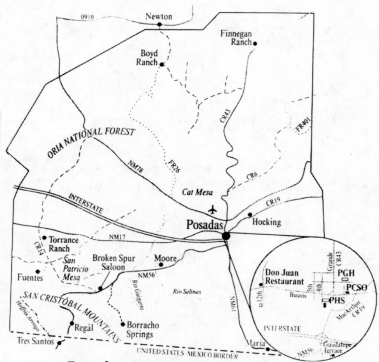

Posadas County, New Mexico

Chapter One

The hat pin rolled easily, six inches of steel shaft with a black plastic head on one end and a filed needle point on the other. Posadas County Undersheriff Estelle Reyes-Guzman nudged it back and forth with her right index finger while the three other people sitting at the conference table waited.

Estelle wasn't paying attention to the weapon. Instead, she watched fourteen-year-old Deena Hurtado. The girl sat between her mother, Ivana, and the middle-school principal, Tessa Dooley.

Deena's mother was trying not to cry, a wadded tissue in both hands. As a longtime District Court employee, she would know something about the law, would know what was coming. As a mother, what she knew would be turning her insides to pudding.

Estelle wished that she could read Deena's mind, but the teenager's face was a mask of studied indifference. Deena never looked at her mother, and Estelle decided that, despite the girl's feigned calm, she didn't enjoy seeing her mother in misery.

"Deena," Estelle said, "you came to school this morning as usual, and then were called out of math class by Ms. Dooley and charged with carrying a concealed weapon on school property. Is that correct?"

"I guess."

"Why would you do that?"

Deena shrugged as if the incident were no more important to her than tossing a gum wrapper on the school parking lot.

"It's my understanding that you were involved in a fight after the volleyball game Tuesday night. Is that correct?"

"Yes."

"And were suspended for three days? Thursday, Friday, and yesterday?"

"Yes."

"Do you feel good about coming back to school this morning?" The girl shrugged. "Did you want to come back to school, Deena?" The eyes rolled. "Deena," Estelle persisted, "do you understand the school's policy about bringing weapons on campus?" Deena grimaced at the notion that there might be something that she didn't understand, but didn't answer. "Do you realize that the school's policy is that you be expelled for the rest of the school year? That it's automatic?"

A tiny chink formed in the girl's armor, and she blinked.

"And that you will not be allowed admission to any *other* school in the state during that time?"

Deena sighed with brave boredom. Her mother dabbed at a fresh flood of tears. "It's not a *weapon*," the girl said to the ceiling.

Estelle picked up the hat pin by the center of its shaft and spun it slowly between two fingers. "Mobsters used to use these things," she said, still watching the girl. Deena slumped a little further down in her chair. "It's as effective as a stiletto, if you know how to use it." She paused. "Do you know how to use it, Deena?" The middle schooler didn't reply.

With her index finger, Estelle tapped the end of the pin gently. "Someone has gone to a lot of trouble to file this *really* sharp," she said. "That's an odd thing to do for a *hat* pin, don't you think?" She placed the pin on the table. "Ms. Dooley called the police because she had apprehended a student carrying a concealed, deadly weapon. Deena, you had this in the inseam of your jeans, is that correct?"

When Deena remained silent, Tessa Dooley said, "Worked into the jeans' inseam at the thigh, Undersheriff. We had a bulletin at an administrators' conference a while ago that this was a new fad in some of the city schools." She shook her head sadly. "First time for us…that we know of."

"How was it discovered?" Estelle asked.

"One of the other students saw it and told her math teacher. That's the class Deena was in at the time. Algebra II, I would like to point out."

"You're a smart girl, Deena," Estelle said. "Do you understand that carrying a concealed weapon onto school grounds is more than just a violation of school policy?"

"Yes."

"Do you understand that it's a fourth-degree felony? That's how serious the state considers the offense."

"Not if you're a juvenile," Deena said. A trace of gloat touched her eyes, and when Estelle glanced at the principal, she saw the flush of anger run up Tessa Dooley's cheeks. Deena *was* a smart girl, evidently. And she was correct as well. If Estelle had asked her what the procedure was, the girl could no doubt have outlined it succinctly—referral to Juvenile Probation, conferencing, counseling, warm fuzzies, admonition to keep the nose clean, and a clean record after a time judged appropriate by the court. In short, nothing. And with more than half of the school year remaining, the expulsion meant a nice vacation besides.

Estelle let the silence hang for long enough that Ivana Hurtado had time enough to change tissues.

"Mrs. Hurtado, I'd like permission to talk with your daughter alone," Estelle said finally. "You don't have to agree to that, but I think it might help."

"Of course," Ivana replied. "Of course, Sheriff." She gathered up her jacket and handbag.

"We'll be just outside," Tessa Dooley said. She heaved her chair backward so that her considerable bulk would clear the edge of the table. In a moment, the door thudded behind the two women. Estelle snapped open her briefcase, found a plastic evidence bag, and dropped the hat pin inside. She jotted a note on the cover tag, her motions not lost on Deena.

"So," the undersheriff said, and closed the briefcase. She leaned forward, folding her hands together. "I've known your mother for a long time." Deena didn't respond. "I remember you and your sister playing around the court offices when you were little. That's a long time ago, huh?"

Deena cocked her head and looked down at her hands. She picked the cuticle of one of her nails, and Estelle saw that they were gnawed raw.

"Tell me about the fight."

"No big deal," Deena said and shrugged. "It was a fight, that's all. Like no big deal."

Estelle ruffled back several pages in her small notebook. "You and Carmen Acosta, with a little help from friends. Carmen was suspended for six days. She started it?"

"Am I under arrest, or what?" Deena said wearily.

"'Detained' would be a better word, Deena." Estelle regarded the girl across the table. She was attractive, fine-featured almost to the point of delicacy. Her light brown hair was cut short enough to see the five gold rings marching up the curve of her right ear. "Have you and Carmen been enemies for a long time?"

"No."

"This a recent thing?"

Deena looked heavenward, and then studied the poster on the wall that listed 101 ways to praise a child.

"Did you make a pass at Paul?" Deena's eyes flicked to Estelle, and her eyebrows furrowed. "Paul Otero is a good-looking young man." Estelle watched the blush work its way up Deena's neck. "You showed him some attention, and Carmen took offense." The fight had hardly been a private affair; half a hundred spectators found the fight more entertaining than the middle-school volleyball game. Two of those spectators had been willing to tell the off-duty deputy who was working security what had happened. Apparently handsome Paul had enjoyed the brawl as much as anyone.

"Soooo stupid," Deena said.

"The taking offense is stupid, or something else?"

"I just said *hello* to him. It's not like we ran off into the bushes or something."

"And Carmen took offense when you spoke to her boyfriend? Well, that happens."

"Soooo stupid."

"Is this the first time you and Carmen have had trouble?"

"Yes. She was my best friend in sixth grade."

"Ah," Estelle said, surprised by the gratuitous information. "Paul moved here last year, didn't he?"

Deena's eyebrows furrowed slightly. "Yes." She glanced at Estelle as if to ask, "How did you know that?" but didn't voice the question.

"What were you planning to do with the hat pin, Deena? Who were you planning to kill?"

Deena startled at the blunt accusation. "I wasn't going to start anything."

"You carried it for self-defense, you mean?" Deena nodded. "You felt that maybe Carmen would make trouble again, and just in case, you sharpened up that six-inch hat pin?"

Deena shrugged.

"Did Carmen threaten you Tuesday night? After the fight broke up?" The shrug had become the standard answer. "Or this morning? You walk to school, right? Did the two of you exchange words this morning? If she threatened you, that's our concern, Deena. That's as much against the law as bringing a lethal weapon to school."

"It's no big deal."

"I think it *is* a big deal that you're going to miss the second half of the school year, and have to go to the JPO as well, Deena."

"Well, I can't help that now, can I?" The girl shook her head in disgust.

"You're on the honor roll, aren't you?"

"So?"

"In fact, you're on the principal's list, isn't that right?" Deena shrugged. "That means you're smart enough to figure things out. Maybe you can tell me something." Estelle shifted position and rested her head on one hand, studying Deena. "Carmen was suspended for six days. That means she doesn't even come back to school until next Friday. What's the hat pin for? She won't even be on campus."

"Well, duh," Deena said petulantly. "I *walk* to school, you know."

"I know that. And I already asked you if the two of you met again this morning, and didn't receive an answer. Are Carmen's friends giving you a hard time now?" Deena shrugged. "Have you figured out how you're going to tell your dad about all this?" Estelle asked, trying another tack.

Deena's eyes closed, and for the first time, the tears were right on the edge. Roy Hurtado had worked for the copper mine until it closed the year before Deena was born. He then joined the Posadas Police Department, attended the police academy, and promptly took a security job with the railroad, working out of Deming and Las Cruces.

"I'm sure Mom has that all figured out," Deena said.

"Maybe she does. And what are you going to do now?" Estelle asked.

"I don't know. I can homeschool. Maybe I'll go up to Albuquerque and live with my sister for a while."

"Did you like school here, Deena?"

The girl took a deep, shuddering breath. "Yeah. Like, some of it, anyways."

"Where did the hat pin come from? Here in town?"

"Yeah. Sure."

"Do you have any more?"

"You can get 'em in the store. It's no big deal."

"That's not what I asked. I asked if you had any more, Deena."

"No, I don't have any *more*," the girl replied.

"Where did you buy it?"

"I just got 'em, is all. It's no big deal."

"No, buying *them* is no big deal, Deena. I can go into the hardware and buy an axe, and that's no big deal. If I bury that axe in someone's head, the deal changes, right? I can buy a nice car, and that's no big deal. If I get drunk and ram that car into someone, the deal changes, doesn't it?" Estelle patted the briefcase. "The hat pin is sort of like that, Deena. You can buy all of them that you want. Except that both you and I know that you have no use for a six-inch hat pin other than using it as a weapon. *That's* what makes it a big deal, Deena...when you carry that concealed weapon into the school. And when you intend to inflict bodily harm on someone else."

"What am I supposed to do, just let 'em jump me?"

"Deena, I know it's a small town, but you're a smart girl." The smart girl looked heavenward again. "Stay away from Carmen. Stay away from Paul. Mind your own business. You've got the rest of the fall semester and then all spring and summer to move beyond this nonsense. Next fall, you and Carmen will be at different schools, even." Estelle smiled sympathetically. "And odds are good that in two weeks' time, Carmen and Paul won't be an item anymore, anyway. He'll be off breaking some other girl's heart."

The undersheriff stood up. "What happens now?" Deena asked, and she sounded like exactly what she was—a frightened middle schooler. Estelle took a step and then paused with her hand on the doorknob.

"Deena, you made a serious mistake. You brought a concealed weapon to school. That's not something you can do without consequences. You know what the school policy is. You'll have a lot of time out of school to think about what you did. And during that time, you'll be talking with Juvenile Probation authorities. They'll want to be as sure as they can be that this won't happen again."

"It won't."

"So you say. But you haven't been open with me, and that makes me a little leery."

"I told you the truth."

"Where did you buy the hat pin, Deena?" The girl didn't answer, and Estelle said, "That's what I thought." She opened the door and waited until the girl's mother had entered. Principal

Tessa Dooley was on the phone and waved a hand for Estelle to go ahead. She closed the door.

"Ivana, I'll be issuing Deena a nontraffic citation," Estelle said, opening her briefcase. "After she signs that, you'll receive a copy." Ivana nodded miserably but remained silent. "The JPO will be calling to set up an appointment for a conference with Deena and with you. You all will decide where this is going to go from here."

"She's been such a good girl," Ivana managed.

"I'm sure she has been, and we all hope that she will be again," Estelle said as she filled out the ticket. "But as you know, the law doesn't care how well she did in Algebra II or in World History when she carries a concealed weapon into school." The office door opened and Tessa Dooley slid inside. "I'm not a counselor," Estelle added, "but if I were you, I'd take full advantage of the school's counseling services at this point." She slid the completed ticket across to Deena, along with a pen. "Sign by the red X," she said. "Think of Deena standing at the top of a long, steep, treacherous slope, Ivana," Estelle added. "She has a lot of choices. Her job is to make sure she doesn't step the wrong way. Your job is to help her make that decision."

Estelle closed the briefcase, resting both hands on the locks and regarding Deena Hurtado. "All right?" When neither the mother nor her daughter answered, Estelle turned to Tessa Dooley. The principal held out her hand, grasping Estelle's in a strong grip. At the same time, she handed the undersheriff a small note.

"The phone call was the elementary school," the principal said. "Myra Delgado happened to look out her window and see you. She wondered if you would stop by for a few minutes when you're ready to leave."

Estelle glanced at her watch. She had intended to catch County Manager Kevin Zeigler when the County Commission meeting adjourned for lunch, but the county manager could wait. Estelle's oldest son, Francisco, was passionately in love with both the first grade and with his teacher, Myra Delgado.

At home, all he had been able to talk about for the past week was the parent-teacher conference coming up Thursday night. Despite her son's enthusiasm, Estelle was well aware that, in seven short years, Francisco would be a middle schooler—and the world for him would never again be so simple.

"Sure, I can do that," Estelle said. "Does anyone have any more questions for me?" She handed one of her cards to Deena. "Use that if you want to talk with me, Deena," she said. "Anytime." She was surprised when that earned a small nod from the girl.

Chapter Two

Estelle started the county car and drove around the perimeter of the macadam acre that served as both the bus staging area and playground for the elementary and middle schools.

Seventh graders on lunch break were already spreading out onto the pavement. Two duty teachers stood by one of the perimeter benches well out of range of the infamous "wall ball" court, where participants became targets for hurled tennis balls. A gaggle of four girls had joined the teachers, all apparently talking at once. One of the girls broke away from the teachers when she saw Estelle park in front of the elementary school fifty yards away. She sprinted toward the undersheriff as if greeting a long-lost pal.

With just enough time to shut off the car, get out, and brace herself, Estelle reached out a hand and caught Melody Mears as the youngster spun into orbit around her.

"Hey, what are you doing here?" the sprite said. She shared the sandy hair and freckles of her father, Posadas Sheriff's Sergeant Tom Mears, and none of his quiet reserve.

"Checking up on you," Estelle said.

"Oh, sure," Melody said, beaming. She did a fair imitation of the broken-elbow, splayed-finger gang-member's point, indicating the two teachers. "Me and them guys are just over there scoring some really bad shit from the teachers."

Estelle cuffed Melody on the back of her head. "I don't need to hear that, *hija*."

Melody grinned an apology and dug her head into the crook of Estelle's arm like a puppy. "Really, how come you're here?"

Estelle looked down at Melody's smiling face and then, as the youngster danced a few steps away, glanced at the inseam of her jeans. "I like to touch bases with Ms. Dooley once in a while."

The girl wrinkled her nose in disbelief as she searched for just the right words. "She is *so* cool," she said, and then with the immediate change of subject at which middle schoolers were so adept, she added, "What's Francisco doing?"

"This morning he's building a skyscraper," Estelle said. "At least that's what he's been chattering about for a week now. I thought I'd go in and see."

Melody danced a circle. "He's so cute."

"Don't tell him that." Estelle nodded at the two teachers. They were watching from a distance, well out of earshot. After the next faculty meeting, they would never look at a set of inseams the same way again. One of the teachers, a youngish woman at least six months pregnant, raised a hand in either greeting or summons—it wasn't clear which. Her authority obviously carried clout, though. Melody Mears' orbit immediately widened, and she waved in farewell.

"I gotta go," she hollered, and then flung over her shoulder, "Tell Francisco I said hi."

Her mind now on her son, Estelle locked the car and walked toward the building. She found herself trying to guess what six-year-old Francisco could have accomplished that would warrant a conference when the parent-teacher's night was just two days away. Her one fear—that the little boy would be bored by the routine of school—had so far been an idle concern.

She pulled open the heavy door, greeted instantly by quiet classical music piped over the intercom. The smell of fresh-baked rolls and roast chicken floated down the long hall from the cafeteria, overpowering even the Clorox-flavored mop water that a janitor was using in front of one of the restrooms. A small sign on an easel pointed off to the right, directing visitors toward administration.

Larry Newberry was leaning on the counter, talking to one of the secretaries. He glanced up when he heard the front door, saw Estelle, and beckoned to her as he stepped away from the counter.

Tall and dark with a brooding face, Newberry could frown and smile at the same time, a peculiar expression that looked as if the elementary principal might break into tears at any moment.

"You came to join us for lunch?" he said, as Estelle entered the office.

"I wish I could," she replied. "It smells wonderful."

The principal held out an ushering hand toward the cafeteria, but Estelle shook her head. "I really can't, thanks. Myra Delgado asked if I'd stop by for a minute. I was just over at the middle school."

"Ah," Newberry said, as if that covered it all. "Wouldn't it be nice if these kiddos never had to grow up."

"I'm not sure about that," Estelle replied.

Newberry chuckled, still frowning. "Myra and I were talking about Francisco just this morning." He looked sideways at Estelle as he stepped out of the office and into the foyer. "That's quite a boy you have there."

"Thank you...I think."

"Oh, yes," Newberry said. His eyebrows relaxed. "Let me find out where Myra is just at the moment," he said, and turned back toward his secretary, who had anticipated his question.

"Ms. Delgado is right there," she said, pointing across the hall toward the faculty room where the first-grade teacher held open the door while she talked with someone inside.

"Ah," Newberry said again. "There she is. And if you change your mind about lunch..."

"Thanks, Mr. Newberry," Estelle said. Myra Delgado turned as Estelle crossed the foyer toward her. She beamed and closed the faculty-room door, then approached Estelle with both hands held out. Not yet thirty years old, the stocky first-grade teacher's round, pretty face was framed by short, spiky hair that looked as if she stuck her fingers into an electrical outlet each morning.

"There you are," she said. "What perfect timing." With Estelle's right hand in both of hers, she paused and glanced in the direction of the middle school. "How's your day going?"

"Well, okay," Estelle replied cautiously. "So far."

"I don't mean to be pushy, but we have about twelve minutes." She linked her arm through Estelle's, ushering her down the hall in the direction of the potent cafeteria aromas. "My aide is with the kiddos during lunch. Usually we both are, but when I glanced out the window and caught sight of you going into the middle school, I thought I'd take a chance and see if you could come over. I'm so glad you did."

They passed the double doors leading into the small cafeteria, and Estelle saw the sea of small heads and hands, industriously shoveling in the chicken, potatoes, milk, and rolls. Teachers hovered and mingled, like fretful drill sergeants.

"This all started about three weeks ago," Myra said, and Estelle glanced sharply at her, intrigued by what "this all" represented. "My first thought was, *Whoa, what's he doing?*" She pointed down a side hallway to the right. "Down here a couple of doors." At the same time she slowed her pace, and Estelle noticed that she made an effort to keep her shoe heels from clacking on the polished hall tiles.

The first-grade teacher sidled up to a doorway and put her finger over her lips. Through the single windowpane of A-12, Estelle saw a set of curved chorus risers. A battered upright piano was turned perpendicular to the risers so that the teacher could sit at the keyboard and direct the students at the same time. The room lights were off, but daylight flooded through the high windows above a row of battered lockers.

Estelle saw Francisco's slight figure standing in front of the piano's keyboard. The white keys were level with the tip of his nose. With his hands clawed over the keys, it looked as if he were trying to chin himself.

"He eats his lunch, and then he slips down here," Myra whispered. "Always by himself. At first, I thought that he was going to the restroom, but he'll stay down here until about six minutes of," and she glanced at her watch. "At eleven fifty-five, we line up to go back to the classroom." She turned to grin at Estelle. "We're kinda regimented around here with the little ones."

"This room isn't locked?"

"No, not usually. Mr. Donner—he's our music teacher—Mr. Donner floats around all the schools, and he's here just three times a week—for all six grades." Myra looked heavenward. "Sometimes one of the regular classroom teachers will bring a class here for something special, and it's easier to leave it unlocked than always having to worry about borrowing a key. When I found out that this is where Francisco was going during lunch, I checked a couple of times to make sure the door was open."

"He just comes here all by himself?"

"Yes. Now, we don't allow the little ones to roam by themselves more than just a little bit, and as long as I'm sure this is where he is, I'm fine with it. So is Mr. Newberry." She leaned closer until her ear almost touched the glass, and looked at Estelle while she listened. "Can you hear him?"

"Yes."

"It sounds like he's trying to work out chords."

"He comes here every day?"

Myra nodded. "By himself. Never with anyone else...and Francisco has a whole classroom full of friends, Mrs. Guzman. He isn't a loner, by any means. But this is a private thing with him, and that's what intrigues me so."

Estelle watched her son as his tiny fingers spidered across the keyboard, seeking whatever sound he heard in his head.

"Do you have a piano at home?" Myra whispered. Estelle shook her head. "Well, I wondered," Myra added. "One day last week, I asked Francisco if he did, and he didn't answer. Sometimes he's stubborn that way, as I'm sure you know. When he doesn't want to talk about something, he just pretends that he doesn't hear. Maybe he was afraid that I would find out about this," and she nodded toward the music room. "Maybe he thought I wouldn't let him come down here."

"Stealthy little guy," Estelle said. "If this was his little brother, I'd be less surprised. Carlos sings to himself all the time. Francisco doesn't."

"Maybe not aloud," Myra said. "But I think it's in his head." She held up her hands, poised over an imaginary keyboard. "Anyway, I wanted you to see this. I think it'll be interesting to see where it goes. He hasn't missed a day here in three weeks. Not one. That in itself is remarkable for a first grader." She leaned toward Estelle and her whisper dropped a notch. "And not to talk to someone about it is absolutely amazing. Given the chance, first graders are pack critters most of the time. Yakkety, yakkety, yak."

Estelle watched Myra Delgado thoughtfully, but her attention was focused on the faint notes from inside the insulated room—some solo, some forming hesitant, simple chords. "We think we know them," she said finally.

Myra reached toward the doorknob. "Did you want to speak with him while you're here?"

"No. Don't interrupt him. He only has six minutes left." Estelle smiled and reached out to touch Ms. Delgado on the arm. "Thanks."

They walked back toward the cafeteria in silence, and as they reached the double doors, Estelle looked up at the large clock. Francisco had four minutes remaining in his private world. "The music that's playing now," she said, nodding up toward the public address speaker below the clock. "Is it piped into the classrooms?"

"Just the hallways," Myra said, shaking her head. "Sometimes, if we don't have music of our own that we want to use, we'll ask Mr. Newberry to throw the switch for our classroom. But usually not."

"Interesting," Estelle said. "Thanks again."

"We'll see you Thursday night?"

"Absolutely. Francis has been talking about his tower all week."

"He and Rocky Montaño are building that thing." She frowned severely. "We are all very impressed with ourselves about that project."

Estelle laughed. "I'm prepared. We're looking forward to Thursday. Thanks again, Myra."

"I hope Dr. Francis can come, too."

"So do we. He's going to try his best."

The clock clicked to 11:57 as Estelle left the school, and she felt a twinge of conscience that she hadn't stayed and greeted her son. He was doing nothing wrong, only slipping away for a few minutes each day for a rendezvous with the piano. The moments were obviously private and intensely personal for the little boy, and for the first time in six years, Estelle realized that there were dimensions to her son to which she no longer had free and unlimited access—and that brought an ache of regret.

"That's a parent's face," a voice said, and Estelle looked up quickly. The Posadas County manager had pulled in his small pickup diagonally behind Estelle's unmarked sedan. He leaned against her unit's front fender as Estelle approached. "Missed you this morning," Kevin Zeigler said. "The village has you working for them already this morning?"

"No…but they had a little ruckus at the middle school involving a couple of girls." She grinned. "I drew matron duty, I guess. Just one of those things when everyone gets busy."

"I know how it goes," Zeigler said, and Estelle didn't doubt him. The young county executive had survived two years of county politics, trying to mold the various county operations into a reflection of what the five commissioners wanted…and what they wanted seemed to change with the phases of the moon. "Are you going to be able to stop by the meeting after the lunch break? I think the commissioners could use your perspective." He grinned. "I think Swartz and Tinneman both got a little impatient this morning."

"The sheriff was going to go today," Estelle said.

"Well, he *did* go. And I think the commission is going to vote in favor of the contract. But…"

"Chief Mitchell was there, too?"

"Yes. And you know, the commissioners were a little surprised. Barney Tinneman is the main voice against consolidation, and

I get the impression that he still counts on Chief Mitchell as an ally." Zeigler crossed his arms over his chest. "But Chief Mitchell told the meeting this morning that the village contracting police services from the county is the only thing that makes sense."

"He's said that all along," Estelle agreed. "Barney needs to listen once in a while. Everybody thinks that, in most ways, it makes sense, except maybe him. The population is just too small to bother with separate departments."

"That's the catch," Zeigler said. "In most ways. Neither Mitchell nor Torrez can convince Tinneman that coverage in the village won't suffer." Zeigler grinned. "And I can see the sheriff's fuse getting shorter and shorter. He doesn't do politics well."

"No, he doesn't."

"I think we mangled the carcass enough this morning. They need a fresh perspective." He glanced at his watch. "I have a few things I have to take care of over lunch, and the commission reconvenes at one-thirty. If you can be there, it would help."

"They're voting on it today?"

"That's the plan. But Tinneman has Swartz wavering, and that's two out of five. I wouldn't be a bit surprised if they forced it to the table."

"Even after the village council voted unanimously to contract services from the county?"

"It's a turf thing," Zeigler said. "Remember, Tinneman was mayor of Posadas at one time. He thinks that the village should have its own police department, no matter what. He thinks that once they give that up, the next thing to go is the fire department, then Lord knows what all else…He even said this morning that if we're not careful, we'll lose our post office." He shrugged at the absurdity of it. "Go figure. It's hard to tell just what his agenda is, except he likes to hear himself talk. He even thinks I'm giving the county dump away by looking at a private contractor."

The county manager pushed himself away from the car's fender and brushed off the seat of his tan chinos. "If you can stop by, it will help. The sheriff told them that the SO would be absorbing the two and a half village officers, but I'm not sure that

Tinneman heard him." He sighed. "I'd like to get this all cleaned up and running smoothly so we can move on to other issues. The world isn't going to hold still for us to dither this to death."

"I'll be there," Estelle said. "I'm not sure what I can say that will make any difference to Tinneman, but we'll see."

"Every bit helps," Zeigler said. He paused with his hand on the door of his idling truck. "Everything staying quiet?"

"Quiet is always relative," Estelle said.

"Boy, ain't that the truth. See you after lunch, then."

As Estelle settled into the county car, she enjoyed an unexpected sense of relief. The county meeting, with the ebullient Barney Tinneman always vying for center stage, could be entertaining—a good way to pass the hours until Francisco stepped off the school bus later that afternoon. She had no idea what she would say to her son.

Chapter Three

Pershing Park was a dusty, forlorn triangle that overlooked the intersection of Bustos and Grande Avenues, the two main streets that crossed through the heart of Posadas. The park featured half a dozen elms, a spread of struggling grass, two picnic tables, and a rusting vintage tank alleged to have been part of Black Jack Pershing's assault on Pancho Villa's forces in 1916. The tank had rested on its concrete pedestal for so long that it had colored to a nice, even patina from tracks to turret. Sheriff Robert Torrez had once irreverently remarked that the tank had been donated to the Village of Posadas by someone who didn't own a cutting torch.

Pershing Street formed the hypotenuse and northwestern boundary of the park. One of the few modern buildings in Posadas, the U.S. Post Office fronted the intersection of Pershing and Bustos. Its nearest neighbor was the former Martinez Brothers A & P grocery store, a flat-roofed, concrete block building. Sometime decades before, an industrious contractor had purchased the A & P, thinking that with a few tons of Sheetrock, the old store could be partitioned into a minimall of sorts.

Of the various ventures that had counted on the neighboring post office to provide a constant flow of daily traffic over the years, only three remained. Arley's Vacuum and Sewing occupied a small corner niche in the old supermarket building, about where the fruits and vegetables used to be. The various cracks and BB holes in the front window had been artfully repaired with duct tape. Arley was semiretired. When Estelle had tried to have her mother's aging Singer fixed, she had discovered that Arley had adopted "You can't get parts for those" as his basic operating motto.

At the other end of the building, the elderly Helen Pierce's retirement project, Junque and Treasure, was filled to overflowing with more the first than the second, and was open occasionally on Tuesday afternoons. Sandwiched between Junque and two vacant opportunities was Great Notions, a little boutique owned by MaryAnne Bustamonte.

The OPEN sign was propped in the window of Great Notions as Estelle's county car drifted to a stop at the curb between the post office and Arley's. She studied the boutique for a few minutes in the rearview mirror, then keyed the radio.

"PCS, three ten is ten-six on Pershing near the post office."

"Ten-four, three ten. Did the county manager find you?"

"That's affirmative."

"Ten-four, three ten. Bobby wanted to be sure you were going to the meeting." Gayle Torrez, the sheriff's wife, leaned hard on the word *sure*.

Estelle grinned as she hung up the mike. It was a safe bet that the sheriff would bow out of the commissioner's meeting the instant he could finagle someone else to represent the department. Despite something as important as the pending dissolution of the village police force, with village patrol contracted through the county, Robert Torrez would rather clean up roadkill than sit in the stuffy commission chambers.

The cork tip protecting the long, polished hat pin was still in place as Estelle slipped the evidence bag out of her briefcase and into her inside jacket pocket.

She had visited Great Notions a half dozen times since it had opened a decade ago, not always as a customer eager to browse through the scarves, handmade vests and hats, incense, or bolts of Guatemalan fabric. MaryAnne Bustamonte had developed a love of other things from south of the border, and generally wasn't too concerned about whether the burning incense samples covered up the aroma of smoldering hemp.

MaryAnne Bustamonte and Ivana Hurtado were sisters, some times to the younger Ivana's discomfort. Ivana didn't find her sister's occasional court appearances the least bit amusing. Perhaps more important, Ivana might find it even less amusing to know—if she didn't already—that her middle-school daughter Deena probably regarded Aunt MaryAnne as the perfect role model. The instant she'd seen the hat pin, Estelle had thought of MaryAnne Bustamonte.

A little brass bell from India jingled above the door as the undersheriff entered. MaryAnne Bustamonte was perched on a two-step ladder, trying to shove a bolt of fabric into the highest spot on an upper shelf. She turned and looked over her shoulder, squinting through the haze.

Except for a thickening of the waist, MaryAnne had changed little from the attitudinal teenager Estelle remembered from an American History class the two of them had shared at Posadas High School twenty years before.

"Hi," MaryAnne said. "I'll be down in a minute."

"No hurry," Estelle said. She remained near the door, trying not to breathe the cloying air too deeply. When not smoking marijuana, MaryAnne lit one nonfiltered cigarette after another. One was smoldering in an ashtray by the antique cash register. Its smoke twined with vapors from a burning incense stick near the pens.

With a final pat to smooth the fabric, and apparently not the least concerned that the expensive cloth would reek of smoke, MaryAnne retreated down the ladder.

"And what is the law west of the Pecos up to today?" she asked. Her voice was raspy, on the verge of a cough. With an efficient twist, she snubbed out the cigarette and then leaned on the small counter with both elbows, watchful as Estelle ambled up the narrow aisle.

The undersheriff stopped in front of a glass-fronted display labeled HEAD CASE. Inside, MaryAnne had arranged an impressive collection of barrettes, combs, and hairpins on a large, open Oriental fan. The eclectic display featured accessories carved from, or studded with, coral, jade, turquoise, amber, enameled copper, even carved wood.

Fanned out on a shelf under the display were half a dozen hat pins, ranging in size from three to six inches. Their handles were utilitarian black plastic.

"MaryAnne, I wanted to talk to you about your niece."

The woman reached across the register and pulled a cigarette out of the crumpled pack. "Need I ask which one?" When Estelle responded only with a tilt of the head, MaryAnne tapped the end of the cigarette against the glass countertop, then held it like a pencil, unlit. "We would be talking about little Deena, right?"

"Yes."

MaryAnne exhaled as if the cigarette were lit and she'd drawn a lungful. "What now?"

"She was charged this morning with bringing a weapon onto school grounds. The school suspended her for the remainder of the year."

"Oh, you're joking."

"No." Estelle pulled the plastic envelope from her pocket and laid it carefully on the counter in front of MaryAnne. The woman didn't change position, but Estelle saw her eyes flick from the envelope to the display on the shelf.

"Deena was carrying *that* in school?"

"Yes."

"*That's* the weapon?"

"Yes, ma'am."

"Oh, please," MaryAnne said, dragging the word out. "And she said that she bought it here?"

"She wouldn't say where she bought it, MaryAnne."

MaryAnne's frown was dark. She glared at Estelle, violet eyes first opening wide, then narrowing to a squint. "Well, so," she said. "That didn't take you long, did it. It just makes me all warm and fuzzy inside to think that I was the first one to come to mind."

"*Did* she buy it here?"

"Well, no doubt," MaryAnne snapped, and straightened up, waving a theatrical hand at the display. "Now you're going to tell me that it's illegal to sell this junk? And you're spending your time roaming all over town telling people what they can or can't sell?"

"No, I'm not doing that," Estelle said patiently. She slipped the evidence bag back into her pocket. "I thought maybe you'd like to know, is all."

"She has this in her little purse, and that earns her a year's suspension." MaryAnne sneered. "Aren't we all just *so* virtuous."

"Deena was carrying it threaded into the inseam of her jeans."

The woman's forehead puckered for an instant. "Now isn't she the clever one."

"MaryAnne, this is one of those dumb fads that kids jump into without thinking," Estelle said. "Who knows where it started, or how they hear about it. It would help *them* if they couldn't just walk in here and buy the things."

"Well, sure," MaryAnne said. "They could walk into any discount store and buy a set of knitting needles, too…sharpen 'em up, and there you go."

"Except knitting needles are too big, and they're nice soft aluminum or plastic. Not steel that holds a point, like those," Estelle added. "And I agree. They could walk into the hardware and buy a hatchet any day of the week, or a steak knife, or a pickax. Or how about a chain saw? They'd be a little harder to conceal, maybe. But those"—and she turned to nod at the display—"aren't intended for sale as *hat pins*, MaryAnne. We both know that. They're intended for sale to kids as weapons that are all the fad right now, that are easily concealable, and are as lethal as an ice pick." She saw the woman's face darken with anger and added, "It puzzles me that you would want to be part of that."

"You can go away any time now," MaryAnne said, turning half around. "This is the dumbest thing I ever heard."

"I tell you what," Estelle said, making no move to leave. She slipped a small camera from her pocket. "Do you mind?" MaryAnne didn't reply. Estelle took her time composing a photo of the hat pin display, stepping close and angling the shot to diminish the effect of flash glare on the glass.

MaryAnne glowered but didn't object as the undersheriff took three photos. On autopilot, the shop owner's hand snagged the butane lighter on the cash register and she lit the cigarette.

Estelle turned away from the case in time to see the angry tremble in the woman's hand.

"I think it's ludicrous that I'm having this conversation with the aunt of a young girl who was just in a fight where she or someone else could have been seriously hurt, and on top of that, who just got expelled from school for the rest of the year." The glower continued, but MaryAnne held her tongue, and Estelle counted that as progress.

"All I'm asking…and what, they're just a buck or so each? All I'm asking is that you sell those things only to little old ladies who want to hold their hats on," Estelle said. "Little old ladies who need a six-inch hat pin." Despite the smoke that MaryAnne made a point of exhaling in her direction, Estelle stepped closer to the counter. "I don't think that's a lot to ask, and I don't think it's out of line."

"Deena is old enough to make her own choices," MaryAnne said.

"Oh, sure," Estelle said. "At fourteen years old? She proved that this morning, didn't she." She smiled. "Remember what we were like back then?"

"No, thank God. I don't," MaryAnne snapped, but her tone had softened. "What was she trying to do, anyway?"

Ah, now we care, Estelle thought. "We don't know for sure. The best guess is that it was a jealous girlfriend-boyfriend thing. She thought that when she went back to school—maybe walking to or from—that she was going to be jumped. She wanted a little protection."

MaryAnne shook her head slowly, thoughtfully turning the ash off the end of the cigarette.

"We hope it isn't anything more than that," Estelle added. "Did Deena talk to you about her troubles?"

"If she did, that's between her and me," MaryAnne said, an edge back in her voice.

Estelle nodded. "Yes, it would be." She indicated the display. "And we'd appreciate any cooperation you can give us."

"I *assume*," MaryAnne said as Estelle turned to leave, "that I'm not the only merchant being harassed about all this?"

"Are there others I should talk to?" Estelle asked pleasantly. When MaryAnne just sniffed, she added, "You have a nice day."

Chapter Four

The sheriff was leaning against the wall, the copier and drinking fountain between him and the double doors leading into the County Commission chambers. His eyes were fixed on the polished tile floor. Like a bobble-head doll caught in a light breeze, his nod was slight but continuous. While he nodded, Posadas Mayor Peter Lujan talked, bent at the waist and intent, one crooked and arthritic finger hooked within striking distance of Robert Torrez's nose.

The sheriff glanced up as Estelle entered. His shoulders straightened, the nod increased, and he reached out a mammoth paw to rest on Lujan's shoulder as if searching for the on-off switch. Before he could disengage himself, a group of four men directly in front of the chamber doors dissolved, three heading inside and one making a beeline for Estelle.

"You've come to join the fun?" Dr. Arnold Gray said cheerfully. He extended a hand, and his chiropractor's grip was firm.

"Sure," Estelle replied. Gray was unshakable in his support of the proposal that the county should provide police services to the village, but his quiet logic hadn't made much of a dent on Barney Tinneman's doubts. As chairman of the commission, Gray's philosophy was to let others talk until the matter was resolved or reached a head. Estelle knew that the issue of the Village of Posadas abandoning its police force in favor of contracted services from the county had been jawed to death during various workshops and public meetings. Half a dozen stories had appeared in the *Posadas Register* before the village had voted in favor of the move, and waited patiently for the county to reach consensus.

Gray glanced at his watch. "Just about showtime." He flashed a quick smile as he turned toward the chambers. "I'll see you inside."

Sheriff Torrez finally managed to break away from Mayor Lujan and strode toward Estelle—or perhaps toward the outside door behind her. "What was the deal at the school?" he asked, voice low.

"A girl with a hat pin," Estelle said.

"You're kidding."

"No. A nice, six-inch-long steel hat pin. She had it laced in the inseam of her jeans."

"That's slick." He nodded at the county attorney who hustled into the building at that moment, favored them with a curt nod, and then vanished into the chambers. Torrez looked back at Estelle. "Zeigler found you, I assume."

"Yes. He said that Tinneman is still a roadblock."

Torrez muttered something and shook his head. "That old fart just likes to hear himself talk." He glanced back toward the doorway. "I guess they're about ready. I was thinkin' that I probably have some work I have to do, somewhere."

Estelle laughed. "Be brave, sir." She took the sheriff by the elbow and steered him gently toward the meeting room. "Is Eddie here?"

"Sure." Torrez grumbled. "He's already been on the hot seat." Estelle found it hard to believe that anyone could make the smooth, quick-witted police chief uncomfortable. "Well," Torrez added with a sigh, "let's give 'em a few more minutes."

The commission chambers were not crowded, but a respectable showing of residents were scattered throughout the small auditorium. Chief Eddie Mitchell had settled halfway back on the right side, one seat in from the aisle. Estelle slipped into that spot, and he looked up from the magazine he'd been reading.

Sheriff Torrez settled with a great creaking of leather and clanking of hardware into the seat directly behind her.

Mitchell leaned toward Estelle, his voice a loud stage whisper. "Weighty matters," he said.

"So I hear." Estelle scanned the room. "Are we going to have a vote today?"

"Ho, ho."

Four of the five commissioners were spaced around the huge semicircular table, a welter of microphones, papers, folders, and files marking each spot, including the empty seat where Tina Archuleta would normally sit. To the right, County Clerk Stacey Roybal hunched over her desk, sipping from a thermal cup and studying a thick computer readout, while at her elbow newspaper editor Pam Gardiner leaned on the edge of the dais, probing something in the document with her pencil eraser. Only Roybal's rimless granny glasses prevented her from looking twelve years old, tiny in comparison with the mountainous editor.

Commission Chairman Dr. Arnold Gray settled in his seat, glanced around the room, hesitated, then hefted the gavel. He leaned and said something to Barney Tinneman, seated to his right. Both men laughed. Gray rapped the gavel twice, and people dove for their seats. Estelle watched Pam Gardiner settle in the front row, voluminous handbag and camera case near at hand.

Gray nudged the microphone a bit. "We're back," he said by way of greeting. "For better or worse." He grinned toward the back corner where a short, sober man stood beside a large tripod-mounted video camera. "You have a fresh tape in that thing, Milt?" The man shifted his feet and looked uncomfortable when several members of the audience snickered. At every meeting she had ever attended in Posadas County, Estelle had seen Crowley filming from beginning to end. He and his camera were a fixture. What he then did with the tapes was a closely guarded mystery, beyond simply owning them as proof should some public servant step out of line. His small ranch was allegedly studded with hand-painted signs threatening trespassers and warning of the dangers of government—whether in the form of tax assessors, the U.S. Forest Service, the Internal Revenue Service, or the Highway Department.

"All right," Gray continued. "As I remember, when we adjourned, Mr. Tinneman had the floor."

"Now *that's* unusual," Barry Swartz said. He was seated at the extreme left, beside the county clerk. Sales manager at Chavez Chevrolet-Oldsmobile, he was a burly man with a quick smile who favored the rumpled look.

Tinneman didn't hesitate. "When we adjourned for lunch, Chief Mitchell was just wrapping up," he said. "Chief, did you have anything to add?"

Mitchell shook his head.

"Then I have a few more questions both for the sheriff and the county manager." He hesitated, glancing toward the rear of the chambers. The county manager's desk was situated in the back of the small auditorium, near the large framed county map. Kevin Zeigler preferred to face the commission from behind the audience, rather than taking a place up on the dais. Frequently needing either documents from his office across the hall or summoned to the phone, Zeigler could come and go from his vantage in the back without disturbing the commission.

"Kevin's on a power lunch," Tinneman said with a smirk. He glanced across the dais. "And so is Tina, I guess."

"She had an errand," Dr. Gray intoned. "And Kevin will be here shortly, I'm sure."

"Well, let's get started anyway." With an audible sigh, Torrez had lurched out of his seat. There were two microphone-equipped podiums in the commission chambers for members of the audience to use—one near the commissioners' dais on the far side of the hall, and one in the back, by the double entry doors. Crowley had set up his camera just to the left of the rear podium, where the sheriff chose to go…as far as possible from the commissioners and as close as possible to the exit doors.

With his camera, Crowley could cover either the speaker at the guest microphone, or the commission—but not both simultaneously. He chose to pan the commissioners.

"Sheriff, I'm still confused about this one basic issue"—and Tinneman held up his right index finger while he scanned the papers in front of him.

"He's confused about more than that," Chief Mitchell muttered to Estelle.

"My concern is coverage," Tinneman continued. "Small as the village department is, we've always got *someone* on duty... even if it's just one person."

"Actually, that's not true," Torrez said, and it sounded more like an aside.

"What's not true?" Tinneman looked up sharply.

"The village department has three and a half employees," Torrez said slowly. "The chief already testified to that. One secretary, one chief, one patrolman, and a part-time, noncertified officer who also serves as the animal control officer."

"We're aware of that."

You're aware of all of this, Estelle thought, wondering how many times the same issue needed to be mauled before a decision could be made.

"You can't cover twenty-four/seven with two and a half people, Mr. Tinneman. It's physically impossible," Torrez said.

"Three and a half," Tinneman interjected.

"The secretary doesn't go out on patrol," Mitchell said from the audience.

"Well, all right," Tinneman persisted. "But we're covered *most* of the time, are we not? During the busy times, like evenings, weekends?"

"I suppose," Torrez conceded. "If you can predict when 'busy' is going to be."

"Well, see...I want to know how the county can provide better coverage than that from *outside* the village. That's all I'm saying. And that's what I've been arguing all along, ever since we first had this notion tossed on the floor."

"Eighty-five percent of our responses to emergency calls are within the village limits," Torrez said. "Not counting traffic stops."

"That's most of them," Tinneman said, and Swartz muttered an aside that drew a chuckle from Dr. Gray. Tinneman ignored them. "So in your mind, there's no trouble picking up the slack."

"I don't see it as slack," Torrez responded. "For one thing, we plan to increase our manpower by two full-time officers."

"Isn't it true that there are times now when there is only one deputy on the road? One deputy for the whole county?"

"Yes."

"One deputy for the *entire* county?"

"Yes," Torrez responded patiently.

"So if there's a call within the village, that leaves no one on the road out in the county?"

"There's usually a state police officer within range."

"*Usually*. But not always." When Torrez didn't respond, Tinneman relaxed back in his chair. "Sheriff, who's on duty for the county right now?" He rapped the dais with a stiff index finger. "Right at this moment? Who's working?"

"Me, the undersheriff, and one deputy."

"Is that deputy certified?"

"No. Not yet."

"So essentially, it's you two, then." He swept a finger to include Torrez and Estelle. "And you're stuck in here. Right now, who's on duty in the village?"

Mitchell shifted in his seat. "Officer Sisneros," he said.

Tinneman frowned, looked first to the right, and then to the left as if caught in a profound conundrum. "See, that's the thing. Is Tuesday afternoon considered a high-crime time around here?" Someone in the audience laughed, but Tinneman held the pose until Torrez responded.

"No, sir. It's not."

"And yet we *have five* officers on duty."

"No, sir, we don't."

"Well, explain to me, then."

"Myself, the chief, and the undersheriff are *always* on call," Torrez said. "We don't work any particular shift. We're around when we need to be. We're here right now because of this meeting. As far as *working* officers are concerned, cops who are out in cars and able to respond to dispatch, you've got Sisneros in the village, and one uncertified deputy in the county." A flicker of a smile touched the sheriff's handsome face. "And if something major happens, you'd see the three of us headin' out this door."

"And so how is that coverage going to improve with this merger?"

"It's not." When Tinneman looked triumphant, Torrez added, "The only way coverage is going to improve is to hire more staff. Merging the two departments saves some money spent on—"

When he stopped short, groping for the right word, Gray leaned forward. "Infrastructure?"

"That's it."

"Now here's the question," Tinneman said. "Is the amount of money that the village will spend to contract with us instead of having their own department *sufficient...*"—he lingered on the word—"is it sufficient to provide the extra patrol officers that you say you need?"

"Probably not."

The silence hung for a moment as Tinneman assumed that the sheriff planned to amplify his answer. When Torrez didn't, the commissioner shrugged his shoulders. "I just don't see how we can take this on," he said wearily.

"No one will *ever* spend enough to do the job right," Commissioner Dulci Corona said. She shook her head in disgust.

"Well, that's not the case—," Tinneman started to say.

"Yes, it *is* the case," Corona snapped, sounding like the grade school teacher she had been for thirty years. "No one wants to pay for police, but everyone will complain when an officer doesn't show up in ten seconds when he's called. We have an opportunity now to do something right. We can have a well-organized department that's responsive in *both* the village and the county. We just *might* have to pay for it."

"And that money comes from where?" Tinneman asked.

"There's *always* money," Corona said. "That's the county manager's job. To find it."

Tinneman glanced back toward Zeigler's still-empty desk. He ducked his head, turning toward Dr. Gray. "Was Kevin coming back this afternoon?"

Gray nodded. "As far as I know."

"I have a couple of budget questions I want to explore with him," Tinneman said. Torrez was already headed for his seat. "Sheriff, do you have your budget with you?"

Torrez hesitated, frowning. He settled into his seat when he saw Estelle raise her hand in response.

"Ah, you're the departmental budget guru, Undersheriff?" Tinneman asked. He smiled benignly as Estelle rose and walked back to the podium. "Do you need to borrow some paper-work?" He held up a thick document.

"No, sir. I don't think so."

Milton Crowley swiveled the video camera so that its glass eye stared at her, and Estelle could hear it adjusting for the distance and dimmer light in the back of the room.

"Undersheriff Guzman, the chief told us this morning that his village department costs something like thirty-seven thousand dollars per person. Do I have that right?" Tinneman riffled through papers, stopped and underlined something with his pencil. "Counting salary, workman's comp, benefits, vehicles, everything else, right down to the tissue paper in the restroom, it comes to just over a hundred thirty-one thousand for the department. That's a little over thirty-seven thousand per person, if we divide it out that way." He looked up at Estelle expectantly.

"Thirty-seven thousand four hundred seventy-three and sixty-nine cents," Estelle said.

"Exactly," Tinneman said with satisfaction. "I was going to ask Mr. Zeigler what the comparable figure for the sheriff's department is. Would you happen to know?"

"If you take the total budget and divide it by the number of employees, the figure is just under forty-two thousand," Estelle said.

"So the village PD actually costs less to operate than the sheriff's department?" Somehow, Tinneman made it sound as if this astounding revelation hadn't been hashed and rehashed in a half dozen meetings and conferences.

"We also run a small jail unit, sir. On top of that, we have civil law responsibilities that the village does not have. We also have a considerable fleet of vehicles. As you know, most deputies now take their vehicles home to cut response time."

"It's my understanding, though, that the village is offering right around one hundred twenty-five thousand dollars for the merger, though. That's not even three officers, is it?"

"No, sir."

"Great deal for the village."

Dulci Corona tossed her pencil on the desk. "I say that we accept the village offer and kick in enough for the Sheriff's Department to hire *three* full-time officers. Let's do this right."

"I'd want to see the figures on that," Tinneman said. "Can somebody give Kevin a call? We need him here. I think he fell into his martini or something."

"Do you have any more questions for the undersheriff?" Dr. Gray asked.

"No, actually, I want to talk to the county manager," Tinneman said doggedly.

"I'll check for you," Estelle said. Torrez turned and shot her an expression of impatience as she left the podium and slipped out the doors, irritated that she'd made her escape and he'd missed his chance. Across the foyer, Estelle saw Penny Barnes at her desk in the manager's office.

"Barney wants to talk to Kevin," Estelle said, and Penny made a face.

"Barney *always* wants to talk," she said. "He's not back from lunch yet?" She reached for the phone, dialed, and waited, then shook her head. "I'll put a message on his pager."

"He told me this morning that he had some errands."

Penny reached forward and pulled the calendar closer. "He wanted to talk to one of the men over at the highway barn about some workman's comp thing. That's the only one I know about." She looked up helpfully at Estelle. "You know…just errands."

"How about at home?"

Penny tried that number without success. "He's about the hardest man in the world to keep track of," she said, snapping off the phone. She tapped a pile of papers at her left elbow. "If you see him before I do, tell him I need to bend his ear, too."

Estelle reentered the commission meeting to find Dulci Corona once more holding the floor, determined this time to head off Barney Tinneman before the commissioner settled into yet another lengthy examination of things already well known. Gray glanced at Estelle with raised eyebrows, and the undersheriff shook her head and shrugged.

Undeterred, Corona offered the motion that would provide police services to the village. To Estelle's surprise, and evidently to Barney Tinneman's as well, Patric Sweeney immediately offered a second. When Tinneman ducked his head and appeared as if he was winding up to launch into another round of discussion, Dr. Gray straightened his shoulders and thumped his pencil down on the table.

"We have a motion and a second. Let's call the question."

County Clerk called the roll, and when his name was called, Tinneman wearily shook his head and voted in favor, making it unanimous. Estelle leaned toward Chief Eddie Mitchell, who had already agreed to return to the Sheriff's Department as its only captain should the politicians actually make up their minds. "Welcome back, sir."

Chapter Five

At first glance, what the political decision set in motion seemed simple enough. The Village of Posadas had voted to dissolve its small police department if the county would then agree to provide law enforcement within the village limits. The centralized dispatch housed at the Sheriff's Department already dispatched both county and village, so Dispatcher Gayle Torrez and her crew wouldn't miss a beat.

The county department had no officers ranked between the patrol sergeants and the undersheriff, and when asked if he'd rather be called a lieutenant or a captain, Eddie Mitchell had shrugged and said, "Captain's easier to spell."

The two village patrol cars, both bright blue and white and boldly lettered with various emblems including the large DARE, logo, would wear out soon enough and would be replaced with county units. Estelle counted all those things as minor concerns.

But she knew that in reality, the changeover would be a paperwork nightmare. Five enormously heavy filing cabinets waited in the small, musty village police office, cabinets filled with confidential criminal records dating back who knew how long—the "secrets of Posadas," as Mitchell called them.

Eduardo Martinez, the affable, low-key police chief before Mitchell, had started the process of updating the village department to the computer age. Some of the material from files generated within the past decade had become part of the NIBRS database system—a pool of information to which all agencies in the state contributed. From those files, it was another instant electronic step to the National Crime Information Center's data files.

Somehow, the vast backlog of village files—all of them, not just a select few—would have to be merged with the existing county records to form a single, cohesive, accessible unit. Physically moving the files from village to county was a simple afternoon's work using one of the county vans. Then the real work began. Someone would have to filter through every last scrap of paper, every photo, every deposition in order to merge village and county files.

"Put it on the computer" was easy to say. That meant that someone actually had to sit at the computer keyboard and type every scrap of information into the system...without error, without omission, without editing.

And, because of the nature of law enforcement, it was a task that couldn't wait to be done over months or years. Estelle knew that Posadas County was as much a part of *mañana* land as the rest of the state, maybe more so. But files and information had to be accessible for ongoing investigations. Further, since there were issues of maintaining both confidentiality and the chain of evidence, the Sheriff's Department couldn't simply hire a couple of high school kids at minimum wage to clean up the records.

After leaving the county meeting, Estelle returned to her office. Without a doubt, her best source for organizational strategy was County Manager Kevin Zeigler. She planned to spend the afternoon preparing a list of questions and proposed strategies to discuss with Zeigler, since she knew that Sheriff Robert Torrez wouldn't.

Regardless of the sheriff's many talents, his allergies to paperwork and bureaucracy were legendary. He had wasted no time in outlining his own strategy.

"If these *politicos* decide to do this," he had said to Estelle Reyes-Guzman before the first exploratory meeting between county and village, "the project is yours." He had glowered at her for a long moment and then added, "If I have to do it, it'll be a major screwup, and we both know it."

When she'd mentioned the conversation to Chief-soon-to-be-Captain Mitchell, he had laughed.

"If I had to go into a dark warehouse against fifty guys with Uzis, there's nobody I'd rather have at my back," he said. "But if I had to figure out a paperwork problem, Bobby is the *last* person I'd ask for help."

But that Tuesday afternoon after her return to her office, the focus to deal with the challenge of merging dusty, yellowing files filled with decades of unhappy moments eluded Estelle. After fifteen minutes and a dozen senseless doodles on her desk pad, she found her mind circling back to the image of her small son standing in the dim light, delicate hands exploring the black and white mysteries of the piano keyboard.

Finally she tossed down her pencil and swiveled her chair around to face the bookcase behind her. She pulled a Las Cruces telephone directory from the bottom shelf and in a moment found the number she wanted.

Holding the book open with her left hand, she reached for the phone and punched in the numbers with her thumb.

"Hildebrand and Sons Music," the cheerful voice greeted. "Good afternoon. This is Ryan."

"Good afternoon. Sir, this is Estelle Guzman over in Posadas. I—" She paused as the office door opened and Gayle's head appeared. "Just a minute, sir." Gayle waited until the undersheriff had the mouthpiece covered.

"They've got something going on over on Candelaria," the dispatcher said. "Eddie's not sure if it's a domestic or not. He wanted you to come over."

Estelle stood up quickly. "Sir, I'll call you back." She hung up the phone as she rounded the desk, not waiting for the salesman's acknowledgment.

"One oh eight Candelaria," Gayle said. "Right next door to Zeigler's."

"Eddie didn't say what it was?"

"He just got there," Gayle said, retreating back toward dispatch. "We've got one ambulance on the way. He said he's got one female down and then he told me to find you."

"I'm on my way," Estelle said, then paused. "If the county manager should happen to call, don't let him escape. I need to talk with him."

"Kevin's probably over there already," Gayle said. "The call is from his next-door neighbors, and you know how they are."

Estelle nodded wearily. "I know *exactly* how they are."

Candelaria Court was a small cul-de-sac off MacArthur on the east side of Posadas—like nearly everything else in the village, less than a minute from the Sheriff's Office on Bustos. As Estelle turned the county car south on MacArthur just beyond the small and shabby Burger Heaven restaurant, she could see the intersection of Candelaria Court, and beyond, filtered through the elms, an array of winking emergency lights.

Burrowed in her office with door closed and radio switched off, she had missed the initial call…but this one was no surprise. As soon as she had heard whom Deena Hurtado had tried to fight at the school volleyball game, as soon as she had heard that Carmen Acosta had been suspended for six days, Estelle had anticipated a blowup at the Acosta residence.

Of all the village domestic disturbance reports that some lucky records clerk would transfer into the computer, half a hundred of them would include the name of the Acostas, stretching back fifteen years.

The postfight commentators at the middle school had agreed that, on the previous Tuesday, Carmen Acosta had won a clear decision over Deena Hurtado before referees had stepped in to separate the two scrapping girls. What the unfortunate Deena might not have realized was that her opponent had had lots of practice. The middle of five children, Carmen regularly thumped on her two younger sisters while her two older brothers whupped up on her.

With five children who had grown too fleet of foot for him to catch, Freddy Acosta regularly took out his frustrations on

Juanita, his fiery spouse. Slow but stout, Juanita usually was able to defend herself, and more than once had sent Freddy to the emergency room for stitches. On one occasion when Estelle had happened to be the responding officer, Freddy had shaken his head ruefully, sitting bloody and battered on the emergency room table. "I guess I said the wrong thing," he had muttered, and refused to tell Estelle just what it was that his *esposa* had hit him with, opening up a gaping hole in his scalp that required twelve stitches.

School usually provided something of a haven for Carmen from her boisterous, hit-first family. The six-day suspension that was supposed to allow her to cool her heels instead merely placed her at ground zero in the Acosta household. Her mother worked long hours in the parts department of Chavez Chevrolet-Olds, but Freddy Acosta had been on disability for more than a year after slipping on a slick tile at Posadas General Hospital—part of the floor he'd finished mopping not two minutes before. He would be home.

As she turned onto Candelaria Court, Estelle saw Mike Sisneros, the full-time village patrolman, running a yellow tape from the back bumper of his patrol car to the fence that separated the Acostas' small cinder-block house from their neighbor's.

The ambulance was parked directly in front of the driveway, back doors agape. Farther on, Eddie Mitchell's unmarked Chevy was nosed into the curb directly behind Sheriff Torrez's department Expedition.

Sisneros jogged toward her as she pulled the county car to the far side of the street. Shorter than Estelle's five seven, Sisneros had inherited his mother's round Acoma Indian face and his father's spare build.

"They really did it this time," he said. "Carmen's inside. The EMTs are workin' on her." He turned and nodded toward Mitchell's car. "The chief has Freddy locked up over there."

The Acostas' driveway was empty. "You need to run a tape on the other side," Estelle said.

"I was just headed that way."

"Did anyone talk to Kevin?" she asked. The county manager's white county truck was parked in his driveway one door east of Acostas'. Nosed in behind his personal car, an older-model Datsun 280Z.

"Haven't seen him," Sisneros said. "I did a quick check, but nobody's home. Not Zeigler or his roommate."

Estelle frowned. "What did Freddy have to say?"

"Not a hell of a lot. He says that he walked over to the convenience store, and when he came back home, he found the place tore up and Carmen in her bedroom, beat to a pulp." He shrugged. "That's all I know."

Twisting at the waist, Estelle surveyed the neighborhood. Five doors north, just before the intersection with MacArthur, Doris Marens stood on her front steps, arms tightly folded across her chest, watching. At least three neighborhood dogs carried on in cadence. In the other direction, beyond Zeigler's house, lay an empty field, the dried kochia four feet high.

"You might talk to Mrs. Marens when you get a chance," Estelle said.

"I'm on it," Sisneros replied. He lifted the tape so the undersheriff could duck under, and she walked slowly along the sidewalk to the gravel driveway. A swatch of dirt a dozen yards wide separated the Acostas' gravel from Zeigler's concrete drive. Choosing her path carefully, she stepped across to the county pickup truck and touched the hood. It was warm, warmer than it should have been even with the afternoon sun dappling through the sparse limbs of the single large elm in the front yard.

"Good question," a voice behind her said. She turned and saw the sheriff standing in the side doorway of the Acostas' home. "Freddy says the truck wasn't there when he left to walk to the store."

Estelle glanced through the truck's closed driver's window and saw that the vehicle wasn't locked. The keys were in the ignition.

Torrez held the Acostas' kitchen door for her until she crossed to the house. "Miss Carmen might have won the first round, but not this one," he said. He propped the door open with a capped ballpoint pen, and he motioned for Estelle to slip past him without touching the door frame. "Someone beat the crap out of her and added a few touches for good measure."

Estelle halted two steps into the Acostas' kitchen. "She's alive?"

"Just." He gently closed the door. "There's evidence that the fight went from here right through the house. She's in her bedroom. They're trying to figure out how to transport her without making matters worse."

"Freddy found her? Or Freddy beat up on her."

"I ain't thinkin'," the sheriff said, shaking his head. "This isn't his style, though." Another siren announced more emergency traffic, and Torrez touched Estelle's elbow. "I want you to see her before they move her. We need to make it snappy, though. They called another crew so they'd have lots of help."

Estelle followed in Torrez's footsteps as the sheriff made his way carefully through the house, keeping his hands in his pockets. They crossed the littered living room, stepping around an entertainment console. The screen of the television was shattered, the entire console skewed toward the wall.

Carmen Acosta's bedroom was part of a small, shed-roofed addition on the east side of the house that included another bedroom and a small bath. The narrow door was open but blocked by the wide shoulders of Nina Burns, one of the EMTs.

"I think right out the front door," she was saying. "But you can't wheel it, Rick." She turned and glanced at Torrez, then at Estelle. "And we need to wait until we have enough hands."

"Here's the hands," Torrez said.

"Nah, we got a team comin' right behind you there." She reached out toward Estelle. "You want to slip in here?"

Carmen lay facedown on her narrow single bed as if she'd flopped there after a hard day picking fights at school. Her clothing—a sweatshirt with an ACTITUD ES TODO logo across the back, jeans, and white socks—were rumpled but roughly in place.

One of the EMTs knelt on the opposite side of the bed near the girl's head, one large hand cupped over Carmen's right hand and the other holding an oxygen mask in place. Beside him, another emergency tech worked to arrange an IV line into Carmen's left arm. Even as Estelle watched, the girl's right foot lifted off the bed a couple of inches.

"It's okay," the EMT holding the mask said, and immediately transferred his free hand in a featherlight touch to the top of the girl's head. He looked up as Estelle approached and made a face, shaking his head at the same time.

He lifted his hand and pointed.

"Ay," Estelle whispered. Blood soaked the back of Carmen Acosta's head, some of it running down into the creases in the back of her neck under her short, spiked hair. Estelle's attention was drawn to an object in the girl's left ear. At first glance, it might have been mistaken for a black hearing aid, or a black plastic dangly earring that had been swept upward into the ear canal. But the girl had not been so lucky. Whatever other injuries Carmen Acosta might have suffered, the hat pin driven into her brain through her left ear would have been the finishing touch.

Chapter Six

The young EMT's ruddy face faded to the color of bleached linen, but he didn't move his hands from Carmen's head. Out of reflex, he ducked so that he could see the girl's right ear as if he expected to see the point of the hat pin protruding there.

"It's six inches long?" he asked, and Estelle nodded. She knelt on the floor, her face close to Carmen's. The girl's eyes were half open, her lips parted. If she was breathing, her respiration was too shallow and fleeting to notice. And the EMT, Cliff Gates, was panting so loud that he was apt to need oxygen himself.

"It *could* be," Estelle whispered. The display in Mary Anne Bustamonte's Great Notions shop included hat pins that ranged from three to six inches—and teenagers would lean toward excess. Estelle rose to her feet and moved out of the way as two EMTs brought the spinal board into the small bedroom. Working quickly, she snapped half a dozen photos of the girl, including close-ups with the hat pin in place, all the while sidestepping the frantic bustle of the rescue crew. She glanced up to see Sheriff Torrez's towering figure appear in the bedroom doorway.

"Did someone notify Carmen's mother?" Estelle asked, and the sheriff nodded.

"She's on the way."

Estelle stepped across the room and took Torrez by the arm, steering him back out of the bedroom. "Someone needs to ride in the ambulance with Carmen," she said. "We're going to need her clothing, for one thing." Chief Eddie Mitchell joined them.

"I'll arrange that," Mitchell said. "Is there anything in particular that you're after?"

"Just all her clothing, Eddie. If there's blood evidence, I don't want that going in the incinerator. And if they cut off her jeans, make sure they don't disturb the inseam." She ran a hand down the inside of her own leg.

Mitchell frowned. "Related to the school business this morning, you think?"

"I don't know yet. But I don't like coincidence."

"It don't look like we're going to get a statement from her," Torrez said. "Everything we can find is going to count for something." He lowered his voice. "You want me to swing around and pick up the Hurtado girl?"

"Not yet," Estelle whispered. "That looks like the same sort of hat pin that I confiscated this morning, but there's no doubt in my mind that there are others in town." She shook her head. "Six inches of hat pin."

"Christ," Mitchell muttered.

"She'll almost certainly be airlifted to Albuquerque if she survives the transfer out of here." She glanced back inside the room. Now five in number, the EMTs were tackling the challenge of moving Carmen's limp body from facedown on the bed to face-down on the spinal board without changing the position of her head relative to the rest of her body. Nina Burns was on the radio. Estelle recognized her husband's voice as the EMT fired information to the physician and received instructions in return.

"No," one of the EMTs said, and took the oxygen mask from Cliff Gates. "You've got to stay away from the ear." Estelle felt the hair stand up on the back of her neck. "Get me an ear cup," Nina said. In a moment they had secured the padded plastic cup— nothing more than half of a set of inexpensive earphones—over Carmen's left ear, sheltering the handle and stem of the pin from contact. With that taped securely in place, they lifted Carmen off the bed in slow motion, ten hands working in concert so that the position of her body didn't shift.

Padded, strapped, and taped, with IVs dripping and rich oxygen flooding her injured brain, Carmen Acosta started her long ride to Posadas General Hospital.

As the EMTs orchestrated their way through the narrow bedroom door with the spinal board and its passenger, Nina Burns caught Estelle's eye. "Dr. Guzman has arranged air transport to Albuquerque," Nina said. "The air ambulance just left Las Cruces, so it shouldn't be long."

They crossed the small living room, and Village Officer Mike Sisneros appeared in the doorway just as they reached it. He immediately backtracked out of the way. Estelle saw Juanita Acosta behind Sisneros, rushing up the sidewalk toward the house. The village officer caught Juanita by the arm. He transferred his grip to a shoulder hug, keeping her out of the EMTs' path.

Someone had released her husband Freddy from the back-seat of Mitchell's patrol car, and he now stood in the dirt beside the sidewalk, hands thrust in his pockets, looking as if he wanted to punch someone.

Juanita's heavy-featured face reflected fury more than anything else, perhaps through long years of practice. But her hands told a different story, clasped tightly together between her breasts as the EMTs approached carrying her motionless daughter.

"Por Dios," she said. "Now what?" Estelle had a fleeting image of the heavy, powerful woman lunging forward, knocking the carefully balanced EMTs and their burden in six different directions.

"Mrs. Acosta," the undersheriff said, and she reached out a hand to grip Juanita's right wrist. Sisneros didn't release his hug, and the two of them guided the woman out of the way. "Juanita, we don't know what happened yet, but they're taking Carmen to the hospital. She'll be transferred by air ambulance to Albuquerque as soon as she's stabilized. It's important that you go with her."

"Por Dios," Juanita said again, and she turned toward Freddy as if he were responsible.

"You can ride right in the ambulance with us, ma'am," Nina Burns added as she passed. "There's lots of room."

"Mrs. Acosta, I'll go with you," Chief Mitchell said, and he replaced Sisneros at the woman's elbow.

A school bus nosed into Candelaria and eased to a stop, the driver facing the sea of flashing emergency lights. Estelle released Juanita's arm with a final pat and crossed the scruffy grass toward Freddy.

"Sir, I need your help," she said. The man nodded absently, eyes locked on his daughter's silent form as it was whisked toward the yawning doors of the ambulance. "Sir?" She touched his shoulder.

"I just don't know what happened," he said, voice distant. "I came home, and there she was…"

"Mr. Acosta, are the other kids on that bus?"

He looked up quickly. "Oh. Yes. Lucinda and Josie." Another Sheriff's Department vehicle had swung into the street from MacArthur, blocking the bus' path so the driver wouldn't inadvertently block the ambulance. Deputy Dennis Collins got out of the Bronco and advanced on the bus, and Estelle saw the door flick open. Immediately behind Collins' unit, Linda Real arrived. The Sheriff's Department photographer weaved her small Honda around the bus and patrol unit, then accelerated quickly down the block, parking directly behind Estelle's car.

"Here's what I need you to do, Mr. Acosta," Estelle said. She moved in front of Freddy, forcing herself into his line of vision. "Do you have somewhere that you and the kids can stay tonight?"

"Stay?"

"For tonight. You can't stay here."

Sheriff Torrez appeared behind her. "Freddy, take the kids on over to Armand's." It didn't surprise Estelle that the sheriff knew the Acostas' relatives; he may have shared a few of them. "Where are Mauro and Tony?"

"There are the girls now," Freddy said, taking a step forward. Five backpack-toting youngsters had stepped off the bus. Deputy Collins ushered them as a group to the sidewalk, talked to them briefly, and ushered three of them around the corner to the first house on MacArthur. The other two children waited with the deputy.

Torrez keyed his handheld radio. "Dennis, keep the kids right there for a little bit," he said. "Mr. Acosta will be up there in a minute."

The sheriff pointed the stubby radio antenna at Freddy Acosta. "Freddy…where are Mauro and Tony? We got to know," he asked again.

Apprehension buckled Freddy Acosta's eyebrows together as if he had just remembered that he had two older boys to consider as well. "They don't ride the bus," he said.

"No shit," Torrez said. "They have their own car?"

"Oh, no," Freddy said quickly. "No…they usually ride with somebody, or walk. You know, when you cut right across, it's not very far."

Torrez leaned his head toward Freddy. "We know where the damn school is, Freddy. You don't know where they are, then?"

"Well, you know," Freddy said helplessly. "Sometimes Tony rides his bike. Well, until it broke, he did. Not Mauro. He usually catches a ride with somebody."

With the ambulance now safely away, the school bus had backed out of Candelaria, and Estelle could see the two Acosta girls sitting on the sidewalk, backpacks making convenient chair backs.

"Sir," she said, "you said that you walked uptown? When you did that, you left Carmen alone in the house?"

Freddy nodded. "I shouldn't have left her like that," he murmured.

"That's not the issue, sir," Estelle said. "When you walked up the street, you didn't see anyone in the neighborhood who you didn't know?" He shook his head slowly. "You don't remember seeing any vehicles?" His head had settled into a methodical rhythm. "Do you remember what time that was?" The oscillation slowed, but Freddy didn't reply.

"Sir, whatever you can remember is going to help us." The dispatcher had taken the father's desperate 911 call at 2:38 p.m.

Estelle could picture Freddy plodding home, ambling up the driveway, entering the house through the kitchen door, and taking several minutes to notice the results of the ruckus. If he had paused in the kitchen, it was conceivable that he wouldn't notice anything amiss for some time.

"I guess," Freddy started slowly. "I guess that I walked up to the car place, there, right around noon. I was going to see if Juanita could break away for lunch, maybe. We sometimes do that. Right there at the burger place."

"And that's what you did today?"

Freddy nodded and then brightened a little. "You know, I walked in and Juanita was on the telephone. I remember her looking at the clock, and then she just shook her head at me. I remember that."

"What time was that?"

"Just like…like twelve oh one. Something like that. Right at noon."

"And then after that, what? You walked downtown?" Torrez asked.

"I thought maybe I'd get a pizza or something. But then I just went to Tommy's and got some chips. I talked to a few people, you know…just people I know. I had a cup of coffee. I guess…"

"When you came back home, you didn't see anything out of the ordinary?" Torrez said, clearly irritated at the man's wandering reminiscence. "Nobody outside, no traffic, nothing?"

Freddy shook his head. "Just like…you know? Like always, I guess."

Like always, Estelle thought.

"And then I came inside…" His lip quivered. "The first thing I saw…the first thing was the telephone on the floor. I almost stepped on it. I looked across the living room and that's when I saw the television set, all smashed." He looked helplessly at Estelle. "Who would do such a thing to Carmen?"

Estelle turned and regarded the house and driveway toward the east. "Mr. Acosta, you said that the county manager's truck was *not* there when you left to walk uptown?"

"It sure wasn't. I'm sure of that. I went out that side door, you know. It wasn't there then."

"But it *was* parked there when you returned?"

He nodded and turned to look at the small white county truck. "He's not home, though."

"We hope not," she almost said, but Freddy Acosta's assumption was a natural one to make. If the peripatetic Kevin Zeigler had stopped home for a quick nap—and he would have had to be incapacitated with the flu, or worse, to do something like that—the hubbub next door would have roused him out of bed. She shot a glance at Sheriff Robert Torrez. He was jotting something down in a tiny notebook.

"I'll give Judge Hobart a call," he said to Estelle, and then turned back to Freddy. "You'll take the kids to Armand's?"

"I guess so. They're going to need some things from inside…"

Torrez shook his head quickly. "Nobody goes inside, Freddy. Not until we're finished. Maybe by later this evening. We'll keep you posted. Right now, you need to go get the kids settled and then make arrangements to meet your wife at the hospital. They might let both of you ride up to Albuquerque on the plane. If not, you'll need the car." Juanita Acosta had parked diagonally, the older-model Fairlane's massive rear end blocking much of the street.

"I got my keys, I guess," Freddy said. He glanced at the house and Estelle saw his eyes flick to the yellow crime-scene ribbon. "You'll let me know?" he asked.

"Of course," Estelle said. "Right now, you need to be with Juanita and your daughter. And you need to find the boys."

He nodded and set off toward the car.

"What?" Sheriff Torrez said when he saw the expression on her face. The sudden question jerked Estelle's head around. He tapped the side of his head and lifted his chin at her in question.

"Where's Zeigler?" she asked.

"That's a hell of a good question," Torrez said.

Chapter Seven

With the Acostas' home cleared of the hubbub of paramedics and members of the family, Estelle stood for a moment at the kitchen door, looking across the side yard toward Kevin Zeigler's neighboring house. There might be a perfectly simple explanation for the truck's presence. But the key ring, loaded with not only ignition keys, but a wad of other county keys as well—office, gates, who knew what all? People didn't go far without their keys.

Estelle forced her attention back to the evidence directly in front of her: the Acostas' kitchen door. A tear in the screen immediately beside the latch looked as if someone had punched through to flip the flimsy lock, but there were so many tears, so many dents and buckles in the door's aluminum frame that it was impossible to tell what was recent and what was simply the result of several seasons' worth of rambunctious children.

The inner door had been flung open so hard that the cheap brass doorstop had broken, and the doorknob had slammed into the wall. A spattering of paint and Sheetrock dust marked the floor below the strike.

"I think she was tryin' to lock the door," Torrez said. With the cap of his ballpoint pen, he touched the brass lock in the middle of the doorknob. It was one of those smooth, difficult-to-grasp things that projected a bare minimum from the knob. "I got one of these that's a real pain in the ass…it hangs up all the time. I can see old Carmen struggling with it, and whoever's on the outside just busts right through."

He turned and pointed at the small table that sat askew, far too close to the kitchen range. "That got scooted back."

Estelle looked from the kitchen toward the small dining room. "And then she headed for the telephone," she said. The telephone answering-machine combination rested on one wing of an impressive oak hutch in the dining room, but the wireless receiver was in the bedroom, where Freddy had left it when he called 911.

"Lemme show you something," Torrez said. He stepped through the doorway into the dining room. "I think she *got* to the phone," he said. "Either that, or they struggled in that doorway between the dining room and living room, right about where the phone *was*. That's the direction she was headed." He knelt down and touched a gouge in the wallpaper beside the doorway that led into the living room.

While the kitchen was smooth-plastered Sheetrock painted in ubiquitous eggshell white, the dining room was mid-'40s fancy, with paneled wainscoting below a painted wood-trim strip. Above the strip, the wallpaper was dark Victorian, the dense curlicues and floral patterns stained in several places from roof leaks.

Estelle knelt beside the sheriff and peered closely. The overhead light fixture wasn't much help, and she pulled a tiny flashlight from her jacket pocket and snapped it on, examining the gouge. The mark began three inches above the wainscoting trim, digging through the wallpaper into the Sheetrock behind it. The gouge stopped abruptly with a diagonal bruise across the horizontal painted strip.

"Took a pretty good lick," the sheriff said.

Going to her hands and knees, she bent low, playing the flashlight beam on the old carpet, her face so close she could smell the musty fibers. She could imagine a dusting of gypsum from the wallboard. If so, that trace was mixed with a fair coating of dust, lint, human and cat hair that the vacuum cleaner had missed.

"The only thing I see in the living room is that busted TV," Torrez said. "One of 'em got into the TV somehow, but I didn't see anything else broken except the busted glass."

Estelle straightened up, trying to imagine Carmen's path through the house. Freddy Acosta had said that he entered the kitchen door, then walked through toward his daughter's bedroom. It would have taken his eyes a while to adjust to the dim light after time spent outside, but he had seen, or almost tripped over, the telephone on the floor, and he would have had to be blind to miss the shattered television.

And Freddy's intrusion had been only the beginning of evidence trampling. Beyond the dining room, traffic had complicated matters further. After Freddy's discovery of his daughter's battered body in the bedroom and his call to 911, half a dozen emergency personnel had mobbed through the place.

"Seein' this mess, he'd head right for the bedroom to check on her," Torrez said.

"Maybe so." Estelle avoided the glass as she crossed the small living room and stood in the doorway of Carmen's bedroom. On the nightstand beside the bed, a much-loved teddy bear leaned against the lamp base. The bed had been bumped toward the wall, and other stuffed animals had scattered as the bedding and pillows were thrashed. A thick, dark stain marked where the blood from Carmen's cracked head had puddled.

"I called Mears, Abeyta, and Taber to give us a hand," Torrez said. "We're going to have to spend a good bit of time combing this place."

Estelle nodded. "I want that," she said, pointing at the telephone receiver. It lay beside one of the pillows where Freddy had tossed it. "Did you find anything outside?"

The sheriff shrugged. "There's about a thousand prints in the dirt. Could be that half the neighborhood's gone in or out that door in the past twenty-four hours. And half a dozen Acostas."

"We need to make sure we don't add any more," Estelle said as she turned from the bedroom. "His tracks are out there somewhere."

"His or hers," Torrez said.

"His."

"You're sure about that?"

"Someone slammed the back door open hard enough to punch a hole in the wall? Then swings something and puts a deep gouge in the plaster of the dining room? And on top of that, Carmen Acosta was a tough little girl. She probably weighs, what, a hundred and thirty or forty pounds? And an attitude to match. This wasn't some tussle with another kid."

"Not someone like Deena Hurtado, you mean?"

Estelle shook her head. "Besides, if the intruder was a kid, Carmen wouldn't have tried to call nine-one-one, Bobby. I get the impression that she's a great one to settle her own disputes. For her to call the cops puts the whole thing in a different light." She hesitated. "But stranger things have happened," she added. "I don't want to rule anything out just now. *Nos vemos.*" She glanced at her watch as she slipped her phone out of her pocket. She walked back across the living room, and before she reached the dining room, Penny Barnes answered the call in the county manager's office.

"Penny, this is Estelle," the undersheriff said. "Did Kevin check in yet?"

"Nope," Penny said. "That rascal's playing hooky."

"You've tried all the easy places? The maintenance barn, stuff like that?"

"Everywhere," Penny said emphatically. "I need his signature on a bunch of checks, and Tinneman is still breathing hard down my neck. They've had to cancel a whole bunch of things off the meeting agenda. I don't know what Kevin was thinking, not letting me know even a little something."

"He didn't leave with someone?"

"Oh, Estelle, I don't remember. At lunch, you know, everyone just sort of scoots. He went out saying he had some errands, and was maybe going to stop at the county barn. What's going on over there, anyway? We're listening to the scanner, and it sounds like the end of the world or something."

"Nothing like that," Estelle said. "If Kevin had some personal errands to do, who would know, do you think?"

Penny hesitated. "He probably talks to me as much as any-body," she said.

"Who did he talk to this morning? Do you recall?"

"A million people. You know how it goes."

"No one out of the ordinary that you remember?"

"I know that William Page called the office first thing this morning, before the meeting. They chatted for quite a while… and Kevin seemed upbeat about something. He didn't say what."

"William Page…?"

"That's his roommate."

"Okay," Estelle said, "I guess I knew that. Do you happen to know where Page works? It's Belen, isn't it? Someplace like that?"

"He's up in Socorro," Penny said.

"You don't know where, exactly?"

"Oh…" A pause followed and it sounded as if Zeigler's secretary was flipping through a Rolodex. "William Page," Penny murmured. "William Page." Estelle waited, and she glanced up as Torrez sidled past her, headed for the front door.

Penny Barnes came back on the line. "Estelle, I don't have it here. I know he has a company in Socorro." She paused again and her tone changed a fraction. "That's about all I know. Big help, huh. But they talk all the time."

"Can you check Kevin's desk for me?"

"Oh…"

"On second thought, don't," Estelle said quickly, hearing the indecision in Penny's tone. "It's not all that important. I'm sure Kevin will show up in a few minutes. When he does stick his nose back in the office, please tell him I need to see him? And I mean before he talks with anyone else, okay?"

"Is everything all right?" Penny asked.

"I just need to catch him," Estelle replied cheerfully. "We have a lot to go over after the commission meeting this afternoon."

"Which he skipped," Penny said reprovingly. "That's the mess he left me in."

"We'll nail him for you," Estelle said. "Thanks a lot, Penny."

"If I find William Page's card or something, I'll get right back to you."

"Thanks. He probably won't know anything, but it's a place to try." Estelle followed Robert Torrez outside. The sheriff was standing on the gravel driveway with his hands in his pockets. He appeared to be regarding Zeigler's pickup truck.

"Zeigler's front door is locked," he said as Estelle approached. "I checked earlier. Nobody answered the bell or my knock." Through the side window off the front step, Estelle could see a neat, thoroughly appointed living room. A mammoth entertainment center faced a large, pillowy, winged sofa.

She and Torrez circled the house but found nothing of interest, nothing that might hint what Zeigler's activities might have been, beyond driving off to work in the morning.

"I have a warrant comin' from Judge Hobart," Torrez said. "Not that we need one. Pasquale's bringing it." Two more county units pulled into the street, and Torrez left to brief the officers.

Estelle sat down on Zeigler's back step and fished her phone from her jacket pocket. After a brief a moment, she jotted down the Socorro phone number for William Page that the electronic voice from directory assistance provided. The phone rang five times before connecting.

"Hello. You've reached the residence of William Page. Either leave a message, or try me at PageLink, Incorporated." The number he gave was also a Socorro listing.

Estelle dialed again.

"Good afternoon," a cheerful voice responded. "This is Marci at PageLink. How may I help you?"

"Hi, Marci," the undersheriff said as if they were old, close friends. "This is Estelle Guzman down in Posadas. Is William there?"

"Sure," Marci replied brightly. "Hang on just a sec."

In a moment, a soft tenor voice came on the line. "This is Page."

"Mr. Page, this is Undersheriff Estelle Guzman, calling from Posadas."

There was a pause. "Yes?"

"Mr. Page, we're trying to reach Kevin Zeigler. An emergency has come up, and it's something where we need the county manager's input. I was hoping maybe he'd called you...that perhaps you knew where he was at the moment."

"I beg your pardon?"

"Mr. Page, apparently Kevin had some urgent business out of the office. He left a meeting of the county commissioners at noon and hasn't returned. He didn't tell his secretary where he was going. I thought maybe you might know."

The line went silent, and Estelle gave Page a few seconds to think before she continued on, keeping her tone conversational. "I thought there was a possibility you might have talked to him this morning."

"I did," Page said. "I called the office and we chatted for a while, yes. It's my impression that there was quite an important county meeting today." Page sounded as if he was leaning into the phone, keeping his voice intimate. "But I have no idea where he might be. I'm not clairvoyant. What's going on, Undersheriff?"

Estelle hesitated, loath to share any more information than necessary. "Mr. Page, we may need to gain access to Kevin's house here on Candelaria. There's been an incident next door."

"At the Acostas', you mean?"

"Yes. I need to talk with Kevin."

"His secretary at the county office always knows where he is," Page said. "But why do you need to get into the house? Did something happen there?"

"I don't know yet. That's why we need to find him. As I said, Kevin left the county meeting around noon. He didn't return."

"I don't understand what you're telling me," Page said. "I thought this had something to do with county business. That's what you made it sound like. Now you're talking about his neighbors. What happened down there?"

"It's an incident involving one of the Acosta children, Mr. Page. Because it's next door to Kevin's, and because his county truck is parked here in the driveway, it's logical that we would want to find out if he saw anything that would be of help to us."

"Is his car there?"

"The little blue Datsun? Yes, it is. But the house is locked, and no one answers. I was hoping that you might be able to help us, since you talked to him this morning."

"You've got me thoroughly confused," Page said. "Look, you said that he was next door at the Acostas'?"

"No, sir, I didn't say that. He *isn't* home. We responded to an emergency call at the Acostas' address. There is reason to believe that Kevin might have been home, next door, at some time during a critical period in that incident. We have a warrant to search the premises, but I thought it would be helpful—"

"A *warrant?* Jesus H. Christ, what for?" Page said.

"It's imperative that we talk with Kevin, Mr. Page."

"Well, I can see that, but look. If he's not at home, then he's not at home, right? He's off somewhere, running errands. His secretary should know."

"His secretary *doesn't* know, sir. And his vehicles are both here."

"The county has more than one truck, for God's sake."

"I realize that, Mr. Page," Estelle said patiently. "And I realize he has a cell phone, and he has a pager. And the county vehicles all have radios. Mr. Page, it's this simple. We need to talk with Kevin, and no one knows where he is. I thought there might be an outside chance you could help."

"Look, you don't need a warrant to get inside the house, sheriff. There's a key under that tin lizard on the front window-sill. Just use that. What happened next door, anyway? You said one of the kids was involved in something?"

"That's how it appears," Estelle said.

"And that's all you're going to tell me? It sounds like I should come down."

"Actually, that would be helpful."

"Absolutely, then," he said. "I can be out of here in ten min-utes. Just a second."

Estelle heard the telephone mouthpiece covered, and then distant voices. Page came back on the line. "If I leave here at four, I can be in Posadas by seven. How would that be?"

"That would be just fine, Mr. Page. I'd appreciate it if you'd check in at the Sheriff's Office when you come into town... before you do anything else."

"I can do that. Now let me ask you a favor."

"What's that?"

"Will you at least wait until I'm there before using that search warrant?"

"I'm sorry, Mr. Page. That's not going to work."

She heard what might have been a sigh of frustration over the line. "Look, it just seems to me that if Kevin saw something next door, if he was a witness to something, he would have let you know," Page said.

"That's what I would have thought, sir."

"There's more to this than what you're telling me."

"We don't know yet what happened, Mr. Page. As far as the county manager is concerned, it may turn out to be nothing at all. If I need to reach you in the next couple of hours, will you have a phone in your car?"

"Of course." He gave her the number. "I'll be there by seven," he said.

"Be careful on the highway, sir." She switched off the phone and remained sitting on the small stoop, lost in thought. Finally, she dialed the county office again.

"Penny, any word from his nibs?" she asked, keeping her tone light.

Penny Barnes didn't buy it. "Not a thing, Estelle. *What* is going on? You know, this isn't like him. Not like him at all. Did you find his friend?"

"No, it's not like him," Estelle said. "And yes, I talked with Mr. Page. Did you happen to think of anyone else to check with?"

"No. But I've called everyone, everywhere. He hasn't been at the county barns, he's not out at the landfill—I even called Jim Bergin out at the airport. Nothing. He isn't answering his cell, or the radio. I've got everyone looking and calling. Like I said, he's playing hooky somewhere."

I hope so, Estelle thought. A still-warm truck with the keys in the ignition, parked next door to an attempted murder, wasn't her definition of hooky.

Chapter Eight

The house key was where William Page had said it was, tucked in a slot in the belly of the small tin lizard on the windowsill. Not allowing her latex gloves to touch the brass doorknob, Estelle turned the key and nudged the door with her left elbow. She could hear Bob Torrez's breathing behind her. Pausing at one side of the doorway, she inhaled deeply, scanning what she could see of the living room at the same time. Nothing appeared out of place, and the air carried the faint, clean aroma of a well-tended home.

"He ain't here," Torrez murmured.

"I don't think so." Estelle moved fully into the living room, and Torrez followed, shutting the front door and leaving Deputy Thomas Pasquale standing outside on the steps.

Loath to probe deeper into Kevin Zeigler's home, Estelle waited. Apparently the sheriff felt the same awkwardness, because he made no move to press by her.

"What do you think?" he asked.

Estelle shook her head, jolted by the intrusion of Torrez's voice. Her senses told her nothing except that the house was most likely as it had been when the county manager left for work that morning. She turned in place, inventorying the living room. Zeigler was a movie fan, and the room was arranged so that all seats, including the large, plush sofa, faced the enormous entertainment center on the east wall, with speakers surrounding the room.

On a small shelf to one side of the VCR, the tape-rewinding machine yawned open, a videotape visible inside.

The curtain was pulled securely over the west-facing window, and much of the remainder of that wall was taken up with a twelve-foot span of bookshelves. An old-fashioned wooden coatrack stood between the window and the corner nearest the door, the hooks empty except for a single dark brown sweater. Estelle stepped to the window and examined the curtain. The pleats hung straight and true, the center seam overlapping precisely.

She slipped a finger between the two curtain halves and pushed one far enough out of place to see outside. The view was directly toward the Acostas' kitchen door.

"There's always the possibility that Freddy is a lying sack of shit," Torrez said matter-of-factly. "He says Zeigler's truck wasn't parked there when he left for the store. He says it *was* in the driveway when he came home and found Carmen. Maybe that's not the way it was at all."

Estelle let the curtain slide back into place. "Freddy might have done a lot of things, but what happened to Carmen isn't his style," she said. "He might not have noticed the truck the first time. Things like that are easy to miss."

She lifted one sleeve of the sweater. Made of lightweight wool, it smelled faintly of Kevin Zeigler's musky cologne. No blood, no gunpowder aroma, no rips or tears. Leaving the sweater hanging on the rack, she turned and walked quickly past the shelves. This wasn't the time for a full inventory, despite her curiosity. She scanned the books and videos as she passed. Zeigler was an organized soul, books alphabetically by author, videos alphabetically by title. By and large, both books and films were all new releases.

The living room fronted a hallway leading to bedrooms and bath on one side, and a large, well-appointed kitchen, utility, and laundry on the other. As Estelle moved through the house, it struck her as clean, neat, and entirely unremarkable, the sort of place where the frenetic county manager alighted for a few minutes out of each twenty-four hours to recharge.

The first bedroom on the right served as an office. The same make and model of computer terminal used in Zeigler's office in the county building dominated the far wall. The metallic county inventory sticker was displayed prominently on the side of the computer's beige tower. Filing cabinets, a map hanger on wheels, even a large copier had all been wedged into the small room—the county manager's office-away-from-office.

The small window that faced the Acostas' was shaded by a standard venetian blind. To open it, Zeigler would have to reach over the top of the copier.

"So much for not taking work home," Estelle said. She turned in time to see Torrez nudge open the bathroom door across the hall. The glass shower door gaped open a couple of inches, and he slid it further, examining the tiled tub.

"Not used much," he said.

With careful planning, the second smaller bedroom could have served as a guest bedroom, if the guest wasn't either claustrophobic or a sleepwalker. In the far corner, a small bunk bed—the kind that would have fitted Estelle's two small boys perfectly—served as a rack for two new-style stunt kayaks. One above and the other below, neither kayak was more than six feet long. They looked like two large fiberglass slippers upended on the beds.

"You got to be kidding," Torrez said. He slipped past Estelle, stepped to the center of the room, and looked at the array of sporting gear with wonder. Near the end of the bunk beds, an aluminum stand held half a dozen kayak paddles. Just beyond, a wall rack engineered to balance itself on two slender legs held a pair of mountain bikes.

Most of the rest of the room was crowded with two exercising machines, one a popular, much-advertised model with integral bench. The exerciser's various arms arched like a giant spider. Toward the door, another gadget rested on the floor, and Torrez eyed it critically.

"For the bikes," Estelle said. "Snap a bike in, and you can pedal indoors when the weather's bad." Her husband had experimented with the idea during their brief stay in Minnesota, but hadn't gotten beyond trying one out in a bike shop.

"Huh," the sheriff replied. "Not this kid." He frowned and turned his attention to what had once been a closet with sliding doors. The doors and door molding had been removed. The space formed an alcove that was home to two more bikes, sleek, razor-tired racing machines that bore the United States Postal Service racing team decal.

"I knew he rode a bike sometimes," Torrez said. He knelt and examined the neatly paired cycling shoes. "This is him and somebody else," he added. "Size nine and size ten and a half."

Without rising, he reached out and spun one of the small skeleton pedals of the nearest bike. "Pasquale keeps sayin' we should use something like this in the village," he said.

"Good idea," Estelle said, and she grinned at the thought of Torrez's six-foot-four-inch frame in black spandex.

They moved quickly to the other side of the hall and the larger master bedroom suite. A king-sized bed filled that room, with just enough space for a small television stand and VCR, a single dresser, and a tiny desk that looked as if it would fit a fourth grader.

Estelle stood in the doorway of the large bathroom. Zeigler hadn't been content with the standard tub/shower combination that would have been so upscale in the '50s when the house was built. A huge, custom-tiled shower, nearly five feet square, filled one side of the bath. A smaller jet tub had been installed on the wall near the commode.

She stepped across and snapped on the light of the walk-in closet. Kevin Zeigler's clothes marched in neat rows. She recognized shirts that the county manager favored, some still in the plastic bags from Keiley's Kleaners.

"I don't think he's been here all day."

"Huh," Torrez mused. He was standing at the foot of the huge bed. "You said this Page guy stays here when he visits?"

"No. I didn't say that."

Torrez shot her a quick glance, and shoved his hands in his back pockets. "Those bunk beds in the other room aren't for no adults, unless they're midgets," he said. "Is this Page guy a midget? If he stays here, he ain't going to be sleeping in one of those, unless he is."

"He may stay at one of the motels," Estelle said.

"Oh, sure."

"Or, he might stay here. Maybe he sleeps on the sofa. I'm not concerned with that right now. And he'll be here in a couple of hours if we have questions."

"Yeah. I got questions," Torrez said. "This place gives me the creeps." He shook his head in disgust. "I'm going to check out behind the kitchen." His radio crackled, and as he pulled it off his belt, he added, "Make sure someone hasn't stuffed old Kevin in the freezer or something." He palmed the handheld. "Torrez."

"Sheriff, there's something kind of interesting out here. You got a minute?" Sergeant Mears asked.

"I'll be right there," Torrez said, and he was already striding down the hall. Estelle followed, and he waved toward the kitchen as he passed it. She detoured and checked the back storeroom, the screened porch, even the small closet that contained the hot-water heater. The freezer was too small to hold anything but a thoroughly processed corpse, but she pulled open the double doors anyway. The county manager was omnivorous, and liked a well-stocked larder.

Satisfied that the house was empty, she left by way of the front door, being careful to lock it behind her. She slipped the key back in the lizard's belly.

As she turned away, she saw that Torrez was standing a pace back from the driver's door of Zeigler's county pickup. Sgt. Tom Mears was crouching low, peering underneath. On her side of the truck, Deputy Thomas Pasquale was head to head with Linda Real, the department photographer. Both were on their hands and knees.

Torrez beckoned to Estelle. "Wanna make bets?" he said as she stepped around the front of the truck. He knelt and pointed.

Estelle dropped to her hands and knees as Tom Mears moved a bit to one side. "A lug wrench," she said. The wrench, one of the generic designs with one end pointed to remove hubcaps and the other with the socket angled off at forty-five degrees, lay in the gravel directly under the small truck's transmission. It appeared new.

"I can reach it," Pasquale said, and Estelle shook her head.

"No. Leave it for now." She glanced at Linda, the photographer's round face flushed from the awkward position.

"Just pictures for now," Estelle said. "When we've documented the truck, we'll roll it back a little bit. That way you can do some close-ups." She pushed herself to her feet. "Good eyes," she said to Mears. "Does it belong to the truck, do you think?"

Mears frowned at Bob Torrez. "I don't remember if the Ranger has one of those kind, or one of the foldy-up things. But it won't take long to find out."

"It's behind the seat, I think," Torrez said. "On the passenger side."

Pasquale opened the passenger door with a single, gloved finger, and stepped back to hold it out of Mears' way. The sergeant knelt and examined the passenger seat. He was about to push the small lever that would slide the seat forward when he stopped abruptly.

"Whup," he said. "The jack's right here, on the floor. It kinda slid under the seat a little." He looked up at Estelle. "No handle."

"What's behind the seat?" she asked.

He pulled the second release, leaning the seat back forward. "A spot where the jack and the handle clip into place. Nothing there."

Torrez had walked behind the truck, and he rested one hand on the back bumper as he bent down. "Spare's gone," he said. He straightened up abruptly and continued around the rear of the truck. "It's mounted on the left rear."

Estelle felt a queasy lurch in the pit of her stomach. Torrez stepped around Linda Real and stood regarding the jack in front of the passenger seat. "He has a flat tire, and tosses the wrench and jack on the floor when he's done. They're a pain in the ass to put back just right, and he's in a hurry."

"Where's the flat tire?" Pasquale asked. The bed of the county truck was empty.

"Beats the shit out of me," Torrez said. "Figure out how the wrench ended up on the driveway under the truck while you're at it." He turned to Estelle. "I was thinkin' about that tore-up Sheetrock in the dining room. Swing a lug wrench hard enough, and that gash wouldn't be hard to do."

"This is Kevin Zeigler's truck, isn't it?" Pasquale asked.

"Yeah," Torrez said. "It's Zeigler's truck." He glanced back at the county manager's house. "It's his wrench, too."

Estelle opened the driver's door. Turning sideways so that she could rest her feet on the driveway, she settled into the seat. Even with both doors open, she could smell Kevin Zeigler… the same cologne that marked the sweater in the house had left its imprint on the little truck's fabric seats, the headliner, even the vinyl of the doors and dashboard.

On top of the cologne, she smelled the unmistakable odor of tobacco smoke.

She motioned at Tom Mears, and he gently shut the passenger door. Estelle swung her legs into the truck and pulled the driver's door shut. With her eyes closed, she sat quietly for a moment. The cloying odor of cigarette smoke was faint but obvious, layered with something else. She sat quietly for a couple of minutes until a knuckle rapped on the window.

"You usin' Zen or something in there?" Torrez said when she opened the door.

"Sit in here a minute," she said.

"What?"

"Sit in the truck with the doors closed," she said. "Tell me what you smell."

Torrez looked skeptical, but he took off his cap and then folded himself into the small truck. He left one leg out, obviously loath to pull himself fully inside.

She reached down and slapped his knee with the back of her hand. "Go ahead. Fold yourself up inside. Close the door." Torrez did so with evident distaste. She watched his face settle, though, and he remained motionless for a full minute. He lowered his head, and Estelle saw that he had closed his eyes in concentration.

He opened the door abruptly, looking up at Estelle. "Same perfume as in the house. And butts. And somebody's had happy hour."

"You smell booze?" Torrez didn't reply immediately, but Estelle knew that there was more than a kernel of truth in the department joke that Robert Torrez could smell an open beer or whiskey bottle from across the county, upwind, with his head sealed in a plastic bag. The sheriff had no need to ask if a motorist had been drinking.

"I think so," he said. "Butts, for sure." He reached out and pulled the ashtray open. It was clean. "It's going to be a long night," he muttered.

Chapter Nine

The painstaking process of combing inside and outside the Acosta household continued until Estelle Reyes-Guzman's eyes teared from concentration…a few grains of Sheetrock dust here, a hair there.

Although there was no road map, it became clear that the struggle had progressed from the kitchen door, through the house, to Carmen's bedroom—and nowhere else. That in itself puzzled Estelle. Nowhere else on the Acostas' property was there a single sign of something out of place, of something tampered with. The backyard was littered with the "stuff" of an active family that didn't put picking up after itself high on the priority list.

Estelle stood beside the bed, trying to imagine how the battle had progressed. It wasn't a fight between equals, that was clear. Despite her combative experience, youthful strength, and Acosta temper, Carmen had retreated, perhaps even bolted, toward what she had thought was sanctuary. Maybe at one point she had ducked behind the entertainment center and its television. A flailing lug wrench would make quick work of the wide screen. Carmen had tried for the telephone, too—to call her mother, to call the police—who knew.

A spatter of blood flecked the burlap shade from the shattered bedside lamp, and after Linda Real had photographed it from every conceivable angle, Estelle bagged the entire lamp. That went out to Deputy Jackie Taber's vehicle, along with the comforter from the bed and the small throw rug from the floor, both soaked with the blood that had gushed from Carmen's battered head.

The blood flow on the bed and rug had been profuse, most likely from the blow to the back of Carmen's head that had laid open her scalp. The blood spatter on the side of the lamp shade away from the bed had been tiny, just a couple of drops. Maybe Carmen had gotten in a couple good licks of her own.

"What do you think?" Jackie said at one point. She had her broad back turned to Estelle and was examining the wall to one side of the door. Palm toward the wall, she swept her arm slowly along, covering an area nearly twenty-four inches long, as much as three inches wide, approximately five feet off the floor.

The wall was a pink-tinged white, latex paint over gypsum wallboard. Estelle stepped close, looking over Jackie's shoulder. Soiling the otherwise clean wall was a swash of discoloration.

"It looks as if someone scrubbed something big and dirty against the wall," Jackie said. She extended a tape measure. "Too big for a dirty hand." She glanced down at the floor. "Too high off the ground for a kid to put his dirty feet on the wall."

"You'd be surprised," Estelle said. "Even the little ones put crud in the most amazing places." She slipped a small, folding hand lens out of her pocket and handed it to the deputy. After a moment, Jackie handed the magnifier back.

"I can't tell. Dirt, maybe."

"Can you get that?" Estelle asked Linda, and the photographer nodded cheerfully. She started to position herself, and Estelle touched her on the arm. "After you finish the close-ups, I need some that show this entire side of the room, including that smear. I need the position relative to everything else. If you can get the corner of the bed, the table, *and* this, so much the better."

Even as Linda was maneuvering to position the camera, Officer Mike Sisneros appeared in the bedroom doorway. "You got a visitor, Undersheriff," he said. "A William Page? He's waiting outside at the tape. You want me to let him through?"

"No, I don't," Estelle said quickly. "I'll be out in a minute." She turned to Jackie. "When you take the sample of that"—and she nodded at the wall—"don't do a scraping. I don't want whatever it is mixed with the base paint of the Sheetrock. Go all the way under so that you lift the plaster and paint and whatever that gunk is, all intact."

"I think the paper layer of the Sheetrock will peel right off," the deputy said.

"Even better." Estelle made her way out of the house. With another roll of yellow tape, deputies had isolated Zeigler's county truck next door, and Estelle paused to look at the area once more. Nothing beyond supposition tied the lug wrench that had been found under the little pickup with either the truck itself or the violence in the house next door—but no other assumption made sense.

Somehow, Kevin Zeigler was involved in the incident, but Estelle refused to entertain the idea that Zeigler had attacked Carmen Acosta. There was no way to predict what trouble would come Carmen's way; she'd proved that over and over again since she'd been old enough to punch out schoolmates. But Zeigler? In trying to inventory what she knew about the man, Estelle could count only a handful of qualities, first among them that Zeigler outworked anybody in his sprawling office.

The only scenario that made sense was that Kevin had come home for lunch and walked into the middle of something. Had he come home alone? He wasn't a smoker, but someone recently had been in his truck who was.

Across the street a small crowd of spectators had clustered, with Deputy Dennis Collins in the middle of them, pad and tape recorder in hand. True to form, few of them would be neighbors. Most would be the idle curious who had heard the scanner traffic.

A charcoal-colored Lexus was parked at the curb, nosed up close to the yellow tape. Estelle recognized the man standing impatiently on the street side of the car; at various times she had seen him with the county manager.

As she crossed the yard, Estelle glanced at her watch. If William Page had left his office in Socorro immediately after her telephone call, he had made the trip in just over two hours…a distance of 192 miles. As she neared the tape, she could hear an occasional cooling tick from the automobile's engine.

Page's head was shaking as he strode toward Estelle. Without breaking stride, he said something to Sisneros as he passed, ducking under the yellow tape with quick grace.

"Mr. Page?" Estelle asked.

"William Page, yes," he said. He extended his hand, his grip firm and in no hurry to release. He lowered his head, fixing Estelle with a hard stare, his extraordinary cobalt blue eyes unblinking. "I'm guessing that you're Sheriff Guzman."

"Undersheriff. Yes, sir."

His eyes flicked past her toward the Acostas' house, and then over toward Zeigler's. "You have to explain all this to me. I need to talk with Kevin."

"There isn't a lot I can tell you yet, sir," Estelle said. She motioned for him to walk with her toward her car, parked inside the tape and farther down the street, well away from the sharp-eared neighbors. Page was wearing a yellow polo shirt, tan windbreaker, black trousers with a razor crease, and expensive running shoes. If he hadn't taken time to change, a hard day at the office certainly didn't show. As they walked, Page raised his arms, locking both hands behind his head as if he expected to be handcuffed at any moment.

"Have you talked with Kevin yet?"

"No, sir. We don't know where he is."

"Doesn't his office—"

"No, sir." They reached her county car and Estelle stopped, turning to stand by the back fender so she could watch both the street and the taped-off area. "How long have you known Kevin, Mr. Page?"

"William. I go by William," he said quickly. "I guess I've known Kevin for three or four years." He lowered his hands and thrust them in his back pockets. Estelle guessed him to be in his early thirties. Blond, tan, perfectly fit, William Page would have looked at home on the pages of a mail-order clothing catalog. All he needed was a perfectly groomed Irish setter sitting in the passenger seat of his Lexus.

"So you knew him before he was hired as county manager two years ago," she said. No one had supposed that Zeigler would be able to fill the shoes of the previous manager, a twenty-eight-year veteran and Posadas legend who had dropped dead during an inspection tour of a recently completed wing of the Public Safety Building. "Where did you two meet? In Socorro?"

"Kevin used to work for the city," Page said quickly. "I was doing a computer consulting job for them." He shifted impatiently, glancing first at Zeigler's house and then down the street.

"Ah." Estelle nodded. "So when he moved down here, you've been able to break away and visit from time to time." She watched Page's face, but the only emotion she could read there was worry.

"Okay," he said, ignoring the statement. He held out his hands a foot apart as if measuring something. "Look…you have to fill me in, Officer. I know these folks here," and he nodded at the Acostas' house. "They go 'round and around all the time. Always scrapping. If it isn't one thing, it's another. So what happened this time?"

"One of their children was assaulted, Mr. Page." He looked back at her quickly. "Carmen," she added. "That's the oldest girl. She's fourteen."

"Of course. I know her."

Estelle nodded. "It appears that neither parent was home at the time. Her father claims that he was gone just for a short time, over the lunch hour. When he came home, he found Carmen."

"Oh…," Page said, and ducked his head, closing his eyes at the same time.

"Mr. Acosta says that when he left on an errand, Kevin's county truck was not in that driveway. He says that it *was* parked there on his return. If you think about that, I'm sure you can understand our concern."

"And you've had no word from Kevin? Nothing at all?"

"Not a thing. When was the last time you spoke with him, sir?"

"As I told you on the phone, it was early this morning. We usually chat once or twice a week. Sometimes more often." He glanced quickly at Estelle, then looked away. "I usually come down early on Friday…sometimes even Thursday, if I can break away. I've been going back up to Socorro on Sunday night, sometimes Monday mornings."

"When you talked with him last night, did he say anything about the neighbors? About the Acostas specifically?"

"No. He was talking about this deal with the village. He thought that was pretty exciting. He thought that it was going to be a real challenge to county resources."

"And that's it?"

Page shrugged. "He was thinking of getting a new car." He nodded toward the truck and car parked beside the house. "I've been giving him a hard time about that old relic of his. He said he'd seen a Porsche Boxster he'd fallen in love with. He wanted me to go with him to Las Cruces this weekend to look at it."

"And you were going to do that?"

He nodded. "Sure. Why not? We go there a lot." He managed a feeble grin. "There's not a whole lot to do in Posadas for entertainment. We go there, catch dinner, maybe a movie or two. We've got some other friends there, at the university." He shook his head wearily and regarded the pavement at his feet.

"I'd like to ask that you go through the house again with me, sir," Estelle said.

The weary expression deepened on Page's face. "You've been in there already?"

"Yes, sir."

He shrugged with resignation. "Sure. Why not." He followed Estelle across the street. "You know, I tried Kevin's cell number about every ten minutes on the way down," he said. Keys jingled as he selected a house key. "I kept thinking, 'Well, he's just out somewhere, probably got called out for some county emergency.'

That happens all the time." He thrust the key in the lock and turned it. "He never answered, Officer."

"No, sir. I don't imagine that he did."

He stepped into the house, walked to the center of the living room, and turned in place, arms outspread. "This is it."

"I'd like you to walk through each room, sir. Just walk through and look. Please don't touch anything. I need to know if anything is out of place, if everything is as you remember it."

Page shook his head, and as he started down the hallway toward the bedrooms, he shouted, "Kevin!" and then, in a small voice meant for his own ears only, William Page added, "God, Kevin, don't do this to me." Estelle kept back, letting Page search the house. He returned to the living room, face pale. "He's not here."

"I know that," Estelle said gently.

"He can't just disappear," Page said plaintively. He turned in a circle. "He can't just walk out in the morning and never return."

"No one said he wasn't going to return, Mr. Page."

He turned and shot her a withering look. "Oh, please, Sheriff. There's an assault next door. Either Kevin was here or he wasn't. If he was here, he would have tried to stop it. That's just the way he was. He would be involved from the get-go. If he tangled with somebody and won, he'd be here, sitting on the guy, waiting for the cops. So he's either in a ditch somewhere, or…"

"Or what?"

"You think he assaulted Carmen?"

"I didn't say that he did."

"No, but that's got to be a possibility in your mind, isn't it? And then what's he do, run away someplace? Is that what your little scenario has him doing? Leave everything behind—house, job, family—and run?" Estelle remained silent. "Kevin did not assault Carmen Acosta, Sheriff. I know that as surely as I know that I'm standing here right now."

"Did he have any other vehicle, besides that little sports car?"

"No. He used the county truck. He hardly ever drove the Datsun. Whenever he did, something on it usually broke."

"No motorbike? Not a fifth bike?"

Page jolted, as if the reminder that others had searched the house had sucked his breath away. "No. At least, not that I know of." He sat down heavily on the sofa, then started to rise immediately, remembering Estelle's request. She held up a hand.

"Relax, sir."

He settled back. "Look, he could have *walked* somewhere," he said.

"Yes, he could," Estelle replied. "The county building is only five blocks from here. We have officers looking for him. His staff is looking for him."

"Did you see him today? I mean, you said he left the meeting at noon?"

"Yes, sir, I did."

"There were no hints then? I mean, *he* didn't mention where he was going or anything?"

Estelle shook her head. "You understand our concern," she said.

He held up his hands again, then let them drop in frustration. "What about the girl. What about Carmen?"

"She's being airlifted to University Hospital in Albuquerque."

"And the assault happened right in the house?"

"That's what we're in the process of determining, sir."

"Is she going to be all right, do you think?"

"No, sir. I don't think she's going to be all right."

He slumped deeper into the sofa. "Raped?"

"We don't know yet, sir."

He heaved a deep sigh and clasped his hands tightly.

"Do you have a place to stay where I can reach you tonight?" Estelle asked.

"I'll be here," he said, surveying the living room as if he expected it to have somehow changed.

"That's not possible, sir. Not until the area is cleared as part of the crime scene. Even the Acostas have made other arrangements."

"Christ."

"It's inconvenient, I know. It can't be helped."

He rose from the sofa, dusting a piece of lint from his trouser leg. "At the Posadas Inn, then, I guess. You've got a lobby down at the Sheriff's Office?"

"Yes, sir."

"Then I think I'll go find myself a chair and just wait. Is that all right?"

"Whatever suits you, sir. I just need to know where to find you should something come up."

"I mean, who can sleep with something like this." He shook his head. "One minute everything is normal as all hell, and the next minute, the world is coming apart." He reached down and repositioned one of the sofa pillows. "I didn't take time to stop by the house to pick up any clothes. How long will it be before I can…before this place is open to me?"

"I'll let you know tomorrow, sir."

He nodded absently, reluctant to leave the room. "Did you know about Kevin and me?"

"No, sir," Estelle said, and let it go at that.

Page moved toward the front door, then stopped. "Can I ask you something?"

"Yes, sir."

He smiled at the clipped, matter-of-fact response. "Kevin's county truck in the driveway…you said that Mr. Acosta claims it wasn't there when he left home, but a while later, however long, the truck was parked there when he returned home and then found Carmen." He paused, waiting for a response. When there was none, he continued, "Is there something else that makes you think Kevin is involved? I mean, the bit about the truck…that doesn't mean much."

"Mr. Page, we have to explore every avenue. That's all I can tell you at the moment."

It looked as if William Page wanted to smile, but couldn't.

Chapter Ten

With one hand over the other ear, Estelle pressed the telephone close so that she could hear Chief Eddie Mitchell. At the same time, she stepped out of the Acostas' living room where Tom Pasquale, Tom Mears, and Jackie Taber were industriously combing the carpet, and found a quiet corner in the dining room.

"You're still out there, huh?" Mitchell's soft voice lowered another notch, as if he was sitting in a crowded library, loath to be overheard. In the background, she heard traffic. "I'm southbound on I-Twenty-five," he added.

"Who with?" Estelle asked.

"Ah, I called in a few favors," said Mitchell. "Hank's giving me a ride to the county line." Estelle heard the Bernalillo County sheriff's deputy say something in the background, and Mitchell replied, "Yeah, right," obviously in response to the deputy. "Valencia's got a quiet night, and one of their deputies is waiting for us on down the interstate a bit. He'll run me south so I can grab a ride with Doña Anna. Won't be long."

"How's Carmen? Have the doctors been able to tell you anything yet?"

"Now there," Mitchell said, and paused. Estelle heard the patrol car's engine noise subside for a moment, then bellow. She wondered how fast Mitchell's "shuttle service" was eating the miles. "She's a lucky girl, Estelle."

"You have the clothes with you?"

"Yup. Every stitch. And I talked with a physician named Hans Deakman at University Hospital. He says he knows your husband. Anyway, he thinks that Carmen will be in surgery for about another hour."

"That's all?"

"Well, an hour *more*," Mitchell amended. "She's a lucky, lucky kid, at least as far as that damn hat pin goes. From what they can tell from the pictures, her head was turned hard to the right when she was hit, and that makes it likely that the pin was driven in from behind. Deakman says that it broke through the ear canal headed forward, so it pretty much avoided her brain."

"Pretty much."

"Yeah, well. We can't have everything."

"There's some brain damage?" Estelle sagged against the wall, suddenly bone weary.

"Not from the hat pin, I don't think. Somebody fetched her a real stout clip from behind, too. Look for something like a hammer, fireplace tool, something like that."

"How about a lug wrench?"

"Sure. That would do it. You come up with one?" She told him about the wrench under Kevin Zeigler's county truck. "That makes sense," Mitchell said. "There's some intracranial bleeding going on. That's what they were working on when I left."

"You have the hat pin, too?"

"Yup. And an amazing X-ray. I think your hubby took some while they were prepping her for the plane ride, too. They actually did the removal surgery up here. You might want to check with him."

Estelle glanced at her watch. Mitchell was on the road at 7:55 p.m. That would put him back in Posadas—given perfectly executed hand-offs and lead-footed deputies in four counties—at close to midnight.

"Tell me about it," she said.

"Well, when her assailant rammed that pin into her head, it angled forward and up." The hair on the back of Estelle's neck prickled. "It kind of bounced around through her hard palette, up into her sinuses, and then glanced off the inside of her right cheekbone. Bent hell out of the pin, that's for sure. Maybe it was a good thing for her that it wasn't the absolute best grade of spring steel. She might have ended up like one of those frogs we pithed in high school biology."

"Can you tell how long it is?"

"What, the hat pin? Just a second. Hang on."

Estelle waited, hearing mumbles from the deputy. Mitchell came back on the line after a moment. "Nobody's written anything up yet, but I got me this handy-dandy pocket rule and a full-size X-ray. Lemme see." After another pause, he said, "It's got to be four inches."

"Four, not six."

"Nope, four. Any longer, and it would have popped out her right eye."

"Okay. Thanks, Eddie. I have some people I need to talk to, but that'll have to wait until we can look at the clothing."

"What are we looking for?"

"I don't think we'll be able to see it without a lens, but I want to know if Carmen was carrying that thing. The spot that's in favor right now seems to be the inseam, up along the inside of the thigh."

"Just like young what's-her-name."

"Deena Hurtado."

"Just like her. Look, I already called Gayle and asked her to have a deputy at the line to play taxi for me. If you guys are all tied up, she said she'd ask the State Police to give me a lift."

"I'd like to look at those clothes the minute you get in, Eddie."

"Hell yes. Why should you have a life?" Mitchell laughed. "It's going to be after midnight."

"That's okay. You said you have the pin with you?"

"That's affirmative."

"Is it handy?"

"Nothing's handy in this car," Mitchell said, and that prompted a guffaw from the driver. "I got a shotgun killing my left knee, the damn computer under my elbow, and God knows what else. I'm not used to being a passenger. Just a second." In a moment, he added, "Here that baby is. Nasty, nasty."

"Do you have enough light to see the tip?"

"Sure."

"Has it been sharpened? Ground or filed down?"

After a brief pause, Mitchell replied, "I would think so. The pin is finished somehow, like gun bluing. The color is ground off around the tip."

"Okay. That's what I needed to know."

"Maybe they dip these things in curare."

"That's all we need," Estelle said.

"We're coming up on my Valencia County ride here in just a second. Anything else you need to know before I get there?"

"Are the Acostas settled down some? Did Freddy get there all right?"

"Yeah, he did. He even avoided all the radar somehow. Damn near drove that old car as fast as we flew. He found the two boys, and brought them up, too. That just leaves the two little girls. They're staying with relatives, Bobby says."

"We'll want to talk with the boys," Estelle said. "No one had a chance this afternoon. Did you have a minute to sit down with them?"

"Yep. I chatted with 'em a little at the hospital. Neither one of 'em knew anything about the hat pin, or where it might have come from."

"If the hat pin was Carmen's that's hard to believe, too. We'll see," Estelle said. "I'll have a talk with the girls. Maybe this evening, if I get a chance."

"Whoa," Mitchell said. "Here's the next leg of my ride. Just a second."

Estelle listened to the muffled conversation, then heard first one door slam, and then another.

"My new chauffeur is Deputy Melissa Gabaldon," he said, and Estelle could hear the car accelerating hard for the run down through the center of Valencia County.

"Tell her thanks for me," Estelle said.

"I'll do that. Now, about this lug wrench thing…You still haven't heard from Zeigler? No trace of the guy?"

"We haven't found him yet, Eddie."

"No shit?"

"Not a trace. His roommate from Socorro arrived not long ago. A guy by the name of William Page. Runs a computer design business up there. He doesn't have a clue either. I believe him."

"That's the guy that Zeigler's romancing at the moment?"

"I guess you could put it that way, Eddie."

"I kinda thought so. I met the both of them a time or two. Interesting, interesting. Wouldn't take a rocket scientist to come up with an interesting scenario for that whole mess. Zeigler comes home just after Freddy leaves, Carmen sees something she's not supposed to see, and old Kevin does a botched-up job. Then he runs. He's smart enough not to take the county truck, and smart enough not to take his own car."

"And goes where?"

"That's what we have to be smart enough to figure out," Mitchell said. "The only trouble is, I'll bet my miniscule paycheck that's not the way it happened at all."

"I don't think so either."

"Zeigler's not a lug wrench man."

The last time Estelle had seen Zeigler, less than nine hours before, he'd been tending to county business, with a couple of errands to fill his lunch break. She could still see him brushing his chinos after leaning against the truck. What else had he been wearing? The sleeves of his dress shirt had been rolled up loosely, the diagonally striped red and black tie pulled away from an unbuttoned collar.

Her last memory of Zeigler had been of a neat, dapper young fellow who might have just stepped through the front door of his college fraternity house.

"No, sir. Kevin Zeigler isn't the lug wrench type," Estelle agreed.

"What's the sheriff think?"

"He hasn't said," Estelle replied. "Ever since he saw there wasn't a guest bed in Zeigler's house, he didn't say much. Apparently that came as a surprise to him."

Mitchell chuckled. "I bet. What the hell. There's probably half the county that doesn't know. Bobby's one of 'em. This whole thing probably touches his conservative nerves. Anything else you need at the moment?"

"I don't think so."

"We'll see you in a bit then, all right? You have this number if something comes up."

"Thanks, Eddie." She switched off the phone and walked back into the living room.

"I don't think we're going to find anything," Tom Mears said, pushing himself to his feet. "How's Carmen?"

She described the injuries, and Mears grimaced.

"It sounds like someone was wrestling her from behind," Pasquale said. "That would take some strength."

Estelle nodded. Once again, she tried to imagine Kevin Zeigler tussling with Carmen Acosta...first slugging her on the head with a lug wrench, then ramming a hat pin into her ear. It made no sense. Even if the hat pin had been jabbed first, followed by the savage blow to the back of the girl's head, Estelle found it impossible to picture the county manager wielding either weapon.

"We have to find him, that's all," she said.

Chapter Eleven

The sheriff regarded the cuticle of his thumbnail for a long moment, glanced up at the wall clock, and then fixed William Page with his best heavy-lidded, unblinking gaze. Page shifted in the military-surplus straight chair that served as most of the furniture for guests in Bob Torrez's Spartan office. The molded plastic seats in the Public Safety Building lobby would have been more comfortable.

Estelle closed the door of the sheriff's office, feeling a stab of sympathy for Page. It wasn't difficult to guess what was going through the sheriff's mind, and it was equally obvious that Page was ill at ease and on the defensive.

"Mr. Page, thanks for being patient," Estelle said. She pulled the remaining straight chair out of its corner where it had been wedged between a gray filing cabinet and a vertical heater duct. The sheriff's office reminded her of a janitorial closet.

As far as she knew, Page had spent the last three hours sitting in the small lobby outside the dispatcher's communications center, waiting for the clock hands to move. His only company had been the comings and goings of various Sheriff's Department personnel, and the various visages captured in the large, framed portraits of the former sheriffs of Posadas County, mounted on the foyer wall. Most of the retired law officers in the photo gallery were either seated behind their mammoth desks or posed beside an American flag. The most recent photo showed Robert Torrez leaning against his patrol unit, binoculars poised. He had glanced at the camera just in time, his skeptical expression captured.

Estelle liked the sheriff's gallery photo that Linda Real had captured. It showed Bobby Torrez doing what he did best: hunting.

"It's been a long day for you, too," Page said.

"And bound to be longer before we're through," Estelle added. Eons ago, she had anticipated the afternoon session of the county meeting as a way to pass the time until the school bus brought home her son. So close. She'd even managed to greet the salesman at the piano store before her telephone call was interrupted.

Now, at 9:45 p.m. on that Tuesday, they sat in Torrez's stuffy little office, and Estelle was sure that each of them wanted to be somewhere else.

"Mr. Page, the sheriff and I need your help."

"All right." He lifted his hands off his thighs helplessly. "Whatever I can do."

"First of all," she began, and found herself hesitating. "It's not reasonable to assume that Kevin Zeigler suddenly remembered he had an important errand out of town somewhere, and that he then left without any notice to his secretary, or to the County Commission who were expecting him to attend an afternoon session."

"He would never walk out on a job," Page said, shaking his head emphatically. "When someone is missing, don't police post something? Like an APB or something like that?" He leaned forward. "Don't you have to wait twenty-four hours or something?" Page asked, and immediately grimaced and rubbed his face with both hands in frustration. "That's stupid, I know."

"As far as anyone can determine, Mr. Zeigler has been missing since shortly after noon. It's unreasonable to assume that in the normal activities of his day, he would disappear for almost ten hours without word to his office, especially in light of some of the important matters before the commission. So no...we don't wait." She paused, and Torrez relaxed back in his swivel chair, hands locked over his belly.

"Not in light of what happened next door," he said.

It was the first time he had spoken since Page had entered the room, and Estelle caught the accusatory edge in his tone. Page took the statement at face value.

"What can I do?"

"Tell us what you know about Kevin Zeigler's habits, Mr. Page," Estelle replied. She scooted her chair closer and leaned forward, resting her elbows on her knees. "Right now, we're grasping at straws. If we had some idea who Kevin saw during the course of his day, other than at work, if we had some idea about where he spends his time—again, other than at work…"

"That's what Kevin does, Ms. Guzman. He works. He's one of those type A people who has to have things done *right* now, if you know what I mean." He ducked his head in a little shrug. "I mean, you must see Kevin around the county offices all the time. You work with him, don't you? So you must know what I'm talking about."

"He's a busy man."

Page nodded. "That's one thing that I've tried to do, I suppose…to slow him down a little bit. I'm a great believer in leaving the office *behind* at the end of the day. Kevin is the opposite."

"How did you two meet?"

"Oh, this and that. He worked for the city of Socorro, I was doing some consulting for them, so we worked together. But mostly it was the biking, I guess. That's been one of my passions for a long time. I invited Kevin along on a couple of rides that our group organized, and he seemed to enjoy it."

"I saw the four bikes in the house."

Page nodded. "Yeah. We just got the new road bikes a couple of months ago. That may have been a mistake. The only place Kevin knows how to ride is out front. He doesn't understand the concept of second place, or of just riding along to enjoy the weather and watch the birds."

"Were there any other bikes?"

"Others? No. Four's enough." He grinned, revealing a movie star's set of teeth, and then his face immediately fell sober. Kevin

Zeigler hadn't simply grown weary of county politics and taken one of his expensive bikes for an extended spin…or crashed one of the mountain bikes, leaving him lying somewhere with a busted hip, waiting for rescue.

Estelle turned sideways in her chair so that she more directly faced Zeigler's roommate. "Mr. Page, did Kevin have any enemies?"

"Enemies?" He blinked.

"Yes, sir. Anyone that you're aware of with a grudge? Any old scores to settle?"

"God , not that I know of…"

"Who was he hooked up with before he met you?" Torrez's question came so abruptly that Page appeared startled.

"I don't follow."

Torrez regarded him expressionlessly, waiting for Page to figure out for himself what the sheriff had meant.

"Any former acquaintances?" Estelle prompted. "Any bad feelings between Kevin and anyone else?"

"No…I mean, I don't think so."

"You're livin' with him, right?" Torrez asked.

"I visit when I can."

"You and him spend weekends together?"

"When we can."

"For instance, were you planning to come down Thursday or Friday, and stay over until Monday?"

Page glanced at Estelle. "Yes," he said simply. "Those were my plans."

"Mr. Page," Estelle said, "when I asked if there were any bad feelings between Kevin Zeigler and anyone else, you replied that you 'didn't think so.' I'd like to ask you to think more carefully about that." Estelle spoke slowly. "Did Kevin ever talk to you about problems he might have had in the past with anyone— anyone at all? Employees, relatives, special friends."

"No," Page said. "Kevin always thought *that* way," he said, and stabbed a finger outward. "He thought about the future… like what he was *going* to do."

"He didn't ruminate much about things?"

Page laughed, a quick, loud, nervous guffaw. "*Ruminate.* That's about the *last* word I'd associate with Kevin."

Estelle leaned back, and the room fell silent except for the faint, occasional creak of leather as Torrez rocked absently in his chair.

"When the two of you go out socially in Posadas," Estelle asked, "where do you frequent?"

Frowning, Page looked out through the narrow window at the plastered wall of the county courthouse. "I like to cook, so we don't ever eat out," he said. "Unless we go to Cruces or something like that for a show." He turned away from the window view. "I guess other than when we go riding sometimes around Cat Mesa, sometimes down in the San Cristóbals, we don't go out much. Not here, anyway."

"Not much to do?"

He shrugged. "I guess you could put it that way."

"Is there a circle of friends or acquaintances whom you've come to know in Posadas?"

"No." Page's answer was immediate, and he didn't amplify the answer.

"Is that because of Kevin's position with the county?"

"I don't follow."

"Mr. Page," Estelle said, "your relationship with Kevin Zeigler is obviously most discreet." She watched a faint flush create a small island of white on the arch of each cheekbone.

"My relationship with Kevin Zeigler is no one's business but our own," he said evenly.

"Sir, I understand that," Estelle said. "And our intention is not to invade your privacy. But we'll dig for any scrap of information that we can. I'm sure you can understand that."

He sighed deeply. "Of course."

Estelle leaned forward and lowered her voice. "That's why I want you to think over every moment you've spent in Posadas with Mr. Zeigler. Is there anyone—anyone at all—who Kevin talked about? Any frustrations he brought home from the office and discussed with you? Anything at all."

"Believe me, Officers, I've been sitting out in that lobby now for quite a while, doing nothing but that." He shook his head, face grimaced. "Of course Kevin and I were *discreet,* as you suggest. Posadas isn't exactly the western hemisphere's cradle of liberal opinion. His job with the county was important to him, if for no other reason than he wanted to do a good job for them, and then move on to something more interesting or challenging."

"Like what?" Torrez asked.

"He was thinking about applying for an administrative position that one of the state universities has posted."

"Where?"

"Albuquerque. He thinks he has a good shot at it."

"He's done a good job for this county," Estelle said.

Page smiled at her. "Kevin refers to Posadas County as 'my problem child,' Ms. Guzman. He keeps talking about 'the long, painful trek toward the twenty-first century.'"

Torrez scoffed. "How about the twentieth first," he said.

"I'm sure that in his work, he's had plenty of disagreements," Page said, and Estelle gazed at him speculatively. "The one thing I *do* know, absolutely for sure, for positive, for one hundred percent, is that Kevin did not go next door to the Acostas' on some perverted whim and attack that girl."

"Do the Acostas know you?" Estelle asked.

"What do you mean, do they *know* me? Of course they do. I've been visiting Kevin almost every weekend and on longer holidays for going on two years. We've talked with them—the parents, sometimes the kids—a lot, mostly just in passing."

"Mostly," Torrez muttered.

Page shot him an impatient look. "Yes, *mostly.* Once last summer, they invited us over when they were barbecuing a goat. And it was pretty good, too. A couple of times, Tony—he's the oldest boy—has gone on bike rides with us. He didn't enjoy it much, I don't think. He's got a mountain bike, but it's one of those really cheap ones. It's broken half the time. We let him ride one of ours when we all went up on Cat Mesa a few weeks ago. I think the ride was about twenty miles too long for him."

"Not in shape, eh?" Torrez said.

"No, he wasn't."

Estelle could picture the chubby, moonfaced Tony Acosta, sweat pouring off in rivers, pushing his bike up the steep switchbacks of County Road 43 while Zeigler and Page rode patient circles around him.

Page restless on the uncomfortable chair, rose and squared his shoulders. "I would think you'd be investigating the obvious, Sheriff."

"And what would that be?"

"The Acostas impress me as a noisy, rambunctious family. Their kids are scrappy. I mean, more than a few times Kevin and I heard rows over there, one kid taking out his aggressions on another, or Fred beating on Juanita, or some other round-robin. And the kids all have some pretty squirrelly friends, too. If Kevin came home for a minute during lunch and walked into the middle of something..."

"Was Kevin concerned about the general behavior next door?" Estelle asked.

Page hesitated. "I think that sometimes he was. He saw Mrs. Acosta—Juanita—wallop one of the little girls with the handle of a garden rake once. I mean, that's not some little willow switch. And a couple of times, the two boys got into a real bloody fistfight, and their parents didn't do anything to break it up. Kevin thought we should do something, but *I* sure wasn't going to step into the middle of that hornet's nest. If mom and dad don't mind the kids beating each other to a pulp, then I guess it's none of my business. It bothered Kevin, though. He told me once that the cops were going to respond to the Acostas' address sometime, and someone was going out of there in a body bag."

"They've come close," Estelle said.

Chapter Twelve

By the time Estelle walked through the front door of the Guzman home on South Twelfth Street, the village had settled into late-night silence. Eddie Mitchell was still a passenger in a patrol car somewhere to the north, speeding down the Rio Grande valley. In the basement darkroom of the Public Safety Building, Linda Real had begun processing reel after reel of film. The "two Toms," Mears and Pasquale, were organizing and processing what little physical evidence had been combed from the Acosta property.

Both Sheriff Torrez and Deputy Jackie Taber prowled the county, and Estelle listened to the muted, cryptic radio traffic as she drove home. And even as she juggled her house keys, Estelle turned and glanced up and down the street, as if hoping that she might catch a glimpse of Kevin Zeigler's trim, dapper figure hustling from one island of light to another under the streetlights.

Before she could slide the key into the lock, she heard the door rattle. Her husband pulled the door open, bowing slightly as he held it for her, then pushed it closed behind her. She set her briefcase down and snuggled into his bear hug. They stood silently for a long time. Francis rested his chin on top of Estelle's head and she swayed gently to the rhythm of his pulse.

"Nasty day," he whispered after a moment.

"And we don't know where it's going, except nastier," Estelle murmured.

"You're going to squeeze in a little sleep, I hope."

"Yes, Doctor." She snuggled her face tighter against his chest.

"Are you ready for some good news?" he asked.

"Con los brazos abiertos," Estelle whispered fervently. She didn't move.

"You missed *Tía Sofía's* call a few minutes ago."

"Ah," Estelle groaned. "Missing her call isn't good news, *oso.*" She thumped her forehead against his chest. "She's coming, I hope?"

"If it's convenient," Francis said.

"It's always convenient," Estelle said. She took a half-step back and looped her arms around her husband's neck. "And I need to talk to her." Francis looked quizzical, an expression that deepened when she added, "I found out about one of my husband's family genes today."

"Mine?"

"Oh, *sí.* At least, that's the easy explanation, since I don't know where mine have been. I had a parent conference with Myra Delgado, this morning." She unlatched from around his neck. "*Los hijos* are asleep?"

"Sure." He glanced at the grandfather clock in the dining room. "*Everyone* with any sense is asleep. I sent Irma home around nine o'clock, when I got here. So…what did Myra have to say?"

"Un momentito." Estelle bent down to retrieve her briefcase. She tossed it into the nearest chair, at the same time toeing off her sturdy, black shoes. The hallway leading to the boys' bedroom sank into darkness. A year or so before, both Francisco and little Carlos had decided that a night-light gave monsters too much advantage.

The door to their bedroom was ajar, and Estelle eased it open. Enough light from the kitchen and living room filtered in that she could see the two small forms, Carlos on the left and Francisco on the right. She stood in the doorway for a moment, listening to night sounds. Francisco shifted, a little rustle of pillow and blanket. Estelle slipped over to his bedside and sat down on the edge. She was sure her eldest son was awake…he slept like a wolf pup, deep in his dreams for a few minutes, then awake to shift and rearrange position before drifting off again.

Estelle knew she didn't have to worry about waking Carlos. The four-year-old slept the night through, polishing his imitation of a sandbag.

"Hey, *hijo*," she whispered. As her eyes adjusted, she could make out Francisco's right hand, and she tickled his palm with her index finger. His hand instantly became a spider, darting a few inches away and pausing, two fingers stretched out and testing the air. Estelle smiled and reached up to stroke black hair out of his eyes. "Did you have a good day?"

He nodded. "Melody said you were at school," he said with just a hint of accusatory whine.

She left her hand on his forehead, her thumb lightly tracing the arch of his thick eyebrows. "Yes, I was."

"She's funny."

"Melody? That's for sure, *hijo*." Featherlight, the tips of her fingers felt the outline of his skull and, with a twinge, she realized clearly what had nagged at her for most of the day—even while the larger share of her consciousness was concentrating on Carmen Acosta and Kevin Zeigler. As clearly as she understood her son in the larger sense, she knew that she had no idea what was going on inside that small, six-year-old head.

"*Tía* Sofía is coming," the little boy whispered, as excited as if he were announcing an imminent Christmas.

"I hope so, *hijo*." One of Estelle's favorite photographs was framed on the fireplace mantel in the living room. It showed three figures, sharply side lit by morning sun and dwarfed by the yawning vista before them. Sofía Tournál, her husband's aunt, sat on the very edge of a rock ledge jutting out from the rim of Cat Mesa, north of Posadas. On either side of her square, strong form stood the two boys, Francisco leaning an elbow on Sofía's left shoulder, Carlos encircled by her right arm.

That day had been quiet, the wind nothing but a whisper, just enough to sweep away the heat as the sun warmed the jumbled limestone. Estelle had snapped the picture, then returned to the van to reload the camera. She'd lingered there, loath to interrupt the quiet moments between Sofía and the boys.

"I thought that maybe Sofía might help us find just the right piano," Estelle said. Francisco didn't reply, but she watched his hands curl together under his chin and felt the slight hunch of his shoulders. She knew that body language well, that curling inward with delight lest a hand too quickly stretched out might destroy the moment of anticipation. "Do you think that's a good idea?"

"Yes."

She smiled at the one-word response. "I think it would be nice to have a piano," she said. She covered both of his hands in hers. After a moment she bent down and brushed his cheek with her lips, lingering for a moment by his left ear. "Then that's what we'll do," she whispered.

Before leaving, Estelle crossed the bedroom and bent down to unwad the blanket from around her younger son's head. Carlos slept deeply. If a four-year-old could ever be described as introspective, that would describe Carlos. The clandestine rendezvous with the school piano wouldn't have surprised Estelle had it occurred in two years' time with her younger son. But for the extroverted Francisco to keep the secret was a genuine surprise.

Her husband had settled onto the large sofa in the living room. "So," he said as Estelle reappeared. He watched as she shrugged out of her jacket and then slipped the bulky, holstered automatic and handcuff case off her belt. She dropped everything in a pile at the opposite end of the sofa and then eased down beside her husband, sitting on the very edge of the cushion.

"So tell me what the kid's teacher had to say," Francis said. "A six-year-old forcing his teacher to call the cops is quite an accomplishment."

Estelle smiled and dug a knuckle into her husband's ribs. "You know, *mi corazón*, I see so many kids in trouble that that's the first thing that crossed my mind when the school called." She shook her head, and then recounted her visit to the elementary school. Francis listened with a bemused expression.

"He just sneaks out at lunch?"

"Well, *sneak* isn't the right word, *oso*. He just goes. He never told his teacher that's what he's doing. She always thought that he was going to the restroom, just across the hall."

"All by himself?"

"Solo."

"That in itself is amazing for a first grader. They tend to be herd animals, don't they? I can imagine Carlos sitting off by himself, but not Mr. Motion." Francis caught Estelle's hand and entwined fingers. "And he bangs on the piano down in the band room."

She shook her head doggedly. "Not *bangs*. I listened to him. It sounds like he's working out particular sounds and combinations."

"Huh," Francis said. "Every day for three weeks?"

She nodded. "Every day."

"And why doesn't Myra just tell him to get his little butt back to the class? Or group." He grinned. "The herd. They generally don't let first graders roam much, do they? Isn't that the grade where they all line up along the wall to be counted? Seems to me I remember something like that."

Estelle paused. "Myra was struck by how much it meant to Francisco to be able to do that. To be able to go off by himself." She turned to face Francis more squarely. "When you think about it…"

He nodded. "I can't imagine him keeping it a secret. That's remarkable."

"But he has. He hasn't told his teacher, he hasn't told any of his classmates as far as we know, he hasn't told me or you."

"What'd he say when you mentioned your visit?"

"I didn't mention it. Melody Mears told him that I'd been at the school."

"Ah."

"What's a six-year-old going to think," Estelle said, lowering her voice. "If the adults find out that he's where he's not supposed to be, what are they going to tell him to do?"

"Get back in line." Francis mimicked the order.

"Exactly."

"You don't think he'll just talk to you about it, if you ask him?"

"I don't want that," Estelle said quickly. "Myra thinks it's fine. I think it's fine. *I* want to leave it alone. He's found this private time for himself." She hesitated. "But we need to buy a piano, *oso*."

Francis untwined his fingers and clamped his right hand on her left thigh in his strong grip. "Probably we do." He grinned. "Next thing you know, they're going to want a puppy or something."

"Then the dog can howl in concert," Estelle said, "and Carlos and I can be one big case of hives from the dog hair. Did Sofía say when she's coming?"

"Ah," Francis said again, making the connection. "She thought this weekend, if we weren't busy."

"Were you going to call her back?"

"I was…or you can."

"Would you ask her to come Thursday or Friday? That way we can drive to Cruces when the piano store is open."

Francis grimaced. "Wouldn't one of those small electronic keyboards work? I mean, to start with?"

"If it will, that's what they'll decide," Estelle said. "But I want to do this right, *oso*. Sofía will know."

"Oh, that's for sure," Francis agreed. Of his vast, extended family, Francis Guzman was the only member who lived in the United States. His Aunt Sofía, widowed for more than two decades, had enjoyed a long, distinguished, and highly profitable career as an attorney in Veracruz…and had been the major financial force behind the new Posadas health clinic.

"But she mustn't buy it," Estelle added firmly. "I want to do that." She leaned toward her husband. "Or we want to do that. But Sofía knows Francisco, and she knows music, and she plays beautifully. That's why I want to talk with her."

Francis looked bemused. "And suppose that this old lady and the six-year-old kid together decide in their own mystical way that the only thing that will do is a fifty-thousand-dollar Steinway, just like the one Sofía has in her parlor in Veracruz?"

"That won't happen."

"She said," Francis quipped.

Estelle laughed. "If it does, I'll find a part-time job."

"Something you can work between midnight and three a.m."

"Is that the time slot that's available?"

"Just about."

Estelle took a deep breath. "If they lose interest in the piano, we can always sell it." She covered his hand in both of hers, feeling the heavy scar that crossed from the base of his thumb to the base of his ring finger, a souvenir from a biking accident several years before. "It would be good for you to play again, too."

He laughed. "Oh, sure. It's been so long I don't know where middle C is anymore. Anyway, this is going to be interesting. What if the only time Francisco will touch the piano is when he's alone? Are we all going to have to stand out in the backyard when he practices?"

"I don't know," Estelle said. "One step at a time. First, I want to talk with Sofía." She relaxed back, comfortable against her husband. For a few delicious seconds, her mind roamed among thoughts of her children. And then the image of Melody Mears danced back into her memory, and Deena Hurtado, and the limp, bloody form of Carmen Acosta. She groaned and leaned forward.

"What?" Francis said. He ran a hand up her back as she leaned over toward her gear at the end of the couch. She retrieved the small cellular phone.

"I need to see if Eddie Mitchell is back yet," she said.

"At midnight?"

Estelle grimaced in resignation. "He's bringing back evidence that's going to determine what direction we go come morning," she said. "It can't wait."

"And come morning, you'll be really sharp without any sleep," Francis said.

"This won't take long."

"She said."

Chapter Thirteen

The blue jeans looked small and oddly pathetic in the evidence bag. Estelle glanced at the photograph of the girl lying facedown on the bed, with two pale-faced paramedics kneeling by her head. Eighteen hours before, Carmen had poured herself into those jeans, tight enough to hinder the circulation.

"Her mother says that she's right-handed, if that's any help," Chief Eddie Mitchell said. He stood with his spine pressed tightly against the wall, trying to straighten out the kinks in his back after four hours in a procession of cramped, speeding patrol cars.

"Something is bound to show," Bob Torrez said. "But even if it does, I'm not sure that it tells us a whole lot."

"Every little bit," Estelle said. She arranged the fabric of the left leg of the blue jeans under the low-power stereo microscope. An instant later, it took no imagination to see the uniformly stretched threads along the inseam. The loops of thread that marched along the seam in the jeans were normally so tight as to be pulled right into the stiff fabric. Under the lens of the stereoscope, Estelle could see the stitching stretched up into a small loop, every half inch or so. She straightened up and beckoned the sheriff toward the table. "Want to place bets?"

Torrez planted both hands on the bench on either side of the microscope and bent over, then released his grip to adjust the oculars. "Huh."

"You can see the loops," Estelle said.

Torrez gazed through the eyepieces for another few seconds, then twisted to one side as Eddie Mitchell ambled over, hands pressed to the small of his back. With a sigh, he bent down and examined the inseam for himself.

"Regular little holster she's got there," Torrez said. "Why not just stab it in twice—once going in, then again a few inches down the pike to hold the tip?"

"That's not very secure," Estelle said. "Thread the hat pin through loops every little bit, and it's going to be held in place, keeping the tip on the outside of her jeans, out of her leg."

"Right now, we're thinking that the hat pin was Carmen's," Mitchell said, and straightened away from the counter. "That makes for an interesting scenario."

"*If* she was wearing it when she was attacked," Torrez said. "We don't know that."

"Let's suppose that she was," Estelle offered. She stepped across the small room and tapped the drawing on the white board. "There's no blood in the kitchen—just furniture that indicates a struggle, a chase of sorts. Whoever attacked Carmen got through the door, busting the already broken screen. Maybe she tried to push the table between herself and her assailant, buying a few seconds."

"Didn't work out," Torrez said.

"No, it didn't. The assailant takes a swing, maybe connects, maybe not. By this time, they're in the dining room, and the assailant takes a good lick with the lug wrench, maybe while Carmen is scrunched up against the wall trying to dial nine-one-one. Or maybe she's holding her hands up, trying to fend him off. The wrench connects with the wall, hard enough to smash the plaster."

With her finger, Estelle traced a ragged line toward the bedroom. "They fight through the living room, back to here. The last stand," she said. "She makes it to the bedroom pretty quickly. If any of the blows to her head connected either in the kitchen, the dining room, or while crossing the living room, she didn't leave a blood trail. And then…" Estelle paused, gazing at the schematic. Without turning around, she reached out, pointing at the jeans under the stereo. "What if she has the hat pin in her jeans. See"—and she looked at Torrez—"that's what we don't know. If she *did*, then she pulled it out somewhere during the fight. She might have been able to cut her assailant with it, a raking blow. Or"—and she shrugged—"maybe she got lucky and stabbed him a good one."

"Just enough to make him mad," Mitchell said. "He either connects at that point with the wrench, or just manhandles her around, wrenching the hat pin out of her hand. And then, *boom*."

"*Boom,*" Estelle repeated.

"Our contact with APD is Frank Hershey," Mitchell said. "He posted one of his detectives at the hospital for us. When the doctors can spring loose, we'll find out some more. But I tell you, I don't see that Carmen's going to do much after taking the blow to the head. She pulls the hat pin, maybe jabs him with it, and that sets the guy off. He's pissed, and *whammo*. That's when she gets it, hard through the ear."

"I think that's when he hits her," Torrez said. He leaned against the counter. "She's down on the bed, stuck through the ear. She's maybe makin' noise, panicked, not knowing what's happened, still fighting. He hits her in the back of the head because that's the target that he's got."

"That's consistent with the blood," Estelle said. "She didn't move an inch after that."

"We're all set for someone to take a run to the state lab in the morning?" Torrez asked.

Estelle nodded. "Tom was going to see what he could do with the blood spatter on the lamp shade. He wasn't really optimistic. There's just not enough there."

"And the crap on the wall?"

"That has to go to the lab. That's way beyond what we can do here."

"Which ain't much," Torrez added.

"One of the docs I talked to at University said that if Carmen survives the attack and the follow-up surgery and everything else, that it might be days before she can answer questions about what happened," Mitchell said. "Maybe weeks."

"And maybe never," the sheriff said.

Estelle picked up the stack of eight-by-ten photos, the first installment sent upstairs from Linda Real's darkroom. "We've got a good start for morning," she said.

"What do you want us to do?" Mitchell asked. Torrez reached out for the photos and began shuffling through them methodically.

"It's important to exhaust every possible place that Kevin Zeigler might have gone," Estelle said. "He's the key. I really believe it. It's just way too bizarre otherwise. We need to talk to all the county folks…again. Maybe something he said in passing during the morning, any little thing. Check with the county barns, see if any of the maintenance crews saw him. Or someone from the village. In the course of a normal day of county business, he must see two hundred people, maybe talk to fifty or a hundred. We need to double-check with every one of them."

"You going to talk with the pink flamingo again?" Torrez flashed a brief smirk when Estelle's face went blank. "Mr. Page," he said. "He's still camped out in the lobby."

"He needs to go home," Mitchell said. "Shit, it's almost one o'clock. *I* need to go home."

"At the moment, he *has* no home," Estelle said. "Zeigler's house is still off-limits. He said he'd get a room at the Posadas Inn."

"Then maybe you'd encourage that very thing," Torrez said. He held up a single glossy print, a close-up of the hat pin taken from Deena Hurtado in the principal's office of the middle school. "You brought the weapon back from Albuquerque, right?"

Mitchell nodded. "Linda took a preliminary picture with it still in the bag. After we get it back from the lab, she'll shoot it again."

The sheriff flipped quickly through the prints again.

"You don't have that photo yet," Mitchell said. "Linda's still working downstairs. Those you have there are just the first batch."

"She workin' all night?" Torrez glanced at Estelle.

"Most likely."

He shrugged. "Won't hurt her. She's young yet," Torrez said. He handed the photos back to Estelle.

"Until we know something to the contrary, we need as many people on the road looking for Kevin as we can spare," she said. "The first step is to comb every piece of county property, every piece of county equipment and real estate. That's a start. And then every other connection we can dig up from Kevin's personal life. Everyone he knows, everyone he's talked to recently. And in that respect, William Page might be of some help."

"First thing we need to do is call it a day," Torrez said. "Every time I try to blink, I got to pull my eyelids back open. You two don't look much better. Who's on the road tonight?"

"Jackie and Mike Sisneros," Estelle said.

"Well, they both know what to look for," the sheriff said. "Maybe come eight tomorrow morning, the county manager will walk through his office door and surprise the shit out of us all."

"That would be a nice surprise," Estelle said. She carefully repacked the blue jeans and then snapped off her gloves.

"And it isn't going to happen," Eddie Mitchell said.

Torrez watched Estelle retag the evidence. "What direction are you takin'?" he asked after a moment.

She sighed, staring at the evidence bag in front of her. "What makes the most sense to me is that Kevin Zeigler walked into the middle of something," she said. "Carmen is no angel. It wouldn't surprise me a bit that the minute she learned that her daddy was taking a walk to the pizza place, she knew she had time on her hands. No one else was home; mom's working, brothers and sisters are all at school…or supposed to be. And then…" She hesitated. "We don't know what happened. But it looks like Kevin came home for lunch at the wrong time. Page told me that they'd witnessed fights at the Acostas' before. And he told me that on at least one occasion, when the two boys were fighting and no one seemed willing to say anything, Kevin wanted to go next door and see what he could do."

"But he didn't," Torrez said.

"No. Page said he talked Kevin out of it. It wasn't any of their business."

Torrez let out a loud grunt that could have meant any number of things. "Sure as hell is now, though."

Chapter Fourteen

Roy Hurtado listened without interruption. If he was surprised that Wednesday by the early-morning telephone call from the Sheriff's Department, and if he wondered about a version of events other than the one he had heard from his wife and daughter, he kept it to himself.

"We'll have her there," he said brusquely.

"Have you talked with Deena about what happened at school?" Estelle asked.

"Sure. And I heard about yesterday with the Acosta girl. You close to an arrest?"

"We're making progress," Estelle replied, and let it go at that. "We'll see you at seven-thirty, then."

"We'll be there," Hurtado said, and hung up.

Across the kitchen, Francisco and Carlos industriously tackled their generous breakfast. As she put down the phone, Estelle watched the two boys, enjoying the intensity of a discussion about whether raisins should float on top of an island of oatmeal or be mixed in.

Dr. Francis Guzman had left the house already, headed for his early rounds at Posadas General Hospital before the day at the clinic began. Francisco's bus would slide up to the curb in a few moments, and he would disappear.

Estelle took a long sip of the strong herbal tea that she had brewed and listened as Francisco chattered nonstop about this and that, inconsequentials that tumbled from his agile little mind

without pause, and that prompted an occasional sage nod from
his little brother. Carlos ate with a studious frown, his eyebrows
puckered in concentration.

The thump of the rubber-capped aluminum legs of Teresa
Reyes' walker announced Estelle's mother as she made her way
along the hallway toward the kitchen.

"What nasty thing kept you up all night?" she asked in
Spanish by way of greeting. She thumped up close to Estelle,
long brocade robe brushing the floor, her iron gray hair gathered
in a single loose braid that touched her waistline. She accepted
a peck on the cheek, running a hand up the back of Estelle's
arm in return.

"You want coffee, *Mamá*?" Estelle reached across the counter
for her mother's cup, an enormous mug with a souvenir logo
of Mexico City.

"Of course I want coffee," Teresa replied. She watched as
Estelle filled the cup to within a half inch of the rim and then
set it on the kitchen table for her.

"Sofía's coming!" Francisco announced loudly. Teresa grimaced at the volume.

"That's good, *Ruidoso*," she said. "Maybe I'll have someone
to talk to who makes sense." She settled in the chair, swinging
the walker out of the way. "What time did you come home?"
she asked Estelle.

"About one, I suppose."

"About one." Teresa shook her head as she took a tentative
sip of the coffee. "All these nasty things going on."

"It happens once in a while," Estelle said. The long weeks,
sometimes months, of serenity in the county made the brief
moments of harsh reality seem all the more intrusive.

"Sofía called last night? Is that what all this means? I heard
the telephone," Teresa said.

"Yes. Francis talked to her."

"Well, that's good. Don't forget to tell *Padrino*," Teresa said.
"Maybe we can all have a nice dinner together." She paused for
emphasis. "If you're going to be home."

"Ah," Estelle said, and set her cup down. She slipped a small notebook from her pocket and jotted a short message. "You reminded me," she said. Bill Gastner, retired Posadas County sheriff, dear friend and godfather for the boys, would want to see Sofía Tournál. The two were unlikely friends—the polished, stately woman of the world and the gruff, paunchy New Mexico livestock inspector. More selfishly, though, Gastner represented the perfect solution to a nagging challenge—although she could imagine his immediate reaction to what she was going to suggest. "I'll make a point of seeing him today."

She glanced at the clock. Irma Sedillos, *nana*, housekeeper, and close friend, would arrive in a minute or so. Later in the morning, Irma would escort Carlos to the Little Bear Day Care Center.

Even with the day organized, Estelle found it hard to leave the warm kitchen. With the lassitude of a brief night's sleep, it would have been comfortable to sit at the breakfast table with her mother, enjoying no schedule at all. Once out the front door, her world was one of unanswered questions.

But ten minutes later, she hefted the packet of photos from her mailbox in the Public Safety Building, the pictures accompanied by a concise report from Sgt. Tom Mears. Dispatcher Brent Sutherland leaned back in his chair, hands clasped behind his head, and waited until she finished reading.

"No word yet," he said when she looked up. "On Zeigler, I mean." She knew he hadn't meant the report in her hand, which he wouldn't have read. Mears' memo told her only that the blood samples on the lamp shade, as well as other physical evidence, had been sent to the state lab in Las Cruces by courier—Deputy Sisneros this time.

If the county manager had been located, someone would have called her, no matter what the hour. "You wouldn't believe the places Jackie's checked out during the night," Sutherland added. "And the sheriff, too."

"I can imagine," she said. The enigmatic Deputy Taber moved about the county like a phantom, working graveyard shift through preference. Ex-military herself, she would have looked at home in one of the recruitment ads that showed special forces troopers lurking with faces painted and uniform and hardware camouflaged.

And through thirty years of hunting and camping since his early teens, Bob Torrez knew every back road and deserted two-track down to the Mexican border…and many beyond. Both sheriff and deputy preferred to work alone and in the cover of darkness. Estelle empathized.

"The sheriff said to ask you about what I should tell Frank or Pam when they come in."

Estelle grimaced. A middle-school student expelled for carrying a weapon on school grounds, another teenaged girl the victim of attempted murder in her own home, and a missing county manager—such would be the stuff for the front page of the *Posadas Register* this week, a monumental break in routine for publisher Frank Dayan.

With a newspaper printed late Thursday afternoons, Frank longed for important news that was fresh during the first part of the week, before events were pounded stale by the large metro papers and television stations. Frank was smart enough to wonder about possible connections, too.

"I'll figure something out," she said. "What time did Linda and Sgt. Mears go home?"

"Just about four, I think. He said for you to call him if you had a question about that." Sutherland nodded at the papers.

There wasn't much to question. Estelle scanned the terse report again as she walked toward her office. She paused in the doorway and glanced up as the "employees only" outer door clicked open between the dispatch island and the foyer. The brawny figure of Bill Gastner appeared.

"Great minds are on the same wavelength," she said, and smiled at *Padrino*.

"You got Sutherland trained yet?" Gastner said gruffly. "Goddamned kid can't figure out how to make coffee."

"That's because he doesn't drink the stuff," Estelle replied.

"Matters not. He should be able to read my mind, know when I'm going to walk through the door, and have the coffee made. I saw your buggy outside." He jerked his chin at the stack of photos in her hand. "Progress?"

"Some, I think. Come on in." She held her office door for him. "I made myself a note to catch up with you today."

"That's generally not too tough," Gastner said. "Consider me caught."

"Sofía's coming up for a visit in the next day or two."

"Well, good," he said pleasantly. "Hopefully, I can pry myself away from my busy schedule long enough to say hello. No word yet on Zeigler?"

She shook her head. "Nothing. It doesn't look good."

"I see what's-his-name out in the lobby...the boyfriend." Estelle looked up quickly. While it was true that Bill Gastner was a walking gazetteer of Posadas County, it surprised her that he knew about Zeigler and Page. Gastner had been retired for most of Zeigler's term as county manager, and wouldn't have worked with him on a regular basis as a livestock inspector. "Has he been out there all night?" Gastner asked.

"I hope not," Estelle said. "I came in the back, and didn't even look out that way."

"You had breakfast yet?"

She grinned at Gastner's reflex question. Any time between midnight and noon was time for breakfast, as many times as convenient. "You're going to need breakfast after I get done with you, sir."

"Uh-oh." He glanced at his watch. "I'm due out at the Triple Bar T in about...a little while." He sat down heavily, stretched out his legs, and folded his hands over his ample belly.

"Yesterday, the County Commission put their stamp on consolidation," she said. "I don't know if you were able to attend any of the meeting or not."

"Actually, they agreed to provide services," Gastner corrected. "And no, I avoided the pleasure of their company."

"Consolidated or services, it amounts to the same thing," Estelle said. "And that's why I wanted to talk to you and twist your arm. What we have to do is merge all of the village records—" She stopped when she saw the grin spread across Gastner's broad face, and brought her hands together, fingers meshed, "—with ours. The problem is about the size of five big filing cabinets full of confidential information, more or less."

"Mostly more, stretching back to the Mexican Revolution," Gastner muttered.

"Just about. All of that has to merge with everything that we have in county records. And you know exactly what's in those."

Gastner straightened up, sitting forward in his chair. "The commissioners didn't think about that little job, did they? In all their infinite wisdom."

"Of course not, sir. Kevin was well aware of what's necessary, though." Estelle saw the older man move his hands to the chair arms and shift his weight forward, preparatory to rising. "The thing is, *Padrino*, we're going to have to go through every file, every scrap of hard copy, and merge, and add, and just generally combine, the two record systems."

"I'm aware of that. More power to you, sweetheart."

"And the other problem, as I'm sure you know better than I, is that this is something that needs to be done by certified police officers, sir. It's not something that we can just farm out to a couple of high school kids, or a couple of office temps."

"God, I hope not." Gastner rose with a loud cracking of knees. He glanced at his watch again. "I need to find some decent coffee. You got time?"

"No, I really don't. The Hurtados are coming in at seven-thirty."

"I don't envy you that."

"This is the deal, sir," Estelle pressed. "You know more about this county than anyone on the planet. You know the law, you know criminal and investigative procedure backward, forward, and sideways, and there probably isn't a single name in those files that you don't know."

Gastner's eyes twinkled. "I probably talk about half of 'em in my sleep. Thank you. Keep going, though. Flattery will get you everywhere."

"There's a time constraint, too," Estelle said. "This isn't something that can drag on and on. It's not something that we can nibble away at, a little at a time. What I need is a team that knows what it's doing, working full-time until the job is finished."

"Sounds like a plan. A ghastly plan, but a plan nevertheless."

"You'll consider heading it up?"

"I didn't say that. I said it sounds like a plan…for someone." He grinned and shook his head. "I think I'd rather go find a nice big pile of rocks and drop 'em on my foot, one at a time, than slog through all that shit." He stepped toward the door. "How's your mother doing? I haven't seen her in a week or so."

"She's fine, sir." She waited patiently. Gastner hadn't actually walked through the door yet, and she could see the wheels turning in his head.

"Who else?" he asked.

"Mike Sisneros…" She couldn't help hesitating. "And Dennis."

"Collins? I don't think so."

"It would give him the opportunity to learn the system, for one thing," Estelle said.

"You're too generous," Gastner said. "I'm sure the experience would do him good, but that's not the point. I can't see him with that level of concentration." He held up his right hand, tapping fingers against thumb. "He talks more than he thinks. He'd be the first one to take shortcuts. I'd shoot him out of frustration before we made it through the first filing cabinet." He held the door thoughtfully, and Estelle waited. "Mike's good. I like him a lot. In fact, he's one of the two best things about this whole merger deal."

"Captain Mitchell is the other," Estelle agreed.

"Ah, 'Captain'? Is that what you guys settled on? You bet he's good. Tell you what. Here's the deal of the century for you. You spring Mike free, full-time…that's one. Give me Linda for the other." He grinned at Estelle's pained expression. "Look, she's not a road deputy, so using her won't cut into your patrol schedule. She's smart. She's meticulous. Well hell, why am I telling you all this. You know what she is. She's probably also indispensable to what you're doing right now, but in a day or so…."

"I wish."

Gastner waved a hand in dismissal. "And guess who also knows how to use a camera, par excellence—who in fact taught Linda most of what she knows about cops and robbers." He swung open the door. "Give me those two, and I'll do it for you."

"I'm not sure Linda—"

"Whoa, whoa," he said, shaking his head. "You're not going to tell me that you were planning to give these guys a *choice*, are you? Linda's a smart girl. She can see that this isn't just busywork that we're talkin' about here." He grinned and swept one hand grandly through the air. "We're talking about building the foundation of a modern, cohesive law enforcement department." He chuckled. "How could she refuse, assuming she had any choice in the matter? Besides, tell 'em I'll buy 'em lunch every day until we're done. You're not going to get a better deal than that today."

He opened the door fully and glanced out into the hall. "Let me know, all right?"

Estelle nodded and picked up the folder of photographs. "One of the things I was going to talk over with Kevin was how much we have in the budget for this sort of thing."

"That's the least of your worries right now," Gastner said. They heard muted voices, and he added, "The Hurtados are here." But instead of leaving, Gastner stepped back and gently closed the office door. "Are you giving some consideration to what Bobby thinks happened?"

"He hasn't talked much about what he thinks," Estelle said.

Gastner nodded philosophically. "Yeah, there is that. But I chatted with him for a minute out at the gas pumps just a bit ago," Gastner said. "He thinks there's reason to believe that it wasn't Kevin Zeigler who walked into the middle of something as an innocent bystander."

"He's talking about Carmen, then?"

"Yup. What if *she* witnessed something that she shouldn't have?"

"You mean that Kevin was up to something, and saw her watching?" Gastner shrugged.

"The obvious route right now is the flip side of that," Estelle said. "I understand why Bobby thinks the way he does. He walked into Zeigler's house, saw the evidence that he and Page share a bed, and his expression looked like he'd stepped in something a dog left behind."

Gastner laughed. "I can imagine." His face settled into sober. "I just wanted to pass the conversation along. That's all. You follow your instincts, sweetheart."

"At the moment, I'm not sure that I have any," Estelle said. "We'll see what Deena has to say."

Chapter Fifteen

"Sit over there," Roy Hurtado said, directing his daughter toward a chair on the opposite side of the small conference table. He pointed to the seat next to the one he had chosen for himself, and his wife, Ivana, settled into it. Ivana was dry-eyed, her jaw set firmly—whether from twenty-four hours of resignation to the ugly events that had caught up her daughter, or from confidence gained from being told what to do by her husband, Estelle couldn't tell.

"Ivana, can I get you something? Water, tea, coffee?" Estelle asked.

"We're fine," Roy said.

Estelle held eye contact with Ivana until Deena's mother found her voice.

"No, thanks," Ivana echoed. "We're fine."

"Deena?"

The teenager shook her head.

"We need some answers," Roy Hurtado said. He stretched out his arms on the table, hands forming a bowl. "We need to know what the hell is going on." The index finger of his right hand extended, aiming at Deena across the table. "From the beginning," he ordered. Hurtado wasn't a large man, but he impressed Estelle as physical—quick with the hands as well as the mouth.

Estelle had placed her briefcase on the table, and she picked up the folder of photographs that was resting on top of it, at the same time circling around the end of the table. She pulled out the chair nearest Deena.

With his order to start talking ignored by his daughter, Hurtado snapped, "I mean, for the rest of the *year*, she's out of school. What the hell are we supposed to do with that?" He managed to make it sound as if the entire incident was the school's fault.

Still ignoring his heated outburst, Estelle slid the eight-by-ten glossy photo of Deena's hat pin in front of the middle schooler. She saw Deena's eyes flick to the evidence tag attached to the upper right corner. "Deena, when you purchased this from your Aunt Mary Anne, the tip wasn't sharpened." Estelle reached across and touched the photo lightly with the tip of her pen, indicating the polished, filed tip. "You can see clearly that it has been. By comparison"—she drew back and riffled through the photos, finding one she had taken of the display at Great Notions—"you can see that none of these have been."

"I don't see what you're getting at," Roy said. "Let me see those." He stretched out his hand, middle finger and thumb going through the soundless motions of snapping.

"In a minute," Estelle said without looking at him. "Deena, did you sharpen this yourself, or have it sharpened for you by a friend?"

"Well, *she* wouldn't have done it," Roy snapped.

Estelle turned and regarded him with interest. "Why do you say that, sir?"

"Well...," Roy began, and stalled.

"You don't have hand tools in the house?"

"I don't see what difference it makes whether or not she sharpened the damn thing. I mean, after all..."

Estelle turned back to Deena. The youngster had settled back into herself, waiting for her father to wind down. Dressed in a simple, frilled white blouse and new jeans with her hair pulled back into a ponytail, she looked exactly like what she was: a frightened child.

Although Deena was wiry and fit, Estelle saw that she could easily encircle the youngster's wrist with thumb and index finger. There was no way that Deena, or anyone like her, had chased the chunky, scrappy Carmen Acosta through the house, wielding a heavy lug wrench so hard that a missed swing had shattered wall plaster and a television set. Had Deena arrived on the Acosta doorstep, Carmen wouldn't have run in the first place.

"Deena, it would be helpful if you'd share certain information with us," Estelle said. "I'm sure that you heard about what happened to Carmen yesterday."

Deena nodded slightly.

"Is she going to be all right?" Ivana asked.

"We don't know yet," Estelle replied. "I wish I could be more optimistic." She tapped the photo again. "Tell me about this."

"Mauro fixed it up for me," Deena said without hesitation.

"Mauro Acosta?" Estelle managed to keep the surprise out of her voice. Deena had done some introspection since the day before. "Tell me about that."

"That little punk," Roy muttered. "Ought to take him out back—"

Estelle held up a hand to stop the tirade. "Do you know about this?" she asked Roy.

"No, I don't know anything about it. I just—"

"Then let your daughter explain without interference, all right?" She let the silence deepen for a moment to make sure that he had finished blustering. She watched his jaw muscles twitch, but then he nodded curtly. She then turned back to Deena. "Tell me about Mauro."

"A while ago, he had one of these, and we thought they were neat," Deena said.

"Neat," Roy grumbled.

"That's where you got the idea? From Mauro? He had one first?"

"I guess so. I mean, I don't know where *he* got the idea, but one day he had one at school and was showing it around out on the parking lot. That's where I saw it."

"Mauro's in ninth grade, right?"

Deena nodded. *Ninth grade and the source of all things important,* Estelle thought. "How long ago was that?"

Deena's head settled back until she was staring at the ceiling. "A while," she said, then looked at Estelle directly, unflinching. "I don't remember for sure. It was back when Carmen and me were talking and stuff, though." What could have been the trace of a philosophical smile twitched the corners of her mouth. "Mauro said that one of his cousins up in Albuquerque had one of those pins, and showed him how to stow it so no one would see it."

"Do you know if Carmen wore hers to school?"

"All the time," Deena said emphatically. "All the time."

"Christ," Roy Hurtado muttered.

"The night of the volleyball game," Estelle said, "when you and Carmen fought. Did you have the hat pin with you that night?"

The girl shook her head. "I didn't. I forgot to take it."

"What about Carmen?"

Deena looked back down at the photo, and Estelle saw the moisture gather in the corners of her eyes. "That's how close you came, Deena," the undersheriff said, and she bent closer. "Carmen had hers that night, didn't she?" Deena nodded. "That's why you wore yours to school?" She nodded again.

"When we were fighting..." Deena paused, looking up at Estelle. "That's all I could think about was what would happen if she got that thing out." She slowly shook her head. "I grabbed on to her left hand, thinking that I could keep her from getting to it. I grabbed on and wouldn't let go." Deena blinked. "Even when she thumped my head against the pavement. I wouldn't let go."

"You thought that she really would stab you?"

"I know she would have," Deena replied. "Carmen? Sure. When she gets all mad and crazy, she'll do anything."

"She's pretty strong, isn't she?"

Deena looked heavenward. "She is *so* bad. There aren't even any *boys* who want to tangle with her."

"What about her brothers?"

"Well, they're different. They're worse."

"So when you purchased this"—and Estelle tapped the photo again—"when you bought this from your aunt, you gave it to Mauro to fix up? To sharpen for you?"

"Yes. Carmen said I should."

"To make it more deadly, or what?" Estelle glanced at Roy Hurtado, who had fallen uncharacteristically silent. Maybe knowing how close his daughter and only child had come to imitating a shish kebab had diluted some of his bravado.

Deena shook her head quickly. "It's easier to thread into the seam of the jeans if it's pointy." She leaned forward and slipped the photo taken at Great Notions toward Estelle. "They're kind of blunt and stuff?"

"And it's a better weapon when it's sharp."

"Yeah, I guess."

"Mauro did this at home?" Deena nodded. "What, you bought the pin, then took it—or them—over to the Acostas'?" The girl nodded again. "When was that?"

"A couple weeks ago."

"And then came the argument about Paul," Estelle said.

"I guess."

"Between the fight at the volleyball game and when I saw you yesterday at school, had you talked with Carmen? Phone calls, threats, anything like that?"

Deena shook her head sadly. "One of my friends said that Carmen was going to get me. But she doesn't scare me."

I bet, Estelle thought. "Going to *get* you—meaning she might jump you at school, or going and coming?"

"I guess."

"But you never actually saw her?"

"No."

Estelle rested her index finger on the photo of the hat pin. "But you wanted to be ready."

"I guess."

"Did you talk with Paul since the fight?"

Deena frowned in disgust. "*No,* I didn't talk with him. This is so stupid. I didn't even really *like* him."

"Have you talked with Mauro recently?"

"No. Why would I talk with him?"

Estelle nodded sympathetically. "After you and I talked at the middle school yesterday…were you home all the rest of the day?"

That prompted Roy Hurtado out of his silence. "Now look, Deena didn't have anything to do with what happened over at the Acostas'. That's ridiculous."

"I don't think she had anything to do with it either, Mr. Hurtado," Estelle said. "And that's not what I asked her. I asked if she was home."

"Of course she was home. She was grounded, for God's sakes. And I mean grounded. She's expressly forbidden to leave the house."

"Deena?"

The girl slumped back in her chair. She picked at the cuticle of her left thumbnail. "After Mom went back to work, I went over to the store and stuff."

"Which store is that?" Estelle ignored Roy Hurtado's whispered expletive.

"Tommy's. The convenience store."

"What time, do you remember?"

"I don't know." She shrugged. "Maybe around one."

"Did you happen to see Mr. Acosta there?"

"No. But Mauro was there. Him and Tony."

"That's after the high school's lunch hour, isn't it?"

"I guess." She shrugged. "But I left right away."

"For where?"

Deena shifted uneasily and glanced at her father, then at Estelle. "I went to talk with Auntie."

"MaryAnne Bustamonte?"

"Yes. She said that you'd come by the store and hassled her."

Roy Hurtado let out a hiss of compressed air.

"That's one way to look at it, I suppose," Estelle said. "Did you buy any more of these, Deena?"

"No," the girl said petulantly. She glared sideways at Estelle and then dropped her eyes.

"I have the others," Roy said quickly. "She had four of 'em." He glowered at his daughter. "In four different sizes."

Estelle caught the trace of gloat in Deena's eyes. *And how many more*, she thought. Taking her time, Estelle tidied the photos and slipped them back inside the briefcase. Before closing the lid, she removed the evidence bag that held the hat pin confiscated from Deena at the middle school.

"Deena," she said, and slipped the hat pin out of the bag, removing the small rubber-tip protector, "I want you to look at this carefully. This is the one that you carried yesterday." She laid it on the table directly in front of the girl, arranging it meticulously to parallel the table's edge. "Someone broke into the Acostas' house and attacked Carmen, Deena. They chased her through the house, and at some point in the fight, Carmen managed to pull a weapon just like this from the left inseam of her jeans." She paused, watching the girl's face carefully, no more than a dozen inches from her own.

"Now, you know how dangerous Carmen can be when she's mad or threatened." That earned the faintest nod. "As tough as she is, the person who attacked her tore the hat pin out of her hand, struggled some more, and then held her from behind while he drove that thing into her left ear."

If either Ivana or Roy Hurtado were still breathing, Estelle couldn't hear them.

"All the way through, Deena, until it bent against her jawbone on the other side of her head. And then whoever did that tossed her down on her own bed and bashed in the back of her skull with a truck lug wrench." Estelle bent even closer and slipped her arm around Deena's thin shoulders. "I *know* you didn't do that. You *couldn't* do that. But we're going to find the person who did, Deena. You can help us."

She remained motionless with her arm around the girl, watching the tears course down Deena's cheeks.

"This isn't something to play with," Estelle whispered, and reached out to touch the hat pin, just enough to make it roll half a turn. "This isn't a toy, and carrying it into a school full of children isn't cool, or funny, or smart."

She withdrew her arm, capped the hat pin, and slid it back into the bag. "If you have any more, get rid of them," she said brusquely. "And if you're not smart enough to do that, think very hard before you threaten someone with it. If you don't, the odds are good you'll be joining Carmen. And that would make me very sad indeed."

"We were thinking that maybe she'll go live with her sister up in Albuquerque," Roy Hurtado said.

"That's up to you," Estelle said cryptically.

"Well, she can't stay at home all day without someone watchin' her. Both me and Ivana work, and I guess we just found out how good she minds."

"How old is Samantha?"

"Twenty-three."

"And she's home all day?"

"Well, no, but…"

"You might want to rethink that idea, then," Estelle said. She stood up and rested both hands on the briefcase, regarding Deena. "Now's the time to prove how smart you really are, Deena," she said.

Deena heaved a shuddering breath. "Do you think she'll be all right?"

"I don't know the answer to that."

"What happens if she's not, then?"

"If Carmen dies, we'll be looking to charge someone with murder, Deena. It's that simple."

Chapter Sixteen

A brief stop at the high school confirmed that Mauro and Tony Acosta had enjoyed more than just an extended lunch. Both had been present in their morning classes; both walked out for lunch and hadn't returned. The attendance records also provided an interesting portrait for the pair.

Margie Edwards, the principal's secretary, beckoned Estelle around the end of her desk, and scooted her chair to one side so that the undersheriff could see the computer screen. The two student office aides had been sent on errands, the principal himself was somewhere out on campus, but Margie still talked as if the walls had ears.

"See here?" she said. "This is our ninth grader. What a pistol he is."

Estelle scanned across the grid. "He's been absent fourteen times since school started, if I'm reading this right."

"That's not counting today, by the way. Neither one of them are here today."

"They're up in Albuquerque with the family," Estelle said. "I see that Mauro was absent yesterday afternoon."

"I'm not surprised. Both of those boys are absent *a lot*. And this is only early November." Margie shifted in her seat, glancing toward the office doorway. "Now mind you, there are some teachers who would say"—and she dropped her voice another notch—"that a day without Mauro is a day improved." The smile was one of resignation. "I kind of like the kid, myself. I can't

imagine what's going to become of him, but he can be a charmer."
She moved the mouse so that the cursor stopped in several places
along the march of days. "Of those fourteen absences, though,
nine are only afternoon skips. He comes in the morning and then
adiós, muchacho. So yesterday's absence isn't unusual."

"And Tony?"

The screen winked and Margie highlighted Tony Acosta's
attendance record. "Here's our good influence," she said. "Mr.
Tony has twenty-three absences since August Twenty-first."

"Caramba."

"And that includes thirteen that are afternoon absences
only, including the one yesterday." She looked up at Estelle.
"You might wonder how he manages to have a three point four
GPA, huh."

"Yes, I would."

"The rest of us, too. I guess he does all his thinking by cor-
respondence." She tapped the mouse. "You want copies of these
two guys?"

"If you can. But I have another question."

"Shoot."

"I need to know if yesterday Mauro and Tony were in their—
what, fifth-hour class? Am I reading that right?"

"Fifth is the one just before lunch. Let me check." She pushed
back her chair and hesitated. "How am I going to do this, now.
See"—and she turned toward Estelle—"the teachers send in a slip
each period…one of our office aides picks them all up. They're
supposed to send in a slip, and if a youngster who is absent isn't
already on the morning's absentee list, they send his name in."

She turned back to the computer. "Fifth period, Mauro has
math with Mr. Hode, and Tony is a library aide. We'd have to
ask the teachers to be sure the boys were there, but Hode and
Kerner are both pretty good about attendance. Would you like
me to do that?"

"Yes, I really would. If it's possible to do it confidentially."

"Well, *quietly,* anyway," Margie said. "There's nothing much
confidential around this place. Let me print these while we're

here." The printer near Estelle's elbow came to life. "And I'm not even going to ask…," she added, then hesitated just long enough to see if Estelle would volunteer information.

"Thanks," Estelle said, knowing exactly what Margie *wanted* to ask.

Margie pulled the pages out of the printer and handed them to Estelle. "Both Hode and the library are just down the hall, so it'll only take a minute. Do you want to wait here?"

"I should," Estelle said.

Margie cleared the computer screen. "I'll be just a minute." She grinned at Estelle. "If the phone rings, just beckon one of the slaves." She nodded toward the two office aides who orbited the foyer, both wondering why they'd been quarantined from the office. "They can get it. Pick that thing up, and you never know what you're going to get into."

"Yes, ma'am."

In less than two minutes, Margie Edwards bustled back up the hallway. She closed the office door, and turned her back as if the two student aides might be able to read her lips through the glass partitions. "Both boys were here until the end of the period," she said, and Estelle heard relief in her tone. "That means they left during lunch." She nodded conspiratorially. "I think that's what they usually do."

"Thanks, Margie."

"I'll be here if you need anything else." Her expression softened. "And we all hope that Carmen is going to be all right. That's such a shame." She beckoned to a disheveled youngster waiting to come into the office. The boy, certainly no older than ninth grade and smaller than many of the middle-school students across the parking lot, held an ice pack against his left wrist.

"Thanks again," Estelle said.

"Come see us when you're not so busy," Margie said. As Estelle slipped past the youngster, his huge blue eyes, a little bloodshot from an earlier bout of tears, looked up at her. Flecks of perspiration dotted his pale forehead.

"Hi," he said to Estelle, hoisting the wrist for better view, sounding pleased that he had a badge of honor to show for his collision with some immovable object. Moving close to Margie's desk, he added, "Mr. Banks said that you need to take me to the emergency room. He says my wrist is broken."

Estelle glanced at Margie, and the secretary looked heavenward. "Let me see it again," Margie groaned.

"Have a great day," Estelle said, stepping out of the way.

Back outside in the car, she perused her notes. Attendance records showed that the day before, the day of the attack on their sister, both Mauro and Tony had been in school until 12:40 p.m. It had been nearly an hour before that time when she'd talked with Kevin Zeigler. Freddy Acosta had called 911 at 2:38 p.m., and if his memory was accurate, he had left his residence sometime around noon to check with his wife at the auto dealership.

Estelle frowned. When she had talked with Zeigler, it was just seconds before noon, straight up. Mauro and Tony were still in class, and Freddy had just left the house a few moments before in search of lunch. By his account, it would be nearly two and a half hours before he returned home.

A two-and-a-half-hour window of opportunity. That the amiable, ambling Freddy Acosta should take a two-and-a-half-hour stroll, talking to this person and that, was entirely reasonable. That he would hustle to the store and back without wasting a moment would have been unusual.

Zeigler would not have arrived home in time to see Freddy leave, but he *might* have driven by and seen Acosta walking into, or out of, the auto dealership on Bustos where his wife worked. He might have seen Freddy on Grande, ambling toward Tommy's Handi-way where the chips, coffee, and conversation waited.

The window of opportunity was there for Kevin Zeigler. It yawned open for Mauro and Tony, too, but Estelle shook her head with impatience. There was nothing about the attack that was characteristic of the two boys, although clearly Mauro was lying when he had told Eddie Mitchell at the hospital in Albuquerque that he knew nothing of the hat pin. That was a typical "I didn't do it" teenager, though. According to Deena Hurtado, Mauro was intimately familiar with the weapon, right down to its neatly filed tip.

Frustrated at no instant response from the state forensic lab to guide her thinking, Estelle drove out of the school parking lot and headed for the county complex. She was certain that Zeigler would not have attacked Carmen Acosta.

That left the possibility that Bobby Torrez was at least partially correct: What if Carmen Acosta had witnessed something next door that she shouldn't have? The evidence fitted two versions of that scenario. If Zeigler had driven home, and had then been confronted by the attacker, Carmen might have been attracted to the back door by the ruckus and seen what she shouldn't have seen.

The inside of Zeigler's home appeared untouched; no struggle had taken place there. If there was an incident, it occurred outside, where it would attract the attention of neighbors. Carmen would have heard it. Farther up the street, five doors to the west, Doris Marens was home, but that was far enough away that all but the most violent sounds would have been indistinguishable.

Mrs. Marens had been standing on the front porch watching the light show as all the emergency equipment arrived, but she had told Officer Sisneros that she'd heard or seen nothing before that. Estelle made a mental note to talk to the woman again. In the flurry of trying to be a helpful witness, Doris Marens might have been searching her memory for the unusual. The answer might have been hiding instead among the usual sights and sounds of the day.

The county building complex was less than five blocks from the school, with the downtown blocks in between. Estelle parked in her own reserved spot and walked around the small brick patio. Just inside were the commission chambers and various county offices, with visitors greeted first by the clerk/treasurer's and assessor's offices. Beyond, just to one side of the doors to the commission chambers, was the county manager's office.

Penny Barnes was on the phone when Estelle entered, elbow on the desk, using the phone as a cradle to hold her head. "I know," she said, and waited a moment. She beckoned toward Estelle. "I know. Believe me, I'll let you know the *instant* I hear anything. Okay?" She waited again, looked wearily at the undersheriff, and at the same time mimed biting the knuckles of her left hand in frustration.

"Right. I know. Okay, I'll get back to you right away, then." She straightened up, and dropped the phone back into its cradle. "Frank Dayan," she said. "That's the *fourth* time he's called this morning, and it's what, not quite nine o'clock? I'm surprised he isn't hounding you."

"I've made a point not to hold still long enough," Estelle replied.

Penny's pleasant face crinkled in misery. "What is going on?" she wailed, and turned to follow Estelle's gaze. The door to Zeigler's office was closed, with a large hasp now screwed on the door and an authoritative lock snapped in place. A short length of POLICE LINE—DO NOT CROSS yellow tape was stretched across the door at eye level. Bob Torrez hadn't lost any time.

"I was so sure that when I walked into the office this morning, Kevin would be sitting in there, all hunched over his computer the way he always is. Instead, all I see is this ugly thing." She waved at lock and ribbon with distaste.

"We don't know any more than we knew yesterday, which is nothing." Estelle drew a chair closer to Penny's desk and nudged the outer office door shut at the same time. "I saw Kevin at the elementary school, right at noon yesterday. That's it. His truck shows up at his house, maybe as much as two hours after that. And no Kevin."

Penny let her hands drop into her lap. She turned and stared through the glass of Zeigler's office door. "I just don't know what to think. I look in there and tell myself, 'Look, it's just been a few hours. He got called away on some kind of emergency or something.' I mean look at that." She held out both hands help-lessly. "His reading glasses are lying right there by his computer, like he just dropped them there for a minute, planning to be right back. When I left yesterday afternoon, his computer was still turned on the way it always is. Even that little radio over in the corner is on, just like it always is." She waved her hands. "Everything is *still* on, as far as I know."

"When you saw him yesterday before the commission meeting, was he upset about anything? Did he talk about anything?"

Penny shook her head. "Just *nothing*," she said. "I mean, he's *always* talking to people, you know. Always. It seems like every single minute, he's on that darn phone. That's the job."

"No particular arguments lately that you can pinpoint?"

"No. He was excited about the vote yesterday, and Estelle, that's how I *know* something is just dreadfully wrong with all this. When the commission broke for lunch, they had some more presentations on the agenda—like you and Bobby and the chief. There were budget questions, a zillion details to discuss. With all that coming up, Kevin would *never* have willingly missed the afternoon session."

"And he would have certainly called, in any case."

Penny's face crumpled in agony. "I'm scared, I guess. I heard about what happened next door with the Acostas, and it just gives me the willies."

"Yesterday morning," Estelle said. "Did anyone call here while the morning session was going on, asking to speak to Kevin?"

"A number of calls," Penny said. "I know that Kevin had a whole list of things to do over lunch break. One of the things he wanted to do was touch bases with you, and make sure you'd come to the afternoon session."

"He did that. But what else? Earlier, you mentioned an errand or two, including something at the county barns."

"He had to see someone over at the maintenance yard about something. Some workman's comp thing." She paused and put her hand over her mouth, deep in thought. "He had to go to the bank. He asked me when he came in yesterday morning to help him remember."

"His own personal banking?"

"Yes. *Normal, so normal.* Just day-in, day-out kind of stuff."

"Was there anything in particular that Kevin asked you to do for him?"

Penny swept her hand over the avalanche on her desk. "Just this," she said. "The county goes on." She reached out and grasped a fistful of papers. "Bids. That's always a popular one. We can't buy a gosh darn pencil without an RFB. Now we have to figure out how to work the village PD financing into the sheriff's budget. *That* will be just a wingding. You and I will be losing sleep over that." She grimaced. "Bobby will just shrug and go hunting."

"But nothing out of the ordinary?"

"No, nothing." She picked up another paper. "Not unless you consider the September landfill records interesting and fascinating stuff, second only to October's landfill records."

"Yesterday," Estelle persisted. "No phone calls out of the ordinary. No errands out of the ordinary. How about right out there?" She turned and nodded at the lobby outside the commission chambers. "You have a grandstand view from here. Did you see anyone that you don't normally see at these things?"

This time, it was a long, slow shake of the head, as if the last straw had been broken. "Same old, same old," Penny said. "But I have to admit, I don't pay much attention. If I did, I wouldn't get anything done."

"You didn't happen to see Kevin talking to anyone in particular? Or no one came in here before the meeting, hoping to have a few minutes alone with him?"

"No, no, and no. If they did, they all just passed me by, you know?" She reached out and rested her hand on the impressive pile that filled the "in" basket. "This is what drives my day, this little friend right here." She fell silent, waiting for Estelle, who was gazing off across the lobby toward the commission chambers.

"You know, if you want to know who attended the meeting, that's simple enough," Penny said. "Stacey Roybal keeps notes. Most of the time, she jots down who-all attends. And then they always pass around that sign-in sheet." She held up a finger in sudden inspiration. "And then, if you're *really* desperate, you could ask Milton Crowley. If it moves, he films it."

"Ah, Mr. Videotape."

Penny nodded. "I'd like to see the inside of his house sometime." She leaned forward and lowered her voice. "The *bizarre* thing is imagining him sitting in his home in the evening, *watching* old tapes of County Commission meetings. That's pretty kinky."

"Milton Crowley," Estelle repeated.

"You're really going to talk to him? You're nuts."

"Probably."

Penny looked genuinely alarmed. "You're not going out there alone, are you? Have you ever seen that sign he has at the entrance to his driveway?"

"No, but I've heard about it. Maybe it's time to see if he really means it."

Chapter Seventeen

The county car thumped through the potholes and ruts, juddered across patches of loose blow-sand, and kicked gravel over the last steep rise in the two-track. The hill was so steep that for a moment Estelle couldn't see the tracks ahead over the hood of the car. The narrow path leveled and within a few yards was blocked by a gate in the barbed-wire range fence.

She could not see Milton Crowley's home. Beyond the gate, the two-track wound through runty piñon and juniper, twisted cacti and creosote bush, skirting the next rise in the prairie. Behind her to the southeast lay the village of Posadas, twelve miles away. She had turned off the state highway a few miles northwest of the airport, following Forest Road 26 around the western flank of Cat Mesa to Crowley's gate.

He had a wonderful view from his property—the San Cristóbals to the south and west, the great sweep of the prairie to the east, the imposing flat-crowned bulk of Cat Mesa at his back door. Estelle sat quietly for a moment with the windows open. A light breeze hissed through the fat junipers that crowded the lane.

It wasn't likely that visitors to this spot first admired the view. Their attention would be attracted instead to a two-foot-square sign of painted plywood wired securely to the top and second strands of the fence immediately beside the gate. The lettering was simple block letters, painted in shiny black enamel on a weathered white background.

Trespass
and die,
fucker.

"PCS, three ten." She palmed the mike and waited, examining the barbed-wire gate ahead of her. The left side, where the wire closure looped over the polished top of the post, was locked with a heavy chain and padlock.

"Go ahead, three ten."

"PCS, I'm at Mr. Crowley's gate." As she spoke, she flipped open the small Posadas telephone directory. There was no listing for Milton Crowley. "Do you have a telephone number for this residence?"

A momentary pause followed as Gayle either pondered Estelle's odd question or looked in the file. Estelle hoped that Milton Crowley was hunched over his scanner, forehead furrowed in suspicion. On her increasingly frequent visits to County Commission meetings, she had always known Crowley was in the back tending his video camera, but she had paid him little mind.

During those meetings, he sometimes posed questions to the commission, or made caustic comments heavily loaded with sarcasm and the not-too-subtle implication that anyone who was part of government was either out to trample his personal rights, or was on the take, or was simply stupid. Without fail, a version of the meeting was reported in the small newsletter that Crowley published and then distributed by mail to his list of like-thinking readers.

"Ah, three ten, that's negative. We have no number on file for that residence."

"Ten-four. The gate appears to be locked."

"You be careful," Gayle said with uncharacteristic informality.

"Three ten will be ten-six this location."

"Three ten, three oh eight, negative that." Sheriff Torrez's voice was startlingly loud, sounding as if he was bending over his wife's shoulder in dispatch.

"Go ahead, three oh eight," Estelle said.

"Three ten, ten-twenty-one." Characteristically, Torrez offered no explanation.

"Ten-four," Estelle replied. Switching phone for mike, she dialed, knowing exactly what Bob Torrez wanted.

"Hey," he said when he picked up the phone. "What's with the visit to the Cat Mesa fruitcake?"

"Bobby, it occurred to me that he might have caught something on video from the meeting yesterday that could be of interest to us."

"Like what?"

"I don't know. But if someone had an argument with Kevin, there's a possibility that something might have been captured on tape during the commission meeting. I don't know what, but maybe something."

"Or not."

"Fifty-fifty," Estelle persisted. "Besides, I'd like to know who was present for the morning session of the meeting, but who didn't return for the afternoon. Crowley should have all of that."

"Maybe so. But you're dreamin' if you think he's going to hand over his tapes."

"That's if he even *has* any in the first place. Maybe he chucks them after a little while. Or records over the same one all the time. But I'm not going to ask him to hand anything over, Bobby. I'd just want to look at them."

Torrez sighed. "You're lookin' at his sign right now?"

"Yes. He doesn't mince words, does he."

"Nope. And that's just how eager he's gonna be to talk to you, let alone let you *into* his house, or give you custody of any tapes he might have."

"How far up this road is his house? I can't see it from here, and I don't know if he's home or not."

"It's about a quarter mile from the gate. Is his gate locked?"

"It appears to be."

"Take a closer look. If the lock is just looped through the chain, he's home. If it's actually locked, then he's off somewhere."

"Just a second." Estelle got out of the car and walked to the gate. The big padlock wasn't snapped shut. "It's open."

"He's probably home, then."

"You sound like you've been out here a time or two."

"Oh, yeah. A couple years ago, Crowley had some disagreements with the Forest Service over that fence you're lookin' at. They loved his signs, too. I guess he compromised and took a bunch of 'em down. Can you wait ten minutes?"

"Sure."

"Then just sit tight. I'll be right out." He chuckled. "Crowley does have a scanner, so you might give your twenty as the gate. If he's within earshot of his radio, he'll be out before long, I'll guarantee that. I'm on my way."

Estelle keyed the radio. "PCS, three ten is on Forest Road Twenty-six, at the private-property gate. I'll…" She paused as she saw the figure striding along the two-track toward her. "I'll be talking with the property owner here. He's on his way to this location."

"Ten-four, three ten. Be advised that three oh eight is en route."

Estelle opened the door, leaving the car idling. She slipped the phone into one jacket pocket and carried her handheld radio in her left hand.

Milton Crowley strode directly to the gate and stopped, one hand resting on the post at the cattle guard. He regarded Estelle quizzically as she stepped from the car. At first glance, Crowley looked like the sort of fellow who would be at home in a commercial for gardening products—homey flannel shirt, buff-colored quilted vest, neatly creased chinos, and waffle-soled boots worn as soft as moccasins. His shirtsleeves were rolled up two folds, revealing hairy, beefy forearms.

His face was broad, with a high, domed forehead crowned by a receding hairline, the same buzz cut that he'd probably first favored as a teenager half a century before.

But there was nothing home and garden about the heavy automatic holstered high on his right hip, butt angled well forward, hammer cocked and locked.

"Good morning, sir," Estelle said.

"Yes, it is." Crowley said carefully. He patted the top of the big juniper post.

"I'm Undersheriff Guzman," Estelle said, even though Crowley would know *exactly* who she was—no doubt even had captured her on film on various occasions.

"Sure enough you are," he said pleasantly. He hadn't changed position an iota, even as Estelle approached the fence. She chose her footing carefully, not because of the rough two-track, but because she wanted the time to consider which approach might work best with Crowley.

At the county meetings, when she paid any attention to Crowley at all, she'd noticed that he wasn't into small talk. He didn't take the opportunity to join the various small groups of politicos hobnobbing between sessions. He didn't appear to talk with Pam Gardiner or whoever was attending the meeting from the *Register*. He watched those groups, watched everyone, for only he knew what reason. He was an easy man to dismiss in a crowd, and most of the county bureaucrats and employees appeared to do just that.

Now, his body language was clear. He stood relaxed, confident, and armed behind his barbed-wire fence. He made no move to drop off the chain, lift off the closure loop, and drag the wire gate to one side so she could either walk or drive past. She realized that this was the first time she had actually talked to Milton Crowley. It would have been easy to stereotype the man as a furtive, anarchistic nutcase, living alone on his little homestead on the bleak flanks of Cat Mesa. But there was absolutely nothing furtive or shifty-eyed about him. Calm blue eyes regarded Estelle, never leaving her face. She decided to try the direct approach.

"Sir, I need your help."

Crowley made no reply, but she saw his right eyebrow drift up a fraction of an inch. At that moment, stereo radios carried first the bark of squelch, and then Bob Torrez's matter-of-fact voice.

"PCS, three oh eight is northbound on State Seventy-eight."

"Ten-four, three oh eight."

Estelle turned the volume up just a bit and keyed the radio's transmit button. "Three ten copies."

The corners of Crowley's eyes crinkled, and he reached around with his left hand without looking and turned down the volume of his own portable radio.

"Looks like the big man himself is on the way," he said.

"Sheriff Torrez knows this country a little better than I do," Estelle said, and stepped up close to the fence. She reached out with her radio and touched the top wire with the stubby antenna. "Sir, I noticed that you were videotaping the county meeting yesterday afternoon. I was wondering if you were there for the morning session as well?"

"What difference does that make?" Crowley's tone was businesslike, calmly neutral.

Estelle took a long, slow breath. She had hoped for a simple "yes," but even though his reply hadn't been contentious, Crowley gave the impression that he was practiced at living each moment with his guard held high, ready to scrutinize the most innocuous remark or question for hidden meaning. She glanced at the sign again, wondering what had prompted his mood the day he'd painted the message.

"The county manager attended the morning session, but didn't return for the afternoon," she said carefully. "I was hoping that maybe you had talked to him sometime during that first session."

"You're talking about Zeigler?"

"The county manager, yes, sir."

Crowley smiled and patted the post again. "Can't help you there."

"Sir, did you film both sessions?"

"It's a public meeting."

"I know that, sir. Your right to film the meeting isn't at issue."

"Goddamn right." Again, his tone was one of pleasant agreement. It reminded Estelle of talking to the old ex-Marine, former Sheriff Bill Gastner, in one of Gastner's more recalcitrant moments, and because of that impression, Estelle found herself liking Milton Crowley. She hesitated, weighing how much to take this man into her confidence. As if he had read her hesitation correctly, Crowley withdrew his hand from the post for the first time and crossed both arms over his chest.

"Why don't you just tell me what you want, young lady? I have things to do, and I'm sure you do, too."

"All right. If you recorded the entire session, sir, I'd like to look at the tape."

"The county clerk records every meeting. It's public record."

"I'm aware of that. But she doesn't use video. You do, sir."

"If you're trying to find out who was there, the clerk has a sign-in sheet."

Estelle smiled. "Yes, sir, she does. But not everyone signs it."

"It's an open, public meeting," Crowley said. "People are free to come and go as they please. They aren't required to sign some silly little attendance list for the county clerk…who has no need of that information in the first place."

"That's true, sir." She heard the sound of a vehicle, and turned to see Torrez's white Expedition nose over the rise and stop immediately behind her unit.

The handheld radios crackled. "PCS, three oh eight is ten-six, Crowley's."

"Your reinforcements are here," Crowley chuckled, a good-natured grin deepening the crow's-feet at the corners of his eyes.

The sheriff took his time, apparently arranging a mountain of paperwork before getting out of his vehicle, no hint of urgency in his motions. When he did get out, Torrez strolled up the two-track toward them as if he had all morning just to soak up the sun.

"Howdy, howdy," he greeted. He paused at one point and looked down at a small scattering of deer pellets beside the path. He toed them with his boot, then glanced up at Crowley. "I was up at Copperton Springs the other day. Pretty good herd hanging out there." Crowley didn't respond, but he unlocked his arms and his right hand drifted back to the comfort of the juniper post. "How you been, Milt?" Torrez stepped up close to the fence, at the same time taking off his Stetson and running fingers through his tousled hair. He wiped his forehead and resettled the hat. "Things going all right?"

"As good as they're going to get, I suppose," Crowley said.

"Sir," Estelle said, "would you consider letting us view the videotape of the meeting yesterday?"

"Not goddamn likely," Crowley said, and this time there was some bristle in his tone. Estelle wondered how much of it was for Bob Torrez's benefit. "If you want surveillance films, you take 'em yourself."

Torrez looked up from his examination of the ground near the fence and grinned. "How come it ain't surveillance when you take 'em?" he asked. Estelle groaned inwardly, but Crowley didn't rise to the bait. The sheriff rested his hand carefully between two of the barbs on the top strand of the gate. He bounced the wire thoughtfully.

"This is what we're lookin' for, Milt. The county manager went missing yesterday." He looked across the gate at Crowley and grimaced in frustration. "We don't know where he went, or with who, or what. Gone without a sign. And it don't look good." He bounced the wire again. "It don't look good."

"That's none of my concern."

"Nope, it isn't. But in tryin' to cover all the bases, your videotape was just something we thought about. Maybe someone came into the meeting, maybe talked with Zeigler. The commission covered a lot of ground in the morning session." He shrugged in self-deprecation. "Hell, it isn't something that I pay much attention to. Other than a few big things, I couldn't tell you what the commission talked about, or what they decided, or who argued with who, about what." He shrugged again. "But a video camera don't miss much."

"I don't turn over my tapes to anybody," Crowley said. "They're not for the government's use."

"Would you consider letting us see the tape in your presence?" Estelle asked. "That way, the tape would never leave your custody. If you don't want us on your property, we could view them at the sheriff's office."

Crowley shook his head deliberately from side to side. "I don't work for the government," he said. His expression had lost any trace of affability, the lines of his jaw set hard. Estelle could see clearly that she was wasting her time. "Get yourself a court order." He drew himself up a bit, unable to resist tossing in the challenge. "And then see if you can serve it."

Estelle looked at him curiously, but Bob Torrez just grunted a chuckle.

"Relax, Milt," he said. He bounced the wire again, as if dismissing the entire conversation and finding the fence far more important. "I thought the Forest Service was going to put in a solid gate for you."

"This one's just fine."

"I'd think messin' with this wire every time you want to go in or out would be kind of a pain in the ass." He gave the wire a final flex and then held up his hand. "We got to go. You have a good day, Milt." Torrez stepped close to Estelle as he passed. "We got some interesting results back from the crime lab that you're going to want to see," he said, obviously not caring whether Crowley heard him or not.

Chapter Eighteen

A gap in the pinons allowed just enough room to turn the vehicles around, and Estelle noticed that Milton Crowley didn't bother to remain at the gate to watch them leave. As they reached the intersection of Forest Road and State Highway 78, Torrez pulled the Expedition over and got out. Estelle parked in the middle of Forest Road.

The sheriff settled on the front fender of Estelle's unmarked Crown Victoria, arms crossed comfortably.

"Two things," he said. "No usable prints on the lug wrench. Mears says that it's either been wiped or someone used gloves. And it's sure enough wallboard plaster on the nose, along with some traces of blood and hair. The blood is type AB, same as Carmen's. We're going to have to wait on the lab for DNA, but there's no doubt in my mind."

"Nothing new on her yet?"

"She's holding her own. Believe it or not, it's the rap to the back of her skull that's going to be the hurdle."

"We need to talk with the boys, Bobby." She recounted her conversation with Deena Hurtado earlier that morning.

"Mauro the little tool smith," Torrez said. "The little sack of shit isn't about to admit diddly. He's probably scared shitless."

"And he wasn't in school yesterday afternoon. Neither was his brother."

Torrez made a face. "I see those two around all the time. School just ain't real high on their list of favorite places. But they didn't have nothin' to do with the attack on Carmen."

"I don't think they did either, Bobby, but we need to talk with them. There's that two-hour black hole between the time when their father left home and then returned to discover Carmen in her bedroom. The boys weren't in school during that time. I'd like to know what they were doing."

"That's the other thing," Torrez said, nodding. "The stain on the bedroom wall? You'll be interested to know what that is."

"Yes, I would."

"How about heavy grease."

"Grease?"

"Yup. 'Contaminated' petroleum grease, the lab calls it. In other words, dirty."

"You're talking like automotive oil?"

"*Grease.* Old, used grease."

Estelle frowned. "That's bizarre."

"Tell me about it."

"There's no grease on the wrench handle?"

Torrez shook his head. "And see, that's the other thing about the boys. If Mauro was out back workin' on his car—and that sure as shit is full of *contaminated* grease—I can't see him puttin' on gloves just at the one moment he loses his temper and lets fly with the wrench."

"So if the grease came from Carmen's attacker, it wasn't on his hands. That's interesting."

"Meaning what?"

"Well, there's no grease on the wrench. That means the grease wasn't on his gloves…and if he had greasy hands, it's a bit much to expect that he would chase Carmen through the house, peeling off his gloves as he went. And I'm thinking about where the grease was on the wall."

"Fifty-seven inches off the floor," Torrez said.

"Right. Maybe Carmen caught him off balance somehow. If the attacker fell against the wall, he might try to catch himself by throwing out a hand. But not this time, apparently. It might have been on his clothes." She reached out and touched Torrez on the shoulder of his light jacket. "A shoulder against the wall. I can see that happening.

"One small catch," Torrez said. "Nobody's established yet that the grease, or whatever the hell it was, is fresh to the wall. It might have been there all along. Maybe from one of the boys a month ago, swingin' around a dirty rag. We don't know."

"No, we don't. I'm just going from the general condition of the room. It's clean, Bobby. That smear is so out of place. Freddy or Juanita will know."

"Maybe."

She looked down, idly drawing small circles in the dust on the fender. "Did the lab have results for the blood on the lamp shade?" The sheriff shook his head and glanced at his watch.

"It's early yet."

"We have to know that," Estelle said, more to herself than to the sheriff. "Penny Barnes said that one of the errands Zeigler mentioned was stopping by the county barns. She didn't know what for." She looked at Torrez. "The flat tire," she said. "If he'd just changed a tire, it might be possible to come away with some grease. Maybe on his clothes."

Torrez shook his head. "You don't believe that."

"I don't?"

The sheriff offered one of his rare smiles. "No, you don't. You don't think that Zeigler had anything to do with what happened to Carmen. So why look for grease on *his* clothes? And besides that, where's the grease with a flat tire? Maybe if he pulled the old tire off, and leaned against the wheel bearing? Nah, I don't think so. Road dirt, more than likely. Grease, no. Not unless he fell against the truck during the process."

"Well, that's possible."

He laughed. "Almost anything is possible, Estelle." He pushed himself away from the vehicle. "The obvious thing is the simplest. Zeigler's truck shows up at his house, but he doesn't. So..."

what'd he do, drive home, and then was grabbed by somebody? Are we going to be seein' a ransom note before long?"

"If that means that Zeigler is still alive, I'll settle for that," Estelle said.

Torrez scoffed. "Well, don't hold your breath." He looked hard at Estelle. "His lifestyle is what needs lookin' at." When Estelle didn't respond, he added, "Mama Acosta is stayin' in Albuquerque. Freddy and the two boys are comin' back later today. At least that's the plan. I'll have a talk with Freddy about the grease. He's apt to be curious about why we hacked a chunk out of his wall, anyway. I'll let you know when they're back in town, if you want to sit down with Mauro."

"I need to do that." She shook her head in frustration.

The sheriff nodded back toward the mesa. "Is that your first chat with the old weirdo there?"

"Yes."

"Ain't too many like old Milton Crowley, that's for sure. I guess maybe that's a good thing."

"I'd like to look at that tape."

"It probably wouldn't tell you a thing you don't already know," Torrez said. "But there's no point in jerkin' Milt's chain. Even if you could talk Judge Hobart into giving you a court order, Milt's still going to refuse to hand over the tape, and if the judge throws his ass in jail for contempt of court, old Milt will just use that as front-page news in his little newspaper." Torrez wiggled his fingers in the air. "The evil government tramples his rights one more time. He's a freaky one. Leave him alone, and he's harmless, though."

"I'm not so sure."

"Yeah, he is. He talks a good talk." Torrez grinned. "I like that sign of his. I've always wanted one of those in *my* driveway." He shrugged. "I'd kinda like to stay on his good side, just the same. There's nobody who knows that mesa country the way he does, and he's been a help to us on a search or two. Sometime when you got nothin' better to do, ask Wild Bill about the incident with Crowley's 'garden.' He'll tell you some interesting stories."

The sheriff dusted off his hands. "You're on your way to the county barns now?"

"That, and I wanted to talk with Doris Marens again. She told the deputy that she didn't hear or see anything, but if we don't count Freddy, Mrs. Marens was the *only* one at home on that block about that time. Maybe there's some little thing…"

"Did Mr. Flamingo give you anything yet?"

"He has nothing to give, Bobby. William Page is in the dark as much as we are."

"How long is he staying in town?"

"Until we know about Kevin."

Torrez grimaced. "That could be a long, long time."

"I know, Bobby. But I don't know what other direction to take."

He nodded thoughtfully. "Lemme know what grease you get into at the county barns." He wagged his eyebrows, but didn't smile. "I gave the go-ahead for Taber to go through Zeigler's house again, one speck of dust at a time."

"I don't think the answer's there, Bobby."

"We'll see. It's something to do. That's about where we're at. Jackie asked if she and Linda could do it." He shrugged. "I said what the hell. If there's anything there, they'll see it." He glanced at his watch again. "I'm meetin' Eddie at Zeigler's office at ten o'clock. We'll tear that place apart, one piece of paper at a time. And I don't think we'll find anything there, either." He lifted a hand in salute. "Keep in touch," he said, and Estelle watched him climb back into the Expedition and drive off toward Posadas.

As she settled behind the wheel of her own county vehicle, the radio clock flashed to 9:46 a.m. Less than twenty-two hours before, Estelle had been chatting with Kevin Zeigler outside the elementary school. She started the car, jabbing at the ignition key with impatience, irritated with herself for wasting time counting the minutes, irritated at wasting time hoping for an innocent explanation of the events that had caught up the county manager, impatient with the waiting while a lab tech removed and tested the tiny blood spatter from the lamp shade.

A few minutes later, with no recollection of the twelve-mile drive into town from Forest Road 26, she pulled through the chain-link gate of the county maintenance yard off County Road 43, just north of the Hutton Street intersection on the outskirts of the village. She parked in front of the office, swinging wide so she had an unobstructed view of the yard and the equipment stored there.

To one side of the towering shop doors, a veteran Highway Department dump truck was parked, its left rear hindquarters jacked high and all four wheels rolled to one side. The massive brake drums had been removed.

Across the yard, two men, one on a front loader and another on the ground, were wrestling a twenty-foot-long, four-foot-diameter section of drainage pipe toward a flatbed trailer. The shop doors were open, and Estelle could see three vehicles inside.

A young man appeared in the shop doorway, a Styrofoam cup in hand. He watched Estelle as she got out of the car and offered a tentative, snaggle-toothed smile as she approached.

"Good morning," Estelle said. "Is Ralph around today?"

"Nope. He's at a meeting." The young man sawed the edge of the hand that held the cup across the back of his other hand, the skin no doubt irritated by the substantial amount of "contaminated grease." Estelle read the stitched name tag on the breast of his dark green work shirt.

"Do you know where that meeting is, James?"

"I think it's with somebody from the State Highway Department," he said. "He was having to drive over to Deming." He crumpled the cup and tossed it in the general direction of a fifty-five-gallon drum near the corner of the building.

Estelle turned and surveyed the yard. It was the sort of place that the meticulous Kevin Zeigler would manage from a distance. "You guys look a little shorthanded today."

James laughed. "We're *always* shorthanded, Sheriff."

"Did the county manager stop by here yesterday?"

"What time?"

"Anytime."

"Oh," he said with sudden comprehension. "That's *right.*"

"What's right?"

"No, I mean I heard about Zeigler goin' missing. One of the guys was talking about that when he came in this morning."

"Is that right?"

"Yeah." James removed a can of tobacco from his hip pocket, and carefully charged his lip. "Weird, huh?"

"I wonder how he happened to hear about it."

"Scotty? His brother's with the ambulance thing there."

"Ah." Estelle wondered if there was a single soul in Posadas who *didn't* know about Kevin Zeigler's disappearance. The "ambulance thing there" had been called to attend to Carmen Acosta—and at that time, Zeigler had done nothing more curious than fail to return to the afternoon session of the commission meeting. James turned and spat brown juice. He wasn't very good at it, and wiped his chin with a greasy hand. "So," Estelle persisted. "Did you happen to see Zeigler yesterday? Did he stop by here?"

"Ah, you know…I don't know," James said vaguely. "I don't pay much attention to who comes and goes. I got me this big old bastard to get out of here." He nodded at the dump truck with the shattered axle. "You could ask Hobie, over there. He kinda keeps tabs on things when Ralph's gone."

"Hobie?"

"The guy on the front loader. Hobie Tyler. He's one of the foremen."

"Thanks," Estelle said. "What's your name?"

"J.T.," he said. "Well, James." He patted his name tag.

"James…"

"Oh. Volpato." He spelled it quickly without being asked.

"You're related to Katie Volpato?" Katie had worked as a custodian in the county building for years, a silent presence who kept the building looking fifty years younger than it was.

"She's my mom."

"A grand lady," Estelle said. "Thanks, James." Across the yard, the huge section of culvert crashed onto the trailer. As the undersheriff approached, the front loader backed off with a blast of black diesel smoke and shrill beeping of its caution horn. The hoist chain dangled from its lower lip.

As he maneuvered the machine away from the trailer, the driver saw Estelle and immediately jabbed the brakes so hard the ponderous loader rocked on its fat tires. The engine died and Tyler swung the cab door open.

"Morning!" he called. "What can I help you with?"

Estelle skirted an impressive puddle of something that would have raised the eyebrows of the EPA and walked up close to the loader. The tires were nearly as tall as she was, and the beast ticked quietly as it cooled, exuding a rich aroma of hot rubber, diesel fuel, and grease.

Tyler leaned out, looking down from on high. At the same time, the other county worker tossed the tie-down chains across the culvert section with a mighty clatter.

"Good morning, sir," Estelle greeted. She rested a hand lightly on one mammoth tire cleat. "I understand that you might have talked to the county manager yesterday."

Tyler shot a quick glance at his companion, then eyed Estelle warily. "Well, he stopped by, is all."

"What time was that, sir?"

Tyler pulled off his left glove and rubbed his cheek with a stubby finger. "He come by yesterday morning early."

Estelle nodded as if the information was old news. "Do you recall what time that was?"

"Well, I get here at seven-thirty, and it was just a little after that. Maybe quarter till." Tyler stretched upward in his seat and twisted his head hard to the right as if to ease a painful kink in his spine. "He had a tire on his truck that he thought was goin' soft."

Estelle's pulse kicked. "Had he changed it, you mean?"

"No. But I told him that he needed to." Tyler shrugged. "I gave him a squirt of air from the pump over there to keep him goin'. He said he'd try to drop it off later in the day. He said he didn't have a whole lot of time."

"And that's it?"

"That's it. He was down to eighteen pounds, though. In that tire, I mean. I told him that if he put it off much longer, he'd be walkin'." He twisted his wrist, looking at a nonexistent watch. "He don't have a lot of extra time."

"So you aired it up, and he left?"

Tyler nodded emphatically. "That's what I did."

"Did you see him after that?"

"No, ma'am." He leaned forward a bit and lowered his voice. "What's goin' on, do you know? Ralph told me this morning that nobody's seen him since yesterday."

"That's exactly what we're trying to find out, Mr. Tyler. That's why I appreciate the information."

"Well, like I said, that's the only time I seen him, all day."

"He never came back to have the tire fixed, then."

"No, ma'am."

"Was anyone with him at the time?" Estelle asked, and Tyler shook his head. "And he was driving that little white Ford Ranger? His usual county truck?" Tyler nodded. Estelle patted the tire once more. "Did he happen to mention where he was headed after here?"

"Ma'am, if he did, I don't remember. Old Kevin, you know. He's kinda different. Keepin' track of him is like trying to nail down one of them dust devils that goes spinnin' across the yard here." He grinned at his own poetic imagery. He reached forward toward the ignition key, but didn't turn it. The hint was clear.

"Thanks, sir," she said, and stepped back from the machine, waving a hand in salute as she did so. The diesel fired up, chuffing out a bilious cloud. As she walked back, Estelle found herself wanting to break into a sprint. She had learned only that Zeigler had stopped by the county yards, concerned about an air leak in a tire. Not many hours later, the lug wrench from his truck had been used to mash the back of Carmen Acosta's skull. The link was invisible, but tantalizing nevertheless.

She slipped into the county car and stabbed the key into the ignition. There was no way that the killer would lean the Ranger's passenger seat forward and unscrew the wing nut and clamp that held the lug wrench in place. The tool had to have been a weapon of opportunity.

What did fit was seeing Zeigler, intent on being four places at once, changing a flat tire in a fury, tossing the wrench and jack back into the cab, to be properly stowed later when time permitted. The flat tire had been tossed somewhere, too—but not into the most logical place, the bed of the truck.

Chapter Nineteen

Simple things. The ideas tumbled inside Undersheriff Estelle Reyes-Guzman's head as she paused at the front door of Kevin Zeigler's home on Candelaria Court. Jackie Taber's county vehicle was parked in the driveway, immediately behind Zeigler's pickup.

The deputy opened the door and greeted Estelle with a sober nod, then looked at her more closely, eyes narrowing. "What'd you find out?" she asked, then added, "Come on in."

"I was just over at the county barns," Estelle said. "Zeigler stopped there early yesterday morning with a soft tire. He added some air, but didn't take time to change the tire. At least not then."

"Really." Taber settled against the arm of the sofa, her latex-gloved hands held away from her clothes. Technically off duty, she'd traded her uniform for an aging pair of army trousers and a brown T-shirt, neither of which did anything to flatter her powerful, stocky figure. "Now that's interesting," she said.

"*If* the tire went flat later in the day, like maybe when he was running errands at noon, that could explain why the wrench and jack were loose. He changed the tire, and didn't want to take time to stow them properly."

"Well, they're a pain in the ass," Jackie said. "So where's the flat tire? It wasn't in the truck."

"That's right—it wasn't. And I don't know where it is. But *if* Zeigler changed the tire, the most logical thing to do would be to clean up a little before he returned to the county meeting." She held out her hands. "I mean, what's anybody do after changing a tire? You can't *do* it and stay clean."

"Huh," Jackie grunted. "I see where you're going. That would be a good reason for Kevin to stop back here. Clean up a little. Maybe." She looked at Estelle skeptically.

"But there's a simple reason he might have come here, rather than just use the restroom at the county building. If he just wanted to wash his hands, a sink is pretty easy to find. There's one or two in the restroom right beside his office."

"Maybe he needed to change his clothes," Jackie said.

"That's exactly right. I picture him kneeling down to put that jack in place, or scrunching down to lower the spare tire out from under the back, drag it out, put it in place, swing the old dead tire up into the truck." She stopped. "And at some point, what if he gets dirty, or tears his trousers or catches his shirt on something—it's almost bound to happen. Especially if he's in a hurry and not paying attention."

Jackie gazed off toward the hallway leading to the bedrooms. "Okay. If that's what happened, then there are some soiled clothes to show for it."

"Maybe. We need to check."

"That still doesn't tell us much, though."

"Jackie, it tells us *something,* and that's a lot more than we had."

The deputy regarded her quietly for a moment. "You don't like the idea a whole lot, do you?"

"No, I don't. What I'm seeing puts a truck lug wrench in Kevin Zeigler's hand. It puts him *here* sometime yesterday."

"None of that means that he swung the wrench against the back of Carmen Acosta's head," Jackie said.

"He didn't do that," Estelle said vehemently. "I know that as surely as I *don't* know what actually happened."

"And there's another possibility, too. What if Zeigler wasn't driving the truck?"

Estelle nodded. "I think it's going to come around to that, Jackie. I sat in that truck yesterday. I could smell Zeigler's cologne, or aftershave—whatever it is. When Bobby and I went through this place yesterday, it's the same smell, right from that bottle on the bathroom vanity."

"Leatherworks."

"That's it."

"Nice stuff."

"Yes, it is. But I also smelled cigarette smoke, and maybe something else, too. I'm not sure. Bobby thought it might be booze, and I think he's right. Kevin doesn't smoke; neither does William Page. Someone was in that truck who did—and it couldn't have been long before, or it would have faded pretty quickly."

"Too bad the aroma won't fit in an evidence bag."

"The assumption is that it's Kevin's truck, so he was driving it." Estelle shrugged. "Maybe not so."

"Or someone was *with* him."

Estelle ran her hand through her hair in frustration.

"*Caramba,*" she muttered. "Too many directions. I came over to check his clothes, Jackie. Let's do that. Then I want to talk with Doris Marens again."

"And she is…"

"The lady who lives up the street. Right at the intersection with MacArthur. She told Mike that she didn't see a thing, but it wouldn't hurt to put the thumbscrews on her a little. There might be something. It's beginning to look as if she's the only person who was home on the entire street at the time—other than Carmen. We don't have ourselves a whole herd of willing witnesses."

"In the meantime, there's a dirty-clothes hamper in the master bedroom," Jackie said. She stood up and beckoned. "Linda's back there now, riffling through his drawers. Sounds kinky, huh?"

In the bedroom, Linda Real was sitting cross-legged on the floor with the bottom dresser drawer open in front of her.

"Hey there," she said as Estelle and Jackie entered the room. She paused, one hand resting on the edge of the drawer.

"Anything?"

"A ton of slides," Linda said, indicating the yellow boxes that filled a third of the wide drawer, "I checked a few at random.

They appear to be what the box labels say they are. Vacations, bike races, that sort of thing. None of them are newer than 2000, the year before he moved here. And these"—and she tapped two large scrapbooks—"are family stuff, newspaper clippings, those sorts of things. I learned some interesting stuff that maybe I don't need to know."

"For example?"

"Well," Linda said, "for example, I didn't know that Kevin Zeigler was married before. His son is in second grade in Socorro."

"Ay," Estelle breathed. "I didn't know that either."

"I always thought he was the swinging bachelor type since day one. Apparently not. Anyway, that and a few other old things." Linda reached up and ran a hand down the three upper drawers. "These are clothes, and this one is memories."

"We need to rummage through his dirty clothes," Jackie said.

The scarred eyebrow over Linda's blind left eye lifted a fraction. "Ooookay. Maybe better you than me, kid. The basket's in the bathroom."

"I'll get it," Jackie said, and in a moment she returned with a small wicker hamper. "We might as well use the bed." They removed each article of clothing from the hamper, shook it out, and laid it on the bedspread.

"This would be a good time for Kevin to show up," Estelle said. "Come home to find three women riffling through his underwear."

"'But I just had a meeting in Deming,'" Jackie said, doing a fair imitation of the county manager. "'Did I forget to tell you?'" She glanced at Estelle, not smiling. "Don't we wish."

Five minutes later, Estelle tossed the last sock into the pile. She snapped the cuff of her latex glove in frustration. "Nothing." Two pairs of Zeigler's habitual light chinos had been in the laundry, and neither showed any soil—much less tears, cuts, or stains. And other than a few wrinkles, the shirts appeared unworn—except for the aroma of cologne, concentrated by the confines of the hamper.

"That would have been too simple," Estelle said with a sigh. She moved the hamper closer to the bed and swept the dirty clothes back in.

Jackie took the hamper back to the bathroom. "We wanted to show you one other thing," she said.

"Okay. And Linda—the slide boxes? If you have the time, we need to check every one. I know it's probably wasted effort, but you never know. He might have something hidden away that'll tell us something."

"I think we're seeing the answer," Jackie said. "This is a house that the owner left first thing in the morning to go to work. Everything's put away, everything's in order. I don't think Kevin Zeigler's been here since yesterday morning." She nodded back toward the bathroom. "If he came home to change his clothes, the offending article would be in the hamper."

"The 'offending article,'" Linda repeated. "I like that."

"Or in the trash, if he just flat ruined it. But we checked. There's nothing other than coffee grounds and an empty orange juice container in the trash under the sink. There's no article of clothing in the garbage can in the pantry. And there's nothing in the wheel-out at the side of the house." Jackie shrugged. "I mean, the guy's just too neat for his own good."

"He could have dropped things off at the cleaners," Linda offered.

"Maybe. And a telephone call will answer that," Jackie said. She beckoned Estelle to follow her out to the living room. "What the hell," she said. "As long as we're going through everything right down to the man's underwear, you might as well see this. I don't know if it makes any difference or not."

She halted near the center of the bookcase and pointed at a Rolodex containing several hundred photos. The one facing the living room was a color portrait of William Page and Kevin Zeigler astraddle their racing bikes, holding a large trophy between them. Zeigler was wearing a helmet, Page was not.

"Family and friends," Jackie said, turning the large black knob on the side to flip pictures by. She stopped at another that showed the Acostas' backyard, smoke billowing from a large barbecue grill. Freddy grinned at the camera, a bottle of beer in one hand, large chrome fork in the other. Behind him, Juanita and Carmen were working at the picnic table. "Lots of things like this." She spun the dial some more. "And a few like this."

The photo that stopped was one of Mauro and Tony. Tony, the chubby one, was twisted, one foot high behind him as he stabbed at the Hacky Sack. Mauro was obviously bellowing something, either curses or encouragement.

"The interesting thing is that this is taken through the window in Kevin's office," Jackie said. "You can see by the background that's where he had to be standing. This"—and she touched the right side of the photo—"is a blur from the window frame. That's what Linda thinks."

"Okay," Estelle said.

Jackie flipped another picture. This one was just of Mauro, standing with one hand on the back of his head and the other on his hip, looking thoughtfully at the ground. He was wearing low-slung, ragged denim cutoffs and nothing else, the planes of his chiseled torso catching the light and shadows.

"A bit on the provocative side," Jackie said.

Estelle sighed. "Okay, again."

"I just thought you should know," Jackie said.

"I *do* know," Estelle said a little more testily than she would have liked. "I know that William Page and Kevin are gay, I know they're living together as time allows. And I guess this doesn't surprise me much either. I mean"—and she flipped the Rolodex several photos beyond Mauro to an innocuous print taken from the top of Cat Mesa—"I could argue that if Carmen looked like a starlet and liked to pose half naked in the backyard, Kevin would probably have snapped her picture, too, assuming that his interests were directed that way…which they don't appear to be. Find me a basement full of whips and chains and black leathers, and then I'll admit that maybe it makes a difference."

Jackie nodded silently.

"We need two things, Jackie. We need Carmen Acosta to pop out of her coma by some miracle of modern medicine and tell us who fractured her skull and then drove a hat pin through her head. And then we need to find Kevin Zeigler, alive and well."

"I don't think we're headed for either one."

"And I wish you weren't right," Estelle said.

Chapter Twenty

From the Marenses' driveway, Estelle could look down Candelaria Court and see the front door of each house. Seven families lived on the little street. It now appeared that only Carmen Acosta and Doris Marens had been home between noon and two p.m. on Tuesday.

According to deputies, Mrs. Marens had chosen not to accompany her husband to Las Cruces that Tuesday on a book-buying trip. Now home with whatever treasures he'd found, it was Clarence Marens who answered the door. Angular and badly bent from arthritis, Marens had to cock his head slightly to look at Estelle. A thick pair of glasses hung precariously from his pocket.

"Good morning, Dr. Marens," Estelle said. She saw the flash of confusion on Marens' wrinkled face, even though the man must have been accustomed to random greetings from college students who knew him, but who had never graced his classes. "I'm Undersheriff Estelle Guzman, sir. May I come in for a moment?"

"Well, of course you can," Marens replied. He fumbled with the tricky storm-door lock.

"Is your wife home, sir?"

"Yes," he said judiciously. "I think she is. Whom should I say is calling?"

"I'm with the Sheriff's Department, sir."

"Oh, certainly." His gaze dropped to the seven-point gold badge on her belt, visible except when her jacket was zipped.

"Just a moment while I go fetch her, young lady." He started to turn away, then stopped abruptly, beckoning Estelle into the house. "Forgive me. Come in, come in."

He pushed at the storm door awkwardly, and Estelle caught the latch. "Where are my manners." He beamed metallically as Estelle entered. "Doe!" he called to his wife. "Doe, you have company." Marens' hands wavered as if he were unsure that Estelle would remain upright if he stepped away. "I'll tell her you're here. I think she's sewing."

The living room to Estelle's left was small, neat, overfurnished, and unused. An old-fashioned paper roller blind was drawn down over the window that faced toward neighbors to the east, and through which Zeigler's home would be clearly visible. Lacy drapes softened the drab effect of the blind. The larger window that directly faced the street was shaded by a modern vertical shade, the sort with narrow slats that both rotated and could be drawn to the side. The slats were currently drawn closed, but rotated so that the view down the street was not obscured.

"How about some coffee?" Estelle turned to see Clarence Marens poised in the archway leading to the kitchen.

"No thanks, sir."

"Tuna sandwich?" He glanced at his watch.

"No, thanks."

"Well, I was just about to make us a snack, and I'd be absolutely delighted to make a third."

"I appreciate the offer, sir. But no, thank you."

"Homemade bread." He persisted, and his eyes twinkled when Estelle laughed. "We have one of those bread machines. You ever tried one of those?"

"They're wonderful, sir."

"I doubt that she's interested in tuna fish sandwiches or bread machines," his wife called. In a moment she bustled into the living room, a small, neat package of energy. Her smile of greeting immediately turned into a frown. "I talked to the young man yesterday. I'm trying to recall his name…"

"Officer Sisneros, I believe," Estelle said.

"Yes. The village officer. What a mess you have over there."

"Mrs. Marens, I wanted to talk with you again about what you might have heard and seen yesterday. I know you've been through it all before, but with a little time now, there's always the chance that you may have remembered something."

"How's the child? I understand that it was Carmen who was—"

"We think that Carmen will be okay, Mrs. Marens."

"Just awful. Really just awful. Well"—and she glanced first into the living room, and then toward the kitchen—"would you like to sit down?"

"Here would be fine," Estelle said, and stepped toward the overstuffed sofa that faced the front window.

"I'm cutting bread," Dr. Marens called, and his wife grimaced with impatience.

"We're going to both end up as blimps," she said. "My daughter-in-law gave Cal the bread machine for his birthday. Now he's Mr. Baker. Anyway, fire away." She settled into a rocker.

"Mrs. Marens, when I arrived yesterday, I saw you standing out on your porch."

"Well, my goodness, such a circus, with the sirens and all. I know that it's none of my business, but the first thing that crossed my mind was, *Oh my goodness, the school bus is going to be driving into the middle of all this.*"

"I'd like you to remember back to early morning, though," Estelle said. "Before any of this happened. You told Officer Sisneros that you didn't hear or see anything unusual between noon and the circus." She smiled. "But before that? Would you tell me about your morning?"

"My morning. Well…my days are so exciting. Cal and I start thinking about getting up right at seven a.m. The clock radio comes on, and we listen to the news. That tells us if the world is still in one piece or not—whether there's any reason to get up. So far, so good. Yesterday, Cal decided to go to Las Cruces. That wonderful bookstore there, in the mall. That's just what we need is more books."

"Everyone needs more books," Dr. Marens said from the kitchen.

Doris Marens held up her hands. "And that's that. I spent my morning doing two loads of laundry"—and she ticked two fingers—"and then I wrote a letter to my sister Agnes. Then I went to work back in the sewing room. I'm a shirt factory now."

"Five grandchildren," Dr. Marens called proudly.

"I took a little break around one or so and had a turkey sandwich. And then back to sewing. And then sirens and lights, and Lord knows what all."

"At any time in the morning, do you recall seeing any traffic on the street? Any at all?"

Doris shook her head. "Most of the time, I was up to my ears in stitchery. That little bedroom back there has just the one window that looks south. There certainly isn't much to see out back. Just weeds and more weeds. But you know, this is a quiet street." She pointed past Estelle. "Not what I'd call *traffic*. Neil across the way goes to work about eight or so. He works at the bank, as I'm sure you know. Mrs. Sanchez next door has been in Tucson for a month with her son and daughter-in-law." Her hand worked down the street methodically. "Both Penny and Ralph Beuler teach at the high school, so they're gone by seven. And the county manager lives down at the end. He's gone early, too. That just leaves the one other house on this side of the street. It's vacant now."

"Kevin Zeigler probably left for work before you got up, then."

"Oh, certainly. We usually hear his little truck, and I fret about that sometimes, too. He drives way too fast on this street. Did you talk with him?"

"She frets about everything," Dr. Marens said from the kitchen.

Estelle jotted a note on her small pad, and her lack of response prompted Doris. "He came home at around noon, you know. You need to talk with him, certainly. Maybe he saw something."

"You saw Zeigler drive by at noon?"

"Well, not *noon*, exactly. When did I see him." She looked down at the carpet. "I think it was when I was coming out to the kitchen. That little white truck of his." She sat back in the rocker, hands braced on the arms of the chair as if awaiting lift-off. "Which is unusual, I suppose. As far as I know, Kevin *rarely* comes home during the day. He's sort of the phantom of Candelaria Court. I don't know, maybe yard and garden isn't his thing. Every once in a while, we see him on his bike—sometimes with his friend. The one with the fancy car."

"Can you recall exactly what time that was? When you saw his truck?"

She frowned and pursed her lips. "What time did I eat lunch? That's the puzzle." She brightened and smiled at Estelle. "You see, if you'd told me *yesterday* that I should remember all this, I would have paid attention."

"That's the way it works, I'm afraid," Estelle said.

"What time? I know that it was sometime after the noon news. I always listen to that. That was over, and I worked in the back for a little bit. So I don't know—I could guess that it was sometime between twelve-fifteen or twelve-thirty and one o'clock. I'm just sure that it wasn't *after* one. Well, one-thirty at the latest."

"Or maybe two or three or four," Dr. Marens said. "Your sandwich is ready, Doe."

"You just be patient," she said, and shook her head. "It wasn't after one-thirty."

"What did you see, exactly? Will you show me?"

"Oh." She pushed herself out of the rocker. "Now you're asking me for impossible details. Let's see…I was walking to the kitchen from the sewing room." She moved to the hallway and turned. "He drove by, *whoosh*, like that." She chopped the air with her hand. "And that's it."

"Why would you remember that?" Dr. Marens asked.

"Who *knows* why we remember what we remember, Mr. Memory Expert," Doris said. "I *didn't* remember that when I talked with the village officer yesterday. But he didn't ask about earlier in the morning, either." She returned to the rocker, sitting on the edge of the seat. "What's Kevin say?" she asked.

"I haven't asked him about that particular moment," Estelle replied.

"Well, you should. It wasn't that long before all the fireworks." Her eyes narrowed a bit as she made the connections for herself. "Was it one of the family who was responsible? They're quite a crew down there, the Acostas are."

"We don't know yet, Mrs. Marens."

"You need to talk with Kevin," Doris persisted. "I know that was him going by. And you know, for once, he wasn't going ninety miles an hour, either."

"He doesn't drive that fast," Dr. Marens said. He appeared in the archway, cup in hand. He held it up toward Estelle. "You sure?"

"He *does* drive that fast," Doris said. "You just don't notice."

"Mrs. Marens, you said that yesterday he *didn't* appear to be in a hurry?" Estelle asked.

"Well, relatively not. Not by his usual standards."

"Was he alone?"

"I think so. But"—and she held up a hand—"now we're really stretching it. I just didn't notice. I did notice that he was going slower than usual. I saw his brake lights come on. And then I wasn't looking anymore. I was in the kitchen."

Estelle rose from her spot on the sofa. "Please show me."

"Show you what, dear?"

"You said that you saw his brake lights come on. Would you stand where you were yesterday and show me...as near as you can remember?"

Doris shook her head, a hand on each side of her skull. "Oh, the things you're asking this old brain to recall."

"You're telling me," Cal said. He leaned against the kitchen's center island, munching half of a sandwich.

His wife ignored him. "Okay. Here I am in the hallway," she said, turning to face the kitchen, chubby arms outstretched as if she needed them for balance. "I walked out here, and I hear the truck. I *suppose* I hear the truck, because otherwise, why would I bother looking out?" She pointed at the living room window.

"The blinds were just the way they are now?" Estelle asked.

"Yes. I saw the truck go by. I'm sure I didn't stop walking. Why would I do that? The brake lights flashed." She stopped and looked at Estelle. "Now, if I take another step, I'm in the kitchen, and I can't see the window past this partition here."

Estelle stood beside Doris. "The lights came on when the truck was about opposite the Beulers', then."

"Good grief," Doris said good-naturedly. "I'm not going to be that exact."

"But standing here, I can't see the little field between the Beulers' and the Acostas'," Estelle said. "I can't see that unless I step out into the living room."

"I didn't do that." She looked quizzically at Estelle. "Why is all this so important? Kevin drove home for lunch, that's all." Sudden comprehension lit her features. "But listen...his truck was down there when all you people were flying around, wasn't it? It seems to me I remember seeing that...and at one point there was quite a crowd of officers looking at it, too. I wondered about that."

"Old nosey," Cal muttered.

"We'll straighten everything out," Estelle said. "It's important to determine who was where and when."

"Well, of course it is," Doris agreed. "I only wish I could be of more help."

"Mrs. Marens, it may be necessary to obtain a formal deposition from you at some point." Estelle withdrew one of her cards from her pocket and handed it to the woman. "I'll be in touch with you if that's necessary."

"You want me to haul her downtown for you?" Cal asked. "I'd enjoy that."

Estelle laughed. "No, sir. If I need anything, I'll be back." She held out her hand, and Doris Marens' grip reminded her of her son Francisco's: tiny bird bones. Back outside, she looked down the street, seeing the white Ford Ranger in Zeigler's driveway. It was possible that the county manager hadn't driven the truck home for lunch...that someone else had. She felt a surge of relief, tempered by a deep wave of apprehension.

Chapter Twenty-one

Leaning against the edge of her desk, alone for a moment, Estelle Reyes-Guzman stared at the whiteboard long enough that the printing blurred into an amorphous mass. She had left the Marenses' with what she considered a key piece to the puzzle—and then the door had slammed shut. For the last two hours, she had scrutinized her notes, her memory, the stack of photographs, the slim folder of lab evidence. Nothing made sense to her, and her intuition refused to make even the most unathletic leap.

"Let me guess." Estelle startled at the sound of Bill Gastner's gruff voice. The retired sheriff leaned against the door-jamb of her office, hands thrust in his pockets, boots crossed as if he'd been lounging there for an hour. His keen gray eyes twinkled. "You haven't had lunch yet, have you."

"Lunch?"

"That's what I thought." He straightened and beckoned with a nod. "Come on. Have lunch with me. Turn loose for a little bit."

"That sounds good."

He stopped short, bushy eyebrows arched in surprise. "You never agree to lunch, sweetheart. Things are that bad?"

"Yes, sir. They're that bad."

He laid a hand over his heart. "I'm flattered, then."

She glanced at the clock. "It's after two, *Padrino*. You haven't eaten yet? I'm surprised."

"As a point of fact, I did not miss lunch. It was early, though. I got myself cornered by Frank Dayan."

"Oh-oh."

"Is right. He's irked with you and Bobby."

"That's not unusual, sir."

"Nope. But I ran a little interference for you." Gastner moved to one side so Estelle could close the office door. The undersheriff locked her office, and then followed Gastner out to the central dispatch island. Gayle Torrez was on the phone, and Estelle waited until she hung up.

"I'm ten-seven, the Don Juan no doubt," Estelle said. "If anybody calls for me, tell them I took early retirement."

Gayle smiled sympathetically. "Can I come, too?"

"You bet," Gastner said. "Just put the 'your call is important to us' recording in the nine-one-one answering machine, and let's go."

"Don't I wish."

"May I bring you something back?"

"No, thanks," Gayle replied. "I didn't mean lunch, anyway, Bill. It's the early retirement that sounds good."

Outside, Gastner gestured toward his state truck. "My chariot?"

"That would be a nice change," Estelle replied. They drove west on Bustos Avenue so slowly that had Posadas had traffic, they would have been a cork. For the first six blocks, they rode in silence. With the Don Juan de Oñate Restaurant in view, Gastner slowed even more, allowing the truck to drift up to the blinking caution light at the intersection of Twelfth Street and Bustos.

"That's the first time I've ever heard you mention the *R* word, sweetheart."

"The *R* word?"

"As in 'retirement.'"

"It was a tired joke, sir," Estelle said. The truck thumped up into the restaurant parking lot.

Gastner maneuvered to park in the near-empty lot with one hand, the fingers of his other hand counting imaginary numbers. "What have you got now, about sixteen years with the county? You were absent without leave for a couple."

"Today, it seems like sixteen years, ten months, two weeks, five days, three hours, two minutes, and fifteen seconds."

Gastner laughed. "That bad, eh." He waved a hand at her door. "Lock that, will you? I've got a bunch of state money in the glove box."

They strolled across the lot to the restaurant. The Don Juan had settled into dimly lit silence after the noon rush, and Gastner made his way to the back where a divider created a small intimate area with only three booths. "Is this all right?" he said, as if there was a choice. The former sheriff had settled onto this same patch of yellow plastic upholstery for decades.

He drummed his fingers on the vinyl tablecloth as Estelle eased back in the booth with a sigh.

"You look tired."

"I am. Tired and frustrated."

"Sixteen years, ten months, blah blah," he said with a smile. "That's part of the package, you know." He waved his hand in dismissal. "Hell, you're still good for another twenty-five or thirty years."

Her eyes rolled and she dropped her head back against the booth's upper roll of padding. "When I click twenty, sir, I'm going to pull the car over to the curb and park it, even if I'm in the middle of a call." She closed her eyes. "I'd like to see what it's like being home when Francisco and Carlos come home from school." She lifted her arm and opened one eye to look at her watch. "Coming up in fifteen minutes, by the way."

"We'll eat fast," Gastner said, and he leaned back as Jana-Lynn Torrez approached. Tall and statuesque, Sheriff Torrez's niece glowered at Gastner.

"You're still trying for that frequent-flyer discount, aren't you?" she said.

"You bet."

"How about you, Estelle? What can I get you?"

"A taco salad with sliced jalapeños would be wonderful." She grinned at the look of mock astonishment on Gastner's face.

"She eats," he said.

"Of course she eats," JanaLynn retorted. "How about you?"

"Coffee and apple pie, if there's any left."

"Sissy," JanaLynn chided. "I'll be right back."

"No burrito, sir?" Estelle asked.

"I had one for lunch. I pried Frank away from his newspaper for a grand total of about fifteen minutes. He would be grateful if you'd give him a call this afternoon."

"I'll try to do that."

"This is a big one, Estelle."

"Ay, I know it, sir. The whole thing makes me sick."

Gastner hesitated while JanaLynn delivered coffee for him and a large glass of ice water for Estelle. She left the plastic coffee carafe on the table.

"I talked with Milton Crowley," Gastner said. He nodded as Estelle's eyebrow shot up. "I happened to swing by the county building this morning. I guess it was a few minutes before noon. Bobby said that you guys had gone out there earlier today."

"Crowley's an interesting fellow," Estelle said. "That's a nice sign he has on the boundary fence."

"That's something, isn't it? But old Milt's okay. I mean, other than being a complete ass."

"I'd give a lot to be able to see the videotape of the meeting."

"That's what Bobby said. Shrewd idea, too. But you know, I agree with him that a court order won't accomplish anything, even on the slim chance that Judge Hobart would give you one. It would just feed the flames. Milt would take a stint in the lockup as a badge of courage. Anyway, I figured it wouldn't hurt to talk with him myself. We get along all right. I got the same answer you did." He shrugged. "I thought maybe he'd lighten up a little."

"He doesn't seem the type, sir. The more we talked, the more he bristled."

"Yup. He does love an audience."

"Bobby said you had some interesting stories to tell about him. Something about his garden?"

Gastner laughed. "Yeah, well…" He took a long, thoughtful sip of the coffee. "His wife died a while ago. I guess it's been seven or eight years now. In the last few months, she was just a bag of hurtin' bones, Estelle. After a while, she refused any more chemo and radiation. Hell, they couldn't have paid for it, anyway."

"How sad."

"Well, that's the way it goes, you know. Old Milt, he had himself a nice stand of that funny tobacco. I'd been there a time or two, and knew it was there." He shrugged. "I didn't give a shit. I mean, so what? He wasn't selling it down at the high school or anything. If the marijuana eased things for his wife even a little bit, what the hell. I don't know if you remember the search we had for those two hunters that got themselves lost on Cat Mesa?" He nodded. "Anyway, that was right behind Milt's property. I kinda steered folks around his place. I knew damn well what would happen if some straight arrow from the Forest Service or State Police saw Milt's crop. There'd be a war, for sure."

"I can imagine. Or even a couple of our own, for that matter."

"So—I suppose in the great balance beam of life, we could imagine that Milt owes me a favor or two." He leaned back and looked wistfully at the mammoth taco salad that JanaLynn delivered to Estelle. "And look at this pathetic little thing," he said to the generous piece of apple pie that she slid onto his place mat. "Thanks, sweetheart."

The jalapeños were fiery, and Estelle felt herself relax. She hadn't thought that she was hungry, but now she found herself digging into the spiced chicken and chile concoction as if she hadn't eaten for a week.

"Anyway," Gastner said. "I chatted with Milt this morning, and that was that. I just wanted you to know I gave it a whirl, for what it was worth—which turns out to be very, very little."

"I appreciate that, *Padrino*."

"Have you stopped by the county manager's office in the last couple of hours? The sheriff and your new captain are tearing the place apart. I didn't dare step too close. They're apt to put me to work."

"I bet Penny's delighted with that mess."

"Penny needs a good, powerful sedative by now."

Estelle hesitated, toying with her fork. "I keep imagining Kevin's face," she said. "We've got people going through his house, his truck…his office. You know how meticulous he is. I imagine his reaction if he suddenly walked into the middle of all of this. As if Penny somehow missed a message that he had to go to Cruces or something—some family emergency. He comes back and walks into the middle of this mess."

"Considering the alternatives, that would be all right," Gastner said. "I don't think it's going to happen."

"No, sir. It's not."

"You have a bulletin out?"

"Everywhere on the planet. Bishop talked to Zeigler's mom and dad in San Diego. Nothing there. No word at all. He has a sister in Seattle. Nothing. We just found out that he has an ex-wife…and a son."

"No shit?"

Estelle nodded. "They're in Socorro. The boy is in second grade. Surprise, surprise." She sighed and looked out the window. "And needless to say, Kevin's roommate is just kind of slowly dissolving."

"Page seems like a decent-enough sort."

"He is. He's not coping with the waiting very well. But then again, neither am I." She pushed the salad to one side, her enthusiasm for food blunted after half a dozen bites. "*Padrino*, we know that Kevin stopped by the county maintenance yard early yesterday morning. He had a soft tire on his county truck, and had it aired up. He didn't change it. But it's *been* changed since then. The spare is mounted on the truck, but the flat tire is missing. The jack was on the floor in the passenger side of the cab."

"Who knows where it might have gone flat," Gastner said. "Unless somebody comes forward to say they saw Zeigler struggling with it along the road somewhere."

"No one has. Not yet, anyway. I talked with Doris Marens this morning, and there's a little piece there. I don't think that it *was* Kevin Zeigler who brought the truck back to his house sometime after noon." She quickly recounted her conversation with Doris Marens, and as she did so, she saw the expression of skepticism settle on the old man's grizzled face.

"Because he's driving slower than usual, and because he puts his foot on the brake? Sweetheart—"

"It makes sense to me, *Padrino*. It makes sense that maybe it wasn't Kevin. Someone brought the truck back, parked it in the driveway. Now"—and she dug her finger into the soft tablecloth—"if that person didn't want to be noticed, he'd drive carefully." She leaned forward and dropped her voice. "If he wasn't exactly sure where Zeigler lived, he might well slow down several houses early—making sure he pulled into the right place."

She settled back and watched Gastner toy with the last scrap of pie crust.

"Why would any of that happen?" he asked.

"I don't know," Estelle replied. "Suppose someone kidnapped Zeigler." She smiled wryly. "Someone after the county's millions. They spirit him away someplace, and return the truck?" She shook her head. "No sense."

"Well, somebody returned it," Gastner said.

"Yes. Someone did. There are no prints, no fibers, no nothing. Just a hint of tobacco smoke and body odor."

"What if the whole mess with Zeigler isn't related to the Acosta girl's assault, sweetheart? Have you looked that way yet?"

"It is, sir. It *is* related. The lug wrench says it is. The grease smudge on her bedroom wall says it is. The whole coincidence of the truck's being there at the time of the assault, and Zeigler's being missing, says it is. I *know* it is."

"Just asking." Gastner poured the last of the coffee. "So let's assume someone grabbed Zeigler—for whatever nefarious reason—and returned the truck—for whatever *bizarre* reason. After he returned the truck, did a buddy pick him up in another vehicle?"

"I don't know. Doris didn't see anyone. Or she didn't *notice* anyone."

"If he wasn't picked up, what did he do, walk? No one saw strangers walking up and down Candelaria about that time?"

"No."

"Or on a bike?"

"No. Zeigler has four bikes, sir. Well, he and Page have four. All of them were in the house. And that's the thing." She leaned forward again. "No one has been inside Zeigler's house since he left for work Tuesday morning. I'm sure of that."

"Not even himself?"

She shook her head. "That's impossible to say. But I don't think so."

"You've pretty much taken all of the Acostas off the hook?"

"Sure. First of all, the attack on Carmen wasn't their style. I mean, getting mad at a sister results in some bruises, some yelling and hair flying. Not what we saw. Freddy may be a tubby little bully, but it's not his style, either. Juanita was at work. And the one thing that makes me certain is"—she held up both hands—"the truck. *Something* happened that involved that. *Someone* pushed his way into the Acostas' home and attacked Carmen. There may be evidence that Carmen managed to hurt the attacker, at least a little bit."

"With the hat pin."

"That's right. She had it with her. When she knew she was in serious trouble, what's she do? She tries to use it. Her attacker wrenched it out of her hand and stabbed her with it. A lucky shot."

Gastner grimaced. "This someone really wanted her dead."

"You bet."

"Why?"

"The only thing that comes to mind is that he didn't want a witness. A witness to whatever he did. Whatever that was," Estelle murmured. "Whatever happened to Kevin Zeigler happened somewhere else, then. There's no sign of a struggle in the house, or in the yard, or in the truck."

"So that narrows it," Gastner said. "What did she see? She saw the truck. And she saw that Zeigler wasn't driving it."

Estelle frowned and shook her head.

"That's something all by itself," Gastner added. "It was important to the killer that the truck not be left at the scene, wherever the hell that is. And equally important to him that he not be seen parking it back at Zeigler's."

"Risky."

"Murder is risky business, sweetheart. But it's a quiet neighborhood. Slip in, park, slip out. Who's the wiser? He didn't know that Carmen was home."

"Freddy could just as easily have seen him, too, sir."

"Sure enough, he could have. But he *wasn't* home. Maybe lucky for him."

Estelle fell silent, her head resting in her hand. After a moment, she turned and looked out the window again, focusing on nothing in particular. Gastner let her ponder uninterrupted for another half cup of coffee.

"Everything is being done for Carmen that can be done," he said quietly.

"Oh, I know that, *Padrino*." She turned away from the window in resignation. "Maybe Bobby will find something in Kevin's office. Nobody says that he had any enemies, but obviously he had at least one."

"Sweetheart, you don't live his lifestyle without making some enemies—that's just the way it is."

"Hate crime, you mean?" she asked, and Gastner shrugged. "It's too calculated, sir. If we had found Zeigler's battered body in some parking lot, then I'd lean that way. Not this time, though." She pounded the table lightly with both fists, just a faint drum roll of frustration. "See, *Padrino*? I'm sure about what *didn't* happen. That doesn't get us anywhere."

"Sure it does," he said, digging out his wallet. He slid a twenty-dollar bill under his saucer. "It tells you which road *not* to take. There's a poem about that somewhere, isn't there?"

She glanced at her watch. "Let's plan Friday evening with Sofía. Is that a good time for you?"

"Sure." He grinned as he pushed himself out of the booth. "You're going to be there?"

"Yes," Estelle said with certainty. "I'm going to be there. And I'm going to my son's open house at school tomorrow night just like a regular parent, and I'm going to enjoy Aunt Sofía's visit, and we're going to Las Cruces on Saturday to buy a piano."

Gastner chuckled. "Don't make too many best-laid plans, sweetheart. You know how these things work."

"Yes, I do," she said, taking Gastner's arm affectionately. "That doesn't mean I can't daydream a little."

Chapter Twenty-two

A yellow crime-scene tape crossed the outside double doors of the county offices, and Estelle used her own keys to let herself in. Sheriff Robert Torrez was sitting on the edge of Penny Barnes' desk, munching on a convenience-store burrito.

"I sent 'em all home," he said when he saw Estelle. "We needed some peace and quiet." Sure enough, the county offices that ringed the commission chambers, including the wing that housed the county clerk's and assessor's domains, stood dark and vacant. County government had been jarred to a halt.

"And by the way," he added, "Arnie Gray called. He wants to schedule a meeting with the county commissioners as soon as we can. As soon as we know something."

"I can imagine he's feeling a little uneasy right about now," Estelle said. "He's just going to have to be patient." She looked into Zeigler's office and could see Eddie Mitchell inside, kneeling in front of one of the manager's map cabinets. "Any luck?"

Torrez shook his head, regarding the last bite of burrito before popping it into his mouth. "One thing. The blood spatter on the lamp shade? Number one, it was blood. Number two, it's type O. And number three, Zeigler's family doctor says that his blood type is AB positive." Estelle caught the intentional emphasis on "family doctor" and knew that Torrez was referring to her husband. "So, you were right. Odds are good that it wasn't our county manager who busted into the house and bashed in the girl's skull." Estelle couldn't tell whether Torrez was pleased or sorry to have reached that conclusion. He chucked the burrito wrapper in the trash can beside Penny's desk. "What'd Bill have to say?"

"That he talked with Crowley after we did. No luck."

Torrez nodded, not surprised. "Marens?"

She recounted her conversation with Doris Marens, and Torrez listened impassively. "I think someone brought Zeigler's truck home," she said.

"What sense does that make?"

"To make sure that it wasn't found somewhere else. Somewhere that might be incriminating."

"What's wrong with the county building parking lot?"

"I don't know what's wrong with it, Bobby. Maybe too many eyes. I just don't know."

"Huh," the sheriff said. "Did you call Frank yet?"

"I was going to."

"What are you going to tell him?"

"As little as I can get away with," Estelle said. "That Carmen Acosta is an assault victim from an unknown intruder. That she was airlifted to Albuquerque, where she's listed in whatever condition she's in at the moment."

"And about Zeigler?"

"'In the meantime, the Sheriff's Department is investigating the apparent disappearance of County Manager Kevin Zeigler, whose truck was recovered at his residence next door to the Acostas'. Sheriff Torrez declined to comment further.'"

"Damn right, he 'declined to comment.'" He took a deep breath. "You know the kind of speculation that's going to be goin' around."

"That can't be helped, Bobby. By now, everyone in town knows that Zeigler is missing. A little publicity might help. Maybe someone saw something, heard something…"

"You never know." He turned and gazed into Zeigler's office, at the same time bending down the little finger on his left hand with his right. "This is the kind of thing that we've found in this mess. If the administrator of Posadas General Hospital was irritated with Zeigler for ordering a rewrite of the bid specs for the new roof, he might have wanted to kill him." He bent down his ring finger. "If what's-his-face out at the landfill didn't want an outside company takin' over the county dump, he might have figured on killing Zeigler."

A third finger followed. "If the County Highway Department was bent out of shape about Zeigler's refusal to buy another twin-screw dump truck this year, Ralph Johnson might have wanted to kill him." He turned to force a half smile at Estelle. "That's the sort of thing we're finding." He held his entire left hand. "Zeigler was tryin' to talk me into accepting compact-sized SUVs for the next round of patrol vehicles. *I* might have killed him for that."

He dropped his hands in disgust. "What a bunch of shit. Maybe he was tryin' to cut Bill Gastner's pension, and Wild Bill bumped him off."

"I thought *Padrino* was a little shifty-eyed at lunch, Bobby."

Torrez grunted with amusement. "Yeah, right. And maybe in a day or so someone in the clerk's office will find a half million in petty cash missing, and we'll know Zeigler's sittin' on a beach down in Colima, sippin' tequila." He managed a full-fledged smile. "And then *Mr. Page* will track him down and kill him." His face almost immediately settled into its usual serious mask. "Jackie and Linda finished up out at the house. Nothing." He held out a hand. "And Jackie told me about the photo of Mauro."

"I don't think it means anything, Bobby."

"Maybe not." He gazed at Estelle, eyes heavy-lidded. "You think Mr. Page might be a little torqued to think Kevin's got another boyfriend?"

"That doesn't matter, Bobby—if that's what it means in the first place. And we don't know that for sure, either. But we do know that William Page was in *Socorro* when Carmen was attacked and when Kevin went missing. He had nothing to do with it."

To her surprise, Torrez relaxed back against the desk and nodded in agreement. "I know that. We're not lookin' at a

solution that simple. Might be nice, but it ain't going to happen."
He shrugged. "Where are you headed now?"

"I'm going to take ten minutes and type out a press release
for Frank, and hand deliver it. And then go looking, I guess."

"Everybody who isn't pinned down with another job is out
searching for Zeigler, Estelle. Come here a minute." He turned
toward Zeigler's office, where a large map of the county rested
on an easel. "I got this from the county assessor before I sent
him home," the sheriff said. He reached out and smoothed the
plastic overlay. As he did so, Eddie Mitchell stood up, a manila
folder in hand.

"Here you go, Holmes," Mitchell said to Estelle, and held
out the folder without waiting for an answer. "The village was
trying to convince the county to sign an agreement with the
Village of Posadas for maintenance out at the airport," he said.
"It's a municipal airport, but the land where it's situated is outside the village limits. So the county collects the gross receipts
tax for things like fuel sales, hangar rental, all that stuff, but it's
the village that has to do the maintenance."

"Whoopee," Torrez commented dryly.

"Well, it's one more thing," Mitchell said. He flipped open
the folder. "'The county is not prepared to assist with Municipal
Airport funding at this time,' "he read. "Signed by Mr. Zeigler."
He shrugged.

"We've got a billion letters signed by him, for one thing or
another," Torrez said. He turned to the map and tapped the
overlay, where a series of quadrant lines had been drawn slicing
up the county. "This is where we're lookin'," he said. "Hell, I
even sent Linda out." He covered the far southwestern corner
of the county that included the village of Regál. "She took her
own vehicle down here, cruisin' wherever she can get to."

Estelle grimaced. Linda Real was a civilian photographer, not
a deputy. Torrez caught her expression.

"She's got a radio, a phone, and she's not in a county vehicle,
Estelle. She'll be all right. She wanted something to do. Anyway,
she's down there. Pasquale is checkin' all the roads, two-tracks,

arroyos, and whatever the hell else, right in here." He indicated the open country between the fork tines formed by the three state highways, Fifty-six to the south, Seventeen parallel to the interstate, and Seventy-eight, northwestbound out past the airport.

"Bishop is up north around Newton, Taber is takin' the area around the mesa, and Mears is snoopin' around between County Road Nineteen and Forty-three, to the northeast. Just lookin', lookin', lookin'. Mike Sisneros is staying in the village, checking every alley, every Dumpster, every empty building, every vacant lot, every culvert. He's got Dennis workin' with him."

The sheriff slapped the lower-right corner of the map. "And Abeyta is down in María." He stepped back and looked at Estelle expectantly. "That's all the people we got, Estelle. And in between, the State Police are giving us all the help they can. If there's a better way to organize it, I need to hear it."

"That's all we can do," she said. "Is Zeigler's truck in the county yard?"

"Yep. We took it over there after Mears was through with it."

"I want to take a digital picture of one of the wheels," Estelle said. "Each deputy should have one."

"A killer's going to bury a body," Mitchell observed. He nodded approval at Estelle. "They aren't apt to bother with a flat tire."

Chapter Twenty-three

William Page sat with his elbows on his knees, head bowed, eyes closed. As Estelle approached, his eyes opened groggily. He lifted his head just enough to be able to turn and look at the undersheriff.

"A long day, Mr. Page," she said. She noticed that he'd changed his clothes. He was now in faded blue jeans and a carefully wrinkled, outdoorsy, brown cotton shirt. Estelle sat down in the hard plastic chair beside him. "Any thoughts?"

He shook his head, discouraged. "You're right. I don't think I've ever spent a longer day than this one."

"Let's take a ride," Estelle said. "Are you up for that?"

"Anything," he replied. "I've never felt so useless in my life."

Page rose stiffly and followed her out of the building. He settled cautiously into the passenger seat of the unmarked county car. Estelle smiled sympathetically. "There's not a whole lot of room, I'm afraid." She reached back and tapped the heavy steel screen and framework that separated the rear passenger compartment from the front. "This keeps the seats from going any further back."

"I'll be all right," he said, and shifted his knee away from the shotgun that stood vertically on his side of the computer and radio cluster. He fell silent, watchful as Estelle pulled the car over to the fuel island where she pumped in fourteen gallons before the filler snapped off. She settled back in the car, flipped open the cover of the aluminum clipboard, and made the required notations.

She closed the log and lifted the mike. "PCS, three ten."

"Go ahead, three ten."

"PCS, mileage is eight seven seven thirty-two. I'm ten-eight, ten eighty-four. Phone's fine."

There was a pause before Gayle Torrez acknowledged. Estelle could picture her glancing over at the ten-code reminder card taped to the corner of the dispatcher's desk. *Informant in unit* wasn't a call that was used routinely enough that it would pop quickly to mind.

"Okay," Estelle said to Page. "Bureaucracy is satisfied."

"Have you been able to establish any leads at all?" Page asked as they pulled out onto Bustos Avenue, eastbound.

"We've established that we're frustrated, Mr. Page," she replied. "I'm sorry that I can't be anymore forthcoming than that. I thought that it might be useful if you would help me locate some of the places that Kevin would be likely to frequent around the area." She glanced over at Page. "Some of the favorite spots that you and Kevin might visit when you're out hiking, or out on your bikes."

"We head up the mesa a lot," he said.

She slowed the car as they approached the intersection of MacArthur and Bustos. "County Road Nineteen goes off to the north here," she said, and he nodded as she turned left.

"We ride this way all the time," he said. "For one thing, there aren't any dogs." Within a thousand yards of the intersection, the village gave way to scruffy prairie. The road was traveled so infrequently that grass tufted through the asphalt along the shoulders. Estelle slowed the car to a crawl as they passed the remains of the VistaPark Drive-in, the huge, looming screen nothing but a ragged framework, all its panels blown out long ago. The speaker posts had all been removed, leaving the ocean-rolls of the parking lot to be taken over by kochia, greasewood, and tumbleweed.

At the entrance a single, rusted chain hung loosely between two posts fabricated out of concrete-filled steel pipes. The midpoint of the chain sagged to within six inches of the ground.

"What do you suppose was *The Last Picture Show* they ever showed?" Page mused.

"Butch Cassidy and the Sundance Kid," Estelle said. "Labor Day weekend of 1970."

He looked at her in surprise. "Now you're going to tell me that you went to that very one."

"No, I wouldn't tell you that." Page waited expectantly, but Estelle didn't offer the details. She'd been five years old that weekend, a little girl enjoying the simplicity of playing among the aging cottonwoods along the river in the tiny Mexican village of Tres Santos. Posadas, and her life in the United States, was still down a long road ahead. "The Consolidated Copper Mine closed that summer," she said.

"Kevin told me about that. It took the heart right out of the village."

"Yes, it did." She pulled the car into the outdoor theater's driveway, angling in so she could look at the ground. There were no fresh vehicle tracks except for the well-worn path the four-wheelers took around the end posts. The drive-in was a favorite spot for kids to crank open the throttle, blasting across the undulations.

"We never rode in there," he said. "Kids used it a lot, though. We'd see them there every once in a while." He leaned forward. "I can't even tell where the projection house and concession stand used to be."

"Right by that little grove of elms," Estelle said, nodding. "All they left behind were some rusty nails." She tapped the steering wheel. *Good for a slow leak,* she thought. But the tracks said that Kevin Zeigler hadn't picked up his nail here.

She pulled back out onto the road.

"We like this route," Page offered. "Up here about a mile, just on the other side of the arroyo, there's a dirt road that cuts over past the landfill and comes out on Forty-three, up by the mine. That hill is a real kick in the tail when you're on a bike." He looked pained at the memory. "Kevin always calls it the *Mur de Dump.*" He glanced at Estelle. "In the European races, they like to name every hill. *Mur* this and *Mur* that."

"Is this the route you took that day with Tony Acosta?"

He nodded. "When we ride the mesa, this is the route we always take. That way, we don't have to ride through town, and we don't have to deal with the traffic on the state highways."

In another half mile, they passed the remains of a mobile-home park, and then a small adobe house. "Kevin told me that the old woman who used to live here was murdered," Page said.

"That's true."

"What happened?"

"An ugly domestic thing with the neighbors," Estelle said. "She looked out the window at the wrong time." *Just like Carmen Acosta,* she almost added. Once more she slowed the car. Fresh tire tracks cut through the weeds that had taken over Anna Hocking's driveway.

She lifted the mike. "Three oh seven, three ten."

"Three oh seven." Sergeant Tom Mears' voice was clipped and efficient.

"Ten-twenty, three oh seven."

"I'm up at the old quarry off Forty-three."

"Ten-four. Did you check Hocking's?"

"That's affirmative. I was there about an hour ago."

She acknowledged and dropped the mike in her lap. "Vacant houses are sort of pesky," she said. "Kids from town try and use this one for parties when they get the chance."

"I'm surprised it's still standing," Page said.

"So are we." The dirt road narrowed and then forked, the route off to the left not much more than a rough two-track. It angled across the prairie, gradually winding up the eastern flank of the mesa. Several miles ahead, Estelle could see the flat bench where the county had long ago established its landfill. Beyond that, higher on the mesa, were the scars from the abandoned copper mine, great pyramidal slag piles and a fenced area where equipment gradually aged and settled into the gravel of the boneyard.

The Crown Victoria thumped and lurched as Estelle turned on to the two-track leading toward the landfill and mine.

"This gets sort of rough up here," Page said. He shifted and stretched upward to watch the ribbon of dried vegetation that the car would straddle. The tracks from Mears' Expedition were clear in the prairie dirt.

"You came down last weekend?" Estelle asked, and Page looked at her quickly.

"Yes. On Friday. I went back to Socorro late Sunday."

"Did the two of you ride?"

He nodded. "Sure. We did about a hundred K on the road bikes."

"That's quite a ride. Where did you go?"

He shrugged, as if riding a hundred kilometers was an after-dinner sort of lark. "We went south to Maria, then circled back up and rode out west as far as the Broken Spur. We were going to go all the way down through the pass to Regal, but it was so windy it wasn't much fun going that way." He grinned. "Sure pushed us back to town, though."

"Did you stop in either place?"

"We got some water at that saloon in Maria."

"That's it?"

"Yes. We've eaten a couple of times at the Broken Spur, but we didn't stop there on Saturday."

Estelle let the heavy sedan find its own route up the two-track, the fragrance from the dried weeds that were crushed by the tires and roasted by the catalytic converter wafting potent through the open window. "Did Mauro Acosta ever ride with the two of you?"

If the question caught William Page by surprise, he didn't show it. "No," he said. "Mauro's not interested in bikes, I don't think. Tony is. But not Mauro. He likes to work on that old Pontiac they've got under that tarp in the backyard." He grinned. "He's pretty good at talking his mother into getting the parts he needs. They have rip-roaring arguments about that old heap. She keeps telling him that they're going to sell it."

"It runs?"

"No. I don't think so. I don't know if it will *ever* run." He reached out a stabilizing hand to the dash as the car waddled over two deep ruts cut diagonally across the road, the beginnings of an arroyo that would eventually obliterate the two-track.

"What was Kevin's relationship with Mauro?" Estelle asked. "Or yours, for that matter."

Page's head snapped around as if he'd been punched. "What?"

Estelle repeated the question.

"I don't follow what you're asking," Page said, although the flush on his face said that he clearly did.

"I'm asking if your relationship, or Kevin's relationship, with Mauro Acosta was anything beyond what we would expect between two neighbors, Mr. Page."

"You've got to be kidding."

"No, I'm not kidding," Estelle said.

"Mauro is just a...just a neighborhood kid," Page said with considerable exasperation. "I mean, what is he, fifteen years old?"

"Just about that."

Page rubbed the side of his jaw furiously, glaring out the window. "Did you ask me to ride along just so you could talk about that?"

"In part."

"I'd like to know what you're getting at."

Estelle guided the car around a sharp curve as the dirt lane swung toward the corner of the tall chain-link fence bordering the county landfill. "Mr. Page, we're investigating a vicious assault of a teenaged girl. We're also investigating the disappearance of her neighbor. There are enough unusual circumstances here to attract lots of attention." She glanced at Page. "We open every door, Mr. Page. Every one. I can tell you that at the moment, the circumstances of your relationship with Kevin Zeigler are of no particular interest to the Sheriff's Department. We don't care what you do in the privacy of your home, or in private moments anywhere else, Mr. Page. We *do* know that either you, or Kevin, or perhaps both of you, had some interest in Mauro Acosta. That's a door that we need to open."

"I don't follow you."

"Yes, you do. I think it's interesting that he is the only member of that family whom you—or Kevin—photographed alone. And photographed essentially surreptitiously from behind the blinds of a window." She looked over at Page. He was squinting straight ahead. "You might remember that Mauro is very much a minor."

"You're very thorough," Page said after a moment.

"I will do everything I can to establish what happened to Kevin Zeigler, Mr. Page. I will do everything I can to find the person who assaulted Carmen Acosta. I believe it's obvious that the two events are linked. I do not believe that Kevin assaulted the girl." She hesitated for a minute, trying to assess Page's churning emotions. "I also do not believe that we will find Kevin Zeigler alive, Mr. Page."

"Christ, stop calling me that," he snapped. "You make me feel like I'm sitting on a steel chair, under a bright lamp shining into my eyes." He heaved a great, shuddering breath. "It's only been a day."

"Twenty-eight hours."

"Christ, you can't just give up hope that easily."

"It isn't easy, William. I liked Kevin. In just two years, he's reorganized this county, moved us out of the dark ages, done all kinds of wonderful things. As far as I can tell, he relished his personal life with you as well, and I'm happy for you both. I sympathize for your loss. But that will not prevent us from exploring every avenue."

"I understand that." He glanced at Estelle cautiously. "I guess."

"Then you can understand why our curiosity is piqued when we look through the collection of photos on Kevin's Rolodex and find something like that provocative photograph of Mauro Acosta—taken with a telephoto lens, through the window of Kevin's bedroom."

"It's just…" Page waved a hand in frustration.

"It's just what?"

"It's no different than if a photographer saw a beautiful young girl posed in the park, or at the beach. She's beautiful to look at, so he snaps her picture. There's nothing wrong with that…and it doesn't matter if the subject of the portrait is a six-year-old, or twelve, or seventeen, or thirty-five...or eighty. It's not illegal."

"Is that what happened? Did you take the photo?"

"What difference does it make?"

"None, I suppose. It would just be helpful to know."

"Kevin took it. He's the photographer. Yes, I saw it, and yes, I thought it was a wonderful study. Mauro isn't much of a deep thinker, Sheriff. But in that photo, he's...well, he looks like he's trying to understand the whole world."

"That's interesting," Estelle said. They both fell silent as she drove along the fence of the landfill.

"Mur de Dump," Page murmured as they nosed up the last hill before the two-track joined with the main, graded county access road to the landfill. "Kevin said this eyesore's days are numbered."

"Maybe so," Estelle said. "He's trying to talk the County Commission into going with a private management firm—a private company to run the village and county's solid-waste operations."

"He *was* trying to," Page said glumly.

The county car kicked gravel as they pulled up onto the county road. "From here out to Forty-three, and then up to the top of the mesa?" she asked.

"Yes."

"This is the route you took that day with Tony?"

He nodded. "With much bitching and moaning," he said. "That kid *needs* to ride about a hundred miles a day to get into shape." He rested his right arm along the windowsill and drummed his fingers on the vinyl. "So why are *you* here?"

"Here where?" Estelle asked.

He turned as far sideways in the seat as the shoulder harness would allow, regarding Estelle. "Why is someone like you working in a backwater like Posadas? Why aren't you in Hollywood, or something like that?"

She glanced at him, amused at his frank, open stare. "Hollywood?"

He pursed his lips judiciously. "You can't be *unaware* of how attractive you are, Sheriff."

"Undersheriff. And thank you."

"So why is Posadas so lucky?"

"Just the luck of the draw, Mr. Page."

"You're from Mexico, originally?"

"Yes."

"How old were you when you came to the United States?"

Estelle sighed patiently. "I was fourteen, Mr. Page."

Page chuckled dryly at her reserve. "Your background isn't the subject of discussion today, right?"

"That's correct, Mr. Page."

"'Mr. Page, Mr. Page,'" he muttered. "Your husband is Kevin's physician. He thinks highly of Dr. Guzman."

"So do I," Estelle said.

Page shook his head in amusement and turned back straight in the seat. In another hundred yards, they reached County Road 43, the paved two-lane road that switchbacked up the mesa past the mine, on into the national forest. "We usually ride up here, past the quarry, and on along the rim. There's that road that parallels the mesa lip that's really spectacular."

Estelle pulled to a halt at the stop sign, and waited as another county vehicle approached from the direction of town. In a moment she saw that it was Bob Torrez, and he swung the big SUV into the landfill road, stopping door to door with Estelle's sedan.

"Anything?" he asked. He dipped his head a little so he could see across the car, looking at Estelle's passenger.

Estelle shook her head. "No. Mr. Page says that he and Kevin used to ride up here regularly. We're following their usual route. Tom says that he checked Hocking's place earlier. No one's been there."

"I heard," Torrez said. "I talked with Brunell at the Border Patrol. I don't know what he can do, but they're lookin'. I think we ought to give Naranjo a jingle, too."

"That's a good idea. Do you want me to do that?"

"Your Spanish is better than mine," Torrez said. "Yeah, give him a call. You never know what his *federales* might stumble on to. Did you talk with Dayan?"

"I wrote a release and left it with Gayle. She was going to call him and tell him it was ready."

"Okay. I'm headed into the outback for a little bit. I gotta get away from the telephone." He nodded at Estelle and his eyes flicked to Page once more. "You be careful," he said. With two fingers lifting off the steering wheel in salute, he backed the Expedition out onto the paved road and accelerated up the hill.

"Interesting fellow," Page said.

"Sheriff Torrez is one of the good guys," Estelle said.

"I hope so. I guess I'll have to take your word for it. But I'm not sure that if *he'd* been the one to suggest a ride that I would have gone along quite so cheerfully."

Estelle's cellular phone chirped just as she pulled out onto the highway. She answered, and almost immediately stepped hard on the brakes, swinging wide.

"I'm on my way," she said and tossed the phone onto the seat beside her. "Make sure you're buckled in," she said, U-turning so hard the tires shrieked in protest. She accelerated hard back in the direction of Posadas. Taking a fraction of a second to check her rearview mirror, she was not surprised to see Sheriff Torrez's big white SUV charging down the hill behind her.

Chapter Twenty-four

A county car with lights flashing blocked the narrow County B-1, the access road that led directly from County Road 43 west to the maintenance yard off Third and Hutton Streets. Deputy Dennis Collins stood at the front fender of the unit, and Estelle slowed enough to avoid skidding broadside into his car. She heard the squeal of brakes behind her. Collins pointed down the road toward the maintenance yard and Estelle nodded, accelerating. The young deputy didn't look pleased.

"Three oh seven, three ten."

"Three oh seven." Sergeant Mears' voice sounded as if he was on the fringes of radio reception, somewhere north beyond the hump of Cat Mesa.

"Tom, we're probably going to need you down here, too. County yard at Hutton and Third."

"Ten-four."

They drove along the fence that enclosed the county maintenance yard. The flatbed trailer with the large section of culvert still rested exactly where it had been earlier in the morning. The front loader was parked next to a pile of gravel on the other side of the yard. Rounding the west corner of the yard and turning left onto Third Street, Estelle braked hard. Mike Sisneros stood beside his village unit. Across Third Street, four county employees were standing in a small group on the sidewalk, facing Chief Eddie Mitchell.

"Stay in the car," Estelle said to Page. She didn't wait for a reply, but got out, hesitating at the door for a moment so that Torrez's vehicle had room to slide to a stop.

Sisneros approached, pointing through the maintenance-yard fence as he did so.

"Right there on the tire pile, just down from the top."

Estelle stepped only as far as the edge of the pavement. Between the fence and the asphalt of Third Street was a narrow, even spread of graveled shoulder, and she knelt and peered first up and then down the street. Inside the fence, the pile of tires was bordered on the south side by a retaining wall of concrete blocks. A row of three fuel tanks stood on tall legs just beyond the wall, and then the large steel building that included repair bays and offices stretched all the way to the yard gates.

"Well, shit," Bob Torrez said as he joined her. The mound of tires was at least ten feet high, a relatively neat pyramid twenty feet in diameter at the base. Many of the tires were enormous, retired from road graders, loaders, dump trucks. The small tire on the north slope would have been easily missed under normal circumstances, hooked halfway through the gaping center of a five-foot-tall behemoth. Sunlight winked off the wheel on which the tire was still mounted.

"Who saw that?" Torrez said, turning to Sisneros.

"Dennis was driving through here," Sisneros said. "I guess he just happened to glance that way, and there it was."

"Well, shit," Torrez said again. "Give the kid a medal."

"He called the chief on the phone," the village patrolman said. He turned to Estelle as she rose from her kneeling position. "I didn't see any tracks on the shoulder, but not much is going to show. The chief looked too, but..." He shrugged.

"Has anybody been in there?" Torrez asked. "I mean, other than those guys?" He nodded at the group across the street.

"No one," Sisneros said emphatically. "The chief put Dennis out at the road, and then his own unit down at the other end, there. We called all the county guys out." He turned to point at the small group around Mitchell. "That's every one of 'em, right there." Estelle glanced over at the chief, wondering why he had exiled Collins to traffic duty right at the height of the young deputy's elation at finding such a critical piece of evidence.

"Okay." Torrez pulled his handheld radio off his belt. "PCS, three oh eight. Have Linda respond to this location."

"Ten-four, three oh eight."

"Real copies," a faint voice said. "ETA about twenty minutes."

"She's twenty minutes out," Torrez muttered and glanced at Estelle. "You want to get started?"

Estelle nodded and walked quickly to the trunk of her car. Page got out at the same time. "Is that the flat tire from Kevin's truck?"

"We don't know yet," Estelle said. She partially closed the trunk lid so that she could look directly at Page. "And I'm serious. You need to remain right where you are, sir. Otherwise, I'll have one of the officers take you back to the office."

With one camera around her neck and the other in hand, Estelle returned to the edge of the pavement. "It's interesting," she said. "It's on the back side of the pile. The guys couldn't have seen it from inside the yard unless they happened to walk around the back side of the pile. Right along the fence." She nodded at the tanks of fuel. "Even over there, the bulk of the pile would keep it out of sight."

"And no one's going to see it driving up this way," Torrez said, gesturing south to north on Third Street. "Just comin' from the other direction, the way Collins was. The kid got lucky."

"He was on his toes, to realize what he might be seeing," Estelle said. "There's a puzzle, though. I'd like photos from above," she said, focusing the camera with the telephoto lens through the chain-link fence. "And we need to do a careful sweep of the road shoulder, too. We need to make sure everyone stays off it."

"We can do that," Torrez said. "Let me go see where the cherry picker is." He turned, then stopped and lowered his voice. "I don't like the flamingo bein' here, Estelle."

She shot him a withering look. "Bobby, I had a valuable talk with him. I would have dropped him off back at the office, but

I didn't want to take the time. I told him to stay right there by the car. He understands."

"I'll have Mike run him back," Torrez said as he turned away. His tone made it clear there was no room for debate. He strode over to Sisneros, stopped for a moment, and Estelle saw the patrolman nod. He beckoned Page, who in turned glanced over at Estelle, frowning.

She met Page as he reached for the door of Sisneros' patrol car.

"I'll keep you posted," she said.

"Thanks," Page replied, his expression a mix of apprehension, impatience, and disgust. Estelle did not try to explain the sheriff's motivations to Page. In a basic, by-the-book way, he was entirely correct in what he was doing, even though she knew perfectly well it wasn't the "book" that motivated Torrez's reaction to seeing Page at a possible crime scene.

"Mike," she added, "after you drop off Mr. Page at the county building, will you take over for Collins at the intersection? I need him here."

"Yes, ma'am."

While Torrez went to confer with Hobie Tyler about a bucket truck, Estelle shot a careful series of photographs beginning on the opposite side of the street, using small red distance-marker flags for scale and contrast. She had taken no more than half a dozen before Collins' unit appeared. She waved him to the grass on the far side of the street, away from the fence.

"Well done," she said as he scrambled out of the truck. "Tell me what happened."

He appeared to have a hard time holding still, like a little kid boiling over with anticipation. "I was just coming through here, on my way over there," he said, pointing toward the neighborhood to the west. "There's a lot of old vacant lots over there that I wanted to check." He turned back to Estelle eagerly. "I was *looking* for the tire, 'cause that's the only thing that's actually missing, you know?"

"Other than Kevin Zeigler," Estelle added.

"Well, yeah…other than him. And here's this stack of tires." He shrugged. "And there it was. Maybe he's underneath."

"That's a cheerful thought. As soon as you saw the tire, you called Chief Mitchell?"

"Yeah, 'cause when I was climbing the fence, I saw his unit on the other side of the yard, over there on Hutton Street."

"Ah," Estelle said, trying to keep a straight face. No wonder Mitchell had exiled the exuberant young man to intersection duty. "You were on the fence?"

"Well," he said and hesitated, the beginnings of a flush on his ruddy cheeks. "I just climbed up a ways so I could see better. I didn't think anything about it. I guess the chief didn't much like that."

"Do you understand why, Dennis?"

"Yes, ma'am. I do now."

I'll bet you do, she thought. In the distance, she saw Bob Torrez accompany Hobie Tyler through the main gate. They walked directly to one of the county's bucket trucks, fired it up, and in a moment, the large vehicle lumbered out of the yard.

"Make sure no one steps or drives on the shoulder, Dennis, other than you. What I want you to do is start all the way down by the entrance, where the truck just came from." She twisted, pointing toward the intersection to the north. "I want this shoulder strip combed, all the way up to that stop sign. Anything at all. Fresh cigarette butts, tire or shoe prints, fresh digs in the gravel…you know the drill. All right? I'll get you some help as soon as I can."

"You think somebody threw the tire over the fence?"

"Likely so."

After some shuffling of vehicles, Tyler had the machine parked where Estelle wanted it, outriggers extended and digging into the macadam, rather than marking up the narrow shoulder. Tyler fussed with Estelle's safety harness until it was fitted to his satisfaction, with the tether hooked through the D-ring on the bucket.

"That way, if you fall, you'll just kinda dangle instead of goin' headfirst to the ground," he told her. In a moment they were airborne, being hoisted high over the fence. As the bucket oscillated gently to a halt, Tyler said, "What are you actually looking for?"

"It's just a good place for an unobstructed view of the pile," Estelle said.

"It's just a goddamn tire," Tyler mused.

"Yes, it is. And once we get in there and move it, the scene will never be the same," she said. The bucket was a tight fit for two people, and she could smell the diesel and grease on Tyler's clothes. "Can you swing us a little more that way?" she asked, and the arm extended into the yard as Tyler jockeyed the hydraulic controls.

Like huge insects hovering over a pile of refuse, they surveyed the pile, the boom reaching out over the barbed wire. With the bucket suspended within a foot or two of the pile, Estelle took portraits of the wheel and tire, trying not to leap ahead with conclusions for which there was no evidence. Tyler stood behind her silently, moving the bucket obediently whenever she asked.

When she was satisfied that there was no direction she had missed from which to view the tire and wheel in place, both from a distance and nearly on top of the pile, so close that she could smell the fragrance of the sun-baked rubber, she nodded that she was finished.

"You sure?" Tyler asked.

"I'm sure."

"Okay, then. Down we go." He swung them back over the fence to the truck. As she was climbing out of the awkward bucket, Linda Real arrived and watched critically as Estelle found her way down to the roadway one handhold at a time.

"Bobby sends me to the ends of the earth, and look what happens," she said. "You get all the fun carnival rides."

Estelle grinned. "We're just getting started, Linda," she said. "We needed some close-ups of that wheel and tire." She drew Linda close to the fence. "Look at the top of the tire. See how it's lying? It's the one that's caught in the middle of that big tractor tire."

Linda cocked her head first this way and that, pacing along the roadway for a better view. At one point, she stood on her tiptoes, stretching herself upward for another couple inches of height. She pointed. "There's a portion of its tread that's underneath that other tire…the one on the very top of the pile."

"Exactly," Estelle said with approval. "And how could it end up like that if it were thrown from the *yard* side of the pile?"

"I don't think it could," Linda said. "It had to come from out here. Is that what you're thinking?"

Estelle nodded. She turned as Robert Torrez approached, this time with Eddie Mitchell.

"No tracks along the road," Mitchell said, glancing over his shoulder at the distant figure of Deputy Collins. "I thought we might get lucky."

"Well, this is a big step," Estelle said. "I asked Collins to do another survey, all the way along this whole strip, right to the intersection up there."

"And perhaps just keep on going," Mitchell said dryly.

"He's young and eager, Eddie."

"Yeah, like an eight-year-old. He looked like a damn monkey on this fence when I drove up." Mitchell regarded the pile for a moment, hands on his hips. "That's a hell of a toss," he said. "What's that fence, eight feet?"

"Not counting the three strands of barbed wire on top," Torrez said. "Unless you were the Incredible Hulk, the only way you'd toss a wheel and tire that far is by standin' in the back of a pickup truck. And even then you'd have to give it a real good fling. It ain't light."

Another vehicle turned onto Third Street from the north. "Here's the man," Torrez said. They waited until Sgt. Tom Mears parked and joined them.

"I'll be damned," Mears said matter-of-factly when Torrez pointed at the wheel and tire.

"We got pictures from every which way," Torrez said. "How do you want to do this?"

"Any prints are going to be on the wheel," Mears said. "And that's unlikely, since nobody messes with the *wheel* when they take off a flat tire. You wouldn't even have to touch it. You grab it by the tire to shuck it off the brake drum. But"—and he shook his head slowly—"you're not going to get diddly off the tread."

"Unless there's blood or something like that," Estelle said. "We're curious about grease, too."

"You got quite a collection of that, standing right over there," Mitchell said, jerking his head toward the four county employees.

"That thought crossed my mind," Estelle said.

Mears took a deep breath and puffed out his cheeks. "The first thing to do is disturb things as little as possible." He turned and nodded at the county cherry picker, idling across the street. "You want to use that. That, and a gaff. They must have some kind of hook like they use for working electric lines or something like that. That'll be a whole lot easier than trying to climb up that mountain of tires."

"Nah," Torrez said. "Let's not make a production out of this." He turned away. "Let me get my gloves." In a moment he returned, pulling on a stout pair of rawhide work gloves. "Let's use your unit, Tom. There's no point in having a traffic jam inside there."

Linda Real traded her still cameras for video, and walked with Estelle into the yard. Mears parked his Expedition a good distance from the tires, and he, Torrez, and Mitchell surveyed the gravel in front of the pile. "Nothing," Torrez announced. "Too damn bad it never rains around this place." He glanced at Eddie. "Nobody saw a thing, I suppose."

"Not a thing," Mitchell said. "I had a good long talk with all four of 'em. They said the last person to drive in the yard who wasn't working there was the undersheriff, earlier this morning."

"And I parked over in front of the garage," Estelle said. "I talked with James Volpato right over there by the dump truck, and then I walked across to talk with Hobie. He and one of the others were loading that culvert."

"You can't see the back of the pile from anywhere in the yard," Torrez said. "That's pretty slick." He pointed at the large metal shop building that included the maintenance bays and offices. "That fronts the fence on Third, so it blocks the view. Whoever it was just drove up and pitched. He'd be parked behind the tire pile, and the fuel tanks there, and nobody would see a thing."

He turned to Estelle. "You got all the pictures you need of it in place?"

"And then some," she said.

"You don't need to film this part." Torrez glowered at Linda, but that just earned him a sunny, lopsided smile.

"Oh, this is the good part," she said. "I have miles of tape."

Torrez picked his way around the base of the rubber mountain, and climbed the pile gingerly. He twisted one boot for purchase, and knelt against the huge tire near the top. "Did you happen to notice how this is sittin'?" he said.

"Do you mean about how it's caught under the one above it?"

"Yup."

"Yes. We have photos of that."

"Kinda interesting." He bent down, put one hand on each side of the tire, and grunted back, lifting it up and out of its nest. Resting it on the pile periodically for balance, he backed down, never changing his grip. Reaching the bottom and firm footing, he flashed an insincere smile in the direction of Linda's video camera.

Mears opened the tailgate of his unit, and Torrez stood the tire gingerly on the plastic mat. "That's a little tire," he said, "but it would be a *hell* of a toss." He beckoned toward Dennis Collins, who was still outside the fence. "Have Hobie come in here," he called, and Collins jogged off toward the small group of men.

Mears closely examined the cast aluminum wheel, rotating the tire this way and that so the light caught the burnished metal finish.

"Like Tom says, nobody handles the wheel when they're changin' a tire," Torrez observed. "That's the whole trouble."

Mears made a wry face and turned the tire so the tread faced him. "Few little things in the tread. Pebbles...tire stuff. And a pretty fair coating of road dust on the wheel." He looked at Estelle. "We'll give it a thorough dusting back at the shop, but it's not going to tell us much."

"It already has," Estelle said eagerly. "I'm positive now that someone else used Kevin's truck." She glanced toward the approaching Hobie Tyler and lowered her voice. "It would be easy to dismiss what Doris Marens told me. She's not my idea of a super-reliable witness. But no matter what he did, Kevin would have no reason to pitch this spare, wheel and all, up on that pile. Someone else did that."

"Not to mention Zeigler not having the muscles," Mitchell observed.

"Hobie," Torrez greeted the yard foreman. "Does this look to you like the tire and wheel you saw on the county manager's truck?"

Tyler paused, not eager to approach too close. He sidled up, and one hand reached out and took Chief Eddie Mitchell by the back of the arm as if he needed the support. "Sure as shit looks like it," he said judiciously. "I can't say as I paid a whole lot of attention, you know. I mean it *could* be the right one. It's flat?"

"Yup," Torrez said. He thumped the top of the tire.

"His truck's right over there in your lockup," Tyler said, as if Torrez might have forgotten the obvious

"Just wanted to hear you say it," Torrez said with a grin.

"This is just about as goddamn strange as it gets," Tyler said. "What was he thinkin'?"

"I don't think he was," Torrez said affably.

Chapter Twenty-five

"I heard the screen door open," Teresa Reyes said. "You know, I'm not very fast." She shifted position on her walker and watched Estelle pick up the package that had been slipped between the screen and the solid door. "I could see out the window, though. I saw this old outdoorsman." She leaned hard on the fourth syllable of the Spanish word, *naturalisto*, as if it were some sort of disease. She shuffled back and gestured out the front window of the living room.

"He was wearing a checkered shirt?" Estelle asked.

"Maybe that's what it was," Teresa said, switching effortlessly to English. "He had on one of those…what do you call it…" She tugged at her own blouse. "A *chaleco*."

"A vest," Estelle offered.

"That's what it was. One of those quilted ones, like the sheriff wears. When I looked outside, this man who didn't have an extra minute to wait for an old lady was walking back down the sidewalk to his old truck. Like the one your Uncle Reuben used to drive."

"An older-model Ford Bronco?" Estelle said.

"I don't know one from the other. It was old and white. That's all I know."

"You didn't happen to see the license, did you?" Estelle asked more to gently kid her mother than because she needed any further verification that the visitor to her home had been Milton Crowley.

"*Ay, cómo soy menso!*" Estelle's mother sniffed with feigned injury. "Silly me. I should have run right out there. You think I have binoculars built right into these old eyes? You're the famous detective who's never home half the time. So who's this old friend of yours, that leaves you things?"

"His name's Milton Crowley, *Mamá*. He lives way out, past the end of the mesa."

"Well, he's impolite, not to knock on the door and come in with his package."

"Maybe you don't want to talk with this one, *Mamá*. He's a little bit *chiflado.*"

"So if he's so crazy, what are you doing with him?"

"I talked with him this morning," Estelle said, and slipped the end of the plain brown envelope open. A single video cassette lay inside, and she smiled with delight. "I was trying to talk him into letting me borrow this."

"I won't ask," Teresa said, and settled into her rocker. "Your husband took the boys somewhere and left me here."

"Sorry, *Mamá*. Where did they go?"

"The engineer needed about twenty-five miles of aluminum foil." She shook her head in despair. "What they do in school nowadays."

"Different, huh, *Mamá?*" Teresa had taught in the one-room school in Tres Santos, and Estelle could remember how stern and formidable this tiny woman had seemed to her then. "I hope you'll go in with us tomorrow night."

"Of course. I have to see what this one is doing." She zipped her fingers across her lips. "I know I'm going to have to bite my tongue."

"You'll manage." She slipped the cassette out of the envelope. None of the stick-on labels that came with blank tapes had been affixed, and there was no note in the envelope. "Thank you, Mr. Crowley," she said.

"Sofía's coming tomorrow."

"For sure?"

"Francis said so."

"Ah, that's good," Estelle said, with satisfaction. "You know what we need to do, *Mamá?*" Her mother lifted her dark eyebrows. "We're going to buy a piano." One of the eyebrows settled a little bit. "I talked to *hijo's* teacher. You know what he does at lunch? He slips off to the music room and plays the piano. All by himself."

"When did you find this out?"

"Yesterday. I saw him do it. All by himself. Ms. Delgado says that he's been doing this for three weeks or more."

"You're just now noticing that music is in his heart?" The question came quietly, without the usual good-natured chiding, and it took Estelle by surprise—all the more so when Teresa added nothing to the question, but just let it hang there, waiting to be answered.

"No, I hadn't noticed," Estelle replied after a while. She tossed the video on to the end table beside the sofa and settled into the deep cushions.

"You watch his hands, *mi corazán*. And you watch him read when he thinks he's alone."

"What do you mean?"

"You may call me *vieja chiflada*, too. But I see it. The stories make music in his head when he reads."

"You mean they remind him of songs?"

Teresa's wrinkled face wrinkled a bit more. "I don't know. I can't see in there." She tapped her forehead. "All I know is that when he reads, he makes music in his head. He does both—*los dos*—at the same time." She shrugged. "What was he playing on that piano at school?"

"I couldn't tell. I didn't want to interrupt him." Estelle leaned her head back and covered her eyes. "I didn't want him to stop. It sounded like he was trying to work out chords, somehow. He didn't know I was there."

"You remember that old piano I had in the school?"

"Yes. Eighty-eight keys, and about forty of them worked."

"Terrible old thing. No one could play it." She yawned. "I think a piano is a good thing, *hija*. Where are you going to put it?" She turned and surveyed the living room of the small house. "In their bedroom?"

"I think right about where your chair is, *Mamá*. If we put it in that corner, it won't be too close to the fireplace."

"Which you use so often," Teresa said dryly. "And then where do *I* go?"

"Well, we're going to have to shuffle things around some, I guess."

"You want some advice?" Teresa mimed pulling on a hat. "I'm putting on my old teacher's hat now," she said. "Buy a good one. That's all I know about it. You remember Pedro Arballo? He was that little fat one who was in love with you all through fourth grade."

Pedro refused to come to mind, and Estelle shook her head.

"No matter." Teresa waggled her fingers. "He was a natural *guitarrista*. I knew it. He had these marvelous, nimble fingers, and when someone would play, you could see the look on his face. Anyway, I told his father, and Luis had this old guitar." She shook her head in disgust. "It was like having a big chunk of cottonwood with strings nailed on. *Imposible*. I told Luis he should take this old thing out and burn it, and he told me that I was being ridiculous, that a guitar was a guitar. You know what happened?"

"No."

"I told Father Tómas about it. I told him what I thought, and about Pedro. The good Father thought about it and then said he'd see what he could do. Before you know it, Pedro had himself a decent guitar. I don't know where Father got it. But he gave Pedro lessons, and before you know it..." She shrugged elegantly.

"And now he plays concerts all across Europe," Estelle said soberly, knowing what was coming.

"No, he doesn't. Luis drank too much one night and drove into the Rio Plegado, which happened to be flooding at the time. He drowned the whole family, including little Pedro with his little guitarist's fingers." She pursed her lips as Estelle tried to avoid bursting out laughing, a combination of fatigue and her mother's version of a moral tale.

"That's a terrible story, *Mamá*," she said, groaning.

"It's true, though. Most of it. The only good thing is that Luis drowned, too. Otherwise I think the whole town would have taken turns shooting him. *Yo también*."

"I promise, *Mamá*. We won't buy a cheap piano."

"Who are you going to find to give lessons?"

"I have no idea."

"Well, you're a detective. I'm sure you can find somebody. You know who I think would be good?"

"Who?"

"Isabel Sedillos. If she'll do it."

"Gayle Torrez's grandmother?"

"Yes. If she'll do it. I don't know. But she plays every week in church, you know. I see what she does with some of the little ones in the choir. It wouldn't hurt—" She bit the sentence off when she saw the glacial calm settle over her daughter's face.

"I'll talk to Gayle," Estelle said.

"I think you should. That's a good idea." She nodded at the video. "You're going to watch that now?"

"It's probably about six hours long, *Mamá*. I'll wait until everyone's gone to bed."

"That's what you should do, too."

"In a little bit."

"Six hours is not a little bit," Teresa said. "And when are you going to buy this piano?"

"Saturday, I think. I'm going to ask Sofiá to go along with us. She plays so beautifully."

"She doesn't just *play, hija*. She is a concert pianist."

Estelle nodded. "I thought she could help Francisco find the right one. Will you go with us?"

Teresa immediately grimaced and waved a hand. "No, no. I don't go to that place. I'll stay home. Are you going to take Carlos?"

"Sure."

"That's good."

"And what do you know about him?" Estelle almost asked, but before she could, her mother took a hold of her walker and pulled herself to her feet.

"And this nasty thing you're working on," Teresa said. "What about it?"

"It's nasty," Estelle said wearily. "I'm hoping this will help." She nodded at the tape.

"What makes you think you'll be able to go off to Las Cruces all day Saturday, then?"

"I'm just going to, that's all."

Teresa nodded with satisfaction. "You can do anything you make up your mind to do, *hija*. This is a good thing you're doing for Francisco. It's too easy, you know."

"What's too easy?"

"Ojos que no ven, corazón que no siente," Teresa said, a pontifical forefinger, crooked with arthritis, raised in the air. "You put them out of sight long enough, pretty soon they're out of your heart, too."

"Mamá, they're in my heart and mind all the time. That's why I do what I do. I think about you, about Francis, about the boys all the time."

"Well, that's good," Teresa said. "But you just remember that being safe and well fed isn't enough." For a moment, it looked as if Teresa wanted to say something else, but she didn't. She began her slow shuffle across the living room, heading toward her room in the back of the house. "I'm going to start on a nap while there's some peace and quiet."

"Close your door so they don't wake you when they come home."

Teresa shook her head. "No. That's the best sound to hear, you know." She blew a kiss toward her daughter. Estelle sat quietly for a few minutes, gazing at the blank spine of the videotape.

Chapter Twenty-six

"Has the feature started yet?" Dr. Francis Guzman settled on to the sofa beside Estelle. The VCR counter showed one hour and seventeen minutes into the meeting, and the sound was turned down to a murmur. He studied the screen intently, watching County Manager Kevin Zeigler methodically making a point about the leaky, one-year-old hospital roof and a possible repair strategy that didn't involve suing the contractor.

"Crowley pays attention," Estelle said. "He catches everyone who speaks, and doesn't waste tape on anything else."

"Fascinating," Francis mumbled. "If it's deadly boring the first time around, the tape must be just spellbinding." He squirmed down into the cushions, resting his head against Estelle's arm.

Estelle pushed the remote's Pause button, and the county manager froze in place, pencil poised, eyes leveled at the commission. "It's strange to see him," she said. "One minute he's here, the next minute he's gone."

"Huh," Francis said noncommittally as the tape continued. "What makes you think that Zeigler's disappearance has anything at all to do with the meeting?"

"Absolutely nothing, *querido*," Estelle said. "And that's how frustrating all of this is."

"Then…," he said, and let it hang.

"Because we have nothing else. There has to be something, somewhere—some little key."

"Maybe he was just robbed. Maybe he went out for a noon-time run or bike ride, got mugged and then dumped in a ditch somewhere."

"That's as possible as any of this," Estelle said. "Except when I saw him right at noon yesterday, he said he had several errands to do. He didn't say anything about exercising in the middle of the day."

"And he probably wouldn't, now that I think about it," Francis said. "At least not on a meeting day. His habit was to run early in the morning."

Estelle touched Pause again and turned, having to duck her head to look her husband full in the face. "How long has he been doing that, Doctor?"

"I would guess most of his adult life," Francis said. "He's a hell of an athlete, you know." He lifted a hand and pointed at the frozen figure on the screen. "He keeps his cool right along with a BP that's down in the basement. His pulse rate might rise to fifty on a bad day. That's where that endurance comes from." Out of idle curiosity, Francis lifted the legal pad on Estelle's lap and scanned the notes. "You don't think it was something from his personal life?"

"Not that I've been able to discover. I had a long talk again today with William Page. There was plenty of opportunity to bring up problems, a lot of time for slips."

"Maybe Kevin was having an affair with somebody else. That's always a good one. What, about ninety percent of homicides are committed by family members against family members?"

"Too many," Estelle said. She sighed. "The problem is trying to determine what sort of casual contacts a person makes during the day that are going to be where the trouble starts. I mean, who can predict that sort of thing? His roommate's not much help with that. Page is only in town a couple of days a week. Sometimes not even that."

"You think there's something there? I mean, with those two?"

"What do you mean, *something?*"

"I don't know. Triangles, rejection, two-timing…all those old tried-and-true ways to wreck a life. Not to mention that they've made it a little more of a challenge anyway. Besides, with Page up in Socorro most of the week, there's both opportunity and temptation."

"I suppose. If there is, though, we haven't found a thing. Except maybe a crush on the boy next door."

"Well, there you go," Francis said.

"I don't think so."

"Page wasn't even in this part of the world yesterday noon, was he?"

"No. I talked to him in his Socorro office. If this is something he orchestrated from afar, then he's doing an Academy Award job of playing the worried spouse. And he doesn't strike me as your basic 'hire a hit man' type."

"But that's been done before," Francis said.

"Oh, *sí*." She pushed the Play button. "I don't know, *querido*."

They watched in silence for a while, and eventually Estelle became aware that Francis' breathing was deeply rhythmic and that his head weighed a ton. She glanced down, loath to move and wake him. Instead, she circled an arm around his shoulders and snuggled deeper herself, resting her head back against the cushion.

The tape plodded on, and each time the camera swung back to take in the commissioners' dais, she could see the back of Robert Torrez's head, a few rows ahead of the camera. Sitting one row ahead of him and one seat to the right was Eddie Mitchell. Once in a while, Torrez would lean forward and say something that the camera couldn't pick up, and Mitchell would respond, occasionally glancing back toward the camera when he turned.

At 10:45 a.m., the commissioners had called a brief recess, and everyone that the camera could see before the recess returned when the meeting reconvened. Twenty minutes later, the camera's mike caught the thud of the commission chamber doors. The camera didn't move, catching every word of Commissioner Barney Tinneman's impassioned plea that the county should sue Colstrup Brothers Construction of El Paso for the shoddy roof job.

At one point, he pounded the dais in frustration. "I mean, if a contractor tore off the roof of your own home, and then replaced it with one that cost what this job did, and then it *leaked,* why in hell would you beg and plead for the job to be done right?" He leaned back in his chair, then surged forward again. "Kevin, what was the date of the final inspection? When we supposedly said the job was finished and approved?"

The camera swiveled deftly to catch Zeigler's answer, and while the county manager explained the July 10 date and what it *actually* meant, Estelle saw that a new face had joined the meeting, this time sitting one row in front of Zeigler's special microphone-equipped desk…perhaps explaining the thud of the chamber's door. Ralph Johnson, the Highway Department's supervisor, had taken a seat beside Don Fulkerson, manager of the landfill. Johnson didn't look like he wanted to be present anymore than did the other department heads in the room, each one of them trying to time their arrival just seconds before the commission might have questions on their personal agenda item. Fulkerson appeared to be dozing.

For another hour, the commission worked its way down the agenda, and as the various department heads said their piece, most then left the meeting. Estelle imagined that they all walked faster toward the exit than they had entered. Ralph Johnson answered a half dozen simple questions, including a brief tussle over bid specifications with Tinneman, who appeared ready to argue about everything, given the chance. When the camera swiveled to watch and hear Johnson speak, Estelle could see Zeigler on the far left, and the full sweep of the commission chambers, with Commissioner Barry Swartz just visible on the right margin of the picture.

Regardless of what was going on with the commission, or what questions they may have had for the various people who took the mike or for the county manager, Kevin Zeigler remained the focus of an almost constant procession of people who entered the chambers to speak with him, bending down for a confidential confab while Zeigler covered the mike with his left hand. Almost invariably, when Crowley's camera swung to cover a speaker, there was Zeigler in the rear of the hall at his desk, talking with someone.

Most of the time, he appeared in good humor, a quick smile his standard greeting for people who needed to whisper in his ear.

At 11:30, the commission launched into its discussion of providing police services for the village. Village Chief Eddie Mitchell walked stolidly to the microphone in the back of the hall, immediately beside Crowley's camera. The chief fielded questions for twenty-five minutes.

When the meeting adjourned for lunch, Crowley kept the camera focused on the commissioners, recording their small tête-à-têtes for posterity. At one point, Tinneman pulled County Clerk Stacey Roybal to one side, his brow stormy. He bent close to Roybal, who was a full head shorter than he was, and it was obvious that Milton Crowley, all the way in the back of the hall, wanted to know what they were talking about, since he zoomed in as close as the camera's lens would allow. The camera didn't waver.

As Tinneman finished, he glanced toward the back, said something else, and gathered his sports jacket off the back of his chair. The camera went dead as Dr. Arnold Gray, the last commissioner to leave the hall, grinned into the lens and said loudly, "Come on, Milt, it's time for lunch. Turn that thing off." The camera winked to snow.

Before the tape had a chance to start the afternoon session, Estelle pushed the Pause button. Francis shifted and lifted a hand to rub the back of his neck.

"Why don't you go to bed, *querido*," Estelle whispered.

Francis pushed himself upright with a groan. "I fell asleep." He regarded the static on the television screen. "That didn't have much of a plot."

"They broke for lunch."

"Are you going to break for bed?" He glanced at his watch.

"I need to see a few more minutes," Estelle said.

"The whole afternoon session is a hell of a lot more than a few minutes," Francis said, and clamped a hand on her knee. "Sofía's coming tomorrow. It'd be nice if you weren't in a coma from exhaustion. Plus we're going to try to have a nice dinner Friday night with *Padrino*, and on Saturday, we're supposed to go to Las Cruces." He grinned and yawned. "I forget what for."

"You win," Estelle said. She pressed the Off button and the television snapped to black.

"Did you ever mention to Francisco that you saw him at school?"

Estelle shook her head. "He's got his secret, I've got mine."

Francis chuckled gently. "That sounds like something *tu mamá* would say, one of her many little *dichos*."

"I'm sure she has several that cover it, *oso*." She frowned, and he reached out with his thumb, stroking the wrinkles over the bridge of her nose.

"What's the matter?"

She sighed and dropped her legal pad on the floor beside the sofa, then settled back into the cushions again.

"I've had one of those 'what if' days, *oso*." He looked quizzical. "Roy and Ivana Hurtado find out that their little darling, their little A-plus, principal's-list daughter, is carrying around a six-inch hat pin for a weapon. And yesterday, or whenever it was, Melody Mears greets me on the tarmac at the school, and I look at *her* inseam, too. What do you think Tom and Deb Mears would say if their daughter pulled a Deena? And it goes downhill from there."

"None of it's your fault, *querida*."

"I know that," she said impatiently. "Carmen is lying in a coma up in Albuquerque, and there's no telling what that's doing to *her* parents. And then when I come home and tell her about Francisco, my mother says to me"—and she switched to a fair imitation of her mother's stately, formal Spanish—"'Are you just now noticing that he has music in his heart?'"

She looked searchingly into her husband's eyes. "*Oso*, did you know that he's musical?"

"No. It doesn't surprise me, but no—I didn't know."

"We've lived in the same house with him for six years," Estelle said. "How could we not know?" Francis didn't reply. Estelle was sure the answer was obvious to both of them. "What if Francisco or Carlos had some enormous talent, and we ignored it?"

"I don't think that they're *ignored, querida*. Sometimes we get busy and maybe we don't spend the time that we should. But we don't *ignore* them."

"Does something like that eventually come out anyway, eventually? Despite numb parents?"

"Something like what?"

"The music that's in his heart."

"I don't know, *mi corazón*. I suppose so."

Estelle stretched her arms all the way over her head, then brought down her hands to cover her face, realizing exactly what her mother had meant.

"What if Teresa Reyes hadn't taken in that little urchin way back when?"

"Estelle…*what if, what if*."

"I'm serious. I was four years old when she adopted me. If she hadn't done that, if I'd stayed a scruffy little *huérfana*, watched over by the good sisters of the Iglesia de Tres Santos… what would I be now?"

"You might be *La Presidente de México*. Who knows."

"*That's* a sobering thought."

"Hey," Francis said with sudden inspiration. "Maybe you would have become a nun yourself and worked your way up to Mother Superior. Or married one of those good-looking Diaz boys right there in Tres Santos and had fourteen children to worry about."

"Ay. What a choice you give me." She pushed herself upright and slipped her arm around her husband's waist. "Promise me something," she said.

"What's that?"

"Help me keep the Saturday promise I made to Francisco."

Francis looked skeptical. "You know how things are, *querida*. If something comes up, he'll have to understand. That's just the way things go."

"Well," she said, "I don't want them to go that way this time."

"Just do your best," he said. "Your mother always says that, I know."

"She also says that being safe and well fed isn't enough."

"Whatever that means."

"That's the trouble, *querida*. I know exactly what she means. And she's right, too."

Chapter Twenty-seven

The German shepherd four doors south sniffed something on the still night air that tickled his attention, and he settled into a rhythmic two-three-two barking. Estelle lay in bed, curled inside the arc of her husband's body, listening. She could feel his even breathing against her left shoulder. Since his earliest days as a medical student, Francis Guzman had been able to grab deep, comfortable sleep whenever the opportunity arose, whether on a hard couch, an empty hospital bed, or even the floor of the staff lounge.

She knew that Francis would sleep until the alarm, the telephone, or one of his children blasted him awake.

Estelle shifted her head just enough to be able to see the digital clock on the dresser across the room. The neighbor's dog stopped barking at 1:26 a.m. For another five minutes, she listened to the sounds of the house and her sleeping family.

Somewhere out in the county, Deputy Jackie Taber was working her regular shift, cruising the back roads, poking into dark corners, leaving the high-speed drone of the interstate to the State Police. Jackie had been sent home earlier in the day to grab a few hours of sleep.

Now, never grumbling about frustration or fatigue, she would plod patiently on, looking and listening. If Estelle turned on the scanner, she knew that she would hear Jackie on the air once in a while, perhaps firing a license number to Dispatcher Brent

Sutherland for an NCIC check, something to do to keep them both awake.

The telephone hadn't rung since early evening, when she'd talked briefly with Sheriff Robert Torrez. The minutes and hours ticked away with the only progress being Carmen Acosta's slow healing, three hundred miles north. The medical staff still would not hazard a guess about how long it might be before Carmen could remember the incident at all. The grim odds were that the blow to the back of her skull had smashed all remnants of the episode from her mind.

Moving the sheet and blanket as little as possible, Estelle slipped out of bed. Her eyes now accustomed to the dark, she crossed to the chair, slipped into her nightgown and robe, closed the bedroom door behind her, and padded out to the living room.

In a moment, the sharp image of Dr. Arnold Gray was calling the county meeting back into session. Estelle plugged in a set of earphones and settled into the rocking chair beside the sofa.

She saw herself enter and take a seat near Mitchell and Torrez. The commission immediately resumed its discussion of providing services to the village, and more than once, one or another of the commissioners would ask about Kevin Zeigler's absence. As if to punctuate the problem, Milton Crowley would swivel the camera each time the county manager's name was mentioned, and even once touched the zoom lens to zero in on Zeigler's empty chair, as if to say, "Aha, see? This is your government in action."

Tinneman made a wisecrack about Zeigler's power lunch, and then Sheriff Torrez rose from his seat and strolled back to the microphone. For the next few minutes, discussion continued, with Torrez answering questions using just enough volume that the commissioners could hear if they paid rapt attention.

Estelle found herself pressing the headphones against her left ear to hear the sheriff. Eventually, their questions for Torrez wound down, and the undersheriff took her place at the small podium.

As she walked to the podium, the camera swung to follow her. Because she had been standing so close to its lens, what the video picked up behind Estelle was fuzzy. Clearly, though, Zeigler's desk was still empty.

Estelle pressed the remote Pause, and then rummaged through her briefcase to find the agenda for the meeting. Item 17 was open for discussion at that moment. Several less weighty items were scheduled to follow, taking the meeting to its projected five p.m. adjournment.

Scanning down the list of action items, Estelle could see that a presentation to the commission by a representative of Baynes, Taylor, and O'Brien of Albuquerque was scheduled to present final paperwork for a bonding issue. Dedication of a portion of a little two-track on the western side of the county as a county road joined a host of other similar items—the sort of day-to-day workings of local government that some folks found fascinating, others found stultifyingly boring, and a few, like Milton Crowley, claimed were cloaks for governmental conspiracy.

Item 28, headed Discussion Items, included such blockbusters as sharing a road grader with the tiny unincorporated village of Newton, a hamlet that lay outside the northern Posadas County limits by about a hundred yards; communication from *The Country Patriot*, which Estelle knew to be Milton Crowley's newsletter; the preliminary report from the county manager about the feasibility of hiring a private contractor for solid-waste and landfill services; and an entry simply titled Resolution of Litigation. The meeting would conclude with an executive session for Personnel Matters and Pending Litigation.

Estelle wasn't surprised by either the personnel session or mention of litigation—that was standard procedure for the county. Employees were hired, evaluated, fired. The county sued and was sued on a regular basis, whether over something as simple as determination of an old fence line, violation of a vendor contract, or failure to pay back taxes. The constant flow of civil paperwork kept Sergeant Howard Bishop busy.

Setting the county meeting back into motion, Estelle listened to herself respond to questions until the tape reached the point where Commissioner Tinneman petulantly repeated that he wanted to talk with the county manager. At that point, it appeared that Crowley wasn't sure whom he wanted to capture on tape. The camera actually wavered a bit with indecision. He swung it hard to the left and recorded Estelle as she left the commission chambers, then panned back to where Zeigler should have been.

Dulci Corona's sharp voice could be heard on the tape, and in a moment, the camera's view returned to the podium. After a few minutes, it filmed Estelle's return as she walked down the aisle and sat beside Mitchell. In a flurry of activity, the final vote was pushed through. The camera caught Tinneman's discomfiture, then captured Estelle leaning toward Chief Mitchell for a final comment before she rose to leave and the commission moved on to other matters.

With a quick stab at the remote, Estelle stopped the tape and ran it in reverse, watching Dr. Gray's gavel spring up from the desk and herself waddle backward to her seat. She kept rewinding until she reached the point where she had left the chamber to inquire about the missing Zeigler, then replayed the tape.

When Crowley panned the camera to the left to catch her exit on tape—and what was so important that he would film that particular moment?—the rear of the chambers was also visible, all the way across the spotty audience to Kevin Zeigler's desk and microphone. A number of people hadn't returned from lunch, including Commissioner Tina Archuleta and *Posadas Register* editor Pam Gardiner. The seat where Don Fulkerson had been sitting, directly in front of Zeigler's desk, was also empty. Predictably, several new faces had joined the audience as well, including an elderly couple at the far side of the chambers. The husband stood his walker in the outside aisle.

Estelle ran the tape forward again. Fifteen minutes after the session resumed, Tina Archuleta returned, grimacing with apology as she took her seat. The others ignored her, except for a pleasant nod of recognition from the commission chairman. Crowley filmed her arrival from the moment the door opened, panning as she walked down through the audience.

The meeting plodded onward through two breaks, and as if concerned that his high-density tape would run out too soon, Crowley became more conservative with his recording, cutting off the video during discussion that he considered to be of no consequence. Estelle wondered how he decided, since not a great percentage of what he taped appeared to be much higher on the consequence scale.

At 4:02 p.m. by the video camera's timer, Crowley panned left once more, as the old man with the walker stood to briefly address the commission about the condition of *his* undedicated two-track that had once been a county road but no longer was and should have been. In the row behind him and close to the aisle, Don Fulkerson had returned, but Ralph Johnson had left, leaving Fulkerson to doze alone.

Estelle glanced at the agenda. The discussion item concerning the contracted services was looming on the agenda's horizon, and Fulkerson had timed it well. Estelle sat forward a little in the rocker and frowned at the screen, but the light in the back of the commission chambers was uncertain, turning individual audience members into shadows.

With Zeigler absent, the commission dropped several agenda items and adjourned early to executive session. The camera panned across the audience, many now standing and milling toward the exits, apparently deciding not to remain and wait for the commission to return from session. The noise level rose as people took the opportunity for chatter and the exchange of gossip tidbits. As she watched their images—some smiling, some sleepy, some bludgeoned numb with boredom—Estelle wondered if someone in those chambers knew exactly where Kevin Zeigler was.

The camera must have been its own form of intimidation, since not one of the audience stopped to talk with Milton Crowley. Maybe sometime in the past, they too had read the sign on his fence, and didn't care to trespass on his personal space.

Far in the back of the house a toilet flushed, its noise muffled by Estelle's earphones. Estelle looked at her watch. She had another hour before Francisco would appear, bright-faced and with mouth in gear.

The tape went blank, then flickered and sprang into life as the commissioners filed back into the hall after the executive session. Dr. Gray pushed them through what little business remained, and at 5:03 by the video timer, he rapped his gavel to end the meeting.

Crowley continued to videotape, the camera intruding into the various private conversations that took place in the natural course of a meeting's end. Finally, the tape ended.

Estelle sat back in the rocker, tapping the remote on her thigh after pressing Rewind. She had seen nothing to pique her interest, other than Zeigler's absence. The huge, numbing possibility loomed clearly. *What if...what if?* she thought. What if she was stumbling blindly down the wrong road entirely? What if Kevin Zeigler's disappearance had nothing whatsoever to do with his work as county manager? Estelle realized with growing frustration that she could say the same thing about every other avenue, too.

For nearly an hour, she sat in the rocking chair, doodling on the legal pad. In half an hour, she'd blackened in enough semicircles to represent a fair-sized pile of discarded tires, with a little one standing at the top.

Chapter Twenty-eight

Behind Kevin Zeigler's home on Candelaria Court, a neat but homely concrete wall four feet high defined the backyard. On the concrete slab patio, two white wire chairs and an umbrella table occupied one side, and a fancy propane barbecue grill dominated the other. Two large ceramic pots sat empty at each far corner of the patio, as if Zeigler had planned something colorful but had never slowed down enough to add potting soil, seeds, and water.

Estelle sat at the umbrella table and watched the morning sun boil up over the eastern prairie. The light breeze out of the north was cool, a delightful mix with the promised unseasonable heat of that early November morning.

Earlier, during the few moments with her family, she had reveled in their simple presence. She had enjoyed little Francisco's excitement as he bundled his cache of aluminum foil into his backpack. The bus had picked him up, and Estelle had driven Carlos to Little Bear, leaving her mother a few treasured minutes alone with Dr. Francis—next to her daughter, the old woman's favorite person on the planet.

But during all of the morning rituals, something nagged in the back of Estelle's mind. Now, she sat quietly at Zeigler's table in his backyard, the insulated cup of hot tea held between both hands, the metal of the table refreshingly cold to the touch. To the north, the prairie rumbled into a series of dips and rolls. The sun shadows created a dramatic dark scar out of Arroyo del Cerdo, and Estelle watched the patterns change, letting her mind roam.

The early-morning report from Albuquerque listed Carmen in guarded condition, but physicians had been optimistic. Although still in a restless semicoma, the teenager's vital signs were strong. Estelle had felt a sharp twinge of sympathy as she tried to imagine what sort of images might still be rampaging in the girl's mind…a torture that would likely continue for years, surfacing without warning to drag Carmen through the experience yet again.

Freddy and Juanita Acosta remained in the city, but Armand Acosta, Freddy's cousin, had driven to Albuquerque and picked up Mauro and Tony, returning to Posadas on Wednesday evening. Armand's home on MacArthur was four doors from Sheriff Robert Torrez's, and Torrez said that he had kept an eye on the place during the night. The boys hadn't roamed. Torrez, who knew the Acosta tribe well, was certain that Armand and Tawnya would make sure that all four youngsters would be in school. Whether the two boys would stay there for the entire day was open to question.

Somewhere on Candelaria, another car engine started, and Estelle arose and stretched. The first bell at school would ring at 8:07 a.m., in five minutes. She strolled back around the house, ducking under the yellow tape, and drove to the high school across town, arriving a minute before the bell. The parking lot and courtyard were flooded with students savoring the last few moments of freedom. Here and there, Estelle saw duty teachers, some standing with colleagues, some mingling with groups of students.

The undersheriff sat in the car, watching. Like a large flock of birds, the students began moving toward the school an instant before the bell rang, as if they could somehow hear the silent transistor circuits click into place. Two minutes later, the parking lot and grounds were empty, the day officially begun.

Estelle got out of the car and walked to the front doors. One of them opened, held for her by a tall, incredibly thin young man with a pageboy haircut and terrible complexion. "Hi," he said, and immediately turned his attention to a mammoth backpack that rested on one of the wooden chairs, all zippers yawning open.

Margie Edwards was trying to hand something to the high school principal, Charlie Maestas, while Maestas talked to two animated young ladies. Maestas saw Estelle, held up a hand to silence the chatter, and then shooed the two from the outer office.

"I'm sorry I missed you the other day," Maestas said, extending his hand. His suit appeared to be two sizes too small for his short, blocky frame, accentuated by his habit of buttoning the jacket over his rotund body. His grip was moist and perfunctory. "Come on in," he said, holding open the door to his office.

Estelle nodded and smiled at Margie, then stepped inside. Maestas closed the door and immediately walked to his desk as if he needed to be in place before a conversation started.

"I need a few minutes with Mauro and Tony Acosta, Mr. Maestas," Estelle said.

"No problem…if they're here," Maestas said. He tapped the keyboard of his computer and waited. "What can you tell me?"

"About what, sir?"

He shot a quick glance at Estelle, and then his eyes shifted back to the computer screen. "We're all concerned," he said, tapped the keyboard again, and straightened up. He brought his hands together in a silent clap and held them that way. "Yesterday at the administrative council meeting, Ms. Dooley gave us a rundown of what happened at the middle school with Deena Hurtado." He paused as if he expected Estelle to add something. When she didn't, he said, "Is this hat pin thing the newest trend? Is that the latest fad? If they're on campus, we need to move on it."

"I don't know, sir. I don't know how widespread they are. I would hope that it's limited, but we just don't know yet."

"Sit, sit," he said impatiently, waving toward a large chair in front of his desk.

"Actually, sir, I need to see the Acosta boys." She glanced at her watch. "We're running sort of tight today."

"Ah, well," Maestas said, with more than a hint of disappointment, "I can understand that." He glanced back at the computer screen. "Who first? Or do you want them together?"

"I'd like to talk with Mauro first," she said.

"He's in Metals One right now, with Mr. Fernandez. I'll call for him."

"It would be helpful if you wouldn't use the PA, sir. Maybe you and I could just walk down there and get him."

"Sure, we can do that. You want to use this office for home base?"

Estelle smiled with just a hint of politic apology. "I'd like to talk with him outside, I think. We might just take a little walk."

"All right," Maestas said, frowning. "Have you been in touch with his parents?"

"Yes, sir."

"How's the sister?"

"Holding her own, I think. We won't know if there's any permanent damage for some time."

He looked askance at Estelle. "You don't think the boys had anything to do with this business, do you?"

"I hope not," she replied.

"Mauro and Tony are the sort of boys—" he hesitated, searching for just the right thing to say "—who really *need* to be here. Do you understand what I mean?"

"I believe so."

He nodded sharply. "Let's go find 'em."

The metals shop was at the far end of the school complex, taking up what looked like it had once been a large garage, complete with two huge overhead doors that yawned open. Nine students were clustered in a small classroom off to one side, most of them attentive as Mr. Fernandez explained something on the chalkboard. Estelle remained just outside, and in a moment the principal appeared with Mauro Acosta in tow.

The ninth grader walked as if he were a hunchback, baggy pants sagging under a long-tailed, checkered flannel shirt. His olive drab army belt flapped a foot too long.

"Hello, Mauro," Estelle said. "I'm Undersheriff Estelle Guzman. I'd like to talk with you for a few minutes."

"Okay." He shrugged and glanced at Maestas.

"If you need me for anything, you know where I am," the principal said. He reached out and patted Mauro on the shoulder. "You too, guy."

"Let's take a walk," Estelle said. As they strolled along the metal building, Mauro shuffled with his hands in his pockets. It appeared to Estelle as if he had to constantly work at keeping his trousers in the perfect position of suspense. Between the gravity-defying trousers and carelessly tied shoes, running wasn't on the agenda.

Estelle paused at a runty elm tree just inside the chain-link fence. The ground around the tree's base was littered with cigarette butts.

"I'm sorry that I didn't have a chance to talk to you before you had to go to Albuquerque," she said. "The doctors say that your sister is making some progress."

"Yeah." He nodded, avoiding eye contact. He managed an assessing glance at Estelle, his gaze running down her figure, and he hunched his shoulders a bit more to make sure he was giving away no secrets.

"I need to know about the hat pins, Mauro." His eyebrows twitched. "We know that you sharpened the one that your sister had with her. We also know that you sharpened at least one for Deena Hurtado."

He shook his head slightly and regarded the distant horizon.

"I don't imagine that Mr. Fernandez knows much about that, does he?" The boy remained silent, and Estelle stepped closer, lowering her voice. Mauro was her height, and she shifted to stand directly in front of him, forcing him to look at her. "None of that is of much interest to me just now, Mauro. You're a smart young man. You know as well as I do what the consequences are if you're caught carrying a weapon on school property. Even if it's just a quickie sharpening job for a friend." She gave him the chance to reply, but he remained silent. "So now you know," she said. "Tell me about your neighbors."

His eyes registered surprise at the sudden change of topic.

"Wha—" he said with a frown, as if the final *t* took too much energy to pronounce.

"Tell me about Kevin Zeigler," she said.

His head jerked back a little as if to say, "Why are you asking me?"

"Did you talk with him in the last couple of days?"

"No."

"How about his roommate, William Page?"

"Why would I talk to him?" Mauro said. "He don't even live here."

"When was the last time you saw him?"

Mauro shrugged.

"Last weekend, when Mr. Page was visiting…did you go riding with them then? On the bikes?"

"I don't ride no bikes," he said, as if the very thought was ridiculous. Estelle managed not to smile at the thought of the baggy Pants and untied laces tangled hopelessly in the bicycle's chain. But then, Zeigler's carefully composed photos had shown Mauro capable of a different image than simply that of the school's thug.

"Did Tony?"

"No. Well, I don't know." He shrugged again.

"Mauro, during the past week or so, have you seen anyone next door besides Kevin and Mr. Page? Anyone at all?"

The boy shook his head.

"They don't have company very often?"

"I don't see nobody there," he said. "Just them two."

"They don't have other folks over? For dinners? Maybe back-yard barbecues? That sort of thing?"

"No."

"Does it bother you that Kevin and Mr. Page live next door, Mauro?"

His eyes became wary. "Why should it bother me?"

"I just thought that it might."

Mauro shrugged. "Why, 'cause they're queer? It don't matter to me what they do."

Estelle relaxed backward and rested a hand against the tree. "I understand that you're a pretty talented mechanic. I saw your car, in the backyard."

"It's okay."

"Maybe you'll have it running one of these days."

"I guess."

"Did you offer to help Kevin change the tire on his truck?"

He looked puzzled. "What tire?"

Estelle nodded. "He had some trouble there. I thought maybe you knew about it."

"I don't know about no flat tire," he replied with a flash of indignation, an instant assumption that some adult, somewhere, thought he was responsible for something he hadn't done.

"Mauro, this is an important question. I want you to think hard before you answer, all right? Do you know anything—anything at all—about the attack on your sister? Do you know who might have done it?" He shook his head emphatically. "Who did she have an argument with?"

"She didn't have no argument with nobody," he said with considerable heat. "Not something like that. Not what happened to her."

"What about the fight at the volleyball game?"

"That wasn't nothing, man."

"No problems with Paul Otero?"

He grimaced with disgust. "He's a wuss."

"Mauro, we need to find the person who broke into your house and attacked your sister. We're going to need your help."

For the first time, Mauro Acosta looked directly at Estelle, his dark brown eyes unblinking and unwavering. "If I knew who did that, I'd tell you," he said, and for a moment he sounded a decade older than he was.

"Mauro, I want to tell you something," Estelle said, and she lowered her voice another notch. "This is just between you and me, okay? Do you know why we're curious about your neighbors?"

"Armand said that Kevin went missing."

"That's right, Mauro. And that's too much of a coincidence, Kevin going missing just when your sister is attacked. Don't you think so?"

"He didn't have nothing to do with it," Mauro said emphatically.

"How do you know that?"

"I just do," he said simply. "Him and Page might be all queer and stuff like that, but he's still okay. I mean, he always treats us okay."

"He's a good neighbor?"

"Yeah."

"He's been over once or twice for picnics, stuff like that?" She smiled at Mauro. "Maybe tried to break up a fight or two?"

The boy looked down at the cigarette butts, close to smiling himself.

"Yeah, maybe."

"If Kevin saw someone next door attacking your sister, what do you think he'd do?"

Mauro shrugged. "He'd probably call the cops."

"He's always got a phone handy, doesn't he."

"Yeah. Or that radio of his in the truck."

"Would he come over himself, do you think? Even before the cops got there? If there was really serious trouble?"

"Sure. He'd jump right in the middle of it. I mean, he's pretty tough."

"But he didn't, this time."

"That's 'cause he wasn't there. If he was, he woulda."

Estelle drew a card from her pocket. "Mauro, I know that talking to the cops isn't your favorite thing to do, but if you remember something—any little thing that you saw or heard—will you call me? Anytime. Even if you wake up in the middle of the night. Give me a call."

He accepted the card, read it carefully, and tucked it into his back pocket. "Yeah," he said. "Did you talk with Tony?"

"Not yet."

He nodded and accepted that as a sufficient answer.

"I'm sorry about your sister, Mauro. We're doing all we can. And I appreciate your help." She reached out and squeezed his shoulder. He didn't pull away.

Chapter Twenty-nine

Tony Acosta looked pleased to leave his Language Arts class, locked down as it was in the middle of a vocabulary test. What Bob Torrez would have described as Tony's "shit-eating grin" faded when he saw Estelle.

"Tony, this is Undersheriff Guzman," Maestas said after the classroom door had closed and they'd stepped far enough away that the other kids wouldn't hear them. "She needs to talk to you for a little bit." Maestas nodded and stretched out a hand toward Estelle. "Stop back by the office when you're finished, all right?" Somehow, Maestas made the question sound as if he'd said, "I'm still the principal around here."

"Thanks, sir," Estelle said. She motioned toward the exit sign at the end of the hallway. "Let's go outside," she said to Tony. The door opened onto a small landing with a railing, a perfect outdoor conference area.

She read the worried look on Tony's plump face correctly, because he visibly brightened when she said, "Carmen's going to be all right, Tony. That's the latest word from your folks."

"Did they say when they're coming back?" he asked.

"No…it might be a couple days yet. Look, I know one of the other deputies has talked to you already, but I had just a few questions, all right? A few things to clear up."

"Sure." He didn't look sure. Estelle watched his face and decided that Tony didn't have as much delinquency baggage as his little brother. The older boy had no trouble making eye contact. He favored simple jeans and a heavy-metal T-shirt that would have gotten him expelled a decade before. While Mauro worked at hiding his lean, trim form under baggy gangbanger clothes, Tony seemed relaxed inside his skin, his pudgy build making him seem the younger of the two brothers.

"When you and Mauro left school on Tuesday after your fifth-period classes—at noon—did you go home, or anywhere near Candelaria?"

"No, ma'am. I went over to a buddy's apartment. I don't know where Mauro went." Tony's version of the afternoon differed in essentials from Deena Hurtado's scenario, but the boy *might* have forgotten his visit to the convenience store…or Deena might have fabricated it.

"So at no time on Tuesday did you happen to see any strangers around your street? Anyone you didn't know?"

"No, ma'am."

"Who does Carmen know that might have assaulted her like that? Is there anyone?" He shook his head. "Not Paul Otero?"

"Nah," Tony said quickly.

"You're sure?"

"Yeah. Paul's a lover, not a fighter." His cherubic face lit up in a broad smile that showed an expanse of braces. "Like me."

"How well do you know Kevin Zeigler, Tony?"

The boy looked surprised. "Well enough to know *he* didn't do it."

"You sound pretty positive."

"Well, I am. He just wouldn't. He's a friend. He's our neighbor. Did you guys find out where he went yet?"

"No, not yet. Tell me about him."

"About Mr. Zeigler? He's a neat guy." Tony stopped suddenly, looking as if he wished he could retract what he'd said. "I mean, you know. He's okay."

"You've gone riding a time or two with him and William Page, I understand."

"Yeah. They got these really bad bikes, you know. I mean, they're about as expensive as a car."

"That's what you rode when the three of you went up on the mesa a couple of weeks ago?"

Tony nodded.

"Not your own bike?"

"I ain't got a bike right now. The frame broke."

"So you rode Kevin's mountain bike?"

"Yeah. He let me take it."

"What did he ride?"

"He took one of the racing bikes. William had the other mountain bike."

"You had fun?"

Tony hesitated. "Well, it was okay." A slow rueful smile crept across his face. "Those guys don't just go out to play around. I mean, they're *fast*."

"Tough workout, huh?"

"Yes, ma'am. *Very* tough. I thought I was going to die."

"All the time you were with them, or any other time, they never talked about trouble with anybody?"

"Trouble?"

"Sure. Arguments they might have had with someone… disagreements, that sort of thing."

"No, not that I heard. They're kind of cool."

"Kind of cool."

"Yeah. I mean, I know about 'em, you know. I think they're kinda funny, sometimes. Like a couple of old ladies." He limp-wristed a small wave. "But they're okay. They don't give me a hard time."

"Why would they?"

"Well," Tony said, and hesitated. "That's what people think, you know."

"Do you know a lot of people who talk about them?"

"No. Not a lot. But it's not like it's any big secret or anything." He shook his head in wonder. "For a long time, my dad didn't know they were gay. When he found out, he didn't know what to do."

"What's there to do?"

"Well, that's what my ma told him."

"Tell me about the last ride you guys did."

"We just went up on the mesa."

"Just?" She smiled at Tony. "That's quite a climb."

"Yeah. I felt kinda dumb. I had to get off and walk, and here these two old guys are, just cruisin' right up. Ridin' circles around me."

"You didn't see anybody on that ride? Or when you came back?"

"No. Well, the guys at the dump. We saw them. Kevin said something kinda mad, but I didn't hear what it was. He said something to William."

"By 'the guys at the dump,' do you mean the landfill manager? Or the young man who works for him?"

"Both. They were both right there at the little house. You know where the scales are? They saw us, and one of 'em lets out this real loud whistle. You know, like you hear on the street."

"A wolf whistle, you mean?"

"That's it. One of 'em did that, and Kevin just waved a little, kinda like this"—and he rotated his wrist. "Like he was sayin' 'asshole.' I was a ways behind 'em, and I didn't hear what he said. Just something to William, you know, like you say to someone when you don't want someone else to hear."

"And then you went on up the hill? Up the mesa?"

"All the way to the rim." He shook his head wearily. "By then I was about half dead."

"It must have been fun coming down, though."

"Not really. The road's rough, and it's just about as much work as goin' up." He flashed braces again. By the time he grew into himself, Estelle decided, Tony Acosta was going to be a lady-killer in his own right. "Maybe a little better on the paved part."

"That's the way you came back into town? On County Forty-three?" Tony nodded. "What did you guys talk about, mostly?"

Tony stared at the steps, thinking hard. "Mr. Page talked a lot about his business. What he does with computer imaging and stuff. It sounds neat. He invited me to stop by his place in Socorro if I got up that way. By his business."

"But neither one of them ever talked about anybody they've had troubles with?"

"No, ma'am."

"Tony, let me ask you something. If Kevin had seen someone—let's say a stranger—assaulting your sister, what do you think he would have done?"

"He would have climbed right in the middle of it," Tony said without hesitation. He ducked his head in embarrassment. "Me and my brother were goin' at it once. My folks weren't home. He was out back and heard us, and came over. I thought Mauro was going to throw a punch at him when he grabbed him by the arm, but Kevin just climbed into his face, you know? Kinda that wild, 'go ahead, punk, I dare you' look? So yeah—he woulda done something. Is that what you think happened?"

"I don't know, Tony. We're not sure what happened. We're hoping that before much longer, your sister can tell us."

He shook his head slowly in disbelief. "I just can't see someone doin' that."

"Did you know that your sister carried a hat pin in her jeans?"

"That dork," Tony said. "You know what I told her last week? In fact"—and he suddenly looked very mature and sure of himself—"it was just before that volleyball game where she and Deena had their fight?"

"What did you tell her?"

"I told her that if she kept wearin' that stupid thing, someone was going to rip it out of her hand and shove it right up her ass." He blushed. "Really. That's what I told her."

"I'm sorry that you were right, in a manner of speaking," Estelle said.

"Yeah. Me, too. Too bad it wasn't her ass." He held his shoulders up and made a face. "They don't think it went into her brain though. That's really gross."

Estelle handed Tony one of her cards, and he regarded it thoughtfully. "This is just in case you remember something else that you think I should know, Tony."

"We're going to miss having them around," he said. "I mean Kevin and William."

"We'll do our best, Tony."

"Yeah, but how often when someone goes missing like this do you ever find 'em alive? I mean, Kevin didn't just go to the pizza place and forget to come back."

"I wish we had an answer for that." Estelle thumbed the latch on the outside door. "You'd better get back to class."

"Hey, no rush," he said with a smile. "It was just a test. I already finished."

"Aced it?"

He cocked his head in easy self-assurance and stepped back inside, tucking Estelle's business card in his hip pocket as he did so.

"What a charmer," Estelle murmured. She walked around the end of the building, cutting cross-lots toward her county car. She didn't bother stopping to chat with the principal, Charlie Maestas. Back in the car, she keyed the radio.

"PCS, three ten is ten-eight at the high school."

"Ten-four, three ten." Estelle waited, but no further message followed. No one else was having any better luck than she was.

Chapter Thirty

A pickup truck loaded with elm limbs towering precariously over the cab was parked on the scales in front of the landfill office, and the attendant leaned on the door, chatting with the driver. His clipboard was tucked under his arm, and when Estelle pulled into the landfill, he glanced back at her and then continued his conversation.

The undersheriff turned hard to the left and parked the county car with its nose to the chain-link fence, beside a flashy motorcycle and a dilapidated imported pickup truck. She got out and stretched. The landfill featured an impressive view, but she knew that its location had been one of Kevin Zeigler's pet peeves. More than once at county meetings, she'd heard his comments about the location. To bury refuse *above* the village, even though the location was five miles out of town, made no sense to Zeigler.

An area in the bleak eastern prairie, out beyond the MacInernys' gravel pit, had been offered to the county. To relocate the land-fill, and perhaps to then hire a private contractor to manage it, were decisions toward which the county moved with the speed of an inchworm.

Off to the left, Estelle could see the dirt two-track that wound up the mesa from town, and she could imagine the three cyclists—one pushing his bike, heart pounding in his ears, sweat soaking his shirt.

"Help you?"

Estelle turned and smiled at Bart Kurtz. "I was sightseeing," she said.

"Hey, no charge for that." Kurtz turned and watched the loaded pickup waddle over the rough ground toward the edge of the current refuse pit. "They don't always go where we tell 'em," he observed soberly. Of medium height and beefy build, Kurtz was working on a potbelly that looked as if he were pregnant.

When the truck turned away from the pit and headed toward a large pile of limb wood and similar burnable trash far in the back of the open, graded area, Kurtz slapped the clipboard for some sort of emphasis, and turned to look at Estelle. "You just cruisin'?"

"As a matter of fact, that's exactly what I'm doing," Estelle said.

"Don ain't here just yet," Kurtz said as if he didn't actually believe the undersheriff's answer. He ambled over to the office door and hung the clipboard on a nail.

"That's okay," Estelle said. "Everything been quiet up here?"

Kurtz laughed. A dentist would have recoiled at the sight. "*That's* the truth," he said. He squinted into the sun, watching as the pickup backed up to the massive pile of branches. A man and small boy pulled the elm limbs off the truck, sailing them onto the edge of the pile.

"Is that your bike?" Estelle asked.

"Nah. That's Don's. That's his toy."

"Nice machine."

He turned and looked at Estelle. "You ride, do you?"

"No."

One of the village garbage trucks groaned off the county highway onto the dirt road to the landfill. "You might want to step over this way," Kurtz said, and Estelle did so. The truck pulled onto the scale, the driver expertly centering the eight rear wheels on the plate. The driver looked as if he might have been one of Mauro Acosta's classmates. He lifted a hand in salute, then lurched the truck forward when Kurtz signaled.

When the big diesel was far enough away that Estelle could make herself heard without shouting, she asked, "Everyone weighs?"

"Everyone. All the time. But if it don't come up to five hundred pounds, we don't charge. Like them over there." He waved a hand at the pickup with its load of tree trimmings.

"I didn't think so. I don't ever remember paying. Did the county manager come by here earlier this week?"

Kurtz wiped his hands on his county-issue dark green work clothes, then groped a cigarette out of his breast pocket. He took his time, examining the little butane lighter before lighting it as if it were a complex operation requiring all his skill and attention. "You mean yesterday?"

"Whenever."

"Didn't see him yesterday. Nope."

"How about Tuesday?"

"We aren't open on Tuesdays, so I wouldn't know. You'd have to ask Don."

The large white sign on the chain-link gate, now pushed open against the fence, announced landfill hours for the public from 7 a.m. to 5 p.m., Wednesday through Sunday. "The boss is here on Tuesdays?"

Kurtz sucked on the cigarette, inhaling deeply. "Well, sometimes he is," he said, as if loath to give away too much information. "Paperwork and the like. He takes care of all of that."

"Are you part-time, or..."

Kurtz shook his head. "Wish I was. No. I'm here, all the time."

"Don, too?"

"Well, sure. He generally takes Saturday off, though. Makes up for coming in on Tuesdays, I guess." He examined the cigarette, ticking off the ash with his little finger. "He don't like to miss the flea market."

"You're talking about the one down in Pershing Park sometimes?"

"Oh, hell, no," Kurtz said. "He goes on down to Cruces for that big one. Hits it every week." He nodded at where the village truck was disgorging its load, like a giant insect expelling a large, compact dropping that crashed out onto the graded apron just short of the pit. "You wouldn't believe the things that some people throw away."

"Oh, I think I would," Estelle said agreeably. "You said Don's coming in today?"

"Oh, he's already been here. We got a blown hydraulic hose on the Cat." He stepped out from the building. "He just ran down to pick up a new one at Clark's."

"There's always something, isn't there," Estelle said. The bulldozer was parked beside an amazing pile of junked appliances. Impressive as it was, the dozer was dwarfed by the collection of hot-water heaters, stoves, refrigerators, washers, and dryers. "I always supposed that with the number of appliances we see shot full of holes out on the mesa, there wouldn't be many left for you guys," Estelle said, and Kurtz grunted a derisive chuckle.

More traffic turned into the landfill road, this time a small station wagon followed by another pickup truck sagging under a load of old lumber.

"I'll get out of your way," Estelle said as Kurtz reached for his clipboard.

She walked out along the northern fence line, taking her time and paying attention to her footing. Bits of metal, wire, plastic, and rotten wood littered the ground, churned and mixed with the red soil by the constant working of the dozer and dump traffic, presenting a thousand ways to puncture a tire.

The appliance graveyard formed a white mountain, beside another mountain created by discarded tires, and Estelle headed for that. The village garbage truck pulled away from the pit, its fat tires churning up thick clouds of red dust.

Skirting the foot of the appliance mountain, she stopped to look at a stove that had either tumbled off like a loose rock after a rain, or had been set aside. The kitchen range was so new that the manufacturer's stickers were still affixed to the enameled top, but the fancy stove was junk. Perhaps it had fallen from a truck, smashing its delicate glass face and circuit boards against the pavement.

The tire mountain was several times larger than the one at the county maintenance yard, the bulk of the collection from passenger cars and light trucks.

Estelle skirted the pile and stopped beside the dozer. Sitting in the hot sun, the mammoth machine exuded its own body odor of diesel and grease. The two great frost hooks were poised like stingers from the bulldozer's rear end. A toolbox rested crosswise on the polished, raw steel of several track cleats, a selection of wrenches scattered around it.

The hose that had blown was small, no larger in diameter than a finger. The rich fluid, jetting out under pressure, had soaked a fan-shaped stain on the dozer's yellow flank. She started to walk around the front of the machine, missed her footing, and managed to catch herself by slamming a hand against the top edge of the blade.

"Careful there," a voice behind her called out. She turned, brushing off her hands, and saw Don Fulkerson walking toward her. He carried a length of black hose, the fittings on the end clean, bright brass. "You gotta watch where you're putting your feet around this place," he said, and winked.

"I got to looking at other things," Estelle said. She extended a hand in greeting, and Fulkerson tossed the new hose into the toolbox, then shook hands. His grip was firm, his hands rough and work hardened. He had cultivated an impressive spade-shaped beard, just starting to turn white around the edges. Estelle could picture him leaning back on his rushing motorcycle, the wind cushioning his beard upward like a platter.

"You thinking of taking up diesel mechanics?" Fulkerson said, and winked again. He pulled at one of the wide suspenders that held up his Carhartts.

"I don't think so," she said. "Bart said it blew a hose?"

"That's what she did. No big deal, though. We'll have her goin' here in about ten minutes." He patted the track affectionately.

Estelle stepped away from the dozer and watched an elderly man unload his Volvo station wagon, sailing one item at a time onto the pile. "I don't think most people understand what a big operation this is," she said.

Fulkerson leaned comfortably against the dozer's left track, crossed his boots, and fished out first a pack of cigarettes, and then a bag of tobacco and sheaf of papers. He slipped the ready-mades back into his pocket and proceeded to roll a cigarette. "Keeps us busy," he said. "You want some coffee?" He nodded at the thermos, nestled in a jacket stuffed in a bed of hydraulic plumbing under the dozer's seat.

"No thanks."

"What's with Zeigler?" Fulkerson asked. "I assume that's who you're looking for. I don't think I've ever seen so many cop cars roamin' around the county."

"I don't know what's with him," Estelle said. "I wish we did."

"You think someone dumped him up here?" The crow's-feet around his sparkling blue eyes crinkled, and he winked—an expression that appeared now to be more of a tic than amused conspiracy.

"We're checking every place we can think of," Estelle said pleasantly. "You wouldn't believe some of the nooks and corners of this county that we've found in the past day or so."

"You know what I think?" He lit the cigarette with a strike match, popped expertly with a thumbnail. "I think he's in Mexico."

"Really?"

"Sure."

"What makes you think that, sir?"

"Well, you think of the opportunity," he said, his round, ruddy face settling into an expression of satisfaction, pleased that he should know the answers. "You think of all the money that guy handles in the course of his job." He inhaled deeply. "That's a heck of a temptation, don't you think?"

"I suppose it could be."

"Damn right." Fulkerson arose, stretched up, and brought down the thermos. He unscrewed the cup and cap and poured. "You sure?"

"No thanks, sir. I'm not much of a coffee drinker." A light aroma other than coffee, creamer, and sugar drifted out to Estelle's nostrils.

Fulkerson spun the thermos cap back on, tossed the container back into its bed, and settled back against the dozer. "So that's what I figure. Cut and run." He took a thoughtful sip. "Mexico's just only over the hill, right? I guess you know all about that."

"Somehow I can't picture Kevin Zeigler down in old Mexico," Estelle said.

Fulkerson shrugged. "You never know what someone like that is going to do."

"I suppose not."

"'Course, nobody asks me." He sipped the coffee, looked appreciative, and winked at Estelle again. "I keep tellin' the president, there, you know, 'Before you go doing something stupid, you just ask old Don, here.' He never does."

Estelle touched the toe of her shoe to the bulldozer's track. "Tell me, then. What do you think happened?"

Fulkerson relaxed back and took a longer pull of the coffee, exhaling smoke at the same time through his nose. "Well, you know…it's hard to say. But I wouldn't be surprised if he just up and skipped. Like I say, there's lots of opportunity."

"But there aren't bags of loose currency just lying around the county building, sir. Everything is done with purchase orders and checks."

He looked at Estelle with sympathy at her lack of under-standing. "There's *always* ways, little lady. There's *always* ways."

"Did you happen to see him in the past couple of days?"

"Sure." Fulkerson ground out the cigarette against a steel track cleat. "He come up here Tuesday early. And after that, we were all at the county meeting, wasting the rest of the day."

"Do you remember what time he was here that morning?"

"Just after I got here. It'd be about seven-ten or so."

"But you're closed on Tuesdays. Did he drive up here for any particular reason?"

"Well, Tuesday was the commission meeting. I was up here getting some paperwork ready. Miss Ziggy had requested some facts and figures, and I guess he thought I might forget to bring 'em along. So he stopped by."

"Miss Ziggy?"

Fulkerson's face lost some of its Santa Claus innocence, and he let his smirk explain the nickname.

"And then he left with the paperwork, and that was it?"

"Yup."

"Huh," Estelle said, and shook her head. "You didn't see him at any other time after that, other than at the meeting?"

"Just at the county meeting. You were there." He winked.

"Did the two of you meet back here over the noon hour?"

Fulkerson frowned, his face wrinkling as if to say, "What, are you nuts?" "If he showed up here, he had the place to himself," he said. "I had better things to do."

"I noticed that the commissioners dumped the agenda item about the landfill," Estelle said. "That was Mr. Zeigler's brainchild, wasn't it?"

"You can say that again," Fulkerson said fervently. "What a goddamn waste of money *that* little boondoggle would have been."

"So you don't agree with him, then."

"Sheeeit," Fulkerson said with considerable disgust. "That's the last thing a little county like this one needs is some outsider company running the landfill. Ziggy's a fan of *consolidation*," he said, emphasizing the word as if it were a whiff of sulfur dioxide. "*Stream*line everything. Like the village giving up its police department. Now he's got his hands on that. You just watch, young lady." He winked knowingly. "You be careful of that one."

Estelle watched an old, battered dump truck wheeze across the soft earth toward the growing pile.

"Why don't they just back up to the pit and dump it in?" she asked, and Fulkerson turned to follow her gaze.

He laughed. "You give a jackass a chance to do something stupid, and he will, young lady. If we let 'em back up to the pit, sure as hell someone's going to go too far." He shrugged at the inevitability of it all. "It's just easier to doze the pile into the pit at the end of the day than have to chain someone's ass out of there."

"Ah—I didn't think about that."

"We keep a watch on 'em, just the same. You tell ten folks where to go and where to dump, and nine of 'em will do like you say."

"And then there's number ten," Estelle said.

"You got that exactly right." He winked.

"I'd better let you get back to work," Estelle said. She handed Fulkerson one of her cards. "Just in case."

"Best of luck to you," he said. "You need anything else, you know where we are."

Instead of returning to her car, Estelle walked the fifty yards to the north edge of the pit, taking her time across the deep ruts chewed by the dozer. She reached the edge and looked down. Ravens working the pile ignored her, talking to each other about their discoveries, occasionally flapping up and out to perch on the boundary fence or soar off toward the mesa.

The landfill was no place for a retired bulldozer with no muscle, she reflected. The pit appeared to be about a hundred feet wide and perhaps three or four hundred feet long. The dozer had bladed at least twenty feet deep, right down to bedrock. Dirt from the original excavation had been pushed up and out the opposite end into a respectable mountain that, when the trench was full of refuse, would be bladed back as fill and cover.

At the moment, the pit had swallowed a tiny fraction of its capacity. Maybe it would be months before Fulkerson had to gouge another trench parallel to this one. She knew that the county owned nearly a thousand acres, enough to bury trash for a long, long time.

Estelle thrust her hands in her pockets, paying attention to the edge of the pit. Far in the bottom where it had bounced clear was a baby carriage. From a distance, there appeared to be little wrong with it. Estelle wondered if it would appear on Fulkerson's table at the Las Cruces flea market.

The aroma from the pile was moderate, but as the sun baked and fried, and by the time the dozer pushed a blanket of soil over the week's offerings, the effluvia would pack a punch.

The sides of the trench were neatly cut and perfectly vertical. In two places, Estelle saw telltale gouges where someone—the one out of ten—had backed too close, crumbling the edge. Most of the refuse was bagged household trash, but Estelle could see where a few customers had managed to ignore directions. A handful of tires were mixed in with the rest, instead of making it to the recycling pile. An old refrigerator, facedown in the dirt, had been pitched in before either Bart or Don could direct it toward the appliance mountain. Twenty feet from the growing pile, a huge tree stump had crashed into the pit and rolled to a stop.

The driver of a fancy dually pickup truck paused after slamming the tailgate shut, and watched Estelle as she walked along the border of the pit toward the dump station.

"You lose something?" he called. A young man, he appeared dressed for a game of golf.

"No, thanks. Just checking for bodies." She smiled at the man, and he started to reply when he noticed the sheriff's badge on her belt. He looked uncertain, glancing back down into the pit.

"Oh, yeah," he said, as if he'd caught the joke.

"You have a nice day," Estelle said. By the time she'd reached her car, two more vehicles had entered, and the constant clouds of red dust settled in her hair and on her clothes.

"Find what you need?" Bart Kurtz asked.

"Thanks a lot," she replied, then stopped suddenly in afterthought. "When do you guys cover the trash? You don't wait until the trench is full, do you?"

"Every Sunday night, Sheriff."

"Just kind of a thin layer, then?"

"Enough to keep things from blowin'," Kurtz said. "Maybe six inches or a foot. Pack 'er down, cover it up."

"And every Sunday you do that?"

"Yup. Sunday after we close. Lots of folks come out on weekends, you know. Come Sunday afternoon, we push the day's drop-off pile into the trench, then we cover it all up."

"Pretty simple. But you push the drop-off pile into the pit every day?"

"Sure enough we do. Otherwise it'd blow all over hell and gone."

"I would think so."

"Yeah, it don't take no rocket scientist." He looked off toward where Don Fulkerson still worked on his thermos of coffee and the bulldozer.

"Thanks again," Estelle said. Back in her car, she sat for a moment, looking out the side window at Fulkerson's pickup truck, an '80s-vintage four-wheel-drive Chevy C20. A black headache rack, the kind favored by plumbers who need to haul lengths of pipe, reached out over the cab. Fulkerson had parked between a trio of fifty-five-gallon drums labeled WASTE OIL PRODUCTS and a trailer loaded with what appeared to be used concrete blocks and paving bricks.

She turned the county car's ignition key. In the distance she heard the staccato bellow as the landfill's bulldozer surged into life, almost as if the one key had connected both machines.

Chapter Thirty-one

"I have a question," Dr. Francis Guzman stage-whispered in Estelle's ear. "What does the work of an engineering prodigy look like?"

"I don't think we need to worry," Estelle whispered back. She straightened up from her examination of something made from Popsicle sticks labeled *Moon Bace* in strong, red crayon. Her husband was doing his best to keep a straight face.

Across the room, Sofía Tournál had both Francisco and Carlos in tow…actually it was Francisco doing the towing while Sofía provided the guidance. A safe distance behind the trio, Estelle's mother shuffled from one display to the next, keeping a firm grip on her walker, with Myra Delgado at her elbow. The two appeared to be exchanging professional secrets.

Sofía was maintaining a resolute face, despite a day spent traveling from Veracruz, Mexico, to Posadas—a trip fraught with more than its share of delays and frustrations. A stocky woman of medium height, Sofía favored tailored suits, with just a touch of ruffle and lace at the collar of her white blouse. She could have been the school's principal.

Immediately upon their arrival at the elementary school, the two older generations had been led on the grand tour of the sky-scraper constructed by Francisco and his partner, Rocky Montaño. The creation did indeed nearly scrape the sky—or the acoustical ceiling tiles of the first-grade room. The two boys had assembled a conglomeration of dowels draped under yards of foil, with windows, doors, and occupants drawn with black marker. Estelle had to turn the small camera sideways to capture the full majesty of the structure, and she managed to include *Moon Base* in the same photo—both structures remarkable for first graders.

Francis frowned and poked at a section of the skyscraper's aluminum foil that had collapsed inward, perhaps because of a massive winter gale off the Great Lakes.

"Emergency exit," he said.

"On the fiftieth floor," Estelle added.

"Neat, though." He nodded at the moon base. "I like the idea of transporting a million Popsicle sticks to the moon to make *bachees*."

Estelle laughed. "Be kind."

"This is the future of the human race—or *rachee*—that we're talking about here," Francis added, and she elbowed him sharply. At the same time, he saw her glance up at the wall clock. "Uh-oh," he said.

"What?"

"You're clock watching. That's not a good sign."

"I will stay until the bitter end," she said. "Until Sofía collapses from jet lag, or Carlos and *Mamá* fall asleep, or Francisco runs out of things to show off."

"How about the best two out of three," Francis said. "Leave it up to Mozart, there, and we could be here after they turn all the lights out." He looked over his shoulder at his eldest son, then back to Estelle. "Show me the piano room," he said. "They won't even know we're gone."

They walked hand in hand down the hall, examining all the other art displays from the various grade levels as they went. At one group of watercolors, Francis stopped short. Estelle saw a fleeting expression of sadness cross his handsome, dark face.

"Look at this," he said. He touched the bottom margin of a watercolor showing what might have been a cabin on the shore of a violet lake, surrounded by jagged, indigo mountains. The image was so advanced it appeared out of place, surrounded by other work so obviously created by children. "Fourth grade," he said. "Sheri Monaghan."

"You know her, *oso*?" Estelle asked.

Francis nodded. "She's a neuroblastoma patient of mine. We just transferred her to Lovelace."

"*Ay.*"

"Uh-huh."

"How's she doing?"

Francis lingered at the landscape. "Well, I don't think she'll be coming home, *querida*."

"Is that the Monaghan who works at United Insurance?"

"Yes." He sighed. "Her mother said that before she got so sick that she couldn't lift a paintbrush, she did two or three paintings *a day*. Sheri's been homeschooled for quite a while." He shook his head and looked down the hall. "Anyway, show me." He quickened his pace, ignoring the remainder of the art.

When they reached the music room, he stood in the doorway for a moment. Estelle hooked her arm through his and didn't interrupt his thoughts.

"Kind of a dismal place, isn't it?" he said finally. He clicked on the lights and looked up at the ceiling. "I always wondered why school roofs leak. I don't think I've ever seen a classroom where at least a few of the ceiling tiles weren't water strained."

"You're not supposed to waste time looking up, *querido*," Estelle said. She jerked his arm in mock discipline. "Pay attention, now."

"So he comes in here, all by himself, and stands at the piano," he said, and stepped over to the battered and scarred instrument. He bent over, spread his hands, and played a chord. Cocking his head to listen, he shifted his hands and played another. "That's just about the sum total of what I remember," he said, and sat down on the bench. He frowned at the keyboard, and then played several measures of a flowing, melodic piece.

"*Fur Elise*," he said, and stopped. "That's all I remember. Everyone who ever takes a piano lesson has to learn it. And learn it. And learn it." He grinned up at Estelle. "Are you ready for this?"

"Sure," she said. "Even *Mamá's* excited."

"*Excited?* Your mother? I don't think so."

"Well, eager, then." A telephone was ringing, and Francis looked at her.

"Is that yours or mine?"

"Mine," Estelle said in resignation. She headed for the exit in the back of the music room, and pushed the heavy door open, letting in a welcome wash of cool air. "Guzman," she said into the receiver.

"Hey there," Sheriff Bob Torrez said. "Where are you at?"

"Down at the school. It's open-house night."

"Oh, yeah. I remember you talkin' about that. Listen, guess who opened her eyes."

"Oh, you're kidding."

"No, I'm not kidding. Carmen managed about thirty seconds of consciousness, according to the patrolman who's assigned to her room."

"Her folks were there?"

"Yep."

"That's wonderful."

"She didn't say anything, by the way."

"That'll come with time. But that's just great news, Bobby."

"Yep. Look, the reason I called—and I don't guess there's anything about this that we can do tonight, but Tom Mears finished processing Zeigler's flat tire. Something kind of interesting."

Estelle stepped out away from the building. "What?"

"Well, there's a pretty good smear—ah, it's not really a smear, but anyway—some flat black paint on the *back side* of the tire. Not a lot, but sort of a little crescent. Might be something, probably not. Linda figured out a way to take some pretty good pictures of it."

Estelle realized that her pulse was racing, and she reached out a hand to the steel doorjamb for support.

"You still there?"

"Yes, I am."

"You workin' tomorrow?"

"Of course I'm working tomorrow, Bobby."

"I thought you were headed to Cruces or something."

"That's Saturday."

"Oh."

"Anyway, we need to talk," Estelle said.

"Yep."

"Are you in the middle of something?"

"Some lasagna that Gayle made. You guys want to come over? We've got enough for about eighteen people. Bring the whole mob."

"Thanks, but how about meeting me at the office in a few minutes?"

"Not too few, now. I'm hungry."

She backed into the room and looked at her husband. Francis nodded wearily and mimed crashing huge chords on the piano.

"How about an hour?"

"Ten-four. What did *you* find?"

"I'll tell you when I see you. I'll be interested to see what you think."

"Uh-oh. I gotta think?"

"Oh, sí," she said. She switched off and slid the phone back in her pocket.

"I heard that," Francis said.

"Carmen was awake for a little while, *querido.*"

"Fantastic. Did she say anything?"

"No. Apparently not. But Tom Mears found something on the spare tire. And I'm pretty sure I know exactly what it is."

She saw her husband's eyes narrow a little as he looked at her. With a sigh, he closed the cover of the piano and stood up. "You've got that hunter's look, *querida,*" he said. "We have an hour though, right? Is that what I heard you tell Bobby?"

"Yes."

"Then let's go back and rescue Sofía."

The other parents, children, and art in the hallway were a blur to Estelle as they returned to the first-grade classroom.

Chapter Thirty-two

The sheriff relaxed in his favorite thinking posture—boots crossed over the corner of his desk, the old swivel chair leaned back far enough that he could rest his head on the heating duct. He had remained so quiet during the portion of Crowley's video that she had played for him that at times she thought he had fallen asleep.

"It's all guesswork, isn't it?" he said. He reached out and nudged a copy of the *Posadas Register* toward Estelle as if with that one comment, discussion of the tape was concluded. "You saw that?"

"Not yet." While Bob Torrez waited, Estelle scanned the front page. It featured a terrible digital photo of Kevin Zeigler on one side of the page and a yearbook photo of Carmen Acosta on the other. Carmen's picture had been cropped out of a larger group photo and then enlarged. Bannered over the photos was the stark headline:

Girl Assaulted, Manager Missing

Although the article never said so, the implication was easily made that Zeigler's sudden departure was somehow related to the assault. Details were meager, but Pam Gardiner—or perhaps Frank Dayan himself—had obviously not been content with the release that Estelle had provided.

The article included speculation from several folks, including County Commissioner Barney Tinneman, who made the point that he hadn't really known Kevin Zeigler all that well...taking the politically safer road of distancing himself immediately when the first sign of trouble arose. The article even featured a wandering, anguished quote from Freddy Acosta, who certainly had no idea "who would do such a thing" to his daughter. Freddy had provided the lurid detail that a hat pin had been used.

"I guess it's the best we could hope for," Estelle said. She folded the paper and placed it carefully on Torrez's desk.

He nodded at the tape. "That's guesswork, I mean," he said.

"For now it is," Estelle persisted. "But there's a pattern, Bobby. For the first time, we've got a motive. Hiring a private company to manage the landfill was Kevin Zeigler's idea...it's not something that the commissioners asked him to investigate. If Zeigler could push it through, guess who stands to lose his job."

"Don Fulkerson, maybe." Torrez nodded judiciously. "And we don't know that, either. There's the chance a private company would hire him."

"True, that's a chance. But he has a nice little empire up there on the hill. In fact, it's a monopoly. Skim the cream off the top, and he can haul a load to the flea market every week. That's a pretty good deal."

"He ain't gettin' rich," Torrez said skeptically.

"No, but it's all his. He says that Zeigler was up there early Tuesday to pick up paperwork of some kind. I believe him. There's no reason for him to deny that. I wouldn't be surprised if Kevin was trying to make sure he had the most up-to-date paperwork on the tonnage that passes through that place. Kurtz told me that they weigh everything, and charge if the load exceeds five hundred pounds."

"Depends who you are," Torrez said. "Do you think Zeigler went back later in the day?"

"I think that could have been one of Zeigler's noontime errands. What if he didn't have everything he needed? What if Fulkerson didn't provide all the data that he wanted? Zeigler was a number cruncher, Bobby—and I don't think Don Fulkerson spends his days in front of a computer. I think it would be natural to have friction between the two men. I can see Kevin zipping up there at lunch to meet with Fulkerson, to get the correct paperwork before the agenda item comes up. Maybe while he was there, the two of them had an argument, and whether by accident or design, Fulkerson took his chance. I get the impression that there was no love lost between them."

"In a manner of speaking." Torrez smirked.

Estelle felt double relief that she hadn't bothered to pass on Fulkerson's "Miss Ziggy" comment. "The landfill is closed on Tuesdays," she said, "so there's no witnesses. Fulkerson dumps the body, and then he's left with a problem."

"No shit, he'd have a problem. For one thing, there's the truck."

Estelle nodded. "Don Fulkerson is one of those clever people, Bobby. I think that he has a pretty high opinion of himself. He's one of those country sages who is quick at contempt for strangers, outsiders, or just plain fancy folks. He *doesn't* have a high opinion of Kevin Zeigler. I can easily imagine sparks between those two. And I can see Fulkerson thinking to himself, what would present more of a clever puzzle than us finding Zeigler's truck right in his own driveway. It would be sure to throw us off."

"Maybe." Torrez still sounded dubious, but Estelle could see the mental gears grinding.

"Look—Doris Marens saw the truck. At least she says that she did. And think about the little things. The truck drives by slowly, not in Zeigler's usual fashion. The driver spikes the brakes a couple of houses early."

"None of that…," Torrez said, and waved a hand. "I'd hate to have this case depend on her testimony. I can imagine what a good lawyer would do with her. By the time he was finished, nothing she had to say would be worth a damn."

"None of it by itself is worth a damn," Estelle said vehemently. "But together? He drives the truck back to Candelaria Court, and parks it in the driveway. Bobby, I could *smell* him in that truck. He pulls in, and there's Carmen Acosta, standing at the kitchen door. She sees him. And the game is up. It's all over, because what would happen if the most thick-witted cop asks her, 'All right, Carmen, did you see anyone at Zeigler's today?' What's she going to say? 'Why, sure. This grubby guy in a greasy coat who sure looks a lot like our landfill manager.'" Estelle snapped her fingers. "Busted."

"Carmen wouldn't stand a chance against Don Fulkerson," Bobby said.

"You bet she wouldn't." She balled her fist. "The lug wrench is handy, lying right there on the truck's floor, in plain sight. He charges after her. Can you imagine him slamming into that door, just as she's trying to close and lock it? At one point, somewhere in the house, she gets in maybe one good lick with the hat pin before he grabs her hand and *wham*. It's all over."

Torrez tossed the pencil down. "I don't suppose you saw a nice wound on Fulkerson's arm or something like that."

"No. But working up there all day long, they probably cut and nick themselves all the time."

Torrez swung his feet down and stood up. "I have a serious question for you." Estelle looked expectant. "Why Zeigler's *driveway*, Estelle. Why not just drive back to the county building?" He held up a hand as he answered his own question. "Sure. Too many people. Too many eyes."

"I thought of this, too. Remember Freddy Acosta? What if Fulkerson saw Freddy, strolling toward downtown? This is a small town, Bobby. It's a certainty that Fulkerson knows Freddy, and he may even have a rough idea where he lives. He saw Tony Acosta riding bikes with Kevin and William—it's entirely possible that he knows where *they* live. Tony told me that when they were out riding, the 'guy at the landfill' wolf-whistled at them, and that Kevin then muttered something not very complimentary in confidence to William Page. Well, think about it. Later, Fulkerson sees Freddy, who's maybe walking right up Bustos, and figures that's a chance to park the truck without anyone seeing him."

"Maybe so."

"And the tire? The tire ends up on the county pile, *not* at the landfill." She leaned forward eagerly. "Do you want to place bets about that black paint?"

"You think Zeigler had a flat tire up at the landfill, then."

"What makes more sense? Sure, the tire should have just been tossed in the back of Kevin's truck. But it *wasn't*, somehow. Forgotten in the heat of argument, maybe. I don't know. When it's all over, what if Fulkerson goes back to the landfill and oops…there it is. He's got to get rid of it. He wouldn't want it at the landfill. It's too risky. If it was found, he'd be implicated right away."

"I don't know. I don't see why it would be apt to be found. He could bury it anytime…"

"Because Fulkerson can't know if Kevin told someone what his errands were. Did he mention to his secretary that he had to go up the hill? The simplest thing is to get rid of it, just in case someone starts snooping around."

"Tossing it on the back of the pile down at the county barns sure does that."

"Even if by chance it's found, Bobby, it directs our attention that way."

"The last thing he'd do, though, is toss the tire up on the headache rack of his truck when he's driving around," Torrez said.

"Maybe he didn't do that. Maybe that was just an accidental scrub when he was getting ready to toss it across the fence. I can see him doing that. He stops, tosses the tire up on the rack, climbs up there himself, and over it goes. A nice high vantage point for a hard toss."

Torrez nodded toward the television set. "The only thing on that tape is that Fulkerson comes back from lunch way late, and Zeigler doesn't come back at all. And when he *does* come back, Fulkerson is not wearing his coat. Well, it ain't exactly cold out, either."

"No, it's not. But it's just one more little point. Why should he be late, on the very day when it's *likely* that Zeigler's going to talk about the landfill thing with the commission? It's not like he has to drive thirty miles to be there, Bobby."

"Maybe he's not the punctual sort. Maybe he just likes irritating Zeigler."

"Maybe." She ticked off several fingers. "Too many little things that point to him. They're adding up. Plus, it would be to his advantage to be at the meeting if they started discussing the landfill in Zeigler's absence. Fulkerson would be in a perfect position to throw a wrench in the whole idea, without fear of contradiction."

Torrez heaved a deep sigh, glanced at his watch, and leaned back again. "I got one naggin' question. You want to guess what it is?"

"Just one?"

"Well, let's start with this one," Torrez said. "Fulkerson parks the truck in Zeigler's driveway. Sees Carmen. Does his thing with the handy lug wrench. That's slick, 'cause folks are going to blame Zeigler, right? Well, then what? Fulkerson is on foot, and the old bat down the street doesn't see him walk by. No one does. Where's he go?"

"Do you know where Don Fulkerson lives, Bobby? I didn't, until I checked this afternoon."

"Yeah, I know where he lives. I think he's the last trailer in that mobile-home park off Camino del Sol. He's got about half of that landfill collected in his backyard."

"And Camino del Sol becomes County Road Nineteen when it leaves the village limits. He doesn't even need to go back out Candelaria Court to MacArthur." She walked over to the small whiteboard bolted to the sheriff's office wall and quickly drew a simple map. "Right out the back of Zeigler's property to Arroyo del Cerdo. Cross Bustos out there beyond Sissons', walk maybe a thousand yards of cross-lots to his place."

"Yup."

"His motorcycle was at the landfill today, Bobby. So was his truck. What if on Tuesday, his bike was at his house? I mean, that's the normal thing, isn't it? He drops off Zeigler's truck, runs cross-lots back to his own place, then rides the motorcycle back to the landfill. Maybe that's when he sees the forgotten tire. He parks the bike and takes the truck. Tire goes on the county

254 Steven F. Havill

pile, he shows up back at he meeting when he's sure that he's covered his tracks."

"Huh."

"He had the motive, he had the opportunity. And he certainly had the means."

Torrez studiously regarded a wart on his left thumb knuckle. "You want to go up there?"

"I think so."

"You *think* so?"

"I want to find Kevin Zeigler, Bobby. Whatever it takes. I'd like to look around up there without either Fulkerson or Kurtz knowing...maybe in the office, around the grounds. Then, if we need to take a crew up there to sift through two days of trash, that's what we'll do."

"Two days? There'll be more than that."

"Not if it happened the way I think it did. Bart Kurtz said that they cover the week's collection on Sunday night when the landfill is closed. It's closed Tuesday, too. So we have the collection from Wednesday and today uncovered in the pit."

"Change your clothes, and let's go take a look," Torrez said.

Chapter Thirty-three

There was nothing surreptitious about Sheriff Robert Torrez's approach. He pulled up to the Posadas County Landfill's main gate, got out with his bundle of keys that included the master for all of the county's heavy Yale padlocks, popped the lock, and swung the gate wide open.

"Let's lock it," he said as he climbed back in the Expedition. "You never know what bunch of kids will be out lookin' for a place to party." He pulled the Expedition forward. Estelle climbed down, closed and locked the gate behind them.

"Where do you want to start?"

Estelle nodded at the small shack that served as the landfill office. "Right there." Torrez swung in close but didn't switch off the ignition. "You know what you're lookin' for?"

"No."

Torrez swiveled the spotlight to illuminate the little building, then swung the light to the left. "The bike's not here."

"He's had lots of time to take it home in the back of his pickup."

The sheriff snapped off the spot and then switched off the ignition. "Darker'n shit," he muttered, and slid the large aluminum flashlight out of its boot in the center console. The new moon was far down on the horizon. A light breeze swirled around the shed, enough to set the symphony of landfill smells into motion.

Torrez unlocked the office door and pushed it open. "Let there be light," he said, and snapped the switch. One of the two fluorescent bulbs flickered into dust-filtered life. The office was stuffy and cluttered. A constant flow of boots carrying mud and dirt had ground the original vinyl flooring bare, leaving recognizable patterns only in the corners, where feet never ventured.

A set of metal shelves bulged with various tools and machine parts, some boxed, some lying loose in the clutter. A single window on the east wall could open, but probably hadn't in years. The glass was opaque, crusted on the inside from smoke, dust, and insects; on the outside from the constant clouds of landfill dirt that shifted with the wind.

Estelle opened each of the three desk drawers, lingering at the last one when she saw the half-full bottle of Canadian whiskey. "I could smell an additive in his coffee this morning," she said.

"Don and the bottle are no strangers," Torrez observed. "I know that for a fact." He didn't say how he knew, but Estelle was well aware that Bobby Torrez was determined when it came to busting drunk drivers; years before, shortly after joining the Posadas County Sheriff's Department, he'd lost a younger brother to a weaving drunk. Other deputies swore that Torrez could now smell an open bottle of beer even before the driver lowered his window. She could not imagine him cutting Fulkerson any slack if he caught the landfill manager—county employee or not—weaving down the highway under the influence.

A computer sat in the middle of the desk, dusty and note-stuck. Directly above it on the wall was the load scale's read-out, the glass of the digital window as filthy as everything else.

"Hi-tech operation," Torrez said. He held a small plastic bag as Estelle transferred a dozen of the freshest cigarette butts from the overflowing coffee can that served as an ashtray. "Which ones are his?"

"Today he was rolling his own," Estelle said, "but he had a pack of Camel filters in his shirt pocket. Kurtz was smoking Marlboros."

"You know we're lookin' at a week or more for a DNA profile off these."

She nodded with resignation. "I don't care if it takes a month. I need to start somewhere. This afternoon, I asked Francis to find Fulkerson's blood type for me, if it was on file anywhere over at the hospital. It's not. Nothing's going to be easy."

"Could be that Bart might have had something to do with all this. That's a possibility."

"I've been thinking about that, Bobby. Maybe he's in on it. He was the more reserved of the two when I talked with them today. I couldn't tell if he was nervous or not. But he struck me as a little evasive."

"Bart's just plain dumb," Torrez said. "He's firing on two out of four."

"Maybe so, but he wasn't the one drinking whiskey at nine in the morning."

"Fulkerson seemed confident, did he?"

"Oh, yes. Pretty smug." She gingerly lifted a grimy jacket off the back of the swivel chair. "This is Bart's," she said. "It's too small for Don." She held out the sleeves, then checked the pockets, finding a butane lighter, a quarter, a penny, and a piece of peppermint candy minus its wrapper.

They spent another five minutes in the shed, but found nothing of interest. Once more outside, Estelle took deep breaths, enjoying the relatively clean air and letting her vision adjust once more to the darkness.

"This is Fulkerson's trailer," Torrez said. "I've seen him pullin' it around." He walked across to it, playing the flashlight on the contents. "Lots of good shit. Looks like somebody tore down an old fireplace or something. Old Don scarfed up the bricks." He leaned on the side of the trailer, methodically examining the load. "I could use some of those."

"They may end up on sale, cheap," Estelle said, and Torrez nodded judiciously.

"Yep, they might." He thumped the side of the trailer, turned and shined the flashlight across the landfill. "Lots of traffic since Tuesday," he said. "That's the frustrating part. And it wouldn't come as much of a surprise to find out that Zeigler had a flat tire up here, either." He walked a couple of paces away from the truck, playing his light on the ground. "Too damn many tracks since then. No way to find where he had the jack." He directed the light toward the pit and the beam reflected off the bright yellow of the dozer. "I'd like to take a look over there," he said. "I ain't walkin', though."

As they drove across the rough, litter-strewn ground toward the pit, Torrez swung the windshield-post-mounted spotlight this way and that. "Did you walk over there?" he said at one point, holding the spot on the large pile of branches, slash, and limb wood a hundred yards away in the back corner of the landfill.

"No. I visited the appliance showroom and the tires. Then I walked across to the pit."

"They burn that pile every once in a while," Torrez said. "Fire department brings the marshmallows and they have a grand old time."

"That's a cheerful thought."

"Next time it'll be barbecue-flavored smoke."

Estelle grimaced at the graveyard humor. "If I was going to dispose of a corpse, it wouldn't be under a pile of branches. That would be both hard to do and time-consuming."

"Me neither." He swept the light back, and Estelle saw that the day's pile of refuse had been dozed into the pit, leaving a neat apron for the next day's offering. Torrez maneuvered the Expedition carefully between the parked dozer and the side of the pit, the left front and rear tires no more than a stride from the edge. He swiveled the spotlight and played it down into the depths.

With barely enough room to open the door, Estelle climbed out and walked around the front of the truck. The sheriff remained inside, and Estelle crossed through the beam of the spot, keeping a hand on the truck for balance.

"Stay away from the edge," Torrez said unnecessarily. "That's a hell of a first step."

"I was over on the other side earlier," she said.

Torrez crisscrossed the spotlight beam methodically across the bottom of the pit, pausing now and then at points of interest.

After several minutes, he leaned his head on one hand, elbow propped on the doorsill. "How sure are you?" he asked quietly.

"I'm not sure at all," Estelle replied. "It's just that in various conversations since Tuesday, the landfill keeps cropping up. It's the only thing that's consistent, and that makes me edgy. Hear it one time, that's one thing. But over and over again, things keep circling back. Tony Acosta mentioned it. William Page mentioned it. The tire shows up down at the county yard, but it's got a paint smear on it that *might* match the black paint on Fulkerson's headache rack." She shrugged and leaned against the truck's door. "That's thin, I know."

"You ain't kidding. Like it ain't the only rack in town. It's going to take the state lab a week to run a match."

"It's just that there is a rack here, too, Bobby. And there are some things that are even thinner. Like the smell in Zeigler's truck. You walk into that shack over there, and it's a megaversion of that same stink."

"It's just cigarettes."

"Well, no, it's not. It's smoke mixed with alcohol, Bobby. I know. I could be wrong. But then you add Fulkerson's motive. That's intriguing, and on top of that it's the *only* motive we've stumbled across that's immediate." She thumped Torrez on the arm. "We know that there are some ill feelings between Fulkerson and Zeigler. At the very least, some dislike. And it runs both ways, beyond just one man's contempt for another's lifestyle. If a private company from out of town takes all this over, Fulkerson stands to lose…and lose big time."

"'All this will be yours one day, my son,'" Torrez intoned. "What a kingdom. Too bad he don't have a son."

"And Fulkerson comes up again in Crowley's video."

"Just because he was at the meeting."

"A little more than that. He was there and then left the meeting, right at the time that Zeigler disappeared. And returned late. It's hard to tell, but it looks like he changed his clothes. Or at least took off his coat."

"He had the opportunity. I agree with that."

"Sure enough he did. Now think about the grease on Carmen's bedroom wall? Fulkerson's the right size, and he works with machines all the time." She jerked her head toward the bull-dozer and shined her flashlight over the roof of the Expedition. "It's not there now, but he stuffs his jacket under the seat and uses it as a pad for his thermos of coffee. There's grease all over the place. These little things, Bobby. They just keep adding up. Fulkerson *could* have walked from Zeigler's to his own place on Camino. It's only a couple of blocks, and makes sense. He wouldn't want to be seen. After what happened with Carmen, he'd want to be out of there. He'd be nervous."

"More'n that. He probably hurt like hell from bein' jabbed with that freakin' hat pin."

"That, too. It makes sense that he'd duck out the back. And suddenly, both his vehicles end up here at the dump. Explain *that* to me."

"Do you feel sure enough to shut this place down? Put a lock on the gate, close it off for however long it takes to dig it all up? I'm thinkin' that a dog will help. I know they have a rescue canine in Deming. Get him up here to nose through all this shit." Estelle didn't respond. "That's what you're talkin' about, you know. That's what we do if there's reason to believe that Zeigler's buried down in that pit somewhere."

"*Ay.* I really hate thinking that he's here."

"Well…" Torrez shot the spotlight all the way down to the far end of the pit again, where the dozer would climb up and out when it dug the pit in the first place, pushing the load of dirt to the storage pile. Each week, a layer of dirt would be graded back as a cover blanket for the trash. "It don't make any difference to Kevin Zeigler whether he's lying down there, or under a juniper up on Cat Mesa, or in the bottom of an arroyo someplace. We go with what we got. So you call it. You've relied on your intuition before."

"I feel really, really uneasy about this place."

He switched off the light and they listened to the silence for a while, broken occasionally by the light rustle of the breeze touching the loose plastic of a garbage bag down below. "That's good enough for me. Let's go take a look," he said after a minute. "What's to lose? Maybe rummaging through trash in the middle of the night is just the ticket. At the very least, we might find some really good shit, and stiff Fulkerson out of his flea market profits."

Estelle moved away from the door, careful to stay back from the edge of the pit. "I'm leavin' the truck right here," Torrez said. "It'll give us something to see by." He turned the spot back on, centering it to cover the most area. "You have your light?"

"Yes," Estelle said.

"Gloves?"

"Sure."

He tossed his bulky handheld radio on the seat. "I don't need to lose that," he said. He got out and stood for a minute with his hands on his hips. "I think we can just kinda slide down over here." He walked back toward the drop-off apron of the pit, where the slope was nearly seventy degrees, as opposed to the gently sloped exit end.

The bed of trash was heaped below the drop-off, not yet pushed out and compacted as it would be at the end of the week. Balancing on both feet as if she were sliding down an icy hill, Estelle slipped and slid down to the pile. Because the collection represented only two days, the pile of refuse stretched out for no more than twenty yards. She stopped and surveyed the pile dubiously.

"I think that if I'd dumped somebody here, I'd make a little more of an effort to cover them thoroughly," she said. "Especially if I owned a bulldozer. I don't think any of this trash has been spread out yet."

"Good-sized pile, though. But I was thinkin' the same thing."

"A sign of confidence, maybe."

Torrez flashed light to the far side, where the smooth dirt layer from the week before was still visible. "Could be over there, too. Could be just about anywhere. The only good way to do this is to get Howard up here on one of the county backhoes."

"He'll love that," Estelle said. She could imagine the stolid Sergeant Bishop on excavation duty, reliving his years as a private contractor.

Bent in a crouch with the light in one hand and the other reaching out for something to provide stability, Estelle made her way across the pile, heading toward the west wall of the pit. Torrez went east, moving with more assurance. The light from the Expedition's focused spot hindered as much as it helped forming harsh shadows that hid treacherous footing.

"Incongruities," Estelle said aloud.

"What?" Torrez shouted.

"Nothing. I'm talking to myself." She worked her way beyond the highest mound, toward the open soil that covered the previous week's collection, and in a moment reached the old refrigerator that she had seen earlier in the day. Battered and dented, the fridge lay facedown, just at the edge of the fresh trash. Several pieces of random-sized, rotted plywood had sailed down on top of it. She pushed the wood aside, and rocked the appliance with one foot. "Why aren't you with the others?" she said.

Fifteen yards away, Torrez was rooting his way through trash, muttering all the while.

"Hey?" Estelle called.

Torrez paused. "What?"

"Help me turn this over?" She waited until the sheriff had made his way over before saying, "Just one more little thing. Bobby. Why isn't this in the pile across the way, there? With all its brethren?"

"'Cause it makes a neat coffin?" Torrez replied. He rocked the fridge tentatively, then grabbed a bottom corner and heaved. With the appliance on its side, they could see that a hasp had been screwed into the door, perhaps when the original latch gave up the ghost.

"I should be taking pictures," Estelle said.

"If the county manager's inside, I promise I'll put it back exactly the way it was." The hasp was latched, secured with the type of staple that passed through a slot and then turned a quarter turn. Torrez pulled a ballpoint pen from his pocket, inserted it in the latch and turned. He then flicked the hasp clear.

He glanced up at Estelle and grinned. "I wish you could see your face right now." He didn't wait for a reply, but worked the door away from the frame, forcing it against the cushion of earth that jammed the hinges. The smell that erupted was ferocious, and even Torrez recoiled back.

"Christ," he blurted. Estelle's pulse was hammering so hard she almost didn't hear him over her heartbeat. He shined his flashlight inside and grimaced. "Somebody got tired of the family dogs," he said. "Looks like one, two, three, four of 'em." He turned his head and grimaced up at Estelle. "You want to take a look?"

"If it's dogs, I'll take your word for it," she said.

He screwed up his face, opened the door a little farther, and probed with the flashlight beam. "Nothin' else." He kneed the door shut and flicked the hasp. "Who the hell would do something like that?"

"I don't know, but they never get charged with murder," Estelle said. She retreated a step, then froze as she heard what sounded like the metallic rattle of chain in the distance.

Chapter Thirty-four

"We know who that's got to be." Torrez's voice dropped to a harsh whisper. "Whyn't you move out of the spotlight. I'll go up and have a chat with him. He don't have to know that both of us are here."

Moving out of the glare of the spot was simple enough. Estelle had only to make her way toward the side of the pit directly below the Expedition. Doing so without falling face-first into various stinking crevices, without losing footing on things that slid and squished underfoot, was another matter. On top of that, she realized that no matter where she moved, if she was out of sight from the rim of the pit, she was also denied any kind of tactical advantage.

As Estelle made her way toward the sheer east side, Torrez crossed directly toward the slope below the apron. Even as he started up, the embankment so steep that he practically had to climb on all fours on the diagonal, Estelle heard the truck approach and saw the sweep of its lights across the top of the pit.

As Torrez worked his way up toward the rim, Estelle tried to move up toward the rubbish pile, in a moment standing directly below the back bumper of the Expedition. She heard no words exchanged. From her vantage point, it appeared as if the sheriff had lost his footing as he neared the lip of the pit. The movement was accompanied by a loud *thwack* and a shout of pain. Before she could fully comprehend what had happened, she saw Torrez careering backward down the steep slope.

Standing in the dark protection of the sheer bank side, Estelle's first thought was to dive toward the flailing Torrez, thirty yards away. Almost immediately, her foot stabbed hard into something sharp and she fell heavily, her chin crashing against metal. Agonizing pain shot through the side of her face and she tasted the hot coppery salt of blood.

Before she could regain her feet, eyes tearing, she saw a man's form appear near the edge of the pit. Only partially illuminated by the truck's headlights, he held something in each hand, and Estelle recognized Don Fulkerson's burly figure. Torrez spun headfirst into a pile of trash bags at the bottom of the slope, and at the same time, Fulkerson dropped the object in his left hand and brought the other to his shoulder.

The report was sharp and staccato as he rapped off three quick shots. One of the rounds whined off into the darkness, and at the same time she heard Torrez gasp an oath. He leaped through the pile of trash ahead of him awkwardly, rolling head over heels into a dark cavern.

Fulkerson stepped first one direction and then another, unsure of his target. Estelle fumbled with her own Beretta at the small of her back. As she did so, Fulkerson raised the rifle again, taking a step to his left. Estelle braced as best she could, blinked to try and clear her eyes, and fired a rapid string of five shots, the reports coming so fast they blended together into one sustained echo.

Rearing backward in surprise, Fulkerson stumbled away from the pit. Unsure if she had hit him, Estelle took one step away from the bank, aimed almost straight up, and fired twice at the spotlight on the side of the Expedition. Glass shattered, raining down on her head. The pit plunged into darkness.

She held her breath, moving in slow motion, one foot at a time. She was twenty yards or more from the slope that would lead her either up and out of the pit, or allow her to cross to Torrez. Above her, Fulkerson's pickup still idled, its headlights illuminating the back of the Expedition. Estelle hesitated. What was he doing? If he found a flashlight, he could stand back from the edge of the pit out of her range, and with the beam and then a bullet, find where Torrez lay, farther across behind the highest peak of refuse.

Flinching at the sharp metallic snap, she popped the partially expended clip out of the Beretta and slipped it in her back pocket. She pushed the full replacement, heavy with fourteen rounds, into the weapon. Even as she did so, the night cracked open with a new sound.

The big Cat's diesel cranked only briefly before the engine caught. "Oh, no," Estelle said, gasping, and before she could take more than two steps or predict what Fulkerson might do, the answer came in a tearing crash of bending metal and shattering glass. The dozer had been parked parallel to and fifteen feet from the edge of the pit. Bob Torrez had parked the county truck between the dozer and the pit edge, with only inches to spare.

Fulkerson pivoted the dozer hard to the right, the blade slamming into the Expedition at the right rear passenger door. A cascade of dirt exploded down from the rim of the pit as the dozer bashed Torrez's patrol unit sideways. The back tires dropped over the edge first, and Estelle yelped and dove to her right, trying to scramble out of the way. The dozer thundered under full throttle as it spun on its own tracks, catapulting the Expedition over the edge.

Hands and feet flailing, Estelle felt for an agonizing moment that she was swimming upstream through rapids like an injured salmon. Immediately behind her, the Expedition hit the bottom of the pit with a resounding crash, landing on its side like a huge, crushed beetle. Something sharp flew up and smacked Estelle in the right hip so hard that she crashed forward on her face.

Without an instant's hesitation, Fulkerson jarred the dozer to a halt, then maneuvered abruptly to the left, the tracks sending up a plume of dust in the headlights of the still-idling pickup truck. The ponderous machine clanked around the pickup truck, swinging toward the pit. Even as he turned the machine, Fulkerson switched on its lights. It became a six-eyed beast, the four lights on top of the cab frame washing the scene when the massive blade shielded the beam of the two headlights in the grill.

For a moment, the lights aimed straight out, far above the bottom of the pit, and as she struggled to her feet again, Estelle's first thought was that Fulkerson was going to use the dozer for cover until he located them and finished the job from a safe range with the rifle. Because of that, she was unprepared for what he did next.

The dozer reached the edge of the steep slope. The blade dropped, the engine throttled back, and with a squealing of dirt-filled rollers and brakes, the huge machine started down. The slope was so steep Estelle would not have thought the maneuver possible.

From her right, a series of flashes burst out of the dark as Bob Torrez cut loose with his .45 automatic, but unless one of the rounds got lucky and struck Fulkerson, he might as well have been throwing rocks. Like a stuntman hanging onto his horse's reins with one hand and firing with the other, Fulkerson used the flashes to locate Torrez and cut loose with another five quick rounds from the rifle.

Still clutching her handgun but with her flashlight lost somewhere in the trash, Estelle's fight-or-flight instinct was to plunge out of the pit ahead of the clanking machine so that she couldn't be cornered. But the dozer bore down on her, lights blazing over her head, before she could turn. Knowing that she could never outrun the machine, she instead lunged off to her left, aware that she was cornering herself behind the crushed Expedition and the steep banks of the pit. Fulkerson had only to brake, pivot right, and crush her to jelly.

Fulkerson was intent on Bob Torrez, and as soon as the machine hit the bottom of the slope, its blade dug into the trash and then surfaced like the bow of a ship in heavy seas. The brakes squealed as he turned to the left. For a moment, his broad body, perched high on the seat, was silhouetted against the lights.

Estelle fell to her knees and held the automatic in both hands, trying to find some sort of sight picture in the haze of tears and blood. She hardly felt the recoil as it punched her hands. The empties spewed out of the Beretta in a stream until the slide locked back. The bulldozer continued inexorably. Dumping out the empty clip, Estelle rammed the second full one into the gun and slammed the slide into the battery.

The dozer rumbled away from her, its slow, ponderous course fixed on Torrez's position. Before she could bring her sights to bear again, she saw flashes from off to the side, five, six, perhaps seven rounds. One of them ricocheted off something and screamed over her head to smack into the bank above her.

The figure of Don Fulkerson had sagged to one side in the seat, but otherwise appeared undeterred. The dozer crossed the sea of garbage diagonally and dug the corner of its blade into the pit's far wall. Estelle heard the engine note change with the force of the impact, and for a moment dozer and dirt cliff appeared to tussle. Then the blade broke loose, and the machine veered right and clanked down the length of the pit.

When it became obvious that Fulkerson wasn't going to spin the dozer in its own length and charge back at them, she shifted position, trying to pick her way in the darkness. She fell hard again, letting out a strangled cry that she bit off in frustration.

"Let him go!" she heard Bob Torrez shout.

Rising to her knees, Estelle shifted the Beretta to her left hand and dug the cell phone out of her jacket pocket. The face was dark, and with her thumb she could feel the smashed plastic. The mutter of the bulldozer's diesel, in concert with the rhythmic, steady clanking of its treads, continued down the pit. Estelle stopped, breathing hard, watching. Away was good.

Reaching the slope up at the far end, the dozer lurched onward, climbing the mountain of dirt. Its lights stabbed up into the sky as it climbed. Estelle saw that as it neared the top, Fulkerson had attacked the pile too far to one side. The right tread dropped off the ramp, and for just a moment it high-centered on the pile until its tracks swam it forward enough that it slid sideways.

With its weight shifted in the one direction in which the massive machine was the most unstable, the dozer executed a slow roll onto its side, then continued all the way over onto its top until the windowless framework of the cab crushed flat.

Without enough momentum to continue the roll, it slid on its top for a foot or two, the tracks still methodically turning. Upside down and jangled, the diesel uttered a strangled cough and died. The headlights continued to burn, lighting the prairie north of the landfill.

"Good shot," Torrez said from somewhere on the other side of the rubbish pile.

A flood of relief turned her joints to pudding. "Are you okay?" Her words came out as little more than a croak, and she coughed and tried again.

"Nope," Torrez said conversationally. "But I'm a hell of a lot better than he is. How about you?"

"I'm okay. Don't move, then. I'm coming over."

"I ain't going nowhere."

A light stabbed toward her. "Leave it off," she said. "I can do better without it."

"That son of a bitch ruined my truck." He coughed and from her vantage point it sounded painful and liquid. "You got your phone?" he asked.

"It's broken."

"Well, shit, that's good."

"Yours?"

"It's in the truck," he said.

"We're a pair," she muttered.

"Just go up and use the one in Fulkerson's office. He won't mind."

"That's the next stop."

"Just go ahead and do that," Torrez said. "I'm okay. I think I got the bleedin' stopped."

"Turn on the light now," Estelle said, and this time she saw that Torrez's location was only a small mountain of trash ahead. The light reflected through the skeleton of an old set of box springs.

Bob Torrez lay on his side, curled awkwardly. "This is a good thing to hide behind," Estelle said. "This is going to stop a bulldozer, all right."

"Hey, I didn't choose it," Torrez said, then sucked in a breath. "Be careful where you step."

"He hit you, didn't he?"

"Yes, he hit me. Goddamn son of a bitch."

"Let me have the light."

Torrez didn't relinquish it immediately. "Go use the goddamn phone and get us some help." The beam crossed her face. "Jesus, what'd he do, drive right over the top of you?"

"I'm fine. Let me have the light."

He slid it toward her, and Estelle could see that he wasn't moving his right arm. She gripped the light and he flinched. "Son of a bitch swung that pipe at me, and I broke the swing with my arm."

"Broke is right," Estelle said. His right wrist angled off in a creative, anatomically impossible direction.

"And then when I went down the hill, I caught my leg on something." She played the light down, but stopped at the blood soaking the back of his trousers.

"More than caught," she said. "He shot you through the butt."

"That's what I thought."

"And your leg's broken."

"Yep. Go use the phone."

"I need to see if I can stop that bleeding."

"Just go find the phone. My goddamn ass will wait."

Estelle stripped off her jacket and wadded it as neatly as she could. There was no way to pad everything. The rifle shot had entered on the right side just behind Torrez's hip bone and punched through, exploding out the left cheek, leaving a nasty walnut-sized hole. There was no flash of bright arterial blood, but internal damage could be massive. Torrez's face was already gray and chalky.

"I'll be right back," Estelle said. "Just hang on."

"Like I said, I ain't going anywhere." Estelle started to stand up, but Torrez grunted in protest. "I need the other clip."

He fumbled and found the .45 automatic, holding it up in his left hand. With a grimace, he pressed the clip release. "It's somewhere around here."

Estelle pulled the loaded clip out of his belt, took the heavy automatic and slammed the clip in, then released the slide. "The safety's on. Don't shoot yourself."

"Just in case the rats start comin' in," he said weakly, and it didn't sound as if he were joking. "Don't be takin' your time, now."

Chapter Thirty-five

Undersheriff Estelle Reyes-Guzman's right hand stroked across the top of William Page's shoulder as the two of them watched the four EMTs starting up and out of the landfill pit. The rescue team made their way carefully, the gurney carrying Kevin Zeigler's body between them. Page stood quietly, but Estelle could feel the trembling and tension, as if he were ready to bolt.

"I'm truly sorry," Estelle said. The words were painful through swollen, stitched lips—and meaningless, too, she knew. Page reached up and covered her hand with his own.

"Thanks for what you did," he whispered, and dropped his hand. She had called him from the hospital shortly after 3 a.m., more than five hours before. He had sounded disoriented, both jarred from a rare, deep sleep and trying to understand Estelle's curious diction. The generous local anesthetic that Dr. Alan Perrone had used when he'd repaired her face hadn't yet worn off when she had made the call. A few minutes before, District Attorney Dan Schroeder had told her that she sounded like a mumbling drunk. She certainly felt like one.

Since 4:30 a.m., Page had kept her company at the county landfill. Estelle made sure that Page stayed out of the way, refusing to let him down into the pit later, when Zeigler's body had been discovered. Aching from the beating she had taken, dizzy from the painkillers, Estelle slumped against Jackie Taber's unit, content to leave the investigation to Eddie Mitchell, Sgt. Tom

Mears, and a host of volunteers. But it was impossible not to watch from a distance.

Page and Estelle had talked little, and that was just as well, since Estelle had collapsed down from her adrenalin high and slumped pale and exhausted against the car. Dr. Perrone had objected to her going anywhere but home to bed, but it had been her husband who had negotiated a compromise. Even as he'd slipped the tetanus booster shot into her shoulder, Francis had looked again at her battered face.

"Pretty sexy, this new look," he said. "Here's the deal," and he tossed the empty syringe into the "sharp objects" recycling canister. "You go do what you gotta do, okay? As long as you don't drive. I'll come up and *get* you when everything is cleaned up here. And you'll come home then, no arguments. Deal?"

"Deal," she had agreed.

Estelle had been driven from the hospital to the Sheriff's Office, where she had met with both Mitchell and District Attorney Schroeder. And then Deputy Jackie Taber had driven her to the landfill, understanding both that Estelle needed to be present for the excavation…and that she probably shouldn't be.

A dozen people had rummaged through the landfill by hand, first under the bright lights of two generators, then in the growing light as the sun first blasted the pit edges and then worked down the west bank. Shortly after 6 a.m., a backhoe arrived, and it seemed to Estelle that William Page had flinched every time the bucket's steel teeth curled into the mixture of earth and refuse.

At 8:16 a.m., Sergeant Howard Bishop had swung the bucket of the backhoe clear and shut off the engine. The remains of County Manager Kevin Zeigler had been found near the east side of the landfill pit, under a foot of cover soil. Sheriff Torrez's mangled Expedition had landed directly on top of the county manager's final resting place.

Now, in the bright morning sunshine with ravens commenting from a safe distance, the noise of machinery had died. It was compassionate handwork as Zeigler's remains were photographed, measured, and inspected by Coroner Alan Perrone before finally being transferred to black plastic and then to a gurney.

Estelle turned a bit to keep the heat of the sun off her battered face. The local anesthetic had worn off and she now realized why Dr. Perrone had shaken his head dubiously when she'd refused more than one of the potent painkillers he'd offered as a follow-up. Her lip felt like a grotesque balloon, and the broken incisor ached. She shifted her weight, favoring her sore right leg.

Linda Real approached at a jog. Estelle watched her, marveling at the young photographer's energy. She had been shooting still and video since she'd raced to the scene in a heart-pounding ride the night before with Chief Eddie Mitchell, beating even the first ambulance.

William Page saw Linda approaching and turned away, as if he couldn't bear to face the thought of the images her cameras contained. "I'm going to follow the ambulance down the hill," he said heavily. "Is there anything else you need from me? Some statement of some kind?"

"I don't think so," Estelle said, extending her hand. Page's grip was lifeless at first, then he squeezed her hand and held it.

"Thanks again." He nodded and Estelle watched him walk off, head down, hands in his pockets.

"Are you okay?" Linda asked. All morning, a procession of people, from cops to EMTs to the district attorney, had asked Estelle the same thing. "You look like you hurt," the photographer added.

"I do," Estelle said. She nodded at Page's retreating figure. "Not as much as he does, though."

"Yep," Linda said, not knowing what else to say. They watched the ambulance carrying Zeigler's corpse leave. "Eddie said that Kevin wasn't shot," Linda said. "Doc Perrone says that it looks like the back of his skull was smashed in."

"I'd bet on the pipe," Estelle said. "That's what Fulkerson hit Bobby with last night. He took us both by surprise." It had been simpler to deal with Don Fulkerson. Eight hours before Zeigler's body was discovered, one of the huge county wreckers had lifted the battered hulk of the dozer at the other end of the pit just far enough to pull Fulkerson's corpse free. The dozer now rested forlornly back on its tracks, its cab framework crushed flat, its exhaust stack lying across the dented hood.

Estelle's radio barked static, and then Deputy Collins was on the air, sounding both officious and still awestruck after learning that Estelle had hit Fulkerson seven times to Sheriff Torrez's zero.

"Ah, three ten?"

"Go ahead," Estelle said, keeping the handheld radio well away from her face.

"Undersheriff, Mr. Dayan is still out here at the gate. He wonders if you can give him a few minutes."

Linda ducked her head in amusement and made a face. "Nah," she said.

"Let him in," Estelle said. She tried to smile at Linda, but flinched instead.

"I was thinking," Linda said, helpfully holding out a fresh tissue to Estelle. "When we put together our new department calendar? I was thinking one of the shots I took of Bobby might be good. Like when the EMTs were trying to figure out how to pad his butt?"

Estelle laughed, then yelped in pain, half doubled over. *"Por Dios,"* she gasped. "You're a sadist." The calendar idea had been a Christmas gift brainstorm two years before. The department's twelve employees made it one a month, using candid shots collected during the year by both Linda and Estelle.

"I think that'd be neat," Linda said. "Maybe it'll cheer him up. He's got to be feeling kinda down knowing you hit a moving target seven times and he didn't connect once."

"It's not something to be proud of," Estelle said. "Besides, the sheriff was indisposed with a broken arm, broken leg, and broken butt." She frowned at Linda in mock reproof. "So don't be giving him a hard time, *hija.*"

Linda beamed her crooked smile. "Here comes Mr. Photo," she said. Estelle looked to see Frank Dayan striding across the landfill apron toward them. "Good luck."

Dayan carried a small digital camera with which he would take amazingly awful photos for the front page of the *Posadas Register*.

"Damn," he said, frowning at Estelle's battered face. "Are you all right?"

"I will be, Frank."

His gaze shifted to the remains of the sheriff's Expedition, now resting on a flatbed car hauler at the far end of the pit. Fulkerson's pickup hadn't been moved. "Is it all true?" he asked, turning back to Estelle. He pulled a small tape recorder from his pocket and flicked it on.

"That depends on what the *it* is," Estelle said. Taking a step back, she settled against the front bumper of Jackie Taber's Bronco.

"Look," Dayan said. "They found Zeigler, right? Is that part true? They said the ambulance that just left had him…"

"That part is true."

"Dead?"

"Yes." She pointed toward where a handful of officers still stood, down in the pit. "He was buried under about a foot of dirt, right where Chief Mitchell is standing."

"How was he killed?"

"A *very* preliminary examination indicates a blow to the back of the head, Frank. You'll want to talk to Alan Perrone later."

"And Fulkerson?"

Estelle nodded, and Dayan held the recorder a little closer.

"I'm told he was shot."

"That's correct. Shot first, and then the bulldozer he was operating tipped over and crushed him."

Dayan shaded his eyes and looked at the dozer in the distance. "Wow."

"Yes."

"Who shot him?"

"I did, Frank."

"What was he doing with the dozer?"

"Trying to kill the sheriff and me."

"Ah. He actually managed to hit the sheriff with the dozer, then?"

"No, he did not. The sheriff was first struck by Mr. Fulkerson with a length of pipe, breaking his arm. He then fell backward into the pit, breaking his leg in the process. He also sustained a single gunshot wound to the hip."

"You're saying that Fulkerson *shot* at you, too?"

"That's correct. He used a .223 caliber semiautomatic rifle."

Dayan looked sympathetic. "You guys were really lucky, you know that?"

"I think so."

"You were up here on suspicion that Zeigler might have been murdered and his remains buried here?"

"That's exactly right, Frank."

"Why would he do it? Fulkerson, I mean?"

Estelle shifted position painfully. "Right now, we think that it has to do with Kevin Zeigler's intent to negotiate with a private contractor for landfill services."

"You've got to be kidding."

"No. I'm not. We think that on Tuesday, shortly after noon, the two of them met here, and that some sort of argument ensued." She shrugged helplessly. "And that's all we know."

"Wow. I talked to the DA a bit ago. He said that he was really proud of the job you did." Estelle didn't respond, and Dayan added, "Is Bob going to be all right, do you think? I hear he's a mess."

Estelle reached out and touched Dayan on the arm in lieu of smiling. "You can quote me on that," she said.

"We're going to bring out a special edition as soon as we can," Dayan said. "I think we can be on the streets tomorrow afternoon."

"Have at it," Estelle said. She looked toward the gate and saw the large figure of her husband crossing the landfill apron. "I don't have a whole lot of time, but I'll tell you everything I know for sure. But we need to talk fast. My ride's here."

"The girl," Dayan said. "Carmen Acosta. Fulkerson attacked her?"

"We think so." She pushed herself away from the Bronco. "We'll be waiting on DNA confirmation of blood evidence left at the scene, Frank. Everything points that way, though. We think that Fulkerson returned Zeigler's truck to his house. Carmen saw him."

"So he tried to kill her?"

"Why not? He'd already killed once."

"What about Bart Kurtz?"

"At this time," Estelle said slowly, choosing her words with care, "Mr. Kurtz is not suspected of any involvement."

"He didn't have anything to do with it?"

"That's not what I said, Frank. Replay that little tape, there." She patted his arm.

"Okay, let me get the basics now, and then maybe I can give you a call this afternoon?"

Estelle shook her head. "Phone won't work, Frank. I'm on administrative leave. That's standard procedure after a shooting. Talk to Captain Mitchell, or District Attorney Schroeder." She turned as her husband reached them and let Francis envelop her in a gentle hug. "Come on," she said to Dayan. "Walk with us to the car. I'll tell you all I can. After that, talk with Eddie. He's going to be running things for a while." She paused in sudden inspiration. "Bobby should be coherent by this afternoon. He'd enjoy a visit."

"The sheriff doesn't talk to us," Dayan said.

"Oh, he will, I think. Just tell him that if he doesn't, Linda Real has some photos of him that she'll let you have."

Dayan looked both hopeful and surprised. "Really?"

To receive a free catalog of Poisoned Pen Press titles, please contact us in one of the following ways:

Phone: 1-800-421-3976
Facsimile: 1-480-949-1707
Email: info@poisonedpenpress.com
Website: www.poisonedpenpress.com

Poisoned Pen Press
6962 E. First Ave. Ste. 103
Scottsdale, AZ 85251

LaVergne, TN USA
16 November 2010
205078LV00002B/12/P